+ +

EDWARD J. DELANEY

BROKEN
IRISH

TURTLE POINT PRESS

NEW YORK 2011

Published by Turtle Point Press

www.turtlepointpress.com

Copyright © 2011 by Edward J. Delaney

All rights reserved

ISBN 978-1-933527-50-5

LCCN 2010938747

Printed on acid-free, recycled paper

in the United States of America

FOR JENNIFER

BROKEN IRISH

+ +

1

Yes, he's driving drunk, but the rarity would be him driving sober, because when he does, he's usually hurrying his way to the South Boston Liquor Mart (the morning run the straightest line he still knows), usually afflicted through miscalculation by a crushing hangover needing to be fed and abated. Jimmy Gilbride hates having hangovers, hates their gravelly insistence and their saddening whispers, which is one good reason why he never truly lets himself sober up. He prefers to flow in the twilight between, that domain of the truly accomplished functional alcoholic. There was a time when he felt guilty about standing in front of the open refrigerator door at eight in the morning, usually naked, knocking down his "breakfast mix" of orange juice, vodka and grenadine. He appreciates the cold sigh of the fridge wafting on his timid loins. He feels no such guilt anymore, nor does he feel okay about it, either; he has simply stopped devoting any thought to it. It's become so automatic that he can sip his ways through most days without forming any conscious thoughts on the matter, because that would be like considering one's own breathing.

It's a hot afternoon, the Sunday of Labor Day weekend. His seersucker sport coat, worn out in the cool of morning, is laid on the seat beside him, too warm to bear now. The heat is getting to him. There's a certain buoyancy to his sodden brain so that he feels, driving, as if his sweating head is the balloon that gives lift to his whole body, the rest just bagged entrails that hang below like the ballast of his life. He feels as if he is floating inside his car as it rolls down a sun-white landscape of pavement and sky. The AC went out years ago in his weathered Ford Taurus, which has a story to tell in its dents and scratches, its emergency bottles rolling empty under shredded seats.

He is thirty-two and in decent shape, if that means thin—someone hardly prone to eating. He's especially slack where the skin gathers around the joints. He is sustained by the nutrients of many beverages, by the gum he chews incessantly to mask his breath, and by some Beer Nuts thrown in for a suggestion of the solid. Getting along, today, the fifth of September 1999, the fifth anniversary of his father's death. He has not called his mother. They have more or less lost touch. But he has really put on a drunk in honor of both old habits and the old man. He's headed somewhere else with a pocket full of cash, and he feels just fine. It's driving sober that has become so unnatural as to be the truer challenge.

Jimmy is driving behind three boys in a beat-up convertible, rolling down William J. Day Boulevard. He has just passed the L Street Bathhouse and he assumes they are coming from there, three shirtless young men with nubbed haircuts and sunburns. One of them is sitting up on the well, his hands stretched back onto the trunk to brace himself. The car is a 1986 Mustang, smallish and with a chipped-brown paint job, the kind of car that gets handed from one brother down to the next, and then gets sold to the neighbor's kid after that. The boy on the back is twenty or twenty-one, with thick muscles that have been, Jimmy assumes, bought dear under barbells and at the dripping ends of needles.

They're goofing, the driver speeding up and slowing down. It's just past four-thirty and Jimmy is woozily drunk, having spent most of this blinding day in the feral darkness of O'Hara's Tap in Dorchester, where the beer still comes cheaply and in pitchers, and then at Triple O's in Southie, where the drinks were clear and hard. As the car ahead of him slows again, Jimmy brakes too hard. The driver running up Jimmy's own bumper, a fat guy in a Dodge Ram pickup, sounds his horn. Driving drunk, for Jimmy, has never been a problem, except when other people complicate the matter. As they are now, front and behind. Squeezing and testing.

The boy driving ahead of him won't let the joke go. He's trying to get the kid sitting up on back to flinch. He jerks the car forward and then slows nearly to a stop. The one on the back takes on more of a hunch, laughing, cursing good-naturedly as Jimmy drops back, not wanting to rear-end him. The Dodge is nearly ramming Jimmy now, inches off his bumper, its driver furious.

This time, the driver ahead really guns the car; almost immediately, Jimmy sees that the kid on the back has lost his balance. The car accelerates further and the boy is now rolling off, still in mid-laugh. Jimmy has been ready with his brakes and now he jams them, other brakes shrieking behind. He can only watch. The guy tumbles down the trunk and, in the oddest kind of effort, the one Jimmy will replay endlessly in his mind, tries to grab the bumper with his hands. It seems later that it must have been all he could think of. The car's driver slams on the brakes, realizing. But it's all too far into motion. It is a body commanded now by physics, sliding sideways and over as if into a somersault, down into the street. As his head hits the pavement, the neck turns. Jimmy sees the face fully, as if it is watching Jimmy watch. It can only be the slightest fractional pulse of time, a single frame of frozen memory, followed instantly by the body. The expression is one of wide-eyed puzzlement, the look of a man who has just begun his other life, that of a quadriplegic. It is a dreamy and emptied stare, all hubris wiped clean, probably forever. Jimmy jams the brakes harder and the car pulls hard left, fishtailing. He doesn't hit the boy, but hears the dull slam of the Dodge Ram's bumper behind him, crushing his own.

It's over that fast. On the road, the boy's neck is humped in a way that is irredeemably bad, and his legs and arms are skinned and bleeding. His friends in the convertible take one look and the driver hits the gas. Jimmy gets out of his car. Still very drunk, he walks around to the boy on the pavement, only feet from his front bumper; the boy's eyes are open but staring at the white sky. Jimmy stands, watching the boy's friends disappear on the curve farther down Day Boulevard, out toward Castle Island. He cannot, at this moment, recall where it was he was going.

+ +

2

Colleen's son barely comes out of his room, and that is the final piece of her desolation. When her husband was killed, the boy was five, and, in those ensuing weeks and months, she had been almost fully sustained not by her parents' attentiveness to him (which was endless) and not by getting back to work (which only made her feel worse), but, rather, by the absolute belief that she and her little boy were in this together, and always would be, and that there would be a closeness that would not simply survive, but become deeper. It did not occur to her at that time, or even until recently, that it would not be sustained, even now, as he plods toward his fourteenth year.

She can see her naïveté in that now. But maybe that's all right. Nearly nine years ago, if she had been forced to confront even the idea of losing Christopher, it would have been too much to bear.

She doesn't know what's normal. She knows that teenagers withdraw; she did too at that age. But not so emphatically. Not to the point of near non-contact. The sense she gets of Christopher is not just that he wants to be left alone but that, in fact, there is some grievance, some anger. He looks at her in a way that borders on hateful and she has no idea why.

She has bought him all the junk: the television for his room, the video games, the CD player with which he shuts her out. None of this seems to have made him a happier person. He seems to have no friends. He comes home after school and shuts the door, and, when she arrives from work, that door rarely opens. Only after she goes to bed does she hear him quietly emerge from his room to use the bathroom and raid the kitchen.

She has been alone since Barry's death. He died far away from her, bleeding to death on a tarmac in the unrelenting Persian sun. He had been an Army specialist working on an Apache helicopter when his arm got caught in the gears. Colleen hadn't wanted to know any more than that, the night they notified her. Barry had always seemed indestructible, from his football days at Southie High to his years in the Army. Barry Coogan, athlete. Barry Coogan, soldier. He seemed to live in uniforms, to love the sense of order they bestowed. She was living in Greensboro with Christopher when they came to tell her what had happened.

She worries that Christopher has forgotten his father, or that he misremembers. Maybe the second one is worse. He was something, Barry was, but he wasn't Superman either, and she worries that Christopher is crushed under the weight of a more idealized version of his father. But all of that is speculation.

So she has decided today to fight with him. To raise him out of his torpor, to reconfigure something between them. She will provoke, attack and incite, because she needs to see something in his eyes that she has not seen in a long time.

The plan, as such, is in progress: she has come home from work early. "Family matters," she has truthfully told her boss at the United Airlines ticket counter, where she has worked for six years. She is lying in wait. It's a little after two and she is sitting on the living-room carpet facing the door, waiting for the sound of a key in the lock. Normally she doesn't get home until after seven. She's parked her car down around the block so he won't turn and run.

She knows so little about him anymore. What he does, where he goes. There had been a time when the after-school things gave her some sense of safety: playing baseball, being an altar server three times a week, being in the science club at school. But he has given all of these up, as he has given up that particular school.

It had never occurred to Colleen that her son might turn out to be one of those who don't fit in. She had always taken it as an article of faith that he would grow up to be more or less like Barry, who had breezed through high school with what seemed like a horde of friends and absolutely no enemies, who had not been the leader of the group but always an easy part of it. She is stunned that her son is not a reconstituted version of his father. She is stunned that it has all become so difficult.

+ +

3

Tuesday morning, after a Labor Day spent shuttered and infused with vodka-rocks, Jimmy called in sick to work, a last-chance tech-writing job he has always loathed. He had somewhat wisely decided not to arrive at work drunk, having not slept and in a virtually psychotic state. Monday morning, he had stumbled to the corner convenience store in the Labor Day dawn to buy the morning newspapers and read what he already intuitively knew: that the boy's neck had snapped, that the two friends have now been arrested. Also, what he didn't: that the guy in the Dodge Ram had a warrant out for his arrest, for stealing that very vehicle. Tuesday morning, Jimmy had likewise retrieved the papers, thinking there would be more, but there was not.

As he drank his way through Labor Day, his mind fixed constantly on one detail of the aftermath: as he stood at the front of his car, watching the paramedics move the boy gingerly onto the board, a heavy, middle-aged woman emerged from the massive traffic jam down Day Boulevard, wandered up past Jimmy, past the cops, up to the edge of the scene, where she got on her hands and knees and began to say, "It's going to be all right, honey . . . it's going to be all right . . ." She was repeating it over and over as the work went on. Thinking about it now, Jimmy feels himself seething, because nothing at all was going to be all right, and everyone, including the boy, who could not feel the torn flesh of his knees or the burning road under his back, knew it. Nothing at all would be all right and it was cruel to tell him that, Jimmy thought, to give him even a moment of hope that anything would be less than what they all knew.

He had come home after watching them load the kid into the ambulance, an excruciatingly attenuated process that would yield no good result, and he had tried to drink himself stupid, and then drink himself to sleep. But instead he had drunken himself awake, and even more sharply focused on the moment.

Having called in sick to work, and having emptied the last bottle in the house, he knew he had to wait four hours for the South Boston Liquor Mart to open, and that sleep would be the only way to bridge the agony. But he couldn't sleep. He sat on his couch nearly inert, thinking about the boy's face, that expression in which there is sudden realization, the instant flash of total recognition when you see you have thrown it completely away and had countless chances not to. Standing unsteadily, Jimmy slid along the wall and into the kitchen, where he vomited down the garbage disposal. His heart pounded heavily, bathed as it was in the alcohol, and while he couldn't wait for the liquor store to open, if there was to be any clarity, it was now. He knew he simply had to stop this, his life.

So, now Wednesday morning, Jimmy shuffles into his office, red-eyed and afflicted with a vertigo brewed from lack of sleep and lack of alcohol. It has been nearly twenty-four hours without a drink. Overnight, on the couch in front of the television at three and four and five, shivering and sweating, he imagined what prison must be like, where the minutes and the seconds seem to stretch endlessly ahead. To him, drinking always defined what people meant when they talked about living "in the moment." Sitting in a bar with a drink in front of him, moments past, and moments to come, had almost no meaning. Now, if he is really going to do this, it will all be measured by the word *since*. A day since. A week since. A month since, which seems to him a near impossibility. Through the night, he tried to turn his mind away from that boy, whom he could only imagine would have a life measured by the excruciating countdown of seconds—the *until*.

Jimmy wants to feel good about the fact that, for the first time in years, he has gone a full day without a drink. But it feels like absolutely nothing except an overpowering accumulation of uncomfortable sensations. The morning shower had provided no curative, and even after brushing his teeth at some length, his mouth feels grungy and dry. His clothes rake his skin as if it is raw. He sees Judy, the receptionist, pointedly awaiting him. "Dick wants to see you," Judy says from behind her reception desk.

This job was supposed to be what he did for the time being. It's been more than two years. He writes instruction manuals for cheap products, translated from Japanese. He knows no Japanese, so he tries to infer from the diagrams what is going on and then write simple commands. He has usually done so drunk, but he works cheaply and rarely misses a day (meaning he shows up something like eight or nine out of every ten), and it seems to Jimmy that no one notices he is drunk—that, rather, they assume this is simply how he walks, talks and thinks. Which it very much is. The office is in a warehouse out by the Southeast Expressway and the boss, Dick, is rarely present, more focused on his real estate schemes. Jimmy tends to show up more or less on time, and fumble with the manuals for a decent stretch, mercifully always livened by the lunchtime cocktail he favors down at Triple O's.

Dick hired Jimmy for this job probably knowing what he was getting, and Jimmy has admittedly never taken the job particularly seriously. Of course he had told Dick he would actually learn Japanese, and that he was committed to a future here. But he has learned that if he endures Dick's occasional cranks, he's fine. Dick knows just as well as Jimmy does that their products are junk, that the whole thing borders on a scam, and that Jimmy is so poorly paid that he is almost being encouraged in his dissolute ways.

But almost at the moment he turns the corner into Dick's office, he knows it's over. Dick is sitting at his desk with the general manager, Dave, the axe man for all manner of company movement.

"Well this is a lynch mob if ever I've seen one," Jimmy says.

"Just in case I was trying to give you further chances," Dick says. Turning to Dave, Dick says, "His memory's shorter than his pecker. I hired him for no real good reason."

Dave chuckles. "Jimmy, enough's enough. Come on. You could be doing other things. You don't need to be blowing off days left and right."

"So this is about yesterday?" Jimmy says.

"And last Thursday and Friday," Dick says, "and the Wednesday and Thursday before that . . ."

"But you came to this decision because I was out of work *yesterday*."

Dick slaps the desktop with his hand.

"Goddamn it, we decided last week, but then you didn't come into work until today."

"That's cold," Jimmy says. "Because yesterday was different. I'm trying to change."

"What the fuck is the matter with you?" Dick says. "Look at yourself. You've been out of a job since last week, and you didn't even know it."

Back on the street, Jimmy gathers himself. Of course, given such circumstances, the urge to sit and drink is more powerful now than anything else he can imagine. He wants to, so badly. And in the next few hours one of two things will happen. Either he will go right now to find a bar stool and some fellow reprobates to whom he will, morning cocktail in hand, spill his guts, not just seeing the accident, but now the larger and more existential question of how he even descended to a job working for Dick, writing incomprehensible product manuals. Or, he will be able to stuff it all back down for another twenty-four hours, based on the premise that a promise made over someone's broken neck should last more than one day.

And he now needs a job. He's had some jobs writing, and when he isn't drunk or hung over (an admittedly small window), he can do so reasonably well. But he's never had anything vaguely resembling a career, other than the vocation of drink, and he is now a good patch into his thirties. He's not from South Boston but has always liked the low arc of expectations in this place, and the vague glee at getting away with something, anything at all. Rarely does he venture into Boston proper. Too big, the height of aspirations as lofty as those clustered buildings. The low-ceilinged bars of this familiar neighborhood have always suited him better. He stands now on the sidewalk of West Broadway, Triple O's within sight, the skyline of the city visible, should he decide to look.

4

He avoids people. Christopher doesn't like the bump and jostle in the hallways of school, or the grabbing and shoving in gym class as everybody fights over a stupid ball. Or even, these days, the more gentle touch his mother applies to him. That soft contact on his shoulder when he's eating breakfast, or the touching of his hair when he's on the couch watching television. He recoils from it now, avoids her in order to avoid it. He is not a stupid baby to be cuddled and squeezed.

He is sick of his friends. They make him feel different. Once they were all just children but now they are each growing into different people, different species, and he doesn't see the common ground anymore. Maybe there wasn't ever any. But neither is he inclined to find anyone to fill that void. He feels fully himself only when sequestered in his bedroom among his things, his video games, computer and television. He strongly prefers the company of televised people, usually superheroes and spies. He appreciates a world in which force is an appropriate response. It seems a more simplified reality, unbound by the complications of the muddled authority that surrounds him. He likes to surf the Internet looking at guns. He is something of a gun expert, in fact, the same way he remembers (in memories that are sharp in the middle but whose edges blur into gray) that his father could look up

at the crabbed and distant imprints of aircraft in the sky and iden-
tify them. His father had planned, after the Army, to service aircraft at Logan Airport, back home. He knew the nuances of each
and would recite them like the rosary. Likewise, Christopher can
tell a Glock from a Ruger at twenty yards. He is fascinated by their
utilitarian elegance, their smoothly potent lines. He is nearly as
taken with armor and weapons, and has lately become obsessed
with the two-handed Scottish Claymore with its long and merci-
less blade. He fantasizes about buying one and mounting it in a
frame that would hang over his bed. He imagines someday having
the kind of friends who would appreciate that—the history and
the beauty. His mother has indulged him in that respect, buying
him books about medieval knights, taking him to an exhibit of
samurai armor at the Museum of Fine Arts, the leather-and-bam-
boo yoroi reminding him of a lobster's hardened shell. He imagines sometimes what it must have been like to be a knight on his
horse, encased in his skin of metal, looking out at the world
through a slot. He wrote an essay in school last year about modern military armament, and the fact that he wishes his father had
been wearing his Kevlar vest when that helicopter's engine caught
him was clearly implied, if not stated. He received a "C" for
problems with theme and spelling. His teacher circled the word
"armer" twenty-seven times with a red pen. He didn't show the
paper to his mother, who worries about his sliding grades.

Each day after school he walks to a park where he sits and
watches cars go by. M Street tops just beyond East Broadway and
rolls down toward the water. Midway between is the Most Holy
Trinity Church and adjacent to that is the elementary school. He
used to attend that school, but last spring he told his mother he

would not go back there. It's such a complete joke. God stopped talking to him a long time ago. He has only just started public school.

He sits on the bench, watching. He has no particular place to go, until he returns home at six to eat quickly and then lock himself into his room. He has homework to do but it bores him and he questions the point of it anyway. He's going to go to Southie High, and they'll have to take him. He can start trying then.

M Street is a narrow passage, hemmed in by a gantlet of triple-deckers, tight as stones in a wall. The traffic is light on this street, most cars taking L Street through to where it becomes Summer Street and jumps over the Channel to downtown Boston. Here, in September, the trees still make the street seem like a tunnel under their spreading leaves, but they will soon enough begin to dry and release, prelude to the always-sudden chill. Down a half-block, some of his former classmates are in the Most Holy Trinity schoolyard having a game of touch football, a game he will never play. If he were to ever take up a sport, it would likely be archery, where everyone yields much distance. Or maybe swimming, the idea of slipping through the fluid grasp, sliding through enemy water.

A car passes, an old woman, who slows and looks at him, then accelerates. Everyone in Southie is inordinately nosy, absorbed in the notion of who belongs and who does not, fixated on what someone is going to do to them before they can be done unto. Christopher wants to stand and scream, "I'm sitting on the bench."

The school is no longer welcoming. If he were to amble on down and observe the ongoing touch football game, he would probably be chased away by boys he once sat at lunch with. Such is the penalty for having left. A presumption of treason. He knows the secrets of a half-dozen boys down in that schoolyard and now they would beat him for showing back up. His exit had been far more drawn out than he could have ever anticipated, at thirteen years of age. Father John had sat with Christopher and his mother and had urged her to keep him in, away from those hooligans down at the junior high school. Christopher's grades were not reflecting his ability, Father John had told Christopher's mother, but sometimes at this age a boy will really turn it around. So she had tried that night to push it, to remind Christopher how he was *wanted* there, where people *took an interest*. But Christopher was not to be dissuaded. Later, Father John even came to the school and pulled Christopher from the classroom (his fellow students nervously watching), then closed the two of them in the principal's office, alone, where he reminded Christopher that sometimes, even at a young age, mistakes could be made that could not ever be taken back, and that it might be wise to instead remain in a place of relative safety, despite its having some admitted drawbacks.

"I want to see you well, Christopher," he said. "Can't you understand that?"

"I do," Christopher had replied, trying to get him to just stop. Now he sits on the bench on M Street, forever cast from the good graces as those were. He does not, in plain fact, feel God's unrelenting eyes upon him. He fancies himself more the watcher— not of God proper, but of His earthly venues, at least as they are in South Boston. His observations have so far yielded a conflict of conclusions. Another car passes, teenagers, packed six to a rusted-out Dodge Aries. One of them hurls an orange-soda can at Christopher, which misses widely and skitters across the sidewalk before pinging the bottom of a chain-link fence. Christopher hears the boy who threw the can being mocked by the others for missing an easy mark, as the car rolls down toward the intersection.

He knows, though, who will come by. He knows that Father John drives to the Catholic Home to administer Communion before returning for the 5:30 Mass. Christopher knows that the black Lincoln Town Car will top the hill within moments and that Father himself, who has not spoken a word to Christopher in all the time since their last meeting in the principal's office, will float by, magisterial in the trappings of the Church and its attendant power, to lay hosts on the trembling tongues of those truest of believers, the elderly and the afflicted. The boys down in the schoolyard break into a shrieking argument, some differing interpretation of the rules that will be settled by who screams loudest and longest. Christopher has foresworn shouting. At times he thinks he should even foreswear speaking. The September breeze kicks up and, for a moment, penetrates his thirteen-year-old indifference. The improbably affecting kiss of a lilting breeze. He relaxes and for a second closes his eyes, stops watching, lets it touch him. He is at an age when autumn is not yet here and winter seems a lifetime away.

He pops his eyes back open. He has registered the near-silent thrum of the nearly new Lincoln Town Car, its glassy-waxed shoulders holding the afternoon sun in a holy shimmer. The car rolls down the grade of road. Christopher's spine tightens. He can see Father's head backlit by the southward patch of sky, but discerns no specific features. Christopher is watching. *Look at me.* And, as ever, the car rolls by with no turn of the Fatherly head, no mash of the Fatherly countenance. Only blankness, silently rolling by.

+ +

5

Jimmy hasn't had a drink in fifteen days. The incessant counting of the fingers (*Sun*day, *Mon*day, *Tues*day) ended on day 10 and now he is on the weekly schedule, two weeks now and another day, re-figuring on shaking hands as if it is going to change sometime before midnight. He has likewise barely slept in these two weeks, and has the general feeling of fogged disorientation that is generally associated with drinking but for him is a symptom of his new, and brief, sobriety. He sits at his small kitchen table at an ungodly hour—seven in the morning—feeling as if he has fought through the long darkness to no effect.

And he has found some work. Not a job, but a shred of work that may get him a job. He is writing items, of all things, for a local society magazine, scant dollars per column inch, a job that may at least get him heading somewhere better. Philanthropical pieces. The work is rote, the preparation of short summaries of gifts and disbursements by various corporations to various local causes. A certain clarity of thought seems the only requirement, and Jimmy is working hard to meet that expectation. Without the drinking, he feels not quite attached to himself, his jones like a hanging piece of skin he cannot quite pull off. There is a faint buzzing in his head and the sense of his being an observer of himself, his supposed better self carefully and nervously watching for the imminent slide.

He keeps thinking of the guy falling off the back of that car. This is his place of strength, to be able to hold that instant. He cannot revisit it without trying to make use of its power, to try to milk it for himself. He's not even totally sure he doesn't want to drink anymore, but he does want to not be sick and helpless, not by the snap of the neck in a sudden tumble, nor from the slow accretion of alcohol that could have been stopped at any time, and now is.

The problem with newspapers is that they don't stay with these kinds of stories, that they trivialize them in the crush of all the others that press for attention. Jimmy reads that the injured party, whose name is Butchie Morrissey, is still hospitalized, and that the driver is in jail on outstanding warrants. The other kid who was riding shotgun has spent time in jail. The one who fell—*Butchie*, he says aloud—was awaiting trial on sexual-assault charges. Jimmy, reading, cannot tease from the lines the real story he needs from them. He throws the newspaper against the wall of his apartment, because these facts are eroding the sanctity of what he saw. For the horror of it to not be pristine would make his sobriety concurrently lacking in its pristine urgency.

When he rises in the morning he has come to a nearly spiritual beginning, although he cannot claim to fervently subscribe to any god at this point. He has begun these days with something akin to a ritual. He has no idea where it came from. The closing of the eyes and the nearly unconscious levitation of the arms. Some kind of gesticulation that feels right and called for, and sets a tone.

But by late afternoon, coming from the absorptions of his part-time temp job, the intentions of the morning have worn desperately thin, stoked by fatigue and the force of habit. The problem with running away from the drinking is that he has not figured out exactly where else there is to go. It is, in some ways, like breaking up with a woman, except that in this case it's more like shunning the entire gender. What now? Ideally, he'd be doing some sort of job that would allow him to simply immerse himself in it with the same compulsion with which he has engaged in his drinking. He finds himself walking in the heat with no specific destination, because he can't go to a bar and he can't really go home, and most importantly he cannot be with himself. The trick is how to keep the particular fire of his self-control burning. People, he supposes, can internalize anything, and he needs to keep the horror of what he saw fresh and present, sharp enough to cut at him again. He needs to steep himself in that, to do what he must do. He can't have the past sins of the victim denying him that.

+ +

6

Colleen awakens, thinking she has heard a door slam. It is dark in the apartment and faint with the sodium-vapor glow of the street-lights out beneath the swaying canopy of late-summer leaves. Christopher's door is shut, a sliver of light coming from underneath it.

He has come in and recused himself. Instead of fighting him, she has missed hours of paid work to come home and fall asleep on the couch waiting, which seems to have been so useless as to be heartbreaking. She knows she didn't want that confrontation. Tomorrow night she will work late to get back the missed hours and there will be no contact with her son then. He had to have seen her sleeping there when he came in, and she wonders what he must have thought. Her retreat into sleep has always been her brand of cowardice. She suspects he will avoid more: she has played her hand, and lost.

Colleen turns on the light and looks at the clock on the mantel. It's nearly ten and she has been asleep for a least five hours. It makes no sense. She will be awake all night now. And any plans to knock on his door and confront him have run out of her like a depressurization. It's too late to argue. He has school in the morning. He needs to stay on his schedule. She settles back onto the couch and flips channels. There is nothing on; there is never anything on. She is tired of the comedies, with their looped laughter and sad conceits of family. Husbands and wives making witty stabs at each other. Sage children adding the running commentary. She is tired of the news, too, with its procession of homicides, car accidents and scandal. She never did like sports. There are never any good movies on. She beseeches the television gods to deliver something that will deliver her from her own thoughts. Her prayers find no purchase.

She thinks instead of her husband. She seems hardly able to believe he has been gone so long, although Christopher himself is the yardstick by which that time is most accurately measured. Sometimes, in the confusion of dreams, she pairs the ten- or twelve-year-old Christopher with his father in what seems such a natural moment. There is rarely action in these dreams, only being. When she awakens, she often feels as if she could easily refile such visions into memory, and trick herself into believing it has all happened. She could build a whole presumed reality from these stitched-together nocturnal moments, in which her husband and son float serenely on some vaguely musical vapor.

There has not been much thought of dating or remarriage, as she feels the widowly idealization of her deceased will not allow for comparison. And, besides, she is scared. She was never fully sure how she was able to come to be Barry's woman, not in those waning months of high school, when he was nearly bursting in his desire to get out of Southie and never return (and had enlisted as his way of fulfilling the desire), and not later as his dutiful wife. Barry, Quiet Barry. He spoke little, shared little. He was a listener. There was something unattainable about his sunny ease with just about everything. She has to admit to herself that she had always waited for some bubble to burst, some upshot. But it never came in the way she expected. He went on being quietly happy, and sweetly good to her, right until the explosion of metal pierced his heart.

Her boss has been sniffing around that prospect and she plays dumb. He makes awkward overtures at which she only smiles numbly. She seems to recall him mentioning a girlfriend at some point, and it reminds her of the blurriness of such matters. She does not want to get fired, either, and so she goes along in a state of suspension, of heightened attentiveness. Here in the living room, the television people natter on, to no resounding effect. They are meant to transport her, to be proxies for her own disjointed mind. But they do not penetrate. They do not come to a place where she can simply be the observer. Christopher is in his room and she has missed her chance.

She has no waking imagination. She just keeps on with things as they are. She daydreams no outcomes for her son, and maybe that's really bad. Should she be wishing him up to great things? Plans come from such imagination, and she cannot make any plans, for herself or her son. She simply rides the given moment. It is her demonstrated lack of imagination that must not allow her to understand how his head is working, and why he will not speak to her. Either that, or, she suspects, this is simply more of the same cowardice.

Flipping channels, she settles finally on a show on the cooking channel. The woman in the smock is cooking some impossibly complicated dish, but it is the simple movement and her soothing voice that gives Colleen some respite. There is the circus of pans and burners, of smoke and sputter. The woman Mmm's and

Aah's but Colleen wants the smell. How can there be a food channel without the aroma, that most crucial factor? But it is what it is. She pulls the throw from the top of the couch and pulls it around her, cocooning. Soon enough, she enters a sleep with no dreams. She awakens again, sweaty and shaking, at somewhere past two-thirty. She pulls herself up and looks over the top of the couch, toward Christopher's room. Even at this deep hour the light under her son's door still burns brightly.

+ + + + + + + + + + + + + + + + + + + +

7

He hopes there will be a party, and that it will be nice. This is admittedly a self-indulgence, but it would be for the occasion of his retirement and that would make for a lovely completion.

Father John sits on his bed on the second floor of the Most Holy Trinity rectory. He is in an undershirt and white boxers, hands on his knees, contemplating these last fleeting weeks of a forty-year priesthood. He feels too young to retire. But so it all goes. He is facing a mirror and, as he regards himself, he is not unimpressed with what he sees. Yes, the hair is white, but in some anomalous fortune it's still thick; and indeed there may be an observed landscape of wrinkles hatching the skin; but beneath all that there is still undoubtedly the boyish remnant, not all that different than the face of the young man who in 1955 first walked through the doors of the St. John's Seminary, where he had already determined his gift to God would be that of himself, body and soul. And indeed the soul was more along than the body, which was still very much that of a boy, still to grow and be shaped by a celibacy that, as he pledged, no woman had touched.

And now he sits, that same body a picture of health, still lean but perhaps just a shade stooped, but a picture of late life nonetheless. And now he has been told, by the Archbishop himself, that it is time to put aside the burden of his duties and move toward a final phase of peace and reflection. He will be going to Arizona, again at the behest of Cardinal Law. Father John can already imagine its pristine dryness, its cobalt skies, the scouring and insistent winds.

He still feels too young for this. He feels as vital as he ever has been, and if he were more vain he could catalog any number of instances that would prove just that. He is indeed not so different than that young boy he was, not knowing the things he would have to do to weather the tests of his loving God.

The party, indeed. He wonders who will come. It is sad that he has no blood family left in his circle, all departed by death or cruel estrangement. It is sad as well that it is the difference between what is holy and what is not that can drive a wedge between such connections. But for now he has much work to accomplish. A young priest will soon be coming to take his place. Mexican, of all. The ranks of American boys have sadly dwindled. There are some of Father John's own parishioners he could guess might have gravitated toward the priesthood, in another era. That Christopher, maybe. But times are very different now.

So tonight he will effect his duties. He will attend a fundraiser for a local politician, Mary Ellen Faherty, whose father was once quite a powerful man at the State House. This Mary Ellen seems of a different ilk: using politics to build her law practice, unlike her father who used his law practice to pave his way into politics. Everything indeed seems upside-down. The neighborhood, from which he came, and where he served his first assignment before being sent to other places, had changed so much when he was brought back—a surprise, three years ago. The mixing of races, of ethnicities, of social stations. This once-Irish bastion is still that at its heart, but fading quickly and losing its center. His own pews are filled mostly with the old, finishing out a particular way of life amid another. Jimmy Kelly, the City Councilor, now spends his time fighting the gays instead of the blacks, his version of changing with the times. Whitey Bulger has evaporated into the ether but his boys still kick around on the street corners while the indictments come down, waiting for Whitey's Second Coming.

Father John has on his dresser a glass of sweet iced tea from the pitcher Mrs. Gaithwright leaves in the refrigerator each summer's night. He had wondered, when she first came to the rectory, whether she would work out at all. She is Haitian. She has become the one person in the world who seems to truly take an interest in him anymore, even if it's because she is paid to do so. Father John can happily admit she has worked out, another example of how time has changed beneath his feet. He's never been afraid of that.

+ + + + + + + + + + + + + + + + + + + +

8

She is free, finally, completely and forever. Four days past her sixteenth birthday and she cannot be unwillfully brought back. Her parents have cranked at her for much too long, her teachers have peddled their own brand of vituperative bile, and her procession of school therapists are like vindictive children. They're all idiots. Despite their own perceptions, they have nothing figured out whatsoever.

She packed this morning and has stowed everything she needs in the single massive backpack that she is now lugging across South Boston to the apartment her nineteen-year-old boyfriend shares with four other guys, all of whom are eighteen. It's a three-bedroom; she and Bobby will now share one of those bedrooms. The others have fully agreed to this, unsurprising given the general awe with which eighteen-year-old boys approach the act of sex, which they presume will happen now and which they want in their apartment even if it is not theirs to have. The general theory seems to be that some yields more, that the general effect may bring them same. But they're all dweebs and they'll figure out sooner than later that they aren't any closer to that particular grail than they were when they first put up their posters of nude women over their beds, like some sort of articles of their faith. They all finished at Southie High in the spring, the end of their education. They're all working a variety of low-wage jobs, of which Bobby's is the best: he is a stocker at the Liquor Mart. He is able to swipe at least a six-pack a night, and sometimes comes home with nips of Jack Daniel's and peppermint schnapps stuffed down his pants.

This is where she's going. To be with Bobby and make something more of a home than the one she is exiting. For now at least, it will still be in Southie. She has some vague aspiration of the two of them going west, which is the only alternative to South Boston unless they're going to row east. But she's thinking *really* west, the west that's east of California. Someplace like Idaho or Montana. There is deep appeal to this idea, and what she sees as she traverses this jammed shithole of a neighborhood is something like one of those trailers, but out on a broad grassy place. Maybe with some mountains off in the distance. She paints them now in this rendering, purplish and undefined. She paints a road going to this place and a pickup truck parked on the side. The idea of having any kind of room in which to exist is a powerful vision, especially having just decamped from her parents' cage-like apartment up on the third floor, above her sour-smelling grandparents and their dozen cats. Her maternal grandparents despise her parents almost as much as she does, but for far different reasons. They want to sell the house and get a condo in Tampa. Their primary complaint, though, seems to be with the weather. Her parents and their refusal to buy their own place, despite her deep suspicion that her father has socked away all kinds of money from his varied dealings, is the deeply related grievance.

Her backpack, and its complicated weight distribution, are creating equilibrium issues, especially given that she has decided on this auspicious occasion to wear the high heels she stole from Filene's two months ago and kept squirreled behind the furnace in the basement, waiting for just such a moment. But with forty-five pounds strapped to her back, and her ankles wobbling atop the four-inch spikes, she looks like someone less than comical but only a little better than pathetic. At East Broadway she holds up a line of honking traffic as she baby-steps across the wide street, chucking a few middle fingers to express her own displeasure with the moment.

She should have had Bobby come and get her, but he's at work and she wanted it to be a surprise anyway. She wants to be there when he comes through the door, to crack him a beer and close the bedroom door behind, and lay with the fan on them in the humid late afternoon.

But as she begins to take on the rising grade of D Street, the blisters on her feet are becoming issues and the sweat has begun to cloud her makeup and drench her top. She stops, breathing deeply.

"You want me to carry that for you?" a voice says behind her. She turns and sees this boy, skinny, dark-haired, swimming in his t-shirt. His face, freckled, is bland and earnest as he shuffles in his sneakers.

"Who are you?" she says.

"I live right on your street," he says. "I'm Christopher."

"I know you?"

"Yeah, like I said."

"What's my name?"

"Jeanmarie."

"Oh, yeah," she says. "Maybe I remember you. I just didn't know you got big. So you know who my father is, right?"

"Yeah, of course."

"You're not gonna tell him you saw me, right?"

"I've never actually talked to him."

"That's not an answer."

"No," Christopher says. "I won't tell him."

"Good, because that would fuck everything up. He doesn't understand what I want. And my mother is no help . . ." She looks suddenly as if she will cry.

"So," Christopher says. "You need for me to carry that for you?"

"I don't know. What's in it for you?"

He ponders this. "Now that you put it that way, forget about it."

She laughs. "Okay then, how about this: Will you carry this for me?"

"What's in it for me?"

"You drink beer?"

"No."

"You want to?"

She slides the pack off and, when he takes it, the weight of it bends him to the ground.

"What do you *have* in here?"

"Everything," she says. "My whole deal."

His knees are the ones wobbling now, but he keeps pace with

her up the rising street. He has burst into a red-faced sweat, and she tells him the place they're going is only three blocks ahead. He grunts back.

"That beer's gonna taste good after you worked for it," she says. "But you gotta do me one favor."

He looks over at her and grunts again.

"You have to take off pretty quick after that. This is my first night living with my boyfriend."

The building is so derelict he might have otherwise assumed it to be abandoned, even on this unimpressive block. But she insists this is the place. When they get to the front door, she gets down on her knees around the side of the steps and finds the key. Inside, they climb the steep, cigarette-butt-strewn steps to the second floor, where the door to the apartment lacks not only a lock but also a knob, and swings open freely.

"Put the backpack in there," she says, and he lugs it into a room carpeted with a tangle of dirty clothes, a grimy futon pushed against one of the walls. The one apparently valuable item is an old computer sitting on a low rough-wood box, its plastic case yellowed at its edges with age, like a neglected block of cheese.

Christopher is drenched now and wipes his forehead on the sleeve of his t-shirt. The apartment seems empty, although both the other bedroom doors are shut. The living room is four plastic lawn chairs (which he immediately suspects have been stolen off some front porches), a shredded couch with a humped middle, a small television on a milk crate in one corner and a boom box with a snapped-off antenna in another.

Jeanmarie looks at home and says, "Yes?"

"The beer," Christopher says, and while the desire to drink his first beer is severely limited, the desire to be paid for this task is foursquare.

"Oh, yeah." She goes to the refrigerator and opens the door.

"Shit, there isn't any," she says. "His roommates stole it again."

"Yeah, that's okay," he says.

"I wasn't shitting you," she says. "It was supposed to be here."

"That's okay," he says. "I'll get out of here."

"You know what?" she says. "Wait a few days and come back. Bobby brings beer home from work all the time. Come in a few days and you can get your beer. Maybe I'll let you meet Bobby, too."

"When?" he says.

"Let's say Wednesday. After nine. Can you be out that late?"

"Uh, *yeah.*"

"Then do it," she says. "And remember that you don't say anything to my father."

"I wouldn't go near the guy, I swear," he says, and that makes her laugh.

After Christopher has gone down the stairs and she has heard the affirmative slam of the front door, Jeanmarie goes to the bedroom. Her backpack is on the futon, but she'll unpack that later; since there is no dresser, she'll eventually make orderly piles of her clothes against one wall. For now, she surveys Bobby's strewn clothes and begins, happily, to gather and fold them, awaiting his return to their home.

+ +

9

Three weeks into it all, Jimmy's life has now become enveloped in alcohol the way his mother has always been wrapped up in religion, with a constancy of attention to things that are not present. The lack of any bottles in his apartment is a nearly dominating presence, like a Godly absence. As is the severe funneling of all imperatives into a single binding preoccupation. All things done now are in a context of his gnawing self-denial. He isn't sure he can live like this for any length of time.

The basic array of tasks seems plodding and inchoate in this life of Since. He has gained no appetite and has felt no surge of energy. Only a keening in the deeper parts of his skull that follows him to bed and into grudging sleep. He sees that salvation lies in a dull sort of simplicity. He will do simple work and accomplish simple tasks. This is more than he ever did drunk, yet it seems so much less.

He has gotten an odd call from the editor at the philanthropic magazine. "I have some extended freelance work if you're interested," the editor says. "But you should come in and talk to me about it."

Jimmy has been doing his assignments well, with a ghost of the stubborn professionalism he was able, at one time, to effect even in the face of late nights and no sleep and pounding stretches between bouts. He can summon a bit of that now, and in that is a whisper of promise.

He takes the T into the city and, at a shade before ten, he rides the elevator up to the offices of the society magazine, pulling at his tie and running his fingertips along the rough collar of his tweed sport coat. He wants to believe that work will be his cure, and he is prepared to say yes to anything. He suspects that if this prospective job were actually appealing, he would already have heard so on the phone. As he gets out of the elevator and goes through the magazine's double doors, the receptionist watches him with the wariness of someone who still cannot pinpoint the problem she knows is hanging in the air. The odorless stink of new and shaky sobriety. The wobble of the weighty pledge.

He sits on a molded plastic chair in the reception area, drinking stale coffee from the stained pot behind the reception desk, and does a slow system check. His feet tingle in an inexplicable kind of sleepiness and his stomach, empty so far today, grumbles sourly from its burrow.

Jimmy has never given a dime to any charity, so his work for a philanthropical magazine recording the expansiveness of millionaires, billionaires and megacorporations seems oddly disingenuous. He is not against them giving away money, but in his assignments it is in the language of self-congratulation, of grave solicitude. The magazine profiles those who give money to others who also have it, in cyclical recognition. Gifts to the art galleries and theater companies and ballet troupes that seem cleaner and worthier than what lies out there beyond. The stories most often catalog the giver's own hard times, as they might have been, and then the eventual triumph of wealth, at which point their heart and selflessness is thereby revealed. It has become, rather quickly, as routine as writing assembly instructions from languages he does not know.

His editor is looming from the doorway of his office. "James, come on in." Jimmy follows him into the office, which, unlike the expansive and wood-paneled outer offices of the magazine, seems a dingy chamber, cardboard file boxes stacked all around. His editor, whose name is Karl, is a dour, fiftyish man with no apparent connection to the wealth he chronicles.

"I got what was a bit of an odd call, and it made me think of you," Karl says.

"I'm not sure whether that's good."

"I'm not sure either, but it could be paying work, and you seem to need paying work."

"Yes, I'll take it," Jimmy says. "So now you can just tell me."

"I got a call from a gentleman who wants to commission a private autobiography. Ever heard of something like that?"

"No."

"A convention of the very rich. Men of wealth have done this for years. Limited edition, leather-bound, linen paper, hand-printed. Old men, usually recounting youthful exploits. Think *Memoirs of Casanova*, except badly written, with a little *How to Succeed in Business* thrown in. It's not intended as literature, believe me. I've done a few, which is why I got the call. The 'authors' circulate them among their club chums and golf buddies. Wives usually don't even know about them, which is very much part of the wicked fun."

"But is the pay good?"

"The pay is great. What's required of you is complete

confidentiality and many signatures acknowledging same. And, as importantly, my assurance to this client that you're trustworthy. No leaking shit to the *Boston Herald* gossip column."

"And you think I am . . . trustworthy?"

"No idea. But I can't spare anyone else. I have the year-end issue to put out. Besides, my impression is that the people you'd tell aren't people this guy cares about. As long as you don't touch his circle, everything's likely fine."

"It doesn't sound so hard."

"I doubt it is. The guy wants a ghostwriter to punch up his story, really just to type his story. The very rich, as you may know, can't type. They need someone to carry out data input. And to keep his mouth shut."

"That's not a problem," Jimmy says. "I don't even have any friends."

The editor laughs. "Quit pitching. I already told him you were the guy I recommend."

Jimmy is out of there by ten-thirty, without a clue as to where to go now. Beyond three weeks ago, he would already be on his favorite use-shined barstool, having ducked out of work for an early "lunch," already in warm-gutted free fall, all productivity stowed away for yet another day. His best work was usually done between the hours of ten-thirty and eleven, and in that narrow window he did enough not to get fired, amazingly. Now he's working five or six hours a day and spending the rest distractedly watching television or taking long walks in which The Itch is a never-failing companion. He finds as well that his walks sometimes loop him unexpectedly back to William J. Day Boulevard, just past L Street, where the pavement holds no answers but where he returns anyway, as if it is a whetstone for his newly found will. There are no more dispatches emerging about the boy who fell from the car. It would seem that his prosecution for matters sexually criminal has been averted, because it cannot much matter at this point.

Jimmy knows he needs this gig, hearing some rich man's boasting recollections, and he will do it well. Maybe this will be his calling, to hear it, and set it down, and secret it away. It's his best prospect and he needs to keep on with this. All he knows is that he needs some sort of continuous movement. But goddamn, does he want a drink right now.

+ +

10

Her father might come looking in that half-hearted way he does everything, primarily to be able to say he did so. He tried to keep Jeanmarie in school; he tried to persuade her to get a job; he tried to get her to stay at home. He makes just enough of an effort to not be questioned or criticized, and he defends from there on. *What could I do? Nothing I could do . . .*

So Jeanmarie sits at the open and screenless window of her new bedroom—hers and Bobby's bedroom—not expecting her father to come looking (he'd have to make an effort to actually figure out where Bobby is living), but ready to go out the back door just in case. No way she's going home. No way.

Feeling the breeze come in off the bay is as nice a sensation as she's had today. The days have been long and eventless; boring, but boring in a different way than they were when she was holed up in her bedroom avoiding her parents, wishing she were anywhere else. Bobby's roommates come and go and they are deferent. She is the goddess in this particular universe, and for now they seem grateful, especially as she lounges in her panties and one of Bobby's beer-brand t-shirts. There's no food in the place but the empty pizza boxes are stacked by the back door, giving the interior of the place, away from this third-floor window, a greasy tang. The pizza belongs to the roommates, usually. Bobby is working his ass off at the Liquor Mart and he's trying to put money away for better things than pizza. He wants a motorcycle.

It's been four days and not a sign of her father. Jeanmarie has pretty much not left the place since she arrived, having decided that a period of prolonged hiding might allow things to blow over as well as give proper time to think about the plan from here, which did not extend much beyond the actual leaving of home and arrival at Bobby's. Meanwhile, Bobby has been doing nothing but working at the Liquor Mart and coming home to sleep. They drink beers he has smuggled out of the stock, they smoke some weed he gets from his roommates, they make love quickly. Then Bobby sleeps while Jeanmarie watches the sky and waits for the knock on the door, if not her father's then one of those lackeys of his, whom she despises just as much.

She's known Bobby since she was thirteen. They began having sex not long after that, in parks and basements and in the scraggly brush up at The Point. He jokes that he'll end up in jail for the pleasure of this, but she promises she won't tell, because she loves him so much. Her father has accused her of this very act, and she has shrieked at him that he is a liar. She has not become pregnant even though sometimes she and Bobby aren't all that smart about things, especially when he's high and drunk. She has begun to wonder if something is wrong with one of them, that she hasn't become pregnant. They have never discussed what would happen if she did. She knows it would make her father very angry, and that wouldn't be good for Bobby.

The traffic over on Broadway is the only sound other than the breeze. She can hear the horns and skids of angry migration, the shouts and shrieks. Up here it's just deadness and a hot wind and the relentless hours. She has washed clothes in the sink and hung them on the rope they've strung across the back fire stairs, and she's done what she can to tidy up her and Bobby's room.

Down below on the sidewalk there are footsteps, but they lack momentum. She can hear whoever it is shuffling in indecision, or maybe waiting. She leans out the window and sees a person down below, a guy. He looks as if he is waiting for someone as he glances up and down the street, shuffling in his sneakers with his hands stuffed in his jeans pockets. Just then he looks up and sees her. It's Christopher.

"Hey," he says.

"What are you doing here?" she says.

"Nothing."

"Well, do nothing somewhere else."

He nods and thinks about that for a second. "Why?"

"Because it's my house and I said to screw."

He nods again. "Why, though?"

"Because you remind me of my neighborhood."

"Really?"

"Yeah. So who are you waiting for down there?"

Christopher shuffles a bit more and then looks up. "You," he says.

When Bobby comes up the stairs with a six-pack of cans in each hand and his t-shirt pulled off and wrapped around his neck, Jeanmarie wishes she could have some food for him, but Bobby's the one with the money so he'll have to decide.

His feet pound the stairs as if he is in a pitch battle with gravity, his legs too bandy to mount the last few steps. When he comes through the door and sees Jeanmarie sitting on the floor of the living room with Christopher, he stops and grins in that way that says he's not happy.

"Who the fuck is this?" he says.

"This is my neighbor," she says. "From my old neighborhood."

"Is your whole neighborhood fucking moving in?"

"Just visiting," Christopher says.

"He helped me move here," Jeanmarie says. "I said I'd give him a beer."

Bobby shoves his six-pack of Natty Lights at Christopher. "So then have a beer."

"I'm thirteen," Christopher says.

"I started drinking when I was eleven," Bobby says.

"Well in that case," Christopher says, plucking a can off the ring.

He has no intention of drinking it, but Christopher opens it as a kind of tribal appeasement. As Bobby watches, smiling, Christopher slugs down a mouthful, and absorbs the brackish and unfamiliar taste. Bobby and Jeanmarie open theirs and Jeanmarie says, "It's warm, though."

Bobby snorts down a mouthful. "I just walked all the way from the Liquor Mart in the heat," he says. "What in the fuck did you expect?"

"I'm just saying," Jeanmarie says.

+ +

11

The CEO's office of Driscoll, Irving, Rafferty Investments is pretty much what Jimmy expected. The hushed domain. The wood paneling and Persian rugs over parquet floor, and brass fixtures. Carved furniture and silver tea services. All of it retrofitted into the girders and sheetrock of a forty-eight story office building, and situated in the seaward corner of the uppermost floor behind a double-receptionist station appointed in the dissimilar black granite and track lights of a far more corporate sensibility. And out again to the next ring of smaller standard-issue offices and the tight skirting of the cubicled masses, the necessary congregation. Beyond the heavy velvet window drapes, pulled back now, one can sight South Boston out across the water, low and dank, wrapped in a steamy summer haze on this unseasonable early-October day. There is a five-foot-long brass telescope on a chrome tripod, and if Jimmy were to peer through it he might see the rooftop of his own place.

"I keep it there for a reason," Terrance Walsh Rafferty says, entering the room where Jimmy has been waiting, having caught the telescope catching Jimmy's eye. "That's part of the story. Want to hear it?"

The man, whose name Jimmy was at least somewhat familiar with, takes him by surprise. He is smallish, and his face could not in any way be characterized as handsome. He is bald with a small mouth and a toothsome grin which, regrettably, reminds Jimmy of a mouse.

"I'm ready," Jimmy says.

"I hope it doesn't prove too boring," Rafferty says. "I hope it isn't too clichéd. The fact is that I have that telescope locked on the projects, The Old Colony, where I came from nothing." He laughs a little. "But I think you know that anybody from Southie who amounted to anything can say the same thing. If they weren't from nothing, they'd have lived in Milton or Westwood—you know, where the people who matter live."

"I understand," Jimmy says. "I grew up in Milton, actually. But not in the really good part."

"Of course, in the larger sense, mine is the story of a guy who does a little business and plays as much golf as he can manage."

"I'm sure that's not the case, sir. I'm sure your story is interesting."

"And you understand all the forms. Confidentiality, liability, consequences. You can have a lawyer look it over if you like. I'm told it's fairly standard language for this sort of thing."

"There's standard language for this sort of thing?"

Rafferty finds this raucously amusing. When he stops laughing, he says, "Yes, apparently."

Rafferty is lean, with a hawk-like nose and that crooked overbite. Yet, not surprisingly, the man is oddly attractive, or at least commanding. There is a presence about him that he seems not to be trying to push. He is slouched back in his leather desk chair, golf clubs leaning on a wall behind him, his suit crisp and hung on him in a manner that speaks of Italian tailors, hand-guided needles and the best thread, and one's own pattern kept in a draw in a quiet North End bespoke shop. It is a pinstriped flannel as befits a man of such stature. But Jimmy can tell even from across the broad oak desk that it is a fabric he has never once touched, something so soft and airy as to have the comfort Jimmy can only imagine in cotton t-shirts and mesh gym shorts. The room is cold, and Jimmy is damp and chilled after the walk up State Street in the sultry morning heat. Fall is said to be coming but the hot weather hangs on and the streets at the bottom of these buildings trap and radiate it. In Rafferty's office, a fire crackles in a hearth across the room and, while it surely must be fed by natural gas, Jimmy can't figure out why he smells the faint air of wood smoke. Jimmy supposes Rafferty to be one of those people who never really has to step into the real air anymore. He can move from climate-controlled office to hushed cool livery cars to his carefully regulated home (wherever and how many there would be). Jimmy expects that Rafferty only has to interact with the climate's vicissitudes on a country-club fairway or the deck of a yacht, which is hardly the same. He supposes that all will be revealed soon enough. If he were to look through that powerful telescope to the projects on which it is fixed, he would likely see someone sitting on his stoop in a wifebeater and shower sandals, escaping the oven of a room in which he passes his life.

"You're a quiet guy," Rafferty says.

"I can tell you whatever it is you need to know about me," Jimmy says.

"No, quiet meaning good. I figure you're a listener. If I'm reading you right. But can I ask you one question?"

"Go ahead."

"Are you hung over?'

Jimmy lifts his head. "No sir. I don't drink."

Rafferty nods. "My father was a lush. I always think I have a sense of these things. You did drink, though."

"Yes."

"When was the last time?"

"Four weeks ago."

Rafferty's jagged grin forms like a coalescing front. "How long did you drink for?"

"Twenty-one years."

"And you're thirty-two."

"Yes." Jimmy shifts in his seat. "If that disqualifies me . . ."

"No, no," Rafferty says. "I'm just getting things sized up. You look like a man who could use a change."

"True enough," Jimmy says.

"And I'm the cure, is it?"

"If you want to put it that way. I'm just after honest work and a simple existence at this point."

"And what do you know about me?" Rafferty says.

"Only what I read here and there in the papers. If you're asking me what my predisposition is, I don't think I really have one."

"Fair enough," Rafferty says. "Because I guess in one's life there are three kinds of stories told about you: There's the one that other people tell about you, there's the one you tell to get yourself somewhere, and there's the one you tell when you've found some reason to look at yourself in the hard light."

"Do you think those stories can ever all be the same?"

"For some people," Rafferty says. "For the people who live those simple lives you're after."

"Which story are you planning to tell?" Jimmy says.

Rafferty laughs in a way that makes Jimmy understand that Rafferty is starting to like him. "Why, the true story, naturally."

Jimmy's eyes wander involuntarily. It seems otherworldly, to be so wealthy, to hold a sum thousands of times more than what most people Jimmy knows could earn in a lifetime of harsh work. His father used to say about people like this that they simply could not find the off switch when they had accumulated as much as they possibly could need. The old man, in fact, was someone who had assembled the kind of simple kingdom that probably gave him all the things that Rafferty had right now, which was a basic deliverance from want. The old man had a car that never failed him, a home that he found endless comfort in, and a level of respect that, while it only stretched a few blocks in any direction, meant something to him. Jimmy, as someone with under a thousand dollars in the bank and prospects with near horizons, knows he could easily be stupefied.

"I'll pay you well for your silence," Rafferty says.

"That's why I'm here," Jimmy says.

12

Bobby, floating in that brief window of time between arriving at the apartment with his pilfered six-packs and falling asleep naked in front of the fan—a slice of time that ranges generally between one hour and two—likes to do it. On top of her in the humid air, sweat beading along his back and dripping in rivulets down his ribs and onto the already-damp sheets, the skin on his hairless belly sliding wetly on hers, he grunts from what seems a great distance; even as his breath blows hot in her drenched face, this is the time when she feels least intimate with her man. She presumes it must be her own issue. When he finishes, it is as if he has just awakened: The overheated room and the sweat stinging his eyes seem instantly intolerable, and he leaps each time to hurry to the shower. When, after, in his boxers, he lies damp on the bed in front of that cheap plastic fan, he is already fading. He tells her that because he spends most of his day inside the walk-in cooler at the Liquor Mart, the summer heat that grips this dark room is even more oppressive, his body thrown off by these lurching shifts of temperature. He tells her that this moment, drying by the fan, is his only real shot at getting to sleep before the heat keeps him tossing in the bed. Jeanmarie observes that it seems to work every time. By midnight she's lying in the dark next to him, listening to the sound through the bedroom door of the television being watched by the roommates, whom she does not care to join, given their fevered knowledge of what has just happened in the bedroom, only a wall away. So she lies in the dark, fully awake, thinking about their future.

Bobby is spending money he probably shouldn't, but who is she to complain with no job at all? She feels neither the confidence nor the inclination to go forward with this, not only because two years at Southie High have fairly well proven she's no genius, but also because it seems as if her looks somehow caught everybody by surprise when she hit about fourteen years of age. Not beautiful in the classic sense but clearly something that makes men stop and look. She presumes that it is this that will take her anywhere at all, and that she must attach it to something or someone sooner rather than later. She does hold in her mind a faint romanticism about this, now, living with Bobby, because she is convinced that their living circumstances won't be this way for long. Bobby works long hours. It's important, he says, as being at the Liquor Mart can put you in touch with the right kinds of people. This is Southie, after all, where the real hierarchy is more deeply embedded than what might at first seem obvious. Whitey is gone, but still hovers over all.

Bobby's father had run afoul of that very hierarchy, shot dead coming out of O'Kelley's Tavern on a spring night in his twenty-fifth year, 1983. Bobby was three, and has since been raised to respect the existing order of things. And what Jeanmarie suspects is that the minor legend of his father's death—Billy Casey, humble and hardworking construction worker, looking for nothing more than a quiet draw on a cold beer after a long day in the unrelenting sun, only to be sucked into a meaningless bar fight with a

Bulger stooge (and then ill-advisedly kicking the guy's ass on top of it)—has made Bobby both afraid of, and seduced by, the brutal plainness of that particular kind of power. Jeanmarie secretly suspects Billy Casey should have damn well known better, but for his own strain of youthful hubris.

Jeanmarie also suspects that, local memory being what it is, there may even be an odd sympathy for Bobby, some engendered guilt that helps him along his way. Indeed, Whitey may have gone on the lam four years ago, but anyone who thinks much has really changed is being naïve. The others float in the aftermath. Bobby, when he first met her and seemed to be trying to impress her, could point them out as if they were the only true celebrities that mattered. There was "Little Kevin," Kevin Weeks, the disenfranchised lieutenant, out at BC High watching his lumbering kid, Kevin Jr., at freshman football practice; up in the splintery bleachers in his shades, awaiting his own prosecution, his own presumed evaporation into either federal prison or witness protection. Or the one they called Big Kevin, Kevin O'Neil, a man shaped like a mountain with the fat foothills of his hips and stomach rising up humped shoulders to the pointed head with its ruin of an acne-scarred face. Some people said he owned Triple O's, but others said it was just a front. Bobby had once gotten to slip into the Boston Athletic Club and watch Big Kevin's Sunday-morning workout, when he put 225 pounds on the bar and cranked out twenty-nine reps on the bench press as his admiring buddies counted them out. Bobby was quietly made aware that this was beyond the capability of most any of the New England Patriots, which was akin to saying someone was holier than the Pope himself. Bobby had been made witness. And Big Kevin was a man approaching fifty years of age. He had messed up many faces to conditions worse then his own staggeringly repulsive mug. Bobby knew all the names—Zip and The Rifleman and Cadillac Frank and the Winter Hill Gang—which he repeated like novenas, all the while rarely mentioning his own father who was presumed to have died in their very nexus.

So Bobby, in that brief window of time between arriving with his six-packs and falling into heavy-lidded sleep, says nearly nothing, an extant sign of his apparent initiation. He allows only that he could use more money, all the hours of work notwithstanding. He used to talk about his gambling but he doesn't anymore, but she has no way of really interpreting the meaning of that turn.

+ + + + + + + + + + + + + + + + + + + +

13

For Colleen the aloneness has never really abated. It seems like a tired joke, that her husband would have died in that quickly forgotten non-war, far away from any of the shooting that may have actually gone on. She has been reminded more than once that what happened was just *one of those things* that could have happened back home, but when she's been told this she hasn't been sure what meaning to take from it. She received a death benefit and was mustered out of the Army soon enough, a now-single mother with a small boy and no real help. She and Barry had told each other more than once that they would not return to Southie. Never. The plan was he'd work at the airport and they'd live up north, maybe over the border into New Hampshire—a cabin, a lake, a commute away. But here she is, again on the couch, lying in wait for her wandering son to come in from those same streets.

It's after nine o'clock. She has twice gone to his room to knock on the door, not fully convinced that he hasn't somehow slipped past her. The third time, she does the unspeakable and enters the room, in violation of all they have negotiated. Her grounds are his own abdication of his pledge, which, while never quite articulated, had a spirit that has now been breached.

He is too young for this. The regret floods her, of decisions poorly made and stands not taken. She never should have let him leave Most Holy Trinity School; it seems to her now to be the pin on which all else was held together. Father John had been right and she can only think of the finality of how things were left. Again, her own fault, the extended trance of having lost a husband and of thinking that was enough, that nothing more could be done to her while at all points her own son was drifting off into a life she could not guess at. Only now as it all collapses does she acknowledge all she should have done.

It's near ten when she finally hears his key in the door, and she stands from the couch to confront him. She is shaking, down through her legs and into her ankles, weak, as if she might sink to the floor. But she does not. He comes in with his head down and she does not speak, waiting for him to do so first. He seems not to even see her. He shuts the door quietly, deep in thought, and walks by her toward his room. And she cannot speak. She cannot find the words, can pull no sound from within her, cannot even remotely imagine how something like this works. She has never shouted at her son. Her voice has barely risen, in all these years, above a whisper. She has drifted as he drifts. She has expected it to turn out all right.

He goes to his room and shuts the door. She has not inhaled since she heard the key in the door. She begins to cry and stands there for a while, even as she hears the music from behind his bedroom door, shutting her out.

In the morning, she awakens on the couch. His bedroom door is still shut. She sits up and takes the phone off the coffee table and calls her boss, saying she slept poorly, promising to be in by noon. He needs her sooner, if she can do that, he says.

For an hour she waits for her son to emerge, sitting on the couch in the rumpled clothing in which she slept, unwilling to budge until he emerges, until they've had it out. She is still shaken by the way he went by her last night, wraithlike, disembodied, as if she could have screamed and he wouldn't have heard her. But she did not scream at him; she slowly comes to the conclusion that she will not scream at him or at anyone else. She screamed when Barry died and is forever screamed out. She can no longer give herself voice.

Her son does not emerge. He is already gone. He is so gone she wonders if she ever had him at all, or whether she had simply been sleepwalking through his childhood, thinking they were connected, that they were overcoming this thing together, when in fact he had always been in a separate orbit, inured to her grieving distance, politely going along with it because there was not much else he was able to do.

She goes to her bedroom and gets her handbag and keys. She should change her clothes but that somehow seems to her a concession, self-absorption. She has an idea— and maybe it's stupid, but all her thoughts and actions may have been ill-considered. This, at worst, will just be another in a long string of bad parenting decisions. She wishes so badly that Barry were here. She thought she'd be over it but, of course, she never truly will be. Christopher is his flesh and blood as well as hers, the gift she shares with this dead man, the son she now realizes, with dire clarity, she has let down so badly.

She comes out of the house and goes up the block to where she has wedged her car into an available space, and finds a note stuck under her wiper: *Stay out of my fucking space.* She rips it up and throws it on the pavement—she does not give a fuck about anybody's fucking parking space. After all these years she feels the urgency, as if she is on fire, engulfed in flames, as if she needs to be saved right this instant. There is only one place she can think to go.

She does not know Father John very well, but she knows that both Barry and Christopher have been, in their times, under this man's guidance. She is the last adult in this familial constellation, all four of her son's grandparents having passed, from smoking and fast driving on the Expressway, from pleurisy and fast driving on narrow streets. She feels the deep aloneness, the orphaned spareness, of this life.

At the rectory, she looks for a parking space. Father John's big black car is in the small driveway cut in through the fence for him at the back of the building. She does not want to miss him. She finds a side street, where she double-parks against an Oldsmobile with a flat tire, and hurries toward the rectory, only then becoming aware of her state of dishevelment. She doesn't want to come at him like a crazy woman, although she is exactly that, or so it would seem. She rakes her fingernails through her hair, trying at least to mat it down. She rings the doorbell and waits. She peers through the window down the dark hallway. There is no sign of motion although she knows there is a housekeeper. Colleen rings the doorbell again, and waits, then rings again. Finally, from the shadows, shuffles the housekeeper, who seems in no hurry. She looks through the door before opening it, and then unlocks it, opening it a bit and filling the small space to block an attempted entrance.

"Yes?" the woman says.

"I'd like to talk to Father John."

"May I ask your name?"

"Colleen Coogan. I'm Christopher's mother."

The housekeeper takes on a look then. "Why don't you just wait here? I don't know if he's home."

"I saw his car in the back," Colleen says. The housekeeper looks down. She pushes the door shut and Colleen paces the porch, waiting. This priest is the only one she can think of who can help. She has a brother she hasn't seen in years. He's trouble and bringing him in would serve no purpose.

The housekeeper is back.

"I'm sorry, Father isn't here," she says.

"Can I come back?"

"I don't know when he will be back," the housekeeper says. "He has a very busy schedule."

Colleen is frozen. There is no place else to go. She stands on the porch, looking at the housekeeper shut and lock the door. When she goes around the block to her car, she sees that Father John's car is now gone from its space.

+ +

14

The mystery, so far as Jimmy is concerned, is why someone like Rafferty needs to be commissioning this vanity project, this private autobiography. The man is richer than Jimmy can really comprehend, endlessly lauded as a business genius, a leader in the community. Everything, in other words, that should make this guy above such crass self-affirmation. But as Jimmy rode the T into the city, carrying in his backpack a newly purchased tape recorder, ten blank tapes and ten blank notebooks, he knew he wanted to hear the story. Maybe he'll actually learn something. Maybe it will point the way.

Jimmy's being given a fifty-minute hour today to begin the work. He figures he will try to move through as much of the man's early years as he can, because already his sense is that time with the man will be scarce. He sits at the conference table in Rafferty's office, waiting as if for a papal audience. Jimmy has three pens in his pocket, and he has loaded a tape in the recorder and set it on the long mahogany table. He stares out the window at the fog of low cloud that has enveloped the building; the changing weather, and whispers of fall behind it. He has not had a drink in more than a month.

Time has seemed, in that month, to be deeply attenuated. He sits for stretches in his apartment, with the television blaring on to no effect. He finds himself swallowing compulsively, as if he cannot contain his own saliva. Nights, he lies in bed waiting for sleep and forcing himself not to look at the clock, which, of course, he then looks at. His heart feels thick, labored, sludgy. The sensation is one he never noticed drunk. But now it seems to pin him to the mattress, to thud ponderously inside him as he tries to find escape. Then there are the dreams. In his drunkenness he didn't dream at all, passing into a state that was blank and dark. Now, in newfound sobriety, the dreams are vivid, come one after another, and are usually troubling. One will startle him awake and he will lie there, convincing himself that what just happened was not real, until sleep comes again and he lapses into a new horror. Many seem to come from years ago, from one averted trap or another. He wakes in the dawn, dry and exhausted. At this moment, he is nearly fading as he sits at a conference table, holding a delicate china cup with a rime of coffee at its bottom and no more refills.

He had gone through the worst of the withdrawal about a week after. He'd never tried quitting before but he knew it would be bad, like a sailor hitting that first barometric drop and feeling the change in the weather before it becomes visible. The storm itself visited him late in an afternoon when fatigue dropped him and left him working his way toward sleep, but then not allowing it. He had ached through days in which he could not eat and the shakes became deeply borne. He had the sense of his body imploding on itself, and the urge to drink was nearly shuddering through him. He paced in a palsied gait, not fully in control; he showered and flipped television channels compulsively; he worked at forcing himself instead to see the image of the boy's head hitting the pavement. He touched it like an amulet, owning it and letting himself be further shrunken and dried by its horror. He sat with a piece of computer paper and tried to draw it, trying to bring it back into the world, an image that could survive the fleeting of that instant. In the mornings of that stretch, he rose from bed shaking and wracked with odd and mysterious aches, some so knifelike he imagined internal bleeding and festering wounds, where, drunk, he had not. He got up and walked to the convenience store for coffee and a newspaper, making it his habit to search the pages for any dispatches regarding the accident or the boy. He looked at the obits and death notices, wondering whether that agony had mercifully ended.

He also pondered why this event was the thing to make him try to change. He had not even contemplated drying out, before that moment. Drinking was too gratifying. But he has since wondered whether this was the cliché of it—that he needed in some way to bless the horror. And if it is a cliché, does it not follow that he will have no hope? He doesn't even know what the motivation is: The premise of some more orderly life? Of some kind of end to his isolation? He has no idea, and yet he doesn't drink, fights the urge, continues to exist in this painful state. It completely contradicts the notion of willpower, because that presumes an outcome.

And now he will record this rich man's rich life, a life so laden with good fortune—the blessing, at least, of brains and instinct, and maybe (the story might admit) of plain old shit luck, the kind you really have to be smart to recognize—and he feels a sickness that has underlaid every thought and motion. He already hates the man deeply at this moment, but it's likely wise to hate one's wealthy boss until otherwise convinced.

The door swings open and Rafferty strides in, big in every way except the physical, his presence sucking up the room. He takes off his suit coat and throws it on the leather couch, then flops into his desk chair.

"I guess it would make more sense for me to make notes, wouldn't it?" Rafferty says. "I guess it's a slow go for me to just talk."

"Whichever way you prefer," Jimmy says. "You're paying me by the hour."

Rafferty nods. "Then we're good, I guess."

"So where do we start?"

"We start by you taking that tape recorder and those tapes and throwing them in that wastebasket over there. Don't worry, I'm paying for it."

Jimmy does as he is told, and takes out a notebook.

"Throw that away, too," Rafferty says. "Everything you do will stay in this building. You will work in a small office down the hall on a laptop computer I provide. I will dictate right into the computer through a microphone. It's all been set up by the tech people. You will work at night. Come in anytime after six at night and make sure you leave by six in the morning. Security has your information. They will show your where to make coffee. You'll leave it all in that room when you leave. No notebooks."

"I just wanted to get my facts straight."

"You will. And I'll review everything you write, and make corrections."

"I'm ready to start when you tell me."

Rafferty looks out the window into the fog. "Right away," he says. "Tonight."

15

Bobby comes home late Friday night carrying a bottle of vodka, which he pulls by the neck from a paper bag, and with a triumphant flourish waves over his head like an Olympic torch.

"Did you *steal* that?" Jeanmarie says. She's sitting cross-legged on the bed in a t-shirt that says, "Angel." It's late and she has stayed in the bedroom in the dark while the roommates ate pizza and watched the black-and-white in the living room.

"I wouldn't call it stealing," Bobby says. "It's more like a tip."

"They knew you took it?"

"More or less. They have to act like they don't so they don't get popped for procuring for the underaged. They know I'm doing it even though they act like they don't."

"Those guys worry about the law?"

"Yeah," Bobby says. "They say they don't need unnecessary trouble. Necessary trouble is another matter."

Bobby sits next to Jeanmarie and unscrews the bottle cap. He sniffs along the edges of it, his eyelids fluttering, then looks at her. "Ever had the hard stuff?"

"No."

"You gonna try it?"

"I'll try whatever you want," she says. This is her bravery, trying anything for her man because she has no way back to anything else.

Bobby hands the bottle to her.

"Aren't we going to put it in glasses, at least?" she says.

"They're all dirty. This is fun."

She takes a swig and comes up coughing. "That sucks!" she says, handing him the bottle. She wipes her tears on the shoulders of her shirt.

"Some things you first think suck turn out to be pretty good," Bobby says, taking a manly belt from the bottle. "I'm gonna have you try a bunch of new things."

Jeanmarie isn't sure how to react to that one.

"I got some ideas," Bobby says, pushing, but she's still not biting. Through the window behind his head, there is a luminescence in the sky where the city lights penetrate the fog, which has hung on the city all day. There is a whiff of sulfur in the air.

"I got some things I want you to try," he says.

"I heard you the first two times. I told you already."

She just doesn't want to hear about it right now. She just wants to lay there with him on the bed and not think about anything else. He's jazzed up tonight, thinking of his new friends and his new plans, the things he'll do. He won't be his father, dumb enough to be on the outside of it all.

The room feels close right now and the way he is swilling the vodka, it'll be a short night after a long wait, unless she does something.

"You want to go for a walk?" she says.

He brings the bottle down and wipes his mouth with the back of his hand. "A walk? Now?"

"Yeah, it's cooler tonight. Let's go down and walk on Day Boulevard."

"Day Boulevard?"

"Yeah, it's nice out. It'll be nice to walk by the water."

"Forget it," Bobby says. "I been on my fucking feet all day."

"Yeah and I been cooped up in this fucking apartment all day, too. Come on. Let's go out."

"Later," he says.

This town, Southie, this criss-cross of narrow alphabetized streets, of deep grudges and of favors carefully cataloged and owed, is as intricate as the chemistry she could not fathom in that overheated classroom, the hidden symbols and interlocking pieces growing into bigger and bigger systems, the combination of disparate elements making something completely new, and often explosive. And like the chemistry, it all exists below what can be seen, the presumed to be, beneath what is hard and visible. Bobby is inserting himself in that volatile mix, and, once in, there is no presumption of his ever really getting out.

He is forcing down another bitter swallow and she touches his leg. "Easy," she says. "We got all night." He looks at her as if she is only a vaguely familiar face. He's already descending.

After a half-hour hoping he'll come back out of it, she leaves him sleeping on the bed and goes out the door, to walk. She needs to, despite the dark. Outside, it does not surprise her that Christopher is sitting on a bench about a block down. When he sees her, he stands, hesitant.

"Yeah, come on," she says.

He runs across the street and falls in next to her as she walks.

"Where's Bobby?" he says.

"Sleeping."

"This early?"

"He worked hard all day. Why are you sitting on a bench at eleven o'clock at night?"

"My mother is waiting up for me," Christopher says. "Where you going?"

"Day Boulevard."

"Really? Why?"

"To get some fucking air by the water, is why. Why does everybody keep asking me why?"

Christopher says nothing, and keeps walking after her.

Down at the sea wall, by McCormack Pavilion, she slows. She stays on the sidewalk along the seawall, streetlights burning above them, a few dark figures on the beach down by the moonlit water. The air is thick with low tide, muck-salty from the tepid wind off the harbor. The cars drift along the boulevard, and as Jeanmarie walks, looking straight ahead, she can feel the burning stares coming from car windows. She knows she gets them. She has ever since she grew a chest. She wonders how often her father, driving, keeps an eye out for her. She wonders why he doesn't leap out of a car now and attempt to drag her home. It hasn't been that long since she moved in with Bobby, but she feels as if she hasn't left the apartment in years. She's pissed at Bobby right now, that he isn't here with her, that he won't do what she wants to do, even just once in a while.

Farther up, they approach the L Street bathhouse. The dealers are out, having rolled up in their cars for an easy night of window business—just kids like Bobby, maybe even working for the same people. A Boston Police cruiser rolls by, undeterred.

"That's where it happened," Christopher says, pointing up ahead.

"What?"

"That's where Butchie Morrissey got his neck broken, right up ahead."

"Serves him fucking right," Jeanmarie says.

"My mother knows his parents. They weren't really speaking to him, but now they have to figure out what to do with him. He's still at Mass. General. Nobody knows what to do with him now. He wants his buddies to kill him, but they won't."

"Those guys? Why not?"

"I heard that he didn't earn enough favors for that," Christopher says.

+ +

16

Father John cannot deny the disappointment he feels. With his retirement fast approaching, he feels as if no one is really doing much to mark the occasion. In these last few months, as he approaches his final official duties, people have simply gone on with their lives. He imagines that this is the way it is, even for a man whose life was one of duty. The holier thing, of course, would be to not mind. But there is that piece of him he doesn't always like that wants what it wants. And most disappointing is that the Archbishop has made no contact at all. John has served his Cardinal well; he has, in these last thirty years, taken transfers to more than a dozen different parishes. Uncomplainingly. Always pushed to move on, almost as soon as he's felt a connection.

Such is the way things are. John climbs the steps of the Chancery, having arrived without an appointment because the Archbishop's secretary never seems to be able to find a time for him, never seems to be able to work him into His Holiness's admittedly busy day. But he has known Bernard for too many years to get brushed aside, despite His Holiness's clear ambitions for greater things, his desire to be the first American Pope and CEO. John has come here on this sunny morning hoping he can be seen before His Holiness's day becomes busy and demanding.

John has not been in the Chancery in three years, since the last time he met with Bernard, on that day of surprising turn. He'd been at a parish way out in Blackstone then and had gotten a sudden call summoning him, and had sat quietly while Bernard told him that he would again be moved. The surprise was that it was back to Southie. He had been there two decades before and he hadn't guessed he'd ever come back to the place he'd worked in as a younger priest, the place as well of his childhood. A month ago, when Bernard informed him that it was time for John to retire, it had been a hurried and stammering telephone conversation, not at all the thoughtful thing. But even then, John had said, *Bernard, you'll come to my retirement dinner . . .*

Oh, sure, sure, I'll be there. You can count on it.

And that was the last John had heard. It seems that an old friend might do well to do more than that. John must admit he feels cast adrift. His new parishioners have their lives and he has not been among them so long; his old parishioners, the ones who had seemed to be stunned by his return after so many years, are not at all in touch. He'd just like, well, *something*.

The Cardinal's Residence is a truly splendid building, the kind that reminds us of God's power, or at least of the Church's. It is a looming building in the Renaissance style, unlike the Chancery itself, which has that vague air of a successful business, all clean lines and neatly squared sensibilities. And so close, all of it, to the seminary in which he had been reared, after his escape from his sad family. There it is, just through the trees, with its pudding-stone walls and conical turrets. St. Clement's had been the junior seminary then. He'd been a boy among boys, learning God's mysterious imperatives. He decides he might take a walk that way, after this matter at hand.

Inside the front entrance, all is quiet. He hears footsteps from afar and wends his way through, looking, admiring, and aware of the contrast with his own modest living quarters. But Bernard was always heading toward bigger things.

"John?"

He comes out of his reverie. It is an old friend, Roger Hart, a Jesuit and aide to the Cardinal. Roger looks baffled. "John, what are you doing here?"

"I thought I'd drop in on Bernard," John says.

Roger is silent, seemingly considering John's words.

"John, one does not just 'drop in' on His Eminence."

"But I've tried making appointments and he never has time . . ."

Roger is shaking his head furiously now, tut-tut-tut, disapproving of that thought.

"Roger, I want him to come to my retirement party. He said he would. It would be an honor to me. For Bernard to sit with me as I finish this life of work."

"John . . ." Roger closes his eyes. "I don't think that's possible. So much going on these days. It's a shame you took so much time coming out here. Maybe you should be on your way now."

"I can wait," John says. "I haven't anything until my five-thirty Mass."

"Oh, John, goodness no. You really have to go."

"No," Father John says. "I'll wait. Maybe I won't get to speak to His Eminence, but I don't mind trying."

Roger seems bested now, tut-tutting still, but quieted.

"Sit right over here, then," Roger says. "I'll see what I can do."

John seats himself on a long wooden bench, folding his hands in his lap. He is ready for a long wait. He feels acutely sad, that he can be ending things so thoroughly forgotten. He'll move to a Jesuit retirement residence; they've suggested one in Arizona, where he will have a small apartment among the other old priests. He'll be a decade younger than the youngest ones there. A bit of golf, he supposes; a bit of reading he could not do amid his duties. He doesn't much look forward to it.

"Father John?"

He looks up and sees a uniformed security guard. This man is not much younger than Father John himself, and he looks like he'd rather not be doing what he's doing right now, which is trying to look imposing. His nameplate says "A. R. Pesare."

"Time to go home," Pesare says. "You can't stay around here."

"I don't mind waiting."

"No, Father," Pesare says. "Forgive me, but I've been told to escort you out."

"By whom?" Father John says.

"By a higher authority than myself," Pesare says, reaching for his arm.

+ + + + + + + + + + + + + + + + + + + +

17

I guess when most people talk about how they learned the ropes, they either cast themselves as the picture of piety or as someone with some kind of remarkable street smarts. But what I've learned, I think, is that the things you do to get ahead are things you might later be ashamed to admit. But the truth is, I'd have fucked anybody over to get where I wanted to get. And like some guys could throw a curve ball down at the ball field, and other guys could charm the girls, I was good at fucking people over.

With his headphones snugged on his ears to receive this dictation, Jimmy types the statement into the computer—the encrypted laptop provided to him, with its complement of security devices that will prevent him from printing, putting on disk, or in any other way walking out of this room with anything other than what's in his head. He has no intention of doing so. All these words are getting way out ahead of him.

Where I grew up, that was the way you had to get through life. No one who could do you a favor wanted to, and nobody who wanted to could. My parents were off-the-boat Irish, hardworking and, sadly and endearingly, simple. Being simple keeps you hardworking. You bust your ass and just stay a few dollars ahead of broke. If you don't mind life like that, more power to you.

I decided early on that I did mind life like that. Part of it was having money—I admit to having found that owning nice things is enjoyable. But I also found out pretty quickly that having things, or money, is only part of the equation. It really relates to power. And power is not about telling people what to do, exactly. Being able to tell them what to do (to fire or promote, to have them carry out your orders) only reminds them not to screw with you. I don't believe that the essence of power is about imposing yourself on other people. I believe it starts out as just wanting to live your life, and that's the simplest of urges.

Take my first real fight. I remember it well, the way all young men remember theirs. And I don't mean third-grade stuff, I mean the first time real bodily harm is possible, at that age when you first get your strength. I think I was thirteen. I was itching for a fight with this kid Murph. He was a loudmouth and a troublemaker, and he got on this tear in which I somehow had become his primary target. I could say I didn't know why, but I knew why: Because he took me for weak. Because that's the dance you dance. He suddenly noticed me, the smaller kid, and he began with it: Hey you fucking homo, hey you fudgepacker. My mother used to say Ignore It but my father used to say Never Ignore It. My mother thought ignoring stuff made it go away when really my father made it go away and then never mentioned it to her. And this Murphy had seemed to attach to me in a way not apparent except for that rule of boys: Pick on the toughest of the guys you think you can beat. Which leads to the first consideration of power: Those of us who estimate their opponents' power best have the immediate advantage. Because if your opponent is significantly stronger than yourself, you need to know that. But most of us spend all our time comparing our enemies not to ourselves but to an inflated image of ourselves. I see guys on the golf course who throw their clubs after a bad shot. "I've made that shot!" they scream. And they have: once, a fluke, a lucky day. And they think anything less is now beneath them, which is both the worst self-flattery and the most crass of self-deceptions. If they were honest with themselves they would have tried the shot they could actually make. The second consideration, then—or maybe Rule 1A—is to truly, truly know your self, even with its flaws and ugliness.

I knew I wasn't as strong, but I knew I was much faster. And I knew Murph didn't really want to fight. He was just trying to keep the bigger, stronger, older kids from beating his ass. So the stakes were significant. If I lost to Murph, I was easier pickings. But if Murph lost, he was fucked.

What is there to be done? It has to come to you. So you wait. You go to school and enjoy the insulation of it, knowing that when you walk out of that building it is the most dangerous time—there's opportunity and there's an audience, primed from a day immobilized in classrooms, bored out of their minds.

I wanted to start the fight, just to get on with it. But protocol was for Murph to do so. Verbal provocation was fine. He had seemed to be hesitating, and I was hung up in this limbo of waiting for him to come. And then one day he did, because I suspect he was sensing he was losing face. The complexities of the schoolyard have served me well in business. They've ruined more kids these days by making the schoolyard civil! Murph came at me that day like we were in some kind of ritual play, which we were: Hey, pussy, hey, homo . . .

So, Rule 2. Once you decide to make the move, you're in it all the way. Murph was coming at me. I tried to use my speed and pretty quickly I figured out that Murph had made tragically poor estimates of both my abilities and his own. He was on the ground bleeding from the nose in under a minute. I had a scraped elbow and bleeding knee from when I pulled him to the ground. My injuries were probably worse but that was hardly the point. I got up from that pavement a new man, with new respect. I went home and said nothing but I felt certain they saw something, my parents did, some air of victory.

But Rule 3 was something I hadn't learned yet. Murph had been trying to prove himself to his older brother (also Murph to his friends, but whom I will refer to as Big Murph). I have an older brother, but at that point in my life he was long gone. Useless and expelled, not at all like Big Murph. This guy only needed a reason to beat ass, and that reason was my reportedly unprovoked attack on his younger brother. So, Rule 3: Never assume there are really rules to anything. That might be the most important rule of all.

Big Murph caught me coming out of school and simply did away with formalities and rather expediently pounded me into the ground. Ever have your head pounded into pavement? You can feel the dull slam of it in this disconnected sort of way, but there's this sound, almost like a spring—boing, boing, that apparently has something to do with the inner ear. It's fascinating, even as it happens.

My head was split pretty good, but luckily the scar would be hidden relatively well by my hair until middle age, when my hairline receded past it and by then it had become shiny and benign. But I dragged it home, bleeding. Scalp bleeding is the worst. I took off my t-shirt and held it against my head. I came through the kitchen door and my mother went nuts about the t-shirt: We have no money to re-place that! I was glad for that; it gave me a reason to not speak to her and therefore not answer her questions. It probably could have used stitches but we couldn't afford them, either. My father came home and looked at me, by then with a cartoonish gauze bandage wrapped around my head as if I'd come from a Civil War battlefield, and he withheld his counsel, because I already knew that thing he might have offered.

What's the old saying about serving revenge cold? I had that in me from an early age. Things settled down at school and Murph seemed, in an odd way, to lord about—he'd been beaten but, because I'd taken a worse beating from his brother, he somehow thought he came out ahead. After school, I'd take the long route home, in order to follow Murph at a distance, see where he lived, watch who came and went, note the neighbors. Refer back to Rule 1. I hung out after dark on that street, getting a sense of things. I was from the Lower End and this was up on City Point. I waited, until I thought the day was right.

It was a Saturday, and I knew which car on the street was theirs, and I knew they had all gone to Fenway Park to watch the Red Sox. You know what it cost for a fucking bleacher seat at Fenway Park in 1955? Fifty cents! Some poor schmoes from Southie could actually afford to go! They had taken the car to go into the city and I went around to the back porch and felt around. You know how people say they used to leave their back doors open in the old days? I'm about to tell you why nobody does anymore: Me. I went there wearing my ball-cap over the bandages still covering my slow-healing wound. I found the door unlocked and I went in about six inches at a time. What I didn't know was whether there was a grandparent in a bedroom up-stairs, or a dog, or some unexpected thing. But there wasn't. The place was completely quiet. I was a kid but I wasn't dumb and, in my pocket, I had a pair of my mother's dishwashing gloves, which she usually kept under the sink and wouldn't miss until after din-ner. I walked around the place. Looking at everything, but unde-cided as to what it was I would specifically do. I knew generally what I was going to do. Here's Rule 4: Fuck Rule 4—always refer to Rule 3 from here on. What you do is find someone's irrationally weak spot. The weak spot they're most afraid to admit. The damage you do should be fair. I wasn't going to take anything, or do anything to benefit myself. I was simply leaving a simple message, which was that to mess with me anymore would be a mistake.

It was a funny set-up. Another Southie shithole. Irish trash just like mine, even though they weren't in the projects. The place was filled with thrift-store furniture and the kind of junk knickknacks that speak of truly horrid taste. The Murphy household was as cheap as it comes, except for one thing: They had a television. This was forty-five years ago and that was unexpected. Televisions cost money then, and this was a big one, the kind that's built like a giant piece of furniture, with a wood cabinet and doors that folded in front of the screen to make it look like a buffet. It probably repre-sented some hopelessly large chunk of the family income. All the chairs were arranged around it, like moons. There were those fold-ing metal television tray tables leaning on the wall by the kitchen.

In the basement I found Daddy Murph's drill. A hand drill with the wooden knob on the end. I put on my dishwashing gloves, took the drill to the living room and knelt in front of the television. Just to be safe, I pulled the plug on it first. Then I slowly drilled a hole *right through the front of the screen. I drilled it deep, and when I got through the glass and hit the next solid thing, there was this gristly, crunching noise. I took the drill bit in as far as it went, then slowly retracted. Glass dust and metallic shavings were on the floor in front of the television. I got the pan and brush from the pantry and swept it up, putting the sweepings in the toilet then flushing it away. I returned the pan and brush to their place, washed the drill bit in the sink and put the drill back in the basement, then folded the doors back over in front of the screen. I checked for any sign of myself— footprints, something I might have dropped. I took my time because I knew this was important and not to be hurried. I then exited the house, pulled the back door shut, and stood on that porch listening for any movement or voices. But no one was around. I went over the backyard fence rather than around the front, into some scrub trees that hid my movements. I emerged a street over and went home to re- place the dishwashing gloves under my parents' sink.*

I had paid back in kind. I had taken in measure. For a scar on my head I see each day now in my bathroom mirror, I had made them pay. The television, not the cabinet but the actual television, was on the street a few days later for trash pickup. I don't know what they did with the wooden part. Maybe they used it for liquor or some- thing. Maybe they used it to display Mommy Murph's fucking knick- knacks.

18

Colleen is getting to that age at which she keeps thinking that the reward for losing your youth is at least the consolation of having earned some comfort in life—some money in the bank, some sense of home. It happens one day that Colleen figures out that she has neither. Grief has aged her hard and made her poor. She lives month to month with little prospect of things getting better. She works at the United Airlines ticket counter, watching the endless egress of people going places. People taking trips and seeing people, leaving for new lives or running away from old ones. She is the constant, punching their tickets out.

She sees her son slipping from her and she's not sure what she'll have left after that. Barry ruined her, in a way; she just doesn't feel inclined to be with another man. It is not so much a sense of loyalty, or fear, but rather a flatness to it all, the incongruity of it. Being alone and broke made sense when her son seemed to know what she was doing mattered. It now seems the basis of the indictment.

Now he wanders. She has stopped by the rectory twice more to try to speak to Father John, but he was there neither time. She suspects she knows the answer to her question anyway: Christopher has made a choice to leave the school and that is it. She understood about their waiting lists, their rigor, their implicit demands of fealty. All now undone.

She pretty much knows Christopher is not going to school at all now. She cannot guess beyond that. He is thirteen and she wishes she could believe there is only so much trouble he can get into. She knows he is lying to her. She knows he is failing to honor any promise he has made. She has never dealt with a teenager before and she does not believe this is anywhere near normal. She has to stop judging everything he does compared to Barry. Barry was preternaturally mature, just this easy manner that seemed to have always been in him. She remembers it from when they were both freshmen at Southie High and she hadn't really even met him. None of the older guys bothered him. There was no cockiness in his hale self-possession.

She is becoming more convinced that this is exactly the problem: That she has simply treated her son as if he was his father. She has, it seems, driven him out with her unclarified expectations. She feels the deep need to talk to someone. She had hoped —presumed, really—that it would be the priest. When Christopher was at the school, Father had seemed to take such an interest in him. Now, nothing. As if her son has become a traitor. So who does she ask for some reasonable advice?

She goes to Christopher's bedroom door. Outside in the hallway, his fresh laundry is left for him, per their agreement. She opens the door slowly, not sure why she feels guilty about it. It seems as it should be. The typical arranged chaos of a teenage boy—messy, but not so messy as to really worry. She goes to the dresser and opens the drawers. Virtually empty, the cleanest spot in the room. She opens the closet. The laundered clothes he's already taken into the room are thrown on the floor. On the top shelf are rows and rows of boxes, the baseball and hockey cards. Barry had started him on that and, for years, Christopher had kept it up in halfhearted homage. It both pained him to do it and pained him not to. She remembers that boyishness Barry took on, back at their base housing, when he spread the cards out on the kitchen table and let Christopher look at them, quietly telling him how they would be more and more valuable if they were allowed to age without damage; she had liked the way he had started Christopher with that kind of lesson, on the rewards of patience.

She takes the boxes out and puts them on Christopher's unmade bed. She slowly pries off the lids and looks at the contents, the rows of plastic moisture-proof sleeves, the cards carefully filed by teams and years, the Red Sox of course the thickest, for Barry never traded away the card of a Red Sox player. She wonders how long it's been since Christopher has even opened these boxes. She wonders if they are really worth anything anymore. You need a market to have value, and she's not sure kids even mess with baseball cards anymore.

They are musty, and this doesn't seem good, or right. She takes the cards and lays them in stacks on the mattress, letting them breathe. She opens the other boxes and spreads out the collection, probably the most valuable possession her husband ever had. Military apartments, junk cars, third-hand furniture: All that was the price of the service life with the presumed payoff—that when war was over he would find work at Logan Airport, servicing for one of the big airlines. It had been a good plan.

She takes the last of the cards out and, at the bottom of the box, is a white envelope. It is unsealed, ripped open with a finger. She ponders for a moment, then slips her own fingers into it, extracting a letter, creased in thirds, plain cream stationery. She unfolds the letter, and sees the money. Thick and neat. She counts, slowly, on and on. Twenty after twenty, crisp bills, rough to the hand. Fifty twenty-dollar bills.

She sits silently on the bed, holding the money, holding her breath as if someone is about to burst through the door. She holds the letter up and looks at it. No letterhead, no return address. Only one line and one initial.

Just something to help you and your Mom. As always, our secret. J.

+ +

19

Jimmy passes by without so much as a hint of recognition, but then she calls out to him. *Jimmy!* He registers his name and turns and she's standing there, a vaguely familiar face, pretty but indistinct. A woman dressed for business, standing amid the morning bustle of Downtown Crossing.

"Jim," she says. "It's me. Shelagh Kenney. From BC, remember?"

He is frozen, trying to see in this face something at all familiar. In fact he remembers very little about his one drunken semester at Boston College, as a freshman who spent those four fleeting months drinking and drugging and sleeping in hallways, drunk in ways more unabashed than under his parents' roof. Months of seeing many dawns and sleeping through many classes, knowing by midterm that he would fail all his courses and lose the scholarship he had totally lucked into anyway. It was then, with the turning of the weather, that he had mounted a truly epic drunk, from late October until Christmas, never remotely sobering up. It was amazing freedom, to awaken on the floor of the dorm bathroom or on a chewed-up couch, to rise and simply keep drinking. Everybody had kegs and few ever got finished, but Jimmy was the man to try. It never occurred to him that it was at all a bad thing. It was a continuing act of self-love, keeping himself euphorically happy in a way he knew he would have to stop eventually, but felt absolutely no motivation to do. By the end of that foggy run he had determined, like a solemn vow, that he would engineer a way of staying drunk and happy and doing what he had to do to maintain some self-sufficiency. And damned if he hadn't, more or less. Technically, he should have been on probation and given a second semester, but they had already determined that he was incorrigible. Being thrown out of Boston College for drinking too much was like being thrown out of carpentry school for hammering too much, and he took it as another point of pride. He would eventually finish school at night, taking classes here and there at good old UMass-Boston. That wouldn't really be going to college anymore, just sitting in classrooms in sporadic bursts and scratching out enough to move forward. He wouldn't get higher than C's, but could later say with a skewed pride that he was doing it drunk, which, as it turned out, was entirely doable.

And the woman is still standing there. He stammers a hello but she makes it easy for him.

"I was Jack McCormack's girlfriend at the time. You remember?"

"Jack I remember," he says. His freshman-year roommate. "You look different, in your business suit and everything."

"So do you," she says. Indeed, Jimmy is in his suit, having exited near dawn from another session with Rafferty's voice, and spent a couple of hours reading newspapers over his coffee in a downtown shop before returning to the austerity of his apartment.

"Where do you work now?" Shelagh says.

"I work for Terrence Rafferty," he says. "Driscoll, Irving, Rafferty, you know?"

Shelagh is clearly impressed. "That's really great. Look how far you've come! I bet you don't drink anymore, do you?"

Jimmy smiles. "No, not anymore."

"I used to really worry about you," she says.

Jimmy is suddenly clenched with emotion, feeling as if he will burst out in tears. He never imagined anybody had ever worried about him. He bites on his lip to pull himself together, and he says, nearly whispering, "Thanks."

"No problem," Shelagh says, more serious.

"Are you still with Jack?"

Shelagh laughs. "Oh, God no. That was a freshman-year thing. I dated a couple of guys you probably don't know, and then a few years after college I almost got married, but, whatever. Jack is someone I've completely lost touch with."

"Yeah, I never heard anything from him after I left. But he was great to party with."

Shelagh nods. "I'm glad you got yourself out of that. Hey, I have to run, but I'd love to have lunch and hear how you're doing." She reaches into her bag and extracts a card. "Or maybe an after-work coffee," she says.

After they've parted, Jimmy feels an odd buoyancy, the exact kind of thing he would generally want to drink to. He walks down Winter Street to catch the T home, weaving through the crowd heading to work now, not quite sure how to contend with this . . . excitement. Jimmy's celibacy is virtually intact, given his greater drive for drinking, and, when he considers his sexual experiences, there is not one that was sober, with someone sober, or emphatically consensual. He had discarded all that, his prick pickled and shelved in all the juicing.

Twenty minutes later, arriving at his stop, he exits the train and wanders up the Broadway, daydreamy, falling without realizing it into the old rutted path. He comes right up to the door of Triple O's realizing he has gone there instead of home, thinking distractedly about lunch with Shelagh Kenney. Here he is. He stands now with but an arm's length separating himself from the well-worn door handle of the bar, but now he steps back, and turns, and begins walking. His heart is already pounding when he hears a voice calling him.

"Jim! Hey, Jimmy!"

He acts as if he has not heard because there is no one he would call a friend who haunts Triple O's, but he can hear the footsteps gaining on him and then feels the firm grasp on his elbow, and he turns to see a face he knows but not all that well. It's Tommy Morton, as notorious a barfly as Jimmy himself, although Tommy, fat and fiftyish and living on state disability, had a big head start.

"Tommy, how you been?"

"How have I been? How the fuck have you been?" Tommy says. The man has a face like a rubber mask.

"I've been busy," Jimmy says. "What does it matter to you?"

"I thought you been avoiding me."

"Why would I be avoiding you?"

"Come on, Jimmy, with the money you owe me . . ."

"I owe *you* money?"

"Jimmy, come on. Don't be like that. Don't fuck with me. I been watching out that window for you for, like, weeks now."

Jimmy hasn't a clue about owing anybody money, but he can't deny it either. He's done it before, not remembered, and settled up. But this Tommy, he's not one of his usual creditors.

"What do you think I owe you, Tommy?"

"*Think* I owe you? Well I know you owe me three-twenty."

Jimmy goes to his wallet and extracts four ones. "I don't have change, so keep it," he says.

Tommy looks at him in what seems to be pain. "Quit crappin' around," he says. They are standing now in a cloud of Tommy's booze breath. "Three-twenty. Three *hundred* twenty."

Jimmy laughs out loud. No way, three-twenty. His debts have always come in the five-to-twenty range, enough to bridge a night of drinking. Even Jimmy couldn't drink three-twenty's worth of that bar's cheap swill.

"Tommy, come on. Quit fucking with me. I don't know about any three-twenty. You must have been drunk and lent it to someone else . . ."

Tommy gets an ugly look on his face.

"Don't mess around, Jimmy. Come on now."

Jimmy shrugs him off. Tommy Morton is as friendless a drunk as Jimmy has always been. That's that. Tommy grabs at him, but Jimmy is younger and stronger, and sober. He gives Tommy a hard push and Tommy goes down to the pavement with a groan, to Jimmy's shock.

"Tommy, come on, sober up. I don't owe you any money. Come on, get up and go back to the bar."

Tommy's elbow is bleeding. He looks at it, then Jimmy, as if he will weep.

"And there I was trying to help you," Tommy says. He pulls himself to his feet and slowly weaves to the door of Triple O's, and then in. Jimmy could be thankful for that, another reason not to return, but he also feels terrible. He has never been one to get physical, and he isn't inclined to start.

20

Jeanmarie is on her back, turning her head to the side to avoid the sweat dripping into her eyes, Bobby's sweat, him above her breathing rhythmically and squeezing his eyes tightly closed, trying with great effort not to finish too soon. After all, this guy Marty has only just started taking pictures, and the plan is to get plenty. Marty, a fat, middle-aged guy who has set up lights here in the basement of his house, which has a false wall and the mildewy mattress on which she and Bobby are having sex, is clearly into it, shooting away, the strobes flashing around Jeanmarie like lightning while Bobby shoves away at her. And then, with a groan, Bobby slumps over her, panting. Bobby raises his head as if he just remembered something.

"Sorry," he says to Marty. "I can do better."

"I'm not worried about you," he says. "Just get the hell off her so I can shoot."

Bobby rolls off Jeanmarie and she closes her legs.

"No," Marty says, looking at her through the lens. "Leave them open. Put your hands behind your head. Straighten your right leg." He's firing away, lights popping as they flash, and she's starting to like it, with Bobby off her and putting on his underwear.

"You're better solo," Marty says as the motor drive on the camera whirrs. "Bobby, I think we're done with you."

"What's the matter with me?" Bobby says.

"Your package is too small and you got a bony ass."

"My ass is *tight*," Bobby says.

"Look," Marty says, bringing the camera down. "You want to make some money, you got to do this right. She looks good. She looks younger than eighteen. You're eighteen, right, honey?"

"Yeah," Jeanmarie says. "Eighteen."

"Good, because these pictures will make us some money."

"We get the money tonight, right?" Bobby says.

"Something got changed on that. You'll get your money later."

Bobby is pulling on his jeans and now he straightens. "What's that about? I thought we get the money tonight."

"Well, you're fired anyway," Marty says. "She gets paid, and it'll be soon enough. I'll definitely be looking to use you again, honey."

Jeanmarie reclines on the musty bed, like a model in a beautiful painting. And she's glad Bobby is off her. It's too hot, with the lights. She doesn't have much sense of who Marty is, or how Bobby made the connection with him, or how much money they're being paid. She's put her trust in Bobby. But right now, to her surprise, she likes what's going on. She hadn't known she would. She's been chosen, just as she's been chosen since puberty by men's eyes, their desires. This is not so great a leap. She's always been the best-looking girl in class, or at least one of the better-looking ones. This feels like the one way she might make her situation into something.

"Where do these pictures go?" Jeanmarie says.

"The Internet," Marty says. "They're going to make everybody rich."

Bobby is fuming all the way home. As they walk along L Street in the dark, she can feel the tightness in the way he carries himself, the clench of his arm muscles, the clamped workings of his jaw.

"We're not going back there," he finally says. "That was *bullshit*."

"It was fine," she said. "We're gonna make some money."

"Did you hear what he said to me? That I have a little dick?"

"It's fine," Jeanmarie says. "It really is. Trust me . . ."

Bobby stops abruptly. "You have other ones to compare mine with?"

"You know I didn't mean it that way."

"I have no idea how you meant it, but we're not going back."

"How do you know him, anyway?"

"He comes into the Liquor Mart. He's a professional photographer. He does prom pictures, graduation pictures, that kind of thing. He was asking around, because this is where the real money is, with the Internet and everything. He asked me if I had a good-looking girlfriend."

"What did you say?"

"What do you think I said? Why do you think we were just there?"

"I was just asking," she says almost inaudibly. She isn't much liking his attitude right now. Right now he's bringing her down. She knows they won't have sex tonight, both because they just did it under the heat of the lights and because he's too wound up. The rattling old refrigerator had plenty of beer when they left, but his roommates are leeches and he'll need something to calm down.

They had gone to Marty's expecting to leave with good money. The whole plan is wrecked, but to her it's not in all that bad a way.

At the apartment, Bobby keys the door and stalks into the bedroom. The roommates are, as usual, arrayed around the television, the empties skirting their feet.

"Did you leave any of my fucking beer?" Bobby shouts from the narrow kitchen. Nobody bothers to answer.

"You should buy some of your own sometime," he shouts.

"You should buy your own sometime, too," one of the roommates shouts back.

Bobby goes into the bedroom and lies on the bare mattress, clearly too agitated to get any rest.

"I'm gonna shower," Jeanmarie says.

She goes into the bathroom and turns the rusty knob to begin a weak trickle of water. She's still thinking about the pops of the flashes, in that one-walled bedroom in Marty's dank basement. It had excited her, not exactly sexually, but more deeply than that, more fully. The idea that her images will be out there, that they will be paid for, seems more than she could have imagined when Bobby first broached the subject—she had only said yes because she was his girl and because she trusted him to get them to some better place. Bobby and his schemes. As she lets the water run down her, she thinks of him, angry in the bedroom; she really doesn't need him being mad at her. It was his idea! She supposes she should feel bad. That's what the nuns would say. But what did the goddamned nuns ever do for her?

+ + + + + + + + + + + + + + + + + + + +

21

He hides in the library when he has no place else to go. He pulls the same familiar books off the shelves and, when he opens them, he still finds fascination. *Arms and Armor. Armour of the Medieval Period. The Art of Warfare in the Middle Ages.* He revisits them like old friends, the same familiar fittings and the odd terms—the cuirass and greaves and vambraces—which he can name from memory and repetition. He marvels at their perfection, their aesthetic of protection. He can turn these pages forever, poring over them. Their brief existence, obsoleted so quickly by gunpowder.

It's late on Saturday afternoon and he has been here since morning, but now the librarian comes around, importuning the last stragglers, most of them the stinking heavy-clothed homeless, telling them it's time to go. Christopher closes the books and pulls on his jacket, following the people funneling out of the low brick front onto East Broadway—not that much unlike school letting out, but with a distinctly sad complement. The men around him grumble and sniff, each pouched in their force fields of pungency and dementia, each as isolated as a human being can be, even as they march in rank. Christopher knows he will see them later, too, skulking by liquor stores or collapsed in the narrow alleys between buildings. His frightened mother, from their second-floor apartment, has sometimes dumped pans of water on them, to rouse and chase them off. She does this saying, more often than not, that when she was Christopher's age there was none of this in Southie.

It's started raining. Christopher pulls the hood of his sweat-shirt up and jams his hands in the pockets. With his head bent low, he knows his mother won't know him if she passes. He has no de-sire to go back there, to her worrying and her observation; he feels as if he's been watched since his father's death and yet she has missed everything important. Instead he wanders down toward Jeanmarie and Bobby's, hoping someone will be there.

The rain picks up. After the leaves fall from the trees that grow from the small holes in the sidewalks, Southie is a gray place. The pavement is slick and the cars whoosh by, but Christopher only watches his feet as they pick up the pace. There is a distant crack of lightning, odd this late in the autumn, and he lifts his head and breaks into a run. But by the time he gets to the front door of Jean-marie's place, he figures he might just as well have taken his time. He's thoroughly soaked. He looks up and sees Jeanmarie looking at him out the window.

"Can I come up?"

"Yeah. Door's open." When she gets up from the window, he gets a flash of skin, the bare upper thigh.

Inside the entry, he pulls off his sweatshirt and tries to wring the water out of it. His t-shirt is plastered to his shoulders and chest. His socks squish inside his sneakers as he climbs the steep staircase to the apartment. At the top, the door is ajar. He steps in and feels surprised at the silence. No roommates for once, and ap-parently no Bobby. Jeanmarie comes out of the bedroom wearing one of Bobby's ratty Journey t-shirts. She looks tired.

"Hey," he says, not quite able to look her in the eye.

"What were you doing, to get that soaked?"

"Just walking. Then it started raining."

"Why don't you go in the bathroom and hang your clothes over the shower rod. There's a bathrobe in there you can put on for now."

"Is it your bathrobe?"

"It's my bathrobe but it's not a girl's bathrobe. I stole it from my father when I left there."

He goes into the bathroom and undresses, but he wrings out his boxers in the sink and puts them back on, then puts on the bathrobe. It's heavy on him, vast and warm. He sits on the toilet and waits.

After about twenty minutes, Jeanmarie yells, "What are you doing in there?"

"Waiting for my clothes to dry," he says through the door.

"You can come out here, you know."

Christopher opens the bathroom door and peers out. Jeanmarie is sitting on the couch in the dark with only the t-shirt on, pulled over her knees. The television is on without sound. He feels a quickening that he is not at all used to. He comes out and sits at the far end of the shambled, food-tinged couch.

"So you been going to school?" she says.

"Not that much. You?"

"I told you I'm done with it. Is anybody doing anything about you not being there?"

"No. You?"

"They can't do anything to me, because I'm sixteen now."

"Yeah. Lucky." Christopher looks around. "Where is everybody?"

"Bobby's at work. The other ones I have no idea."

"Any food?"

Jeanmarie laughs. "You're shitting me, right?"

"What do you have to eat?"

"I'm dieting."

"You? Why?"

"Because I got a new job."

"Really? What is it?"

"Modeling."

"Wow. Is the money good?"

"The money is really good."

"What are you going to do with it?"

"Bobby looks after it for me," she says.

"Why?"

"You're like a three-year-old with all the fucking why's, you know that? Because he's the one who got me into it. He got it going."

"Oh."

"But I do keep a little he doesn't know about." Her jeans are on the floor and she picks them up. She digs into the pocket and comes out with some money. "Here's something. Why don't you get us some food when your clothes are dry? I think the rain's letting up."

"I thought you were dieting."

"Just get something for yourself and I'll have what you don't eat." She pushes the money into his hand. "Just take it, will you?"

Christopher relents, and puts the money in his pocket. It doesn't seem right but that's now something between them. "So what else is new?" he says.

"What's ever new? What's new with you?"

"I want to move out of my house. I don't want to be there."

"Sweetie, moving out at your age is called 'running away.' You have to wait a few years."

+ + + + + + + + + + + + + + + + + + + +

22

I never thought of myself as having done anything that might be called "bad" unless it was absolutely necessary. Maybe some people grow up in protected environments, but others of us have to do what is necessary to rise out of our circumstances. For reasons I am not completely clear on, I knew from a young age that I was destined for more significant things. In high school I was someone who had already established what one might call an aura: I was never someone to take overt action. As a smaller boy, I had to present the perception that one would be ill-advised to take me on. I had a way of being scary, like one of those puffing lizards. But the key was that it was not about force in the classic sense. Virtually anybody could beat me up if they chose to; it was the promise of an aftermath that would make them regret it. I worked alone, not foolish enough to trust anyone; my methods were well thought out and well executed. It was a matter of finding those soft spots. It could involve anything from orchestrating a backstory that could not be traced to me—such-and-such a girl was caught blowing so-and-so down by Carson Beach—to slow punishment in a myriad of ways—the poisoning of a favorite dog. All of this led not just to me being left alone, but also being accorded a measure of fearful respect. My methods, as we shall see further on, were of much use when I later entered the world of business.

Let me tell you the reality of a place like Southie, at least as it was:

What you have is something like eight or ten guys causing real may-hem, and about ten thousand others trying to act the part. In Southie, everybody thinks he's a tough guy but, when you get right down to it, nobody likes to actually fight any more than they do over on Beacon Hill. You get a lot of chest-puffing and talking out of the side of the mouth, and most of it comes to absolutely nothing. But, like any myths that people buy into, there's a reason they buy into it. It's because it serves them, because it camouflages their weak spots. The spots are still there, mind you, just not so nakedly visible. And they can always be exploited.

What I found, though, was that, as I quietly operated in my ad-mittedly proactive way, I was not satisfied simply to hold my place in the pecking order, as it existed in the musty confines of Southie High. I actually wanted to rise above it, albeit in a very muted way. Unlike my older brother, who had gone off on his path trying to fit into the established order, I saw the whole thing more like the game that I believe life truly is. I volunteered for choir and then poured Clorox into the lockers of those boys who dared to mock me. I gently asked select peers for the favor of some pocket change—a pittance—and, if denied, quietly receded; sadly, some one or another of these intractable peers found that not only had the principal gotten word of their threatening notes to some of the newer teachers, but that it would not be taken so lightly. Mine was an asymmetrical kind of re-sponse, and while I might have been suspected, the boys who mocked me usually had other enemies, and it drove them crazy trying to figure out whom to get back at. It also honed many skills in me.

I eventually felt the call to public service and asked for the sup-port of my peers in my quest for the class presidency, and gratify-ingly found myself unopposed. Then I got the principal to create a fund I could access that would cover incidentals. I may have been the only sophomore class president in school history with an expense account for dinners and travel.

Of course, no one gets along like this without frequent challenges. It starts in high school and goes on from there, right into the business world. And of course there is the matter of "talent," as one would apply the word in this instance. I began to sense rivals, people who were aware of my game and wanted to beat me at it. There was one who I will refer to only as "McX," because even at this advanced juncture the battles are not yet over.

But for now I will say that McX was someone who dismissed me at first, believing that I was hardly worth paying attention to at all. He was a football player, and he got girls, and had a general attitude that he was above it all. He simply ignored anything that didn't interest him. Which might have indicated we would coexist, as if that were ever really possible. But human nature being what it is, he had in due time arrived at the conclusion that he needed to squash me.

McX was a tall and muscular boy with red hair that he wore in a crew cut, a splash of freckles across his cheeks and blue eyes that faded nearly to gray, all of which seemed to drive the girls of our high school into a feverish ardor. He was broad-shouldered and thin-waisted, and while the obvious conclusion to draw was that he was not very bright, in fact he was shrewd in surprising ways he did not parade. Never once in all these years has McX ever actually acknowledged me, much less spoken to me. Nor I, him. By all appearances, by all possible witness and documentation, we don't know each other at all. But what began back then has lasted nearly forty years and isn't necessarily finished yet.

And it all started with something fairly minor: He had his fa-
vorite jacket stolen. He was in the cafeteria and when he came back
to his seat from the soda machine it was gone. Apparently it had
been his varsity jacket with his football letter, and these were the
days when such a thing was crucially important. McX was nearly
weeping with anger, and I heard later that he asked Coach Crotty
for a replacement and was told no: If every boy who misplaced a
jacket got a replacement, etc., etc., learning responsibility, etc., etc.,
you had your chance. After that day, McX wandered the hallways in
a shabby corduroy work coat that must have been handed down from
his father. No one had money back then; in most cases not even the
parents owned cars, and McX was one of those cases, his father a
construction laborer right off the boat from Ireland who didn't fully
respect football ("It's the same as rugger 'cept for all the pussy
padding") and must have really coughed up for his son to have that
jacket ("How could you just leave it 'round? How could you not have
your eye on it?").

McX had never anticipated such a brazen daylight theft, for two
significant reasons: One, the accrued respect of his peers would have
kept someone from attempting such a theft, or from denying they
had witnessed it; and, two, no one in his right mind had any prac-
tical use for the jacket. To wear it around Southie was both foolish
and dangerous; to wear it anywhere outside Southie was foolish and
dangerous in a different way. Southie was looked upon as a bunch
of trashy, inbred Irish thugs, even in neighborhoods you'd think had
nothing to brag about. You didn't want to go walking around
Malden or Chelsea sporting a Southie varsity jacket.

So what even McX's slow wits could reasonably deduce was that
the jacket had been stolen as some kind of statement. The kind of

statement, in fact, that someone like myself might have made, for I was intent then, sophomorically so, on making statements. But I hadn't touched his jacket, nor had it been stolen on my behalf. I was sitting there at my usual table, eating a roast beef sandwich I'd just had delivered by taxicab to the front steps of the school (something done as much for effect as for nutrition: It impressed my constituents). And in a moment of my own weakness, I didn't realize that McX thought I had stolen his jacket. That was my mistake, indeed, and one I didn't absorb until a day later, when the fire alarm suddenly went off and we all marched out to the frigid sidewalk. Boston Fire rolled up G Street, grumbling about us and moving slowly, and got things under control. Some of the firemen were fathers of students, and those children were yelled at, in proxy for the culprit. We stood shivering in the cold as we had not been allowed to retrieve our coats. The firemen, taking out their packs of cigarettes and lighting up, seemed to draw it out, as a case in point.

When we all went back inside, I was immediately summoned. I was led by the principal to what turned out to be my fire-gutted locker. It seemed that gasoline had been run into it through the vent and then a match applied. In it, besides my books and jacket, I had some crucial documents and records—loans to classmates, a payment ledger tracking the rather healthy interest rates I had imposed—that would have been hard to fully dredge up from memory. In a financial sense, I was temporarily ruined. But it was the issue of respect that was far more important. My interest rates (which were really no worse than any of the numerous credit cards any of these people now possess) were apparently viewed as a malignant usury rather than a vital financial service. Over my shoulder, I heard people laughing at me. Smoke still hung in the hallways, and we were forced to sit in the acrid aftermath. I found myself for days afterward unable to concentrate at all on my lessons, given my pressing need to decide how to answer McX's attack. A few days after that, Coach Crotty (with a great flourish before the assembled lunchers) handed McX back his varsity jacket, which Coach had stealthily lifted from that cafeteria chair as an object lesson about responsibility. Everyone, even McX, laughed with a moment's sense of relief. But at this point, there was no going back for anybody.

23

Colleen finds herself always drifting toward his room, always easing open that closed door, always finding her way back to the money. Three or four times a day, to that tomblike box of baseball cards, to the envelope. Always dumbfounded then. A renewable discovery, a repeated shock. She counts quickly and always then again to be sure it's always a thousand dollars, always, and the small note is always there, attached. She looks at it over and over, as if it will say something different on further examination. She barely sees him anymore, just hears the late-night stirrings as he comes in, and she is disconsolate in her own inability to confront him about this, about everything. She only lapses into sleep near dawn, lying in bed, willing herself to rise and go to his door and pound on it and demand things. Which she never does. She has been awakened from her long grief only by this new grief, and the realization that her son is as gone to her as her husband has been. And when she comes from work to the silent home she again goes to her son's room and takes out the money and the note and stares at them, looking for some hidden answer.

As she sits cross-legged by his closet door, riffling through the box one more time, she wonders if taking it would make a difference. She can't be certain he ever checks it. She wonders if she might plant a companion note, the way she would, in his second-grade days, plant "I love you" notes in his lunch bag before sending him to school and retreating to the couch for another blank day of paralysis. The day she was told Barry died had been the last in which she had felt any real place in the world. But that also may have simply been her youthful naïveté. The cycle of responsibility she had been shielded from—the paying of bills and the consequent money worries, the tasks and demands—should not have been that hard, this long after. Life insurance, military benefits, her job, all of them made it so that things should have been simpler by now. But with the money in her hands she wonders who her son is, to have this.

She wants to take it, and to force a reverse dynamic. To make him confront her, for him to make the demands, opening the clash that she cannot. All she has to do is take this cash, fold it, slip it into the pocket of her jeans and leave the room. Not for herself, either. To buy him things he needs, to put it in a college fund, to buy him a savings bond. But she can't get it away from that shoe box. Failure is on her, a coating, a glaze. Following him somehow seems a more doable task. To skulk and spy is the coward's way of finding out what's going on, and she will do that. But she needs help.

The closest thing she has to friends are the people at work, as surface as they all are. The girls at the front counter are nice enough, but she thinks now of the guys handling the baggage and doing security. One of the security guards, Chuckie Connelly, has always been mildly flirtatious with her, and she has always resisted. Who else is there? She has a brother she barely hears from any more; his problems are something she tries to keep away from her son. The priest won't even see her.

She puts the money in order and folds it back up with the note. She must gather herself. The crucial turn, she decides, will be the moment that comes when he has taken the money to use it for whatever plan he has in mind. She's clenched with the clear premonition of him leaving, whenever that may be. She hasn't any idea why. Why doesn't he just take the money? It has a latent power that comes from its puzzling origins. She can touch it, count it and examine it, but she cannot move it from here, for there is in it a psychic weight beyond her strength. This discovery from among Barry's baseball cards, those of which she cannot touch or examine at all. She has far less than a thousand dollars in the bank. That is, however, beside the point.

What paths does he take that she cannot see? She needs to know. She needs to know while the money still lies dormant. She thinks again of Chuckie Connelly, who wanders in the airport with a certain self-possession that she doesn't see in the others, and she knows he would do her a favor if she allowed it. For any other reason than this she would recoil at the notion. She needs for her son to be followed, his movements discovered. She will see to it that this happens. If she must endure Chuckie's friendship for this, she will, despite her better judgment.

24

Jimmy awakens with a start, a little after three in the morning. The first shock is the taste on his tongue, the dry acidity that is clearly the alcohol still working through his body. Then he can feel it in the front of his head, the gelatinous throb of the frontal cortex, up over his eyebrows. He tries to swallow and feels how his throat has closed up. And then the wetness down below, where he has urinated on himself. He runs his hand along the night table then up the neck of the lamp and turns it on.

He stands up unsteadily and takes off his shorts and undershirt. His clothes are coiled on the floor, the pants inside-out in a heap, his shirt over near the door. It has been seven weeks since he saw the accident. Seven full weeks before he has finally fallen.

He strips the sheet off the bed and drops it on the floor. There are no bottles or glasses, no sign he brought the drinking home. He's shaking. *Where have I come from?* This hangover feels new and different, like a familiar state now made unfamiliar by its new context. He goes into the bathroom and starts the shower going. The water warms slowly. The wedge of headroom beneath the slant of the staircase shrouds in steam. Jimmy sits on the toilet seat, trying to piece it together. It's as if all the weeks and intentions have now disappeared. The most recent major memory he can dredge up with any clarity is of Tommy Morton and their altercation. From there, just shards and notions, the nocturnal sitting and working on Rafferty's recollections, of making himself dinner at dawn and watching television to sleep (if that wasn't the night before). Then he remembers Shelagh Kenney. It seems nearly obvious that he has been with her the night before.

He steps into the shower, letting the water nearly scald him. Punishment, forfeiture, atonement. His knees are shaky in his grief. He further dredges the last hours. He seems to recall phoning Shelagh to go to dinner in the city, but he may have only meant to. Under the shower head, Jimmy thinks he can remember, more clearly, leaving Rafferty's office and walking with the pleasant anticipation of something like a date, although he wouldn't have called it that, exactly. But that would have been in the morning, not the afternoon. It's all upside down.

He rewinds further, as if beginning his recounting from farther back is something akin to a running start. He called the number on her card; they met last week in the late afternoon at a sandwich shop down in the Financial District. Shelagh actually seemed happy to see him. He didn't know why that would have been: He was not a model of good behavior in his days at Boston College. She had judiciously picked the liquor-free locale, a credit to her; she was there waiting when he came through the door. He still had no recollection of anything about her back at BC, and very little of Jack McCormack, despite the oceans of beer he and Jack had consumed together: His memory of Jack was like a photograph, both their elbows perpetually cocked, beer cups poised at their mouths. In fact he remembers no substantive conversation between them—it's not that his memory is so bad, just unlikely that one ever happened. And Jimmy makes a judgment that presumes this: If Shelagh dated Jack and now has an interest in Jimmy, something is desperately wrong with her.

The shower runs until it loses heat, and he's still trying to dredge up last night. He has a recollection he cannot trust of sitting with her in a restaurant. He worries that he's compositing the image. He can't see if he is drinking in this recollection, but he must be, given the sorry condition he's in now. And she had seemed so impressed that he wasn't a drunk anymore.

He reaches down and squeezes his penis. There's no soreness. He has only ruined his sobriety, apparently, with nothing else to show for it. He turns off the shower. Cold and wrinkled, he stands on the bath mat, dripping and nauseated. *What now?* He has lost that power, of what he saw, of what happened. He cannot conjure it at all; it is as if that deeply etched horror has been leeched all away. And, as suddenly, he feels all the bile coming up, and bends over to vomit in the sink. It's all liquid, all string and sputum. No trace of food. He thinks he was in a restaurant. He distinctly remembers being there, with her.

25

Christopher comes up the stairs and finds the front door ajar, as always. The place is quiet but for the low issue of the television, which he has never seen switched off. Saturday afternoon, the sky clouded and giving the room an anomalous glow. This is unusual, this recusal, because there is always someone here, at the very least Jeanmarie but often those roommates wedged into the couch with their weed and their beer. But here he is. It makes complete sense that no one locks the door, as there is nothing of the remotest value here, not even beer in the refrigerator. It is the most abject of circumstances, but he envies Jeanmarie and the others, in their own house and beyond their parents' intrusions and implications. He breathes. It will be years before he can really have this but he feels this place is his, a little bit.

He seats himself on the couch. The television is old and its picture has become blurred at the edges. There's nothing on anyway. Some kind of game show. People screaming over prizes. It seems to him something deathly, that deep lust for things mundane, a dishwasher or range, the ballast of that kind of life. He already knows he will never have that, will be a creature living by movement, a traveler. He can't wait to get out of this pisshole.

The couch smells a little but is otherwise comfortable. The roommates seem like palace guards, always milling about, always thwarting his advance when he is here. It's clear they don't like him. They always seem to be worried about the mooching of their food. Christopher goes to the bedroom, where the door is half open; he feels the desire to be in the place where she spends so much time. He feels an urge to lie on the bed and feel some connection. He doesn't think she'd mind.

He pushes the door open; it is dark and he feels his way toward the window. The ratty curtains are tight together and he parts them. Outside, the clouds look fit to burst. His mother always rushes around closing windows at moments like this, as if she thinks the lightning will bend through the window and chase her through the rooms. She worries too much. He knows that she is worrying about him even more now. But in his harder moments he thinks she should have worried when it actually mattered.

He scans the sky for lightning but sees none. Satisfied that his mother is not freaking, he turns toward the bed. He nearly jumps, because they are in bed, right there, naked. Bobby is dead asleep, his arms wrapped around Jeanmarie, but she is awake, uncovered, unabashed. He stands, unable to look away. She is sprawled across the bed with her legs parted, one knee bent and the other straight, the hairs burning his eyes, the nipples different than he imagined, like coins, her breasts wide and flat. He looks to her eyes and they are on him; she smiles, and he cannot bear it.

Outside, he runs, and as he does his mind shifts to Bobby, the scumbag with his stupid, pathetic mustache, his loser face and pale gray skin, wrapped around her like an intrusion. He tries to outrun his own body, and the ache in his chest. He feels as if someone is chasing him but, if he turns around, he will see that no one is, as no one ever is in the way he imagines or wants. And no one probably ever will be. His lungs burn, his feet feel fried and he is fighting the tears that sear his eyes. He stops, gasping, bending, choking. He doesn't even know what she means to him but he feels homicidal toward Bobby with his arms around her, that horrific clench. He wants to do something to himself, because he is so stupid. Bobby is her boyfriend and he lives with her and somehow that smile is a betrayal; he does not know of what.

He goes to the beach and sits there for hours, and no one approaches. Darkness comes but the humidity does not abate. The clouds finally burst very late, and, soaked, he moves ahead of the lightning flickering out on the harbor, illuminating far clouds in a sculpted instant. He walks to the Liquor Mart, which is already closed. After eleven, then. He stands in front as if something might happen. He goes from there to the Most Holy Trinity School and sits on his familiar bench and seethes. He goes everywhere but home and, finally, he is in front of the church, the stone hefted in his hand; when he aligns and hurls he waits for that interminable moment until he hears the shatter of the glass, the heavy stained glass that breaks like sugar candy, leaden and dull. He knows that window exactly. *Christ Falls For The First Time.* And now it comes from him, the sobs and ache. He runs into the dark, leaving a trail of his own keening.

26

"What's the matter with you?" Rafferty says as Jimmy slumps into the chair in front of the broad desk. This is their progress meeting, early over tea before people come in to start the day.

"I got the flu or something," Jimmy says.

"You told me you don't drink."

"Right."

"'Right' you don't drink, or 'right' you told me that?"

"Both, at the time. And both now. But I had a slight relapse."

"You're a drunk, then."

"Actually, 'was' is more the way I think of it. It was just one night."

"Why that night?" Rafferty says. "You said you were clean. Why right then?"

"I just had a few drinks."

"That's not what you said," Rafferty says. He has a fierce look that doesn't surprise Jimmy at all.

"I had a lapse."

Rafferty is sitting in his big leather chair with his tie loosened and a glass of scotch on the rocks in his hand, the eye-opener Jimmy craves.

"I need you to stay focused," Rafferty says. "This is important. I only want to go through all this once."

"You have nothing to worry about," Jimmy says, as evenly as he can.

"I have a brother who was a drunk," Rafferty says. "He started out as an altar boy, nipping the mass wine. So why this one night?"

"I was out with a girl."

"And she's important to you?"

"I didn't think so," Jimmy says.

Jimmy returns to the recollection of meeting Shelagh at the sandwich shop. He remembers not worrying that he'd drink. As it grudgingly comes back to him, he realizes that, if he can focus on one detail, then perhaps the next one will suggest itself. He comes then to that moment of muted anticipation, coming through the door of the shop, in which he tried to imagine how guys who went on dates for real conducted themselves. With no experience and a libido macerated by a couple of decades of drinking, it didn't seem likely that much was going to happen.

He had made note, the first time he saw her, that she was a woman with an oddly astringent face—not the expression on it but the very way it was built. She had to make a real effort to look pleasant. It seemed to him that it may have been a face that fit her back in those college days, at that age when passing judgment was something to live by. Or it may simply have been milder, more softened and round, more benign. But now, with the subtle shift of topography, she had a look that seemed fierce in its exertion.

"How are you?" she said, her enthusiasm odd for someone who remembered him as a drunk and nothing more. He was a happy drunk in those days, admittedly, but not a conversational one, nor an affectionate one, nor even an entertaining one. He couldn't imagine they had ever spoken, unless he was inveigling her to fetch him another drink.

"I'm good," he said, smoothing his shirt on his chest. She was dressed in jeans and boots and a black turtleneck, the weekend uniform of the young professional woman in the Back Bay. He assumed she owned a small apartment, had a cat, left for work early in the morning. And yet, inexplicably, here she was, smiling mightily at him.

"Are you okay?" she said. "You look a little green or something."

"I feel fine," Jimmy said. He was, it was true, having small battles with the nausea of continuing sobriety. He was not about to tell her he'd only stopped drinking six weeks ago.

"I can't believe you work for Terrence Rafferty," she said. "I mean, that's really something. Do you actually work with him in the flesh?"

"I do," Jimmy said. "He has me on a project."

"So you know him well . . ."

"No, not much."

Jimmy was shifting in his chair and she could see that. "Not to be pressing you," she said, "it's just that I'm impressed."

"I can tell," Jimmy said.

It gets hazy from there. It is morphing into other memory, the one he's not so sure about. There is the vague recollection of food and small talk, mostly about her. He remembers steering it all back: better not to be asked to recount his own sorry progression. He remembers little of what she said, but that in itself is not of great concern. His sense is of an excruciatingly dull tale of a woman's success in the field of finance. He might not have tolerated it even if he'd not had a drink. Yet he sees nothing on that account. Maybe it is a bridge to what came later? He tries to summon up what he can.

There is the image now of them parting, late, of walking with her on Newbury, of a key in the door. Memory or desire? His head aches with that. The intersection of the remembered and the imagined plagues him. Is he concocting the notion that he was in her bed? The thought, as it now knifes in his head, has no solidity, no grounding. Just a scene that may or may not have happened.

He has to discard it. Reality has to be more real than that. Jimmy cannot trust his mind's own testimony, its fragmentary and stolid manner of materialization.

"You still with me?" Rafferty says.

"Yes, sir."

"I can't have you flaking on me. There are some stakes to this you need to understand."

Jimmy sits up straighter.

"You're not going to be drinking *now*, are you?" Rafferty says. "Because I'd have to get rid of you."

All experience tells him that, once drinking, he will drink. But maybe he can will something different right now. Maybe he can believe that all things start now. Again.

27

"We're going back to Marty's," Bobby says as Jeanmarie sits up on the bed. She has fallen asleep early, and now he is standing over her at the foot of the bed, just home from work.

"We are?" she says groggily.

"He's paying us two-hundred fifty."

"Us?"

"Yeah, come on, he's waiting. Hurry up!"

She rolls off the bed and stands naked, the cold air of the apartment raising bumps on her skin, making it tighten down along her thighs. She is a different person in the cold air, colorless and shrunken, trembling in the unheated apartment. Not like when she sweats under Marty's array of hot photographic lights. Yes. She wants to be there.

She pulls on a pair of jeans and a big sweater she stole from her father, not bothering with underwear or socks as she tugs on her boots.

"What time is it, anyway?" she asks Bobby.

"It's about one in the morning." The smell of alcohol gusts off him as he speaks.

"How are we getting there?"

"Marty lent me his car."

It is indeed out there at the curb, a glistening Sedan de Ville of unknown vintage, wine-dark red, its cream leather seats soft and cold as Jeanmarie slides in. Bobby starts the car and the heat registers blow hard, the warmth building quickly.

"Why now?" she says, but Bobby does not answer as he steers the car fast over the rain-glazed streets. She hears the skimming water under the carriage, and thinks of those blinding lights. Bobby brakes too hard as he approaches Marty's street and the car goes into a nose-down fishtail, but he steers out of it and just misses banging into a parked car. The car shudders sideways to a stop. She looks at him and he is shaking.

"Are you cold, too?" she says.

"Yeah."

"Are we still going?"

"Yeah." He takes his foot off the brake and eases the gas, rolling the car down the street and into Marty's parking space. She can see the glare of the lights in the basement, illuminating the edges of the small curtains in the foot-level windows. Bobby leads Jeanmarie, still shivering, through the side alley to the entry and then down the basement steps. He opens the basement door and Jeanmarie sees Marty, twisting a lens onto one of his cameras. What surprises her are the three men sitting on the shredded coach pushed up against the wall behind the lights. Entering the room, she smells the alcohol stink, sour and laden. The men look to be in their late twenties and early thirties, dressed in jeans and t-shirts and work boots, leering unabashedly at her. It's becoming clearer that they're beyond drunk. One of them slumps precipitously, propped onto the arm of the couch.

"I just hired these guys," Marty says. "They all say they have big ones. We'll see who really does."

"That's me," one of them says in a bar-hoarse voice. He has a thin face with pockmarks that keep him from being handsome. "How much am I getting paid?"

"Twenty bucks," Marty says.

Jeanmarie grabs Bobby's arm and pulls his ear to her mouth. "I thought you said I get two-hundred-fifty," she whispers.

"We do," Bobby says.

Marty looks at Jeanmarie standing there in her jeans and sweater. "You got makeup?"

"No," she says.

"Jesus Christ," he says. "You got to go get some." He pulls a wad of bills from his pants pocket and hands Bobby a hundred. "You two go get some makeup for her. The works. And hurry up."

"Where do I get makeup at one-thirty in the morning?" Jeanmarie says.

"There's a CVS over on Newbury, in town," he says. "They're open all night."

"That'll take at least an hour," Bobby says.

"So go," Marty says. "She's got to be in makeup."

Outside, they get into Marty's car.

"What's this about?" she says. "Who are they?"

"Don't you trust me?" Bobby starts the car. "Do you know how to get to Newbury Street?"

"No," Jeanmarie says. "I've really never been into Boston."

"Fuck," Bobby says. "I mean, it's right over there." They can see the buildings looming up in the mist. "How is it possible not to know how?"

"So you haven't been either," she says. "So don't yell at me."

"I'm not yelling," Bobby says.

"Look, I know where to get makeup," Jeanmarie says. "And how we can keep the hundred."

She finds the key where it has always been left for her, under the potted plant on the back porch. She knows every nuance of this tiny place, the creak of every step and the small uneven places she must negotiate. They will all be asleep in this sad building, and as she keys the back door lock with excruciating slowness she is already listening for any sound, although she knows there will be none.

Inside the kitchen, she sees the same small nightlight, a molded-plastic frog that her mother bought for her but which is now nearly devoid of its green coat, all yellow and weird. She moves slowly toward the bathroom. She can hear her father's weighted breath from the bedroom at the far end of the hallway, past her own bedroom, into which she will not look. They keep their door open a few inches, an old convention they have not abandoned even in her absence. She moves slowly, letting each floorboard bear her weight silently. In the bathroom, she leaves the light off and edges out her mother's drawer, which is filled with the piles of cosmetics she uses only for holidays and funerals. Jeanmarie feels her way through, everything familiar from her stealthy childhood investigations. She lifts the easily identifiable shapes from the drawer: lip gloss, eye shadow, mascara, powder. She is filling her pockets when, suddenly, she hears the creak of her parents' bedroom door and her father's sliding, half-asleep footsteps.

She steps into the bathtub and slowly draws the shower curtain across, the plastic rings scraping the corroded rod with a slow moan. She hears him pushing back the door. Instinctively, she drops into a defensive crouch. He enters the bathroom without turning on the light and she can hear his movements through the translucent curtain, him sniffing in his tiredness, fumbling. He lifts the toilet seat and she then hears his urine spattering into the bowl. He goes for a long time, the nightly beer drinker, and then he clanks the lever to flush. The water rushes in. The footsteps recede. The bedroom door creaks to its near-shut position. She stays in the tub for another fifteen minutes before she finally begins her escape.

And that will come back to her, even under the lights, as the drunk with the second-longest one, a guy named Norm, slams his hips against hers and breathes his stench in her face, as Marty shouts at her to act like she's in love with the guy, act like she wants him. The longest one, whose name she did not get, sleeps through it on the couch. Bobby stands behind Marty, watching, his face gray and slack. He is out, for good. She is in. She knows now that she can be famous, that she can have life how she wants, as such people do, and that Bobby will not make it there. She is, with her mother's makeup rubbed now across her raw face, turning into somebody else in the heat of these burning lights.

28

It became obvious to me midway through Southie High that grades were not nearly as much of a consideration for future success as other, more basic qualities, such as innate intelligence and what may be an inherited guile. It was no mistake that the populace of Southie were who they were: They were descendants of people who had been willing to cross an ocean to try to find something better, but then not smart enough to have succeeded in the ways of the other Irish, who had, within a generation, come to people the more affluent suburbs of Boston—the Newtons and Needhams and Brooklines —where they lived among the Jews and Protestants in a far more comfortable fashion. Southie was like a purgatory from which many could simply not escape. And what that bred, I think, was not only a very wary relationship to authority (how upstanding could the Boston police have really been if filled with the boys of Southie?) but also to education (the province, after all, of people over on the other side of the Fort Point Channel). Being the possessor of said inherited guile, I quickly realized that in order to get on, I needed both a piece of paper attesting to my superior intellect but also no hint of that communicated to my fellow students. They may have quoted Ovid and Cicero with impunity in the private schools of which I could not be part, but, in the classrooms of Southie, those who did so became disenfranchised losers who might, if lucky, get out and not return. But the quality of Southie was so inbred and tightly woven that, for most, a full break from the place was in some ways a form of self-erasure. The goal was to be in plain view but also to move beyond, whether that be the leafy suburbs, the pages of The Boston Globe *business section, or the* Record-American's *crime columns. Being a criminal in Southie had a homey joviality to it, the conventional wisdom being that the only people risking harm were the ones engaging in the same business. The code of silence that enveloped Southie and Charlestown and Dorchester was a nod in the direction of that premise.*

So for a young man growing up there in those days, it was a tough choice between becoming a cop or a criminal. It was about an even wash, the cops' primary duty being the containment of either a) assholes, or b) people from outside Southie who came in to make trouble; the subtext being that there was compensation beyond that of the union pay scale: A blowjob received from an inebriated girl transported home after being found in the park, performing the same act on her boyfriend, insured everyone's silence. A "Southie handshake," a bill of reasonably impressive denomination folded and placed on the palm, was clearly a form of tipping that signaled a job well done, or to be done.

But either of these choices condemned one to remaining in the ant farm. My mother may have been too lavish in her praise of me, because I grew up believing I was going to be something pretty nifty. And unless you were a Kennedy, who had attained all of the above in nearly otherworldly fashion, the path was clearly not to Harvard, but to that second-tier commuter school for the young men of the near Commonwealth, Boston College. And like a chief executive officer who must delegate, I realized that my absorption in the busi-

ness of being myself (with all its incumbent ledgers, both written and extratextual) required me to involve others in the process. A lesson from those days was as follows: To enlist underlings to battle a rival is a waste of one's effort, and involves enough leakage as to always put one in a less advantageous position than simply, methodically, and tactically overtaking the rival oneself.

I had five teachers, all in subjects for which I had little interest. Beyond that, it was a truism to me that whatever material one was to painstakingly absorb was going to be gone from memory again by the conclusion of summer recess. What, really, was the point? Schooling is a faulty notion, I reasoned. Experience was the eminently better education.

I also knew that a significant cohort of the Southie student body was simply being passed up and out, to their lives as tradesmen and laborers (the girls, as well, on the simple premise of their impending marriage and motherhood). So I reasoned that, based on intelligence alone, I deserved to orbit above that altitude. I also knew that I did not want to rise so high as to assume any visibility, be it as valedictorian or honoree. Just enough to get to where I needed to be. The task of getting five different teachers coordinated and on task was something better steered directly to their supervisor.

I was already learning that the best way to manage people is to let them think they had the idea themselves. The principal, a Mr. Duffy, seemed to have a look of reticent fear, sitting askance in his creaking wooden swivel chair as I earnestly voiced my desire for his advice and guidance on how to progress to the Right Places. It was a Friday afternoon in winter, the place cleared out save for the janitors languidly buffing the waxed hallways. I was telling him I needed his help. In short, I said, I was putting my future under his experienced auspices. I laid myself figuratively at his feet, and he looked as if he were about to cry.

"Can you give me a hint of your general direction, son?" he nearly whispered.

"I want to be in business." I knew that "business" could be a liberally applied euphemism for all manner of escapade, so I said after that, "maybe banking."

"Banking, you say?" Mr. Duffy seemed nearly startled.

"Yes, sir," I said. "Or finance. The business world would seem to suit me. Do you think I need to attend Harvard for that? And if so, may I ask your assistance in getting there?"

He paled a bit, his eyes darting as he was thinking, then shook his head furiously.

"No, no, no, no, no," he said. "A fellow from South Boston? They're all Protestants over there—it's not the kind of place a man from here would want to be. And Boston University is nothing but Jews from New York. I think Boston College is the place where you would find yourself most comfortable."

"But if I could get in to Harvard—didn't all the Kennedys go to Harvard?"

"I suppose."

"But I should settle for Boston College?"

"Well, we can be sure we get you admitted and settled in," he said. I nodded gravely.

"Mr. Duffy, as long as that's guaranteed, I see what you mean." Then I looked at him in a way that was both gentle and unyielding. He finally broke his sad glance away and nodded. "We'll see to it."

I smiled broadly and jumped up to shake his hand. "Thank you so much for taking me under your wing," I said. "I'm excited now about Boston College."

Mr. Duffy mumbled something I didn't catch.

"And sir, I noticed your new Plymouth out there in the principal's parking space. If you ever need it washed . . ."

"You want to wash my car?"

"I'd see it's attended to," I said.

The following Monday I returned to school with an altogether new sensibility, that of a man expecting results; so too did the teachers seem to have taken on a new attitude toward me, one of nearly undisguised anger. One, a young algebra teacher named Slade, who had once been a lacrosse player at some oak-shaded college out in the Berkshires, stopped looking at me, or calling on me, or nodding to me in the hallway. The next test, I was appalled to see he had given me an F. When I looked up from the mimeographed sheet he was looking at me in full, quietly simmering, perhaps even suppressing a smile. I looked away bloodlessly. But, after Mr. Duffy's new Plymouth suffered some sort of fuel-line problem that caused it to inexplicably catch fire upon ignition, my math grades began to rise like the dark smoke from that conflagration, and not long after, Slade made it loudly known that he had accepted work at an even-lower-paying parochial high school on the South Shore.

+ + + + + + + + + + + + + + + + + + + +

29

Chuckie Connelly has a soft and open face that might suggest to someone not at all familiar with him that he is slow, but Colleen has come to see that it is merely the expression of a mechanical person, the kind of man for whom the world is a mesh of interlocking pieces, not all of which function, some of which are worn or poorly maintained, and some of which are, gratifyingly, solid and dependable. Chuckie had been a mechanic at a Quincy gas station before they went self-serve; he says the gig as a Massport security guard was compliments of his cousin, the state rep from Chelsea. Colleen can see in his face a vague satisfaction she cannot muster, of the admittedly Catholic view in which there is a design to all that happens and a mechanism to all fortunes—not only the positive kind but also the occasional plane crash.

She is sitting with Chuckie in the Brewpub in Terminal C, drinking a Summer Lager from a heavy glass. Chuckie is on his second, masticating the details of what she has just told him, and what she is asking him to do. He has a look of heavy sorrow, the look of someone who just realized his alternator died, mucking up the whole system. But then again, his face seems to say, there's a way of fixing that.

"Okay, I'll follow him," Chuckie says. "There's no way he knows me. And no way he'll figure out I'm following him. After all,

I'm a trained security professional." He waits for her to laugh but she is too deep in it all to have the joke register. He takes another draw of his beer and looks at her face, flickering with woe and indecision. He smiles on her behalf.

Chuckie is in his blue nylon windbreaker so that his uniform is concealed. He's not supposed to drink or dine in the airport when he's off-duty. That's the first advance of risk on her account. And this for a job with good pay and a pension. She had come to him, finally, long after he had expected her to. He feels now that he must try to help.

"It'll be fine," he says in sunny reassurance. "I'll figure out what he's doing."

"I half don't want to know," she says.

"But the half that wants to know is probably fifty-one percent," Chuckie says. "I mean, we need to know what your teenage son is up to, don't we?"

The "we" jolts her, as if Chuckie in his casual choice of words has staked some kind of claim. There is a disquieting triangulation to this, and the fact is that she is sitting here with this near-stranger while the other half of the true "we," her son, is off in his murky recusal.

"Colleen," Chuckie says, and she comes back into focus.

"Yeah, Chuckie."

"You do want to know what your son is doing. You do want to know, even if it's bad. From what you tell me, there's something not so good going on, unless someone's giving him money for carrying out saintly deeds."

She nods, and nods. He's lost her again. He lets her recede into herself only because he knows she can't help it, knows that it is no great place, inside there, bumping up against the insides of her own skull. He's been there himself. He sees Colleen each day at her place at the airline counter, her mind flickering with the discharge of her worries; he knows that, no matter how many times they're processed, they do not recede without action.

Chuckie doesn't have children, so he isn't quite sure what he will find. He guesses it won't be good, but that it also won't be as bad as Colleen thinks it is. The airport is not a good vantage point from which to understand what kids are all about; the ones who pass through these portals, despite their shuffling indifference, are children of means and direction, off to one place or another. The fact is, the kids all look the same, dress the same and talk the same these days, although there are still subtle differences between the kids from Wellesley and the kids from Southie. It may have to do with something as abstract as expectation. The class system isn't gone yet, as much as the kids on L Street wander along in designer shirts while the ones from the prep schools slouch in their tangled dreads and dirty jeans as they board their flights to Switzerland and Honolulu. Chuckie didn't have either of those kinds of childhoods—really didn't have much of one at all—and he considers that no great loss. There's too much brooding self-regard in it for him. He has borne his responsibilities without any sense of being cheated, and indeed his life now is pleasantly rounded, simply built and easy to service.

Which is why he can't fully understand why he is even here. He doesn't want to be feeling sorry for her, exactly, but he doesn't feel affection for her either. He just wants to see her stop looking so powerfully sad, the kind of sadness that sucks all the peace out of the room. He has spent at least a moment of each day warily contemplating her, watching the travelers look at her tightened face as if it is an omen. He has gone home feeling bad at her expense; at night he has lain awake in his small bed in his small apartment, wondering why she is affecting him this way.

30

Jimmy sheds his rumpled suit and stuffs it in a plastic grocery bag, not wanting to commit the money on dry cleaning but knowing he will meet with Rafferty again in a couple of days and, that he'll need to look clean. In his bedroom, still in his underwear and un-showered as it approaches four in the afternoon, he retrieves a pair of jeans from the rug and pulls them on. He is being paid well; while he knows he needs to save what he can for the uncertain times beyond this Rafferty job, there is something more to his aus-terity—the built-up instinct to see all money in terms of its con-version rate to alcohol. He never had much money, but neither did he spend it on anything but the drinking. So the currency and un-cashed checks mostly accumulate in his drawer, which he takes from only for rent and basics. He needs to get the money into his bank account. Sober and in this dingy place, he could live off Rafferty's pay nearly forever.

He still carries on a drinker's schedule, except that he now stays up all night in his small office, slowly transcribing Rafferty's long recollections into the computer. It piles up and up, and he tries to find the thread. It takes him three hours to type out a half-hour's tape, and the rest of the night to give it some sort of shape, to smooth the rambling and repetition that is the nature of the spoken word. Jimmy is familiar now to the janitors and security guards who float through the late hours, and they seem to regard him with grave respect, an acknowledgment that he is clearly doing very important work for the company. A man no one really knows, working in Rafferty's vicinity. By day, Jimmy still gets intermittent work from Karl for the magazine. He sleeps in the late morning and afternoon, shades drawn tight against the glint of day, and commences his days in the falling shadows. Many mornings, he walks home from downtown Boston, across the channel and up Broadway, as the illegal third-shift bars let out, something he nearly wants to see. He tries to see the drunks for what he once was, before he settles into his restless advance toward sleep.

Jimmy picks a t-shirt off the floor and pulls it on, and slips his feet into his rubber shower sandals. He looks in his closet, at the ball of clothing that has sat there on the floor since before he stopped his drinking. He must push forward with all this, and it suddenly occurs to him that to clean this place would be a purging of things past that still cling to him. Out the window, a gray rain falls. He needs some new push to set the drinking at bay once again, and it seems to him that a recommitment to neatness and order is just the thing to underline the differences between who he was and who he is now.

What he lacks are the actual devices and implements of cleanliness. Brooms and mops and sponges always seemed a sad fate for perfectly good beer money. He takes his most threadbare undershirt from the pile in the corner and runs it under hot water at the sink. Right to it, he wipes the veneer of settled dust-roughed stickiness from surfaces he has traditionally avoided touching. He has no actual cleaning agents other than his bar of soap in the shower, so he uses that to suds up the counters. He wrings the wet t-shirt and resoaks it with clean water. The work feels foreign but not all that bad; he is perspiring soon enough and throws open the windows to let in the cool air. He then ties another t-shirt around an old hockey stick he has in the closet, something he has kept as a remnant of his childhood. After soaking it, he begins to swipe it back and forth across the floor and then under the couch, putting at least some kind of scare into the dust balls that lurk underneath.

He's into it now, making transition once again. In his head he compiles a shopping list of the kinds of exotic paraphernalia he recalls from his mother's broom closet, the stuff one uses for a serious job. He takes a handful of balled-up plastic shopping bags from under the sink and begins to stuff them with his dirty clothes, which he has traditionally carted to the basement laundry room wrapped in his sheets. He will, for the first time in his life, have a living space in which all the laundry is clean, all the counters are shiny, and all the spoiled food has been thrown out. A place with a certain kind of agreeable neutrality, without smells or sounds or the pall of memory making it seem eternally tainted.

After five hours, now into late afternoon, he looks at a place that makes him feel as if he has moved to a new city. He feels a thirst for clean cold water. His hunger is honest, and healthy. He gathers bags of dry cleaning, pulls on his coat and goes out into the street. It's getting cooler out, late fall losing what warmth it had. In his heavy work coat, he walks down toward the dry cleaners on Broadway. He has in his bags three suits, five ties, six button-down shirts, all to be made spotless, to be worn with a certain change in approach: not to be slept in, puked on or pissed in. The dry cleaner will solve all evidence of his iniquities.

He has not called Shelagh. He can't think what to say, given he still cannot faithfully recall the events of that particular night. While the idea of seeing a woman had begun with a healthy motive geared toward a different kind of living, the fact that it became a night of relapse means she's probably someone to be relegated, with the spoiled food, to the category of Done With.

At the cleaners, he empties the bags onto the counter and waits while the grayed and stooped Chinese woman makes unintelligible marks on her pads and then sorts the clothes, her hands dipping in and out of pockets, producing loose change, a couple of ballpoint pens and three beer-bottle caps. She goes deep into one of the summer sport coats, the seersucker, where the pocket has split, and her hand moves under the lining, searching.

"Ah!" she says, smiling and nodding as she hands him a thick fold of bills secured with a paper clip. "Found this in lining!" she says.

"I wonder how long that's been there," Jimmy says; he pulls the wad open and sees it's all twenties, and he counts out sixteen of them. Three hundred and twenty dollars he didn't even know he had.

+ +

31

The first cold days blow into the city on a hard wind, and the apartment is like a refrigerator. Jeanmarie sits in sweatpants and a heavy sweater, watching out the window for Christopher, who no longer appears. The window onto the street has become frosted and Bobby stays out most of the time, be it at the Liquor Mart or wherever he goes after that. The roommates have withdrawn to the point that they seem to be frightened of her as she comes in and goes directly to the bedroom. They know all about what has been going on; Bobby has told them for sure, although she doesn't know whether he has done so in a tone of pride or revulsion. The fact that it was all Bobby's idea has nothing to do with where it's gone. Jeanmarie has had a half-dozen men on her, sweating and gasping and groaning while the whirr of Marty's motor drive and the flash of the strobes distract her and remind her that she is just acting. Bobby doesn't know about any but the first two times. Marty picks her up at the apartment while Bobby is at work, and drives her to his studio where he shows her the photos he has taken. It is an epiphany to see these pictures, and who she is in her makeup and heels in the flattering light, with Marty's retouching of small blemishes and characteristics in herself she has always hated. Marty says he's selling the photos on the Internet and that if things keep on this way they'll both be making good money.

"You're a star," he says. "You're a name." She doesn't know much about all that; it's 1999 and her parents have never bought a computer. It was to have been her reward for the good grades that never came.

The roommates say nothing when she goes off with Marty. When she comes through the door they stare at the television and don't speak; but when she turns away, she senses them watching her. She feels the power in this dynamic. What she possesses is what they worship and obsess about, and she is the flame they cannot touch. She has hidden all the cash from Bobby, in envelopes, one behind the cranky furnace in the basement of the building, another under the box spring, through a slit in the fabric Bobby will never notice. She submits to him when he does come home, but without enthusiasm, feeling his beer-steamed breath on the side of her face. He doesn't always use his rubber but he also doesn't speak to her about what happens next.

She is restless. She feels she needs to get some air. She pulls on one of Bobby's leather jackets and then her boots, and looks out the window. The rain is beginning to taper but it's still raw out. Past the roommates again, without words.

Walking, there is almost no one on the street. She passes a man carrying laundry in plastic shopping bags, but he hardly looks at her. She sees three young guys heading into Mulvaney's. She has seen these kinds of men in Marty's basement and she likes the way they stared, that night. But in these clothes, oversized and grimy, she is cloaked in invisibility.

She wanders down Day Boulevard, watching the rain fall on the monochromatic waters of the harbor. Cars swish by along the glazed pavement. Her hair is soaked and the water runs down her face, collecting at the neck of her sweater. Someone honks a horn but she doesn't look. When she swings back down toward the apartment, she makes sure to take the longest way around her parents' house to get back. Down by the elementary school she sees Christopher, sitting in a rain slicker on the bench across the street from the school. He sees her coming but stays put. When she gets to the bench, she slides alongside him as if he might suddenly bolt.

"Where have you been?" she says. "I haven't seen you around much."

"What do you care?"

"Oh, that's so sweet. You're hurt. You're jealous."

"I don't want to talk about it," he says.

"Look, honey, when you saw me and Bobby—there are just some things you're not old enough to understand."

"You're sixteen!"

"Yes, and that's *older*. I'm older than you in a lot of ways. And if it makes you feel any better, I'm moving out from the apartment, without Bobby. But Bobby doesn't know yet."

"Are you going back home?"

"Yeah, right. I'm moving into a place Marty got for me."

"Who's Marty?"

"He's the photographer I model for. He's kind of my manager now. He got me a little place down toward the park. It's a basement studio. It'll be mine, but he'll pay for everything."

"Is he your new boyfriend?"

"Marty? Don't make me laugh. It's strictly business."

"What do you think Bobby will say?"

"Bobby's not gonna care."

"Are you sure about that?"

Jeanmarie notices the rain picking up. Christopher has a heavy coat on that doesn't let in the water, but she's soaked through, and cold, and the apartment is freezing and the shower will, at best, dispense tepid water. She may have to boil a pan of water to warm up a shallow bath for herself.

"It's just not going anywhere with Bobby," she says. "I don't really care what happens. He's got to be making money but I don't see any of it."

Christopher nods.

"But you're making money, too."

"Yeah, and no way I start spending it on him if he's making me live like that."

Christopher realizes suddenly that he doesn't want her here on this bench. It is his place, and his place alone; he needs for it to be that way.

"You need to go get dry," he says.

"Okay, I can take a hint!"

"No, you just don't want to get sick."

"So sweet, always looking out for me. I'll tell you what: Maybe, when I make this move, you can stay for a while, in case Bobby gives me trouble. There's just a little extra space. It'll give you a little place to be when you don't want to be home."

"Okay," Christopher says.

"You look really skinny."

"I haven't been eating much."

She reaches into her jeans and pulls out a handful of wet, crumpled dollar bills. "Here's some," she says. "Go sit inside somewhere and eat something warm."

He puts the money in his pocket. "Okay," he says, and when she is still looking at him, "in a little while."

"Well, I'm not going to get pneumonia sitting here," Jeanmarie says, rising from the bench. She feels the clamminess of her wet clothing against her skin, the bumps rising on her flesh. She starts down the hill and sees a man standing at the corner, looking at her. But he says nothing, and she says nothing, and she moves on to the apartment, her home, another place she no longer wants to be.

+ +

32

And so I was a college man, the first in my family. I walked each
morning from the Old Colony projects to South Station, where I got
the Red Line to Park Street Station, then switched to the Green Line
out to its termination point at Boston College. Everyone wore coats
and ties in those days, and mine had been secured through a thor-
ough scouring of the closets of some of the older men in my building.
I found the ones who roughly approximated my size and then explained my dilemma, going through their closets to find appropriate garb. They were, to a man, completely cooperative, and I in turn
penned them notes promising return of the garments for holidays
and, on request, in special circumstances.

Therefore I arrived on campus with the look of a more traditionally tailored man, pinstripes and dark worsteds and Irish tweed at
a time when my contemporaries, mostly from more monied suburbs,
favored loud plaids and narrow lapels. More than one smirked at
me or made a remark, and of course I understood this: I was, to
them, no one of consequence. I made note of each of them in my mind
as if in the neat green lines of a ledger.

I knew my modus would have to be different with this particular
population. The language of Southie was not spoken in this light-
dappled place at "The Heights" of Chestnut Hill. No, in my first
days of college I sat down in my bedroom late one evening and, with

pen and paper, charted out a four-year plan with which I would achieve the success I fully expected. For the first year, one of my goals was to perform credibly in each of my classes; also, I intended to be invited to the homes of at least a half-dozen of my freshman brethren, preferably those with fathers who were captains of the business community. And, finally and perhaps most importantly, I needed to engineer a situation in which I would be understandably provoked but yet able to respond publicly and decisively. I had already learned that a key to attaining power is to orchestrate the situations in which you can make your show of strength.

I began in a quiet and solicitous way to find common ground with my peers. One immediate way was to share the load in the work we were assigned by those dour Jesuits. Ovid and Cicero were out in the open now, and The History of the Peloponnesian War *became part of my lexicon. I now commenced the studying I had tabled in high school. Thucydides spoke truths my compatriots could not touch. I was never against learning—no, I knew all along it was crucial; it just hadn't made sense to waste time with it in high school. But now I found myself taken by the wisdom of the ancient warriors and philosophers. And in my enthusiasm I could steer my classmates as well toward that knowledge. It was revelatory, and for a certain group of young men I was fast becoming a leader. Of course I chose them carefully, unbeknownst to them. I had done my research, knew who their fathers were and knew the nature of the companies those fathers ran. As for me, I did not lie but neither did I tell them about my background. The majority of the boys I was surrounded by didn't seem to understand that I didn't live on campus, and I tended to float through the dorms late into the night to further that perception, often catching the last train into the city and then* walking the rest of the way. Sometimes I slept in the small chapel where I knew I would not be disturbed, in the pew with my bookbag as my pillow.

Finally, the first crucial invitation came. It was the first main holiday of the term, Columbus Day, and the dormitory was clearing out. But the catch—that we had a Classics test the day we returned—had put everyone into an anxious mood. A somewhat dull but fully blessed fellow by the name of Driscoll, throwing some dirty clothes in his laundry bag, saw me in the hallway and called out.

"Rafferty! Why don't you come out with me to Weston?" Driscoll said. "We can bone up for that Classics test."

Jackpot. I knew from my previous research that Driscoll's father was the new president of Irving Investments, which was a major financial house in the old, quiet sense, the kind of organization you wouldn't even know existed unless you were deeply embedded in that world. So of course I feigned the kind of complete ignorance that would be understandable for a callow college freshman. I'd always tried to express an interest in Driscoll himself, almost excessively so. There were times when he caught me looking at him just a moment too long, and when he did I'd look away, suddenly bashful, as I thought of his father's fortune.

Driscoll hired us a cab from Cleveland Circle and I rode with him, watching the trees with their riotous colors against the backdrop of deep blue sky. I felt phenomenally serene, as if by traveling in the opposite direction of Southie I was finding a new place within myself.

We arrived in Weston, at what I can conservatively describe as a mansion. These were the days when an Irish boy other than a Kennedy could not have found his way into Yale or Harvard, but

Driscoll had confided in the cab that his father was bitterly disappointed in him, the implication being that it was because he had ended up at Boston College. It seemed, looking at that house, that the elder Driscoll must have truly come to believe that nothing at all was unattainable to him. But when the man himself came bursting out the front door to shake my hand and slap his son on the back, it seemed he still had all the Irish in him, the informality of personality that distinguished us from those pinched and proper Bostonians.

"Call me Red," Mr. Driscoll said, as we repaired to his library for what was to be my first glass of Laphroaig single malt scotch and my first expensive cigar. Red focused in on me, asking about my background very directly. My honest answers seemed to surprise the younger Driscoll, and Red proceeded to tell me about his own struggles rising out of tough circumstances, in his case on Winter Hill over in Somerville. The son seemed happy to let me be the focus; in fact, I began to realize that my presence was happily postponing the conversation he didn't want to have—namely, how he was making out in his first semester at school. The answer was not well. Driscoll tended to disappear for long stretches, sometimes days, and no one around the dormitory much cared. He was something of a cipher and if not for the knowledge of his lineage I have to admit I'd have paid him little attention. His inviting me to Weston was clearly a desperate move, born of the knowledge that he was about to fail Classics. His father, sitting in the library, seemed utterly delighted that his son had befriended someone as purposeful and clearheaded as myself. Driscoll the son sat steadily ingesting his expensive whiskey.

Red seemed impressed that, even as a freshman, I had some real sense of direction. I suspect he may have seen a bit of his younger self in me, far more so than in his son, who had grown up in the rarefied place of privilege Red had created for him.

Mrs. Driscoll was not present, apparently attending to a charity event to be held that evening, and Red had the cook serve us in the library so we could continue our conversation about the business world and how a young man might make his way through it in these modern times. I looked over to my classmate Driscoll, who was by now slumped into his clothes in drunkenness and boredom. He seemed almost angry, as if willfully choosing not to join in the conversation. At nine, Red clapped his hands and announced that we should turn in, and that breakfast would be served at seven sharp, at which time the lovely Mrs. Driscoll would be present.

We boys went to the bedroom, where twin beds were an odd touch, since I knew Driscoll had no siblings. Driscoll fell drunkenly into his bed, looking at me as if he was angry. I snapped out the light, stripped to my underwear and pulled the blankets over myself, and was quickly enough sleeping deeply. Somewhere in the night I could feel that familiar nocturnal erection, stronger than usual even. I was an eighteen-year-old with much sexual energy and it wasn't all that unusual for me to remain aroused throughout my many vivid dreams. In this particular dream, a woman from a film I had recently seen was sliding her hand along my proud organ. It was a pleasure and seemed very real, as if she was actually mine, and even in my sleep I noted my success. But, awakening suddenly, I realized it was actually Driscoll's hand touching my leg as I lay on my back.

I honestly reacted with no intent other than to reclaim some personal space. I slammed my fist into his face and landed it too perfectly, no pain to me at all but yet a resounding crack that made Driscoll fall off the edge of my bed. I thought at first he was crying but the sound was of blood gushing from his nose and mouth. He pulled himself off the floor—I could see in the weak light that he was naked—and rushed into the bathroom, where I heard running water and then real sobs of pain. He stayed in there through the night and my suspicion was that he was sleeping, drunk and bleeding, on the cold bathroom tiles.

As seven o'clock approached, I prepared myself to be banished from that big house. At six-thirty I began lightly tapping on the bathroom door until finally I heard a groan. Driscoll opened the door and brushed by me, shivering and pained. He pulled on some clothes without looking at me. Both eyes were nearly swollen shut and his nose was plugged with wads of tissue. Dressed, he left the bedroom and made his way downstairs. I heard Mrs. Driscoll's shriek—I never did meet the woman that weekend—and then the shouting to someone to get a car ready. I could hear the slamming of doors and I simply sat on the bed, waiting it out. More than a half-hour later there was a tap on the door of the bedroom, and Red came in and sat on the bed opposite mine.

I was trying to figure out how to start, but he said, "As you can see, my son has a problem."

"He caught me by surprise," I said.

"He deserved it," Red said. "You're the first of his buddies who hasn't come down the stairs looking like a blushing bride."

"People sometimes have a mistaken impression of me," I said. "And I have no choice but to straighten them out."

It was that last remark that seemed to catch Red's attention. He leaned in as if someone might hear.

"I'm not asking you to be his friend or be responsible for him," he nearly whispered. "But if you can have an impact, there are ways I can benefit your ambitions."

33

When Colleen looks up from her computer monitor at the ticket counter, she sees Chuckie giving her the raised eyebrow, as in *talk to me.* She nods and goes back to her work, but for the next hour and a half until her fifteen-minute break she is nearly hyperventilating, because, as much as she wants the answer to what her son is doing, she is terrified of what that answer might be.

When her break comes, she finds Chuckie down by the metal detectors. He nods to his boss who nods back, and he says, "Let's walk."

On the concourse, he says, "I have a sense of what's going on. I've been keeping a close eye on him."

"Do I want to know?"

"That's the part I can't answer."

"Just tell me," she says.

"So I made contact at your house after hanging out there on and off for a couple of days. The kid hardly ever comes home, huh?"

"I don't know sometimes whether he's in his room or not."

"Well, I tailed him finally, and some of the things he does don't seem so bad. He goes to the library, he sits down by the beach, he goes to the convenience store for milk and a donut. But in the late afternoon he hangs around on this bench down on M Street, by the school."

"Most Holy Trinity School?"

"Yeah."

Colleen is nearly ready to cry. "I never should have let him leave that school," she says.

"Yeah, he just sits there," Chuckie says. "But a couple of nights ago something happened. A girl came by, sat with him for a while, then gave him money."

"How much?"

"I couldn't see."

"Who is this girl? Like one of his little friends?"

"Older. A blonde. I'm not good on ages. Sixteen? Eighteen? So she heads out and I went with my gut and followed her. She lives in a shitty apartment building down by Broadway. I decided to wait a bit to see if anyone else came or went, and what happens is that a middle-aged guy in a Cadillac pulls up, and out the girl comes, high heels, makeup, short skirt, tits hanging out . . . I'm sorry, *breasts* almost coming out of her top. And off they go."

Colleen's head is spinning. "Tell me what that means. I can't think."

"I'd guess it means the girl who is giving your son money is a hooker."

Colleen stumbles to a row of seats along the window and collapses down. She looks at Chuckie, pleadingly. *"What the hell is going on?"* she whispers.

In Chuckie's car she feels like a sneak, and angry at herself for feeling so. She needs to know what's going on! She wants to tell Chuckie the truth, of what a terrible mother she's been, what a terrible widow. There are those turns you cannot handle, and she knows her son needs more than she can give him. She almost thinks Chuckie could help, but he is such a pale comparison to Barry it would almost seem unconscionable to ask.

"See that window with the light on?" Chuckie says. "Just keep an eye on it."

So she watches, seeing nothing. It's about ten o'clock and she is usually home at this hour. She has left a note for Christopher, with a heart at the bottom, saying she's doing errands. She wonders if this might be the night he intended to begin talking to her again, while she's sitting in a car with Chuckie Connelly.

"Whoa, here we go," Chuckie says, and she turns to see the Sedan de Ville slowly gliding up the street. It drifts across the street and parks along the opposite curb, in front of the apartment building. A moment later, the girl comes out, as advertised. She's wearing tight jeans and high heels and a puffy short fake-fur jacket. She comes around the front of the de Ville headlights and Colleen gets a clear look at her. The makeup is so heavy she knows Chuckie must be right. She gets in the car and slams the door hard and the car eases back out and down the block.

"So that's what you have," Chuckie says. "There's the money."

"That girl looks almost familiar," Colleen says. "But I can't place her."

"You want to follow that car?" Chuckie says.

"I'm afraid to. We don't know who that guy is, or if he might think we're cops or something."

"Yeah, okay," Chuckie says.

"Take me home now," she says.

"No problem," Chuckie says.

They do not speak on the ride back. Colleen feels sick. Chuckie lets her off and she whispers thanks and goes inside, just maybe hoping. Her note is sitting right where she left it and, as far as she can tell, no one is home. It's after eleven. She goes to his closed door and knocks.

"Christopher?"

There is no answer. She turns the doorknob and pushes the door open.

"Christopher, are you here?"

There is no one here. She stands in his empty room and feels the desolation of it. In the closet, she finds her way to the shoe boxes, to the money, which she again counts, like a compulsion. All there, as always. But, putting it back, she lifts her head and something touches her hair and there is a tinkle of wire hangers. She looks up. His clothes, except for those that no longer fit him, are gone.

She sits on his bed. She is thinking about the girl, trying to place her, and it is only when she starts to get herself ready for bed that it comes to her.

Jeanmarie.

Oh my god.

It is a few minutes after eight o'clock in the morning when she arrives at the rectory door, sleepless, pounding on it so hard the window rattles in its leading. She stabs her finger at the doorbell ten times, counting it out, and then begins pounding with the side of her fist. The black housekeeper comes rushing from the back but doesn't open the door. "Stop!" she barks from behind the door. "What is it you want?"

"I want to speak to him," she says. "I need him to help my son."

"Wait here," she says. The woman's shadow recedes into the dark and Colleen is ready to pound the door again if the house-keeper doesn't come right back, but she does.

"Father says come back in a half hour," she says.

Colleen feels better. Finally. Finally something can begin to happen. Maybe she will go to work today with some small shred of hope. As much as she does not want to encourage him, she will thank Chuckie, because now the matter has been forced.

She doesn't know what to do with herself. She doesn't want to appear the stalker, so she exits the rectory steps and walks down M Street, to a convenience store where she buys a small cup of coffee. She drinks it slowly on the way back, checking her watch again and again. She is back near the rectory by eight-twenty, pacing along the sidewalk a block away while the hands of her watch seem not to move at all. Finally, at eight-twenty-eight, she bursts forward.

Coming up the granite steps of the rectory she sees the envelope taped to the door. *Mrs. Coogan.*

I deeply wish there was anything at all that I could do to be of help to young Christopher. I considered him a friend and wished he had not turned his back on us here at Most Holy Trinity. But at this point, there is simply no assistance I can lend, especially given my imminent retirement and departure. J.

This is the handwriting, the cramped hand that she has studied and agonized over. This is it. It is his.

+ +

33

Jimmy wakes up, although it is not so much waking as pulling himself with great force into some semblance of consciousness; he is lying on his bed fully clothed, his newly pressed suit now rumpled, bunched on him, his tie wrapped around his neck. His head is throbbing. His body feels wracked with aches. The despair he feels howls through him like a ghost, chilling his soul. *How did I let myself do this again? Why has this happened?*

He looks at the clock and it says 6:42, and he hasn't any idea which side of the day he is on, the faint light outside insufficient to draw any meaningful conclusion from. His mouth feels dry and crusted, and the pain in his abdomen is searing. He lowers his head back down to the pillow and closes his eyes.

He awakens again at 9:30, in the darkness of his shrouded room, not sure if he has been out three hours or fifteen. His apartment is a chamber in which he floats without petition from the outside world. It is the chamber he has forged with his drinking, his own isolation. It is not new. But what is new in these recent lapses is the pursuant inquiry, of where he has been and why he was there, questions he used not to ask of himself. He needs to latch onto one detail if the story is to rise from out of the fog, but he cannot find it.

The urine on the crotch of his best suit has dried into a circular and horrifyingly large stain. He sits up on the bed and looks around, but sees no sign of his indulgence, no bottles or glasses or paraphernalia. He does feel a rising pain from his knees and looks down to see bloody rips in the gray flannel, from what must have been either a fight or a fall—it doesn't really matter which. He checks for his wallet and of course it is gone.

He is slipping back into being the man he thought he had left behind. The urge to drink now and to stanch the flowing pain is nearly overwhelming. The lack of alcohol within arm's reach is the salvation of the moment, for he feels too sick even to get up to find a drink. Even sobriety has not truly been a pleasure: The dull, everyday pain seems to be his body finally registering those mundane sensations every other adult must feel, the various tics and complaints of adulthood. He had thought it might be better—a thought that could easily constitute a rationale back to the bottle, even as he finds himself now, spent and amnesiac.

This makes twice in three weeks. It feels as if his body must have tried to balance the accounts by ingesting all the alcohol missing from the excruciating dry weeks. He feels as if he might die right now, but imagines he won't, if only on principle. Days matter now, as they did not in the past. He knows that his little office is sitting empty tonight and that, if Rafferty comes by to drop more material off in the morning, he will see that the previous package is sitting untouched next to the computer.

He stands up and feels the head rush of pain and vertigo. His hands feel as if they're asleep, and he slowly pulls off his clothes and lets them drop to the floor in a pile. He is standing naked now in the cold air. His penis is shrunken and receded, his legs wobbly. He is slipping back into his darkness and he is afraid he doesn't know how to stop it.

He starts the shower going. The bathroom smells of vomit and he wonders if that might have spared him. He can imagine his guts splattered along the sidewalk like a trail that can lead him back to the source. In the shower, he feels more bile rising and it comes out of his mouth before he can think to turn. He looks at the puke floating in the backed-up water, then gets out of the shower and extends each leg to rinse his feet. He was never like this, even when he was a drunk. The ghost blowing through his body feels suddenly like his father's. He feels its benevolence, but that has never helped. His father was too good a man for him to ever live up to. Jimmy had betrayed the old man's love, guidance, concern and worry, had betrayed all of that with a million insidious cuts, and still the old man had come back to him, gently, openly. That kindly face was its own torture to Jimmy. He could keep no pictures out.

In the shower, with the water beating into his face and chest, Jimmy recalls without really wanting to that twilight phase in which his father was in his final decline and Jimmy's own drinking had reached the point of true illness. His father was going with pancreatic cancer and Jimmy mostly stayed away, too drunk to pull himself together and just sit with the man, in his throes. Jimmy was told at the wake that he was forgiven for all that, one of his father's final proclamations, and it was a harder truth than to not be forgiven at all. He got drunk and missed the funeral. And still, with all that, it never occurred to him that he should stop.

His legs are bruised. For some reason, the first click of memory from the night before comes to him, and somehow he has a vague notion that it involves Shelagh. But the notion seems false and scrambled, mixed up with the other time. He hasn't even seen Shelagh since that last binge. His memory is a failing thing now, treacherous. The memories of Before are in him like an over-healed burn, but these new ones scatter and formulate themselves, badly.

The shower runs and runs and finally goes cold; he turns it off and pulls his towel around himself. He feels empty now of all worth, desperate to find his way back. And he realizes what he must do, what he must see if he is to point himself back in the general direction of his own salvation.

+ +

35

She is down there, pounding on the door again, but he will not succumb to it. Father John is steadfast now in his refusal, has indeed hardened into it after this unconscionable badgering. She could as easily ring the doorbell, which has a gently mellifluous chime. The housekeeper has stopped asking whether he wants her to open the door, and has been sent home through the back door, to await a call to return. All the doors are locked, and Father John has left a message at the chancery to say he is ill and that his Masses will have to be covered by someone sent in from elsewhere.

He cannot help that boy anymore. Though still a child, the boy is old enough to know that he has left the auspices of this church, and its God, and all its ancillary agents and privileges. The boy is now outside of its embrace and its guidance. The mother should recognize that, for it was she who allowed it to happen, but clearly she does not. John cannot make up for her failings, which she must not at all embrace, as it is taught that she must do.

And this, in the final days of a long career. This nonsense. Granted, religion is not what it used to be, and most people no longer make the Church a central part of their lives. But for all the Communion he has served, for all the baptisms he has performed, for all the couples he has wed, who is here now? His parish seems reduced to the elderly and the infirm, bowing their heads at morning Mass in some last-ditch routing of perdition. Even they, the old ones, barely mumble a word to him. But it is the saddest thing that these children he had tried to influence and love have now turned their backs on him. How many years of tending to them, of developing those connections? He remembers the awe and the fear he himself felt as a child, under the gaze of those priests, and he remembers as well the way he and the other young seminarians submitted to the demands and needs of the older priests. As much as it sometimes lacked comfort, it also somehow made it seem more real, this passage to the sanctum of true holiness. Not all, of course, enacted this initiation. But it seemed that those who did not were like ghosts, floating around it in some fundamental denial, trying to be holy in some hopelessly simplistic way. Everybody knew, though. These odd rituals were a benediction of their own, and perhaps he would admit to having wanted to bring other, similarly innocent acolytes into the full realm of God. And now it seems they had come to resent that very special, very intimate treatment accorded them.

The day Christopher and his mother came to the rectory, to announce his impending decampment, the boy had not even looked John in the eye. Of course Christopher was a shy child, almost to the point of being withdrawn. But in this instance, as priest and mother spoke, the boy seemed to be shrinking into his own clothes, his heavy, oversized coat. He would not say anything, as none of them ever did. Ah, the sullen youth of South Boston. The Church and its infallibility, its most special place under the ever-vigilant eyes of God, were not to be trifled with. John had indeed expressed the desire that day that Christopher stay on. In fact, the boy was among a handful over these years who had not stayed when asked. And when Father John pressed, the boy seemed only to reduce himself to shrugs and grunts.

"Christopher, wouldn't it make sense to finish school with all your friends and classmates?"

The boy shrugged and continued staring at the floor.

"Now I have assured your mother that if money is the issue, I will see to it that you can continue here without an unfair burden on the family finances, especially given the situation."

At this, the boy had said nothing. John knew, looking at the two of them now as he had when she first brought him through the front door of the school, that the boy would never share anything with his mother. John felt emboldened to press on.

"We'd really miss you here," John said. "*I'd* miss you." And at that the mother had nearly begun to cry.

Dressed as always in his black trousers and shirt but without the irritation of his white collar (which stays in the top-left dresser drawer with all the others, of various fabrics and yellownesses of age), John sits in the chair in his small upstairs study with the blinds drawn on this brilliant late-autumn day. It was odd that he had been compelled to take an interest in the first place. He had taken a like involvement in the boy's father, to no good end, before John was sent away that first time.

The boy's father had not turned out to have the same calling at all. John had heard, one way or another, that, after his departure, Barry had gone on to do many impressive things, had gone on to athletic success and service to his country as if on a mission no one else could fully understand. Or so he had heard from those few people who had bothered to stay in contact with him after he'd moved on to the more remote postings. The son, this Christopher, seems not to possess the kind of single-minded drive his lineage would suggest.

And now this madwoman at the bottom of his stairs, looking for him to revisit what has already been done as he passes these final days before retirement. The pounding on the door is a final intonation in a career in which he could not help everyone. The sounds come intermittently from below, and there are times when he thinks they have ended, when they cease for a few hours or a few days. Then, when he begins to think he can call his housekeeper and ask her to stop on the way and bring some food and supplies, the pounding begins anew and again he shrinks back into the dark.

36

The new apartment is tiny, but it has everything that Bobby's drafty, dirty hovel of a place lacks. It is a small, furnished efficiency apartment built into the basement of a brick apartment building near Day Boulevard. It might have served at one time as a home for the janitor, closet-like yet outfitted. The narrower-than-normal doorway opens out on a long hallway, which leads to an exterior door that requires a key for entry. Most of the upstairs residents are old people or Section 8 housing cases, people who do not mingle or call in on neighbors, transitory and wary.

The apartment is overwarm (due to its proximity to the boiler at the other end of the basement) and simple: white walls and blue shag carpeting, and a twin bed along the wall with bolsters that make it into a couch by day. The bed takes up almost the whole room, except for a small black-and-white television on an old telephone table. There's a small two-burner stove, a clean stainless-steel sink, a mini-refrigerator and a counter separating the kitchen, with its newly laid white linoleum, from the carpeted living room. The smell of the newly applied latex paint has not died down yet, and Jeanmarie associates the smell with new life, after the admittedly failed experiment with Bobby. Two steps now from her parents and their sad lives, she can feel them receding into a more distant past.

She doesn't know what the rent is; Marty is handling everything, taking it from her earnings. He has explained that to sign a lease might hurt her, since she does not declare her income or pay any taxes. Marty handles it all now, saying that it's better to keep her hidden away, and when he hands her thick rolls of money, a hundred or two hundred at a time in fives and tens, she knows she is well taken care of. She moved this morning, although there wasn't very much to move: the same bag of clothes with which she had arrived at Bobby's, a case of newly acquired makeup and a bag of "working clothes" that she kept hidden in the basement.

Not that she suspects it matters to Bobby, or that he would be surprised. They had barely spoken in weeks, had really not made love since that last time in Marty's studio, and had slept out on the far edges of the bed before Bobby dressed and shuffled sleepily out to the street for his walk to work. He'd come in late, drunk, and when he showered she slipped her hands into the pockets of his jeans to confirm what she already knew, that there was no money, that he had again gambled it away with his goddamned poker and goddamned pools. It was as if he wanted to hit her but was afraid, maybe of her father. And as with her father, she had gotten out before she got dragged down to some bad place. She waited until the roommates cleared out and then packed and dragged her things down to the convenience store two blocks down, where she called Marty to come and get her. He did so in a circuitous approach, rounding the block a couple of times as if anxious that someone might be watching him; when he pulled to the curb he had already popped his trunk and was motioning for her to hurry up. The stakes had been raised with all this.

"Are you worried about something?" she had said, and he had laughed and said, "What would I be worried about?"

Bobby is the problem—not just what he might do, but who he might tell. She keeps trying to figure out why she ever thought she was in love with him. Well, she'd been younger. She doesn't want to see him, but Southie isn't that big to think she won't. But she is changing, evolving, and she thinks a time will come when he doesn't even recognize her anymore. She imagines herself transforming in such a way that no one—her father, Bobby, the fuckers at Southie High—will connect the woman passing by them with the girl they did not appreciate enough.

She hasn't seen any more of the pictures of herself that Marty took, except for a head shot that he brought her a few days ago, saying that it would come in handy for pursuing other jobs, eventually. For it, he had set up the studio and brought in a woman named Claire to do her hair and makeup, and all the while Jeanmarie was not allowed to look at herself in any mirrors. The picture had shocked her, the face of someone altogether not what she thought of herself as being: In other words, someone more glamorous, confident, sexual and self-possessed than she knew she could ever be by just continuing on as herself, stupid old Jeanmarie. She needs a new name, Marty says, and the beauty of a new name is that you get to choose it yourself. In the studio, he had set up a couple of fans, to blow her hair and make it look like a model's hair in a magazine. It had been a day in which she had nearly felt as if she had come to some new version of herself.

The windows of the apartment are high on the wall and at street level, just like Marty's studio, and that is the one thing she misses about Bobby's: Sitting on the bed by the open window, looking down at the street. Watching the leaves rustling on the trees through the fall, or the rain on the pavement, or the movements of people, or the march of clouds on a windy day. Sitting up there gave her a feeling of both serenity and safety. Now, below ground, she sits on the bed with her *Glamour* magazine and her tea from the box of groceries Marty brought her when they moved her stuff into the place. It is so small—almost cocoonish—and she realizes now that it is all she ever wanted. She looks up over the stove at the small crucifix that has been on the wall so long it is almost obscured by layers of paint.

+ +

37

I hardly need say that, almost immediately upon coming back from the Driscoll manse, I set about a rather far-reaching plan to create in Driscoll the changes that had been deemed necessary. The problem, of course, was that I had shattered his nose, had made clear my lack of interest in the sort of liaison he must have imagined, and that it was simply not in me to go begging him to be my "pal." Furthermore, I decided, it was going to take something different than friendship to get him to take it at all seriously—he had, in my mind, abused our friendship beyond repair the moment he grasped at my merry peter. There was no going back after that. So I decided that the best approach was to come at him as someone trying to repay the hospitality afforded by the larger Driscoll family.

The next time I saw him, I had to laugh. He was bandaged to a degree you would never see in the Old Colony projects, where the conventional wisdom was that a) you were obliged to display the results of a beating so that the one who inflicted it would not be forced to brag, and b) fresh air was the best salve for all manner of wound. Driscoll, by covering his damage in thick gauze, was nearly exaggerating how bad it truly was. I came up a staircase heading for my Ancient Philosophy class when I saw him at the top, looking like a mummy-in-progress in a blue blazer and rep tie. He turned and was gone. I could have given chase but it was going to be a more subtle game than that.

It became clear not just that he was avoiding me, but that he was terrified. I wasn't sure of what—that I was going to inflict more physical damage, or that I would tell everyone what happened? I had no such intention. He could not have guessed I was trying to help him. So I subtly stalked him so as to have an opportunity, one Friday afternoon as the cold sun made its early exit into the treetops. He was in the lower depths of the library when I eased up behind him and set my books on an adjoining table, just another student trying to get his work done.

"Driscoll," I said softly, "How are you doing?"

He turned and froze at the sight of me.

"Rafferty," he said. "How are you?" I could tell his impulse was to gather up his books and bolt out of the place, but, in those days, the idea of courtesy was still enough to trip you up.

"The nose looks good," I said. "You'd never know what happened. Which was an accident, of course. You took me by surprise and I simply am not into that sort of thing."

Driscoll was looking down at his book as if he would cry.

"I didn't do anything," he said. "You were saying something, apparently in your sleep."

"You really oughtn't do things like that," I said.

"I don't know what you're talking about," Driscoll said.

"Then how do you account for that nose?"

Driscoll looked up at me with as much courage as he could muster. "I was sleepwalking, and I scared you, and you hit me," he said.

163

I let out a leaden sigh that was meant to communicate my deep disappointment that he was taking this route. I have always had an unconventional sense of ethics, but this was clearly a breach, not simply a face-saving, because Driscoll clearly sought to cast me as a frightened boy overreacting to his innocently sleepwalking host.

"I have to study now," Driscoll said. "Would you let me?"

I reached down, took his book and quietly closed it.

"First of all, you don't want to come close to messing with me," I said. "And secondly, I have taken it upon myself to make sure you don't bring any further embarrassment to your family or Boston College." Understand that I did not give a shit about Boston College—it was a deflection, nothing more.

When I saw the small glint of recognition on his face, I read it this way: That he knew his father was directly behind this, and that this wasn't the first time someone had been recruited for such duty. Indeed, Mr. Driscoll had not said he had not tried before. That only made me more angry.

"Watch your step," I said to Driscoll. "And keep your nose clean or there'll be trouble."

A smirk spread across his face, and I put my finger to his lips. "That right there is a mistake."

Driscoll assumed I didn't have enough stake in all this to go beyond a few words, but he was wrong on many accounts—that I knew who his father was, that I didn't care for people crossing me, and especially that I wasn't just some dope from Southie High. I had my motivations, on many dark levels.

The question of where he disappeared to on so many nights was easily answered with just a bit of effort. Over several autumn weeks,

I kept an eye on his dorm; when he emerged of an evening I followed him from a safe and secretive distance. I had no idea where he was taking us, and had, for the purpose of protecting myself, brought along a length of cast-iron pipe, eight or ten inches in length but thick and weighty, taped at one end for better grip. I was not a violent person but I was smart enough to care about self-defense.

I followed him on the T, boarding the car behind him and watching through the windows, jumping off when he did. We got off at the Theater District station and then continued on foot down into Bay Village, not far from the Common, where he ended up at a bar called Jacques, the reputation of which was well known among the locals. I watched from down the block as he went in, then sat on a stoop waiting for him to emerge. Which he eventually did, hours later, with a middle-aged man in a gray overcoat. I gleaned no prior acquaintance, and that they were both drunk. They found their way down one of the darker recesses between a couple of brick buildings, where Driscoll was soon enough on his knees, the older man standing back against the brick wall, head up as if looking at the stars. The obvious thing would have been to strike one or the other with the pipe in my coat pocket, but what I was after was far more existential—that they simply be made aware of themselves under watching eyes. What I did was throw the pipe down the alley, an overhand toss so that it spun in the air like a baton before finally crashing onto the trash cans down against the back wall. I expected them to scatter like rats as I watched from my safe shadows, but the noise was far louder than I expected, followed almost instantly by a shriek from the older man. Driscoll had apparently champed down, out of fright.

The man was now thrashing wildly at Driscoll, throwing him

on the pavement and beating him savagely. Driscoll was making no noise at all. After an attenuated five seconds of this, I came out of the shadows and grabbed the man by the throat, and, at the same time, thrust my hand into his pocket, pulling loose his wallet as he tried to fight me off. And then he was running, holding his loosened pants around his waist, crying in pain. Lights were snapped on in the windows above us, and I could feel the gathering of those watching eyes I had wanted to summon.

Driscoll was in a fetal ball on the ground, breathing softly. I looked in the wallet and brought out the three twenties that were in it. I threw them at Driscoll, where they lay along the side of his coat. "He left this for you," I said.

Driscoll, who until now had not registered that a third person was in the alley, looked up at me in pure disbelief, then brushed the money off himself. "I don't need anybody's money," he said. "I have more money right now than you'll ever imagine, Rafferty."

"I'll see to it you never behave so fucking shamefully again," I said. "Mark what I'm saying." I picked up the money and pocketed it myself. I pulled the driver's license from the wallet and could see in the faint streetlight that the man was from Hingham, the kind of perfectly picturesque suburb that people from the Old Colony projects could only imagine. The man's name was Archibald Greenway, which made me laugh. I could picture him arriving home with no wallet and a tooth-marked penis, trying not to wake the wife or kids. It was a pathetically sad thought, although I could not prove it.

I rode back on the T with Driscoll, who had neither asked me to accompany him nor told me not to. Blood had crusted around his mouth and he had an abraded welt on his forehead where it had

166

slammed into the pavement. He said nothing. I could smell the al-
cohol on him, like a glowing halo. He was terrifically drunk.

"Are you stupid?" I finally asked. "You don't know what this guy
could have done to you."

Driscoll looked at me and shook his head. "He's a good man," he
said, slurring the words. "He only hit me because I hurt him."

"Are you telling me you know this guy?"

Driscoll nodded, and a sob escaped him before he could hold it
back. "And now I'll probably never see him again."

"Oh, Jesus Christ," I said.

"Do you even understand the notion of love?" he said.

At the end of the line he got off the trolley without saying anything
more, as did I. He walked unsteadily up the hill to his dormitory,
even more drunk now as the alcohol and pain took effect. He stum-
bled across the lawn with me trailing behind him, continuing
silently to make my point until he entered his residence hall and
slammed the door shut behind him. Archibald Greenway's wallet
was still in my pocket. I planned to throw it into the Chestnut Hill
Reservoir. It was late and I found my space in the dark-but-un-
locked chapel, rolled up my coat as a pillow and tried to get some
sleep before first light, when I would find a quiet spot in the depths
of the library and sleep more, then shower in the gym or up on one
of the dorm floors. My excursions back to the old neighborhood had
become less frequent and strictly out of necessity for a change of
clothes. I imagined Driscoll up there, sleeping in the bed his father
had paid for as I lay on the hard and ascetic board of a pew.

I was wrong that he made it into bed at all. In fact, that was not
the end of Driscoll's night. I found out later the next day, by over-

hearing a group of students talking excitedly in the library, that he had apparently entered the men's bathroom, which, although cavernous in scale with many showers and stalls, was empty at that late hour. He took off his alligator belt (which I had admired and even coveted more than once) and looped it over a hot-water pipe that ran along the ceiling; he must have stood (with great difficulty in his inebriated state) on the edge of one of the sinks, refastened the belt buckle, and then slipped his head into the loop. I can still almost imagine him stepping off that sink and into the void.

Driscoll had never eaten well or often enough, and his pants did not tend to stay up without that belt around them. The next student to enter the bathroom, some time later, was a beer-sodden football player named Bailey, a simple boy just following his urge for a cathartic nocturnal piss. Enough time had passed that no one would be saved. Driscoll hung from the creaking pipe, with his flannel Brooks Brothers trousers down around his ankles, having apparently thrashed in his final seconds. Bailey woke fully in that instant, and the thing that would burden him for years after, even decades later (when he would drink too much at reunions and begin to describe that moment, in a way that made it clear he was still haunted by it) was Driscoll's apparently not-insignificant death erection, projecting obscenely from his white monogrammed boxers.

At the wake (to which I traveled using Archibald Greenway's money to hire a car), Mr. Driscoll spotted me and came across the room quickly before clenching me in a fierce hug.

"I wish you'd become his friend sooner," he said softly. "I'm sure it would have helped."

"I tried to do what I could," I said. "I am deeply sorry for your pain."

Mr. Driscoll put his arm around me and walked me to a quiet corner. He was completely composed, even as the woman I presumed to be Mrs. Driscoll wept uncontrollably by the casket.

"The truth was, he would have humiliated the whole family," Mr. Driscoll said. "All anyone ever wanted was for him to act like a man. A man like you."

"Thank you, sir," I said.

"He had all the opportunity I could possibly give him," Mr. Driscoll said, almost angrily. "And then here's someone like yourself, doing anything you can to get a fair chance."

"This is true."

Mr. Driscoll leaned his head in to me. "After the funeral, I want you to come to see me up at my offices," he said. "I'm going to see to it you get the opportunities that my own son chose to throw away."

He reached out his hand and I shook it. "I will do that, sir."

He patted me on the shoulder and then wandered back toward the casket. I didn't go close, but I could see Driscoll's face, his head laid on its satin pillow. His face looked radiant, white, unmarked. The welt on the forehead, the broken nose, the marks on the neck— all now excised by the undertaker's art. It was as if, I thought, looking at him in death, he had suffered no real injuries in life at all.

169

+ +

38

He has found his way back, as he so often has, to the refuge of the library stacks. Christopher can hear the rain drumming hard against the windows, but he does not look up from the pages of his book, which has a deeply and satisfyingly detailed illustration of the heavy swords of those days. He is somewhat versed in their uses, both offensively and defensively, and he knows that the truest measure of a swordsman is not how he attacks but, rather, how he deflects the thrusts and lunges of others, rendering his own armor a largely redundant system. Christopher tries to imagine the times in the world when matters were settled within arm's length, close enough to hear an opponent's breathing, enough to feel the deceleration of a blade as it hits flesh. It shames the more cowardly remove of a far-off gun. As he reads in *Medieval Combat: A Manual of Swordfighting and Close-Quarter Combat*:

> Combat with the longsword was not so barbaric and crude as is often portrayed. Codified systems of fight existed, with a variety of styles and teachers each providing a somewhat different approach. The longsword was a quick, effective and versatile weapon capable of deadly thrusts, slices and cuts. The pommel and cross of the longsword was used as a hook for tripping and knocking an opponent off-balance . . .

He studies every word, pulls it in, savors it. He has not gone to school in a month. He has stopped going home except when his mother leaves for work, when he will let himself in and go to his room to briefly sleep, go to the kitchen to eat only what is necessary. Nights, mostly, he wanders, out on the other side of things, sitting on doorsteps and walking down along the trees behind the rectory, where he sees the light from the upstairs windows, the shadows on ceiling of nocturnal movement, of unsettled mind that cannot sleep. The weather is colder now—the overnight chill of late fall—but it will soon be worse, more than his heavy hooded sweatshirt can withstand. He will find places, because he cannot face the thought of being around his mother, whose face reveals each of his failings as another wound to her, whose quietness is clearly silent indictment. He shuts the book. He needs to get out in the air.

Outside the library he sees, at some distance, a figure on foot, whose movement is hazily familiar. The build and the rolling gait, the bow of the head. It's Bobby. With no distinct sense of why, Christopher follows, hanging back, pulling up far enough behind to not be noticed. He does not want to be seen, but Bobby doesn't seem at all interested in what is behind him anyway. Bobby moves along with what seems like deliberation, but then at times he stops abruptly, sometimes skirting off to the side where he seems to be waiting for something to momentarily pass. Then he starts again, and so does Christopher, who keeps the distance carefully measured and makes no effort to close it.

It occurs to him now that Bobby himself is following someone. Christopher swings out onto the street and sees a woman, in heels and a long fur coat, walking up ahead. Christopher cannot be fully sure that Bobby is following the woman, but the three of them are walking at nearly even intervals up Broadway. And, in some odd way, Christopher feels that he too is being followed. He glances back behind him. There are indeed people down the sidewalk, but, other than his mother, he can't think of anyone who would particularly care.

Christopher isn't even sure why he's following, except that maybe he feels some vague affinity with Bobby from that dingy apartment. And their shared affinity for Jeanmarie, which, in the simpler times as detailed in his favored books, might have been fought over with swords and shields. But Bobby has been cut loose anyway, and in some ways Christopher has been cut loose as well.

The woman up ahead turns right onto L Street and when Bobby gets to the corner he turns right as well. Christopher reaches the corner, peeks around, and sees that the pursuit continues. Bobby watches the woman with a bowed head apparently meant to minimize the chance of recognition, but that walk, a kind of schlumping apologetic shuffle, would give him away to anyone who knew him. The woman looks older, her hips swinging under her coat as she maneuvers on her heels. She is carrying a plastic grocery bag on her arm. Again, Christopher reflexively looks behind him without knowing why.

When she turns north again at Seventh, and then Bobby does, Christopher knows for sure. The woman begins to labor up the rise in the road, and Bobby slows accordingly. Christopher stays back around the corner to let the distance between them grow on this quiet street. The woman brings out her keys and, as she turns toward the front entrance of her apartment building, Bobby falls into a tacking motion, circling back on himself and then picking up the chase again. But she turns and sees him.

"What the fuck are you doing?" the woman shouts, and Christopher startles at it being Jeanmarie's voice. He peeks around the corner and sees Bobby's hands rising to his side, palms out.

"I just wasn't sure if it was you," Bobby says. "I just wanted to say hi."

"Bullshit," Jeanmarie shouts. Even knowing it's Jeanmarie, Christopher still can hardly recognize her.

Bobby walks toward her, his hands still at his sides.

"Leave me alone," Jeanmarie says. "I don't have anything to say to you."

"You didn't even talk to me," Bobby says. "I came home and you were gone."

"It was the easiest way," she says.

"Easiest for you, you cunt."

The word hits Jeanmarie like a slap across the mouth. Her chin quivers, as she tries to stay composed.

"I gave you everything I fucking had," Bobby says, his voice quaking.

"Get out of here," Jeanmarie says more evenly. "And you, too," she shouts, and Christopher realizes he has wandered out into sight.

"Hi," he says. Bobby, turning, is startled.

"I can't believe you're with him on this," she screams.

"I'm not," Christopher says.

Bobby is coming at Christopher now and even when he sees Bobby raising a fist, his brain just does not seem to compute it. Bobby swings an unpracticed roundhouse that nonetheless con-

173

nects solidly on Christopher's ear. Falling, Christopher is thinking more than acting, his mind working on the question of why he has been hit when, really, he has done nothing. Then, as quickly, someone is on Bobby, knocking him down. Christopher is glad Jeanmarie would defend him. But he looks up from the pavement to see that Bobby is now in a scuffle with a red-haired man he's never seen before.

"Pick on somebody your own size," the man says as he bunches Bobby's jacket in his hands and swings him onto the ground.

"Who the hell are you?" Bobby says, trying to sound tough even as his voice cracks.

"Nobody, shithead. Leave the kid alone."

"I don't need you defending me," Christopher says, trying to pull the guy's arm off Bobby.

"Why don't you go home to your mother," the man says, releasing Bobby and dumping him onto the pavement. "It sure as hell looks like you need someone defending you." The man is breathing heavily, someone not used to such exertions anymore. He wipes the spittle from his lips and straightens his overcoat. He looks down at Bobby and says, "And why don't you go home, too, before you get yourself in a lot more trouble than you want. Just like your damned father."

The man shuffles down the street, shaking his head, still trying to get his breath back. Bobby pulls himself to his feet and, after glaring at Christopher, heads in the other direction. Jeanmarie, in all of the commotion, has disappeared.

39

The place is a shithole, prison-like, with fluorescent-lit, window-less inner hallways strewn with the detritus of the day's routine: Paper cups and cigarette butts littering the linoleum floor, emp-tied food carts piled with trays and dirty dishes, rags and bottles. Jimmy has entered the place through the loading dock, and here, in the part of the building that is not for visitors, it is like the dis-eased organ of the outwardly healthy body.

It's not a hospital, exactly, and not a nursing home, but a "long-term care facility" in a far suburb, a locale Butchie Morrissey had likely never come to before being brought in on a hospital bed rigged with the computers, wires and hoses that make any move-ment at all monumental and rare. Jimmy has tracked him down by close and unrelenting reading of the *Herald*, where it was noted in a tiny item headlined "Sex-assault charge may be dropped for accident victim" that Butchie Morrissey was being transferred, and to where.

And so here Jimmy is, stealthy, avoiding the front door where he might be asked who invited him. Up the service elevator, try-ing to look as if he belongs here, he goes to the top, the fourth floor. But no one even acknowledges him. He wanders the hallway past indolent nurses and slow-moving aides, no one as much as saying hello. He reads the name tags on each door he passes, looking in with a quick glance at all manner of sad cases. Not all are old, either: people damaged and contorted, frozen in some sort of trap. Through one door, Jimmy sees an older woman lying in what surely must be a coma, her mouth formed wide into a silent O, a scream not heard. In the next room, a man lies on his side, emaciated to bone and slack, ash-colored skin, his hospital johnny open to reveal a bony ass and ruddled, bed-sore back.

Jimmy moves on, glancing, trying not to look lost. He finds nothing on Four, ducks into a stairway, and on Three sees that he's among the paras and quads, one and then another. To exist on this floor would be to feel as if the state is nothing so special, the succession of unmoving bodies and of darting eyes, installed in their grottos of tubes and wires and monitors.

Now he sees the name "Morrissey" handwritten on the Dry-Erase nameplate by the door, which is ajar a few inches. The room is dark and Jimmy stands outside, listening to see if there are visitors. Hearing nothing from within except the gastric, gurgling hiss of a respirator, he enters.

"Who are you?" Butchie Morrissey says in a near-whisper, his voice bled of any bottom it might have had. It is a tired-sounding exhalation, almost a wheeze.

"You don't know me," Jimmy says.

"Are you a doctor or something?"

"No."

Butchie Morrissey seems then to fall back into himself, as if he has just again realized that it does not at all matter.

"I saw the accident," Jimmy says. "That day. I was the car behind you."

"What's your name?"

"Does it matter?"

"Were you on the witness list? For the insurance claim?"

"No. I was shitfaced. So I couldn't talk to the cops. I avoided them."

"Are you shitfaced now?"

"No."

Butchie waits and Jimmy doesn't say much.

"I came here to look at you," Jimmy says. "Seeing your accident happen right in front of me was what finally got me to stop drinking."

"Wow, awesome for you," Butchie says.

"But now I'm sliding back into it," Jimmy says. "I can't keep myself from it. I wake up in the morning and it's happened without my remembering."

"So you think I have advice for you?"

"I didn't think that at all. I just thought, you know, to look at you . . ."

Butchie Morrissey lets out a breath. "Wow, and there's nothing I can do to beat the piss out of you right now."

"I guess not."

"No one here's going to do anything about it. I was always a real asshole, but especially now. Nobody here can fucking stand me."

"That's too bad."

"I haven't had anyone visit in a month," Butchie says. "My family disowned me after the rape charge, mainly because it was true. I would have been going to prison for sure."

"What about your buddies in the car that day? Do they see you?"

"No way. I got a personal injury lawyer and I'm suing them to get coverage from the car insurance, because I got no medical."

"Oh."

Butchie seems already to need to rest from the talking. He closes his eyes and works to inhale. Jimmy stands by the bed and Butchie opens his eyes again.

"So they let you in without my permission."

"I sort of snuck in."

"No one saw you?"

"Nobody seems to pay much attention around here."

"So have you told people? About how you saw this happen to me?"

"I haven't," Jimmy says. "Nobody. I don't have any people I confide in."

Jimmy stands looking at this man in his vessel and he wants to feel what he's come all this way for. He wants to re-channel that moment in the car, but it is gone, somehow processed and filed, never to be as real as it was in those first days after he saw it, when it could have bent metal and crushed coal into diamonds with its energy. Jimmy has, it would seem, acquired another hard layer to his shell. He turns because there is otherwise no reason to be here. He has come for nothing.

"I want you to kill me," Butchie croaks out.

"Excuse me?"

"No one saw you. You have no connection to me that anybody could ever figure out. You can just do it and they'd probably think it was one of the staff here, or the father of that girl I raped, or the guy I'm suing. They all have motive, and you don't."

"You want to die?"

"Look at me," Butchie Morrissey says. "Like this, in the fucking care of The Commonwealth."

"It's not my responsibility," Jimmy says.

"Just be a fucking human being," Butchie says.

"I still have enough to live for, not to take that risk."

Butchie's eyes are wet now, shining in their fury. Jimmy imagines what this man must have been like with an able body, the waste of how he had used it and inflicted it on others, for no better reason than that it was his instrument—young and strong and filled with urges that he had apparently never tamed. Now it is an appendage, a millstone that weights down whatever hope he might have found after the fact. Just viscera. Jimmy wonders if Butchie Morrissey thinks, ever, of how he might have otherwise lived his life—the one he wants back, not the one he is now begging to have ended.

"Get out of my room, then," he wheezes. "I hope looking at me helped you out, you fucking douchebag."

Maybe it has. For now. Jimmy walks out into the empty hallway feeling lifted, in the horror of all this, feeling resolute again and maybe, possibly, conceivably able to save himself, as Butchie Morrissey could have once, but did not.

40

Colleen has no appointment and no entrée, but she has arrived now outside the Official Residence with full intentions of gaining audience with the Archbishop. The dry leaves above her rustle in the wind and float down, spiraling, meeting those already fallen. Coming out on the Green Line, she has contemplated the madness of someone of her low station thinking she can be brought face-to-face with this man. She has been raised to do anything but that, to in fact regard this man as she might regard God Himself. She can recall from her childhood the awe she felt at those shining and archaic garments, that pointed mitre and curled staff, and she can equally recall the chill she felt at her own confirmation when that era's archbishop, Cushing, laid his shaking and elderly hands coldly on her forehead. Even that night as she slid into bed with this newly afforded status (and the party afterward and the toasts of relatives certainly reinforcing to her the importance of that act) she felt, as she lay in the dark, a holy tingling along her hairline.

She is dressed appropriately, in the dark outfit she keeps for wakes and funerals, for the reading of wills, for the probating of modest accumulations and bequests. The wool, hot for the weather, smells of cedar and stale perfume, and is too snug in the waist and hips. That tightness only adds to the discomfort of all this.

She collects herself once again, running through the things she will say, and how she will say them. No panic, no anger, no accusation. Nothing that would lead them to see her as a nut, as a crank, as someone presenting with unfounded grievance. No one, really, is much more devout than she has been through her life; even in those darkest of days after Barry's death, she swallowed the urge to raise her eyes and ask *Why?*

An urge comes over her now to flee, to return home and to regroup. She knows this is something she must do but it feels suddenly as if today is simply not the day to do so. She realizes she is shaking. She will be seen shuddering, like a drunk or a psycho. It will be seen, in her eyes, that she is not thinking straight. She wants to feel, more pointedly than she has in years, the eyes of God, and to meet their gaze. But above her there are only curled leaves, shaking themselves free and spiraling down to earth.

She steps forward and, at the main entrance, she pushes open the heavy door, fighting its weight and then slipping through. She does not see an obvious place to go, and it surprises her, as if the Swiss Guard themselves should be coming at her with brandished weapons. It has instead the feel of a bank, hushed and moving, the soft register of footfalls and whispers and transactions.

"Hello?" she says. Her voice rebounds back at her and she hears someone approach—a young priest, serious-looking and squinting behind steel-rimmed glasses.

"Yes, ma'am?" he says with quizzical and quiet affect. "Is there something you want?"

"I'm here to see Cardinal Law," she says.

The young priest seems for a moment to freeze, as if confronted by a trick question. His smile belies a careful search for the right words.

181

"You have an appointment, then," he says.

"No."

"I see, I see," he says. "May I ask the nature of the visit?"

"It's about my son."

"I probably need more than that."

"My son is in trouble," she says. She is someone who rarely raises her voice but right now is attempting not to shout.

"Have you tried Social Services?" he says.

"I want to explain but it's something I need to speak to *him* about," she says. "It involves a priest."

The young priest before her nods in a way that does not fully communicate assent.

"You know it's really not possible to simply show up and expect Cardinal Law to be available," he says.

"Then I want to make an appointment," she says.

"I don't think we can really do that," he says. "I'd suggest you should start at the parish level. Have you spoken to your parish priest?"

"He won't see me," she says.

"Yes, I see," he says, in a way that suggests he now considers her a troublemaker. "Well, showing up at the Cardinal's home is hardly the appropriate thing to do." He reaches out and puts his hand on her upper arm. "I think the proper thing is that you should go."

She can feel the tears building. Her rage right now seems to be picking up everything that she has so carefully pushed down for so many years, beginning with Barry's death. "Get your *fucking* hands off me," she says in a fierce whisper.

"Okay, this conversation is officially over," he says. "Please leave before I have to call someone."

"Doesn't the Cardinal want to know what this priest is doing?" she says. "Doesn't he want to know?"

"Please just leave," he says.

"I'll wait outside until he comes out," she says.

"You do what you want," he says. "Just please leave."

Outside she bursts into tears. It has happened so fast, and she has sworn at a priest, another damnation upon all the others. She sits down in the fallen leaves and attempts now to compose herself. It seems almost instant that a police cruiser pulls up along the curb. The officer, an older man, comes out of the car slowly and seemingly without agenda. He reaches his hand out and she takes it and lets him pull her up to her feet.

"I can arrest you or just give you a lift back off the property," he says.

"I don't give a shit," Colleen says.

"Let's not make this ugly," he says. "Get in the car."

She slips into the back seat, in the cage, and the officer gets in behind the wheel. He makes a U-turn and goes back down through the front gate. He says nothing to her. At the T station he stops and looks at her through the steel mesh.

"I'll let you out if you don't go back up there," he says. "You need to promise, though."

She's started to cry again, but she finally nods, and he gets out of the car and opens the back door.

"I stopped thinking a long time ago that anybody's listening," he says to her.

41

And so, upon my graduation from college, I was brought into the investment firm of Driscoll, Irving. I worked as an aide to Red Driscoll himself, now chairman, who at times seemed to see in me not only a protégé but a successor, someone from the same place and with very much the same ambition. At other times he seemed distant and angry, and it made me wonder how much I brought to his mind his son's suicide, which, after the wake, he never again mentioned in all the time I knew him. I was young but he knew, I think, that I had some seasoning that the men around me, somewhat older but having kept their hands clean in their matriculations through prep schools and elite universities, did not; I think as well that Driscoll had a sense of all this as a blood sport. As much as we all dressed in our pinstripes and at meetings in the boardroom were served tea from a silver service, it was rough trade for him.

Driscoll decided to put me in tandem with another young newcomer, a Harvard graduate named Saltonstall—a tall, angular man with a long horsey face that didn't quite make it to handsome. He was raised, from what I could gather, not more than a few miles from me, but Beacon Hill was an altogether different universe. He was a nervous fellow, newly married and clearly not sure of himself; I did not realize at that moment that Driscoll had set it up this way, and that I would, for my own survival, have to overtake

Saltonstall, would have to humble him and, through doing so, develop an even sharper edge to my own already sharply honed nature. I had also gotten a whisper that Saltonstall, a clever fellow, had come up with a nickname for me that apparently captured my small stature and pinched face; he was, or so I heard, referring to me as "The Rodent." When I heard this, I did not completely mind it, only because it made me realize that Saltonstall was occupying himself with me more than I thought, which was entirely to my advantage.

What I did know was that there was a position to be filled—it had been announced by Driscoll, not more than a few months after Saltonstall had joined the firm. When he described it, there was no doubt that the competition could only be between Saltonstall and myself; in fact, our two positions were to be merged into a single, more highly paid position, but no mention was made of what would happen to the man who wasn't chosen for promotion.

The irony was that Saltonstall, clearly the product of too much refined breeding, actually seemed to become more friendly to me at that moment.

"Well, Terry," said the young new husband to me, his sudden nemesis, "we're both going to give our best, no doubt, but that doesn't mean you shouldn't come with your wife some night to dine with me and Margaret."

I suspected he was taking the measure of me. The fact was that I not only wasn't married, but that I was still a virgin. This was not nearly so unusual a state for a twenty-two-year-old then as it would be now, and in fact the nature of things in the early Sixties was that, if you wanted some, you were going to have to marry the girl who was going to give it to you. And I was never one to make much of my looks. I was living in a shabby one-room apartment out by Coolidge

Corner and putting all my money into something new and exciting: Golf. I had come to it because I knew it was the lingua franca *of the kind of people I was doing business with, but what I failed to anticipate was how much I would take to it. I'd never been big enough for the usual sports, other than some pickup baseball at the park, but I apparently had the helical strength of a tightly wound spring, with which I could hit a golf ball with surprising range. I did not have the usual growing pains of shanks and slices and hooks, finding in myself the ability to simply put the ball right up the middle of the fairway. I scraped together enough money to go out to the Presidential in Quincy; my Saturdays, lacking any other distractions, saw the sun rise and set on that course. I would fall into foursomes with anyone who needed an extra, and would shun conversation whenever possible. On the day of the summer solstice I would play seventy-two holes, walking, my pagan ritual. At nights after work I'd stand in the confines of my small room, swinging a club. I had hardly considered the idea of a woman, because I knew that smaller men like me—and this is a sad but truthful statement—simply looked more attractive to women when standing on their money. I was, as always, willing to patiently execute my plan.*

So I came into Lafayette Square on a cool late-summer evening, carrying a bottle of burgundy and a bouquet of flowers, looking along the black-painted doors for the residence of Oliver and Margaret Saltonstall. I was trying to suppress my resentment that a man my own age could live in such grandeur, and it only reminded me that Saltonstall really didn't even need a job, while I would have to struggle for every rising step. Saltonstall was at the door instantly, where he shook my hand and motioned me into the living room, where his wife, Margaret, sat in a diaphanous dress as if this was to be an audience with her. She was, like her husband, someone who had just missed being attractive. Her eyes were a bit too wide-set and her lips just a little too thin, and I could tell by the look on her face that this was not a pleasant moment, that she knew what was going on between us, and that she was likely being put up to this. I went to her, knelt before her, and kissed her hand. At that moment, I was both acceding to and mocking her; she knew it, and immediately burst out laughing.

Throughout the drinks and dinner, I kept all my attention on her, asking her everything about herself and exclaiming at her answers. Brearley and then Wheaton? Remarkable! An equestrian as well? Capital! A member of the Junior League? Where do the accomplishments end!

You would think she could see right through me but it was clear she did not. Saltonstall sat sullenly next to her on the sofa while I sat rapt in my armchair. It was clear she was a woman who did not get the attention she craved, and it became clearer, as Saltonstall descended into a deeper funk, that she liked even better the idea of two men not only competing for a job in their firm, but also for her favor. She was the type of woman a wiser man avoids at all costs. I was no more than a modest rook on this board, but I had the queen in check and the king at my mercy.

Through dinner (boxed and delivered from the kitchen of a nearby restaurant and heaped on china in what was Margaret's apparent definition of "preparing dinner"), I kept on. I knew Saltonstall really could say nothing, because I was in no way being overly flirtatious, even as Margaret ate up my every attention. I had, indeed, come into his home and subverted the order he clearly enjoyed there; it was as if, in my absorption with Margaret, I had not even noticed what I had been brought here to witness, which was Saltonstall's obvious place in a hierarchy I could not ever be part of. It was tough going, working as vapid and unengaging a woman as Saltonstall's wife, but I pushed on. By the time we sat before our dessert plates, Saltonstall was nearly in a state of complete distress. I can imagine he knew that he did not have the wherewithal to match the attention I had given her, as I myself could not have for much more than those few hours—and still she seemed to crave more.

"Well," I said as I finished my raspberry torte, "I shouldn't presume on the time of a pair of newlyweds."

"Oh, that's perfectly all right," Margaret said, and Saltonstall looked at her, unabashedly hurt.

The next Monday morning, Saltonstall had nearly nothing at all to say to me, and the lines were clearly drawn. And when I got a phone call from Margaret later that week, asking me to meet her for tea at the Park Plaza, I wasn't completely surprised. I had provided her with the purest form of the drug she craved—unexpurgated attention. Despite the fact that I had very little money (having poured it into my golf), after our tea that Friday I got a room from a clearly disapproving clerk, and within the hour lost my virginity to the young and homely wife of my archrival. She admitted to me afterwards, naked in the sheets as I put my wristwatch back on and sorted out my clothes, that what had intrigued her most of all was her husband's apparent fear of me. She said she was contemplating divorcing him. I got dressed almost without hearing her, instead thinking through my first sexual experience as if it had been a round of golf, trying to square my expectations of the act with what had just ensued. Women would come somewhat easily from there on, and

188

I would learn soon enough that Margaret had been truly wretched as a lover. There was a fumbling, cowish nature to her entire being. But even if she had been brilliant, it hardly mattered. I had no further contact with her, refusing to take her calls and letting our nervous and matronly executive secretary, Jane—who never directly asked why Saltonstall's wife was calling me with such regularity— put Margaret off with the requisite decorum, laced as it was with the genteel opprobrium we hired people like Jane to have. The calls stopped and the next time I saw her was just before Christmas, during cocktail hour at the firm's Holiday Dinner at The Ritz. I had a date that night, in fact, a Vassar girl to whom I had been introduced by her father, a golfer I had met at the club. Margaret looked contemptuously at me even as I introduced my date to them, and when I directly addressed her, inquiring as to her well-being, she pointedly refused to answer. Saltonstall looked sick, as if some feared confirmation had now been delivered. By the first of the year he had resigned from the firm, and I must admit I never heard his name mentioned again, even in the relatively small world of Boston business. I, of course, had won my promotion through what appeared to all to have been his default.

+ +

42

She finds him at the usual time of the afternoon, sitting in his usual place. As always at this time of day, Christopher occupies the bench across the street from Most Holy Trinity Elementary School. The weather has grown colder, the trees are stripped of their leaves, and he sits with the hood of his sweatshirt pulled up tight and his hands jammed in the pockets. Down the street there is still a plywood sheet covering the broken stained-glass window. As she finds him, Christopher is bowed forward, hunching to try to conjure a bit more warmth. Looking at him from a half-block's distance, Jeanmarie thinks of a monk at prayer. She is more warmly dressed, in sleek boots and her faux-fur coat, and as she gets closer he hears the click of her heels on the sidewalk and looks up. Then he looks away and bows his head even more deeply as she approaches and sits on the bench next to him.

"I guess I *do* know you weren't with Bobby the other day."

Christopher says nothing.

"But what I can't figure out is why you were there."

Christopher straightens up. "I followed him. I saw him walking down West Broadway and decided to see where he was going. He was following you, so I followed him."

"Well, now he knows where I live, more or less."

"Are you afraid of him?"

"I'm not sure. I definitely don't feel like dealing with him, though."

Jeanmarie looks at Christopher's bony wrists jutting from the sleeves of his sweatshirt. "You look skinny," she says. "Are you living at home?"

"Not really. Sometimes I go there but mostly I stay away."

"What does your mother have to say about that?"

Christopher turns and looks at her. "Nothing yet," he says. "You said I could stay with you."

"You can stay with me, then," she says. "It's a small place, though. The floor has carpet but you'll need something more than that for sleeping. Maybe a piece of foam or something."

"I can do that," Christopher says.

"And Marty can't know you're there," she says.

"Marty?"

"You know, my manager?"

"Yeah, your *manager*."

"A model needs a manager, stupid."

Christopher contemplates this. "I guess I already figured out what kind of modeling you do."

"Does it shock you?"

"Hey, none of my business."

"I know you don't think so because you see me around here, but I'm already kind of famous, you know."

"What do you mean, 'famous'?"

"You know, *famous*. Like, a lot more people know who I am than I know. Marty says my pictures have gotten, like, a couple of thousand hits on the Internet."

"That's not what 'famous' means."

"Yes it is."

"I don't think so."

"Okay, whatever," she says, suddenly seeming indignant. "Then you tell me what it is."

"It's sort of like . . . that you matter."

"I don't matter? Is that what you're saying?

"No, you do."

"Then I am famous, the way you just said it."

"It's more than that, though. I just can't explain. I mean, everybody knows who Whitey Bulger is, but he's not *famous*."

"No, he definitely is famous. He's the most famous person from here. It's not like you have to be on the Red Sox or be an astronaut to be famous."

Christopher shrugs, beaten in the argument. "So why do you want to be famous like that, anyway?"

Jeanmarie is smiling triumphantly. "So that I matter," she says. "Lots of people know who I am. The thing is, though, they know me by my new name. You know how actresses and celebrities usually don't go by their real names?"

"Yeah . . ."

"The name I chose was 'Sandra Shields'. I think it sounds elegant."

"Where did you get those clothes?" Christopher says. "You didn't used to wear clothes like that."

"Hey, I'm getting older, do you mind? Marty got them for me. He took me shopping for stuff. I picked what I wanted and he paid."

"Does your father know about Marty?"

"My parents don't give a shit about where I am," she says. "Just like yours."

"My father would if he didn't die."

"Yeah, that's nice to think," Jeanmarie says.

In the ensuing silence they listen to the dry leaves rustling up against the school playground's chain-link fence.

"Why do you sit here?" Jeanmarie says.

"Just to sit."

"I'm going to the drug store for some makeup and then walking home," she says. "You want to come with me? It's warmer inside."

"I'll come over later," he says.

"I wouldn't mind if you came with me now," she says. "After that situation with Bobby."

"I can't right now," Christopher says. "I'm going to stay here a while."

"Well, I can stay and wait."

Christopher turns to her and says more quietly, "I just want to sit here by myself for a while."

Jeanmarie stands. "*Fine*," she says. "So you know my street, so I'm in the gray apartment building. You can ring my bell—G1. I'll be there in a half-hour or so. But if you get there before me, be careful not to let Marty see you waiting for me. He's kind of fat and drives a Cadillac."

"That could be a lot of guys around here. How would he know I was waiting for you?"

"I don't know. But just don't do it, okay?"

"Okay."

She walks off toward East Broadway and Christopher shrinks back into his sweatshirt. It's nearly time. The wind suddenly dies down and the quiet envelops him. No after-school games go on this afternoon in the schoolyard, and the leaves for a moment are still. He can hear a car over the rise and when it comes over it is the familiar black Lincoln. The car moves slowly, drifting a little from its intended path, and the same familiar head is at the wheel. And, in infinitely repeated ritual, the head does not turn, does not look, does not acknowledge. And then the car passes by. Christopher stands. It is over, once again, for today.

43

Him, there again. As always. John has wondered, each day, about when the foolishness will end, this boy and his mother both, their boorish games. Time grows short now, the last slack weeks of these rounds of duties. He drives as always to the retirement home, trying not to entertain the thought that he will soon be headed to a similar destination himself, albeit not one of the dank and medicinally tinged places where he goes to offer hosts and to anoint the sick. His place of retirement will be a tennis-court-ringed, arid enclave at which he can hardly imagine being. He hears it's hot down there. He has never been the scholar many of his peers try to be, sublimating other impulses into their careful readings and writings. He does not anticipate a late life spent rereading Augustine and Hobbes, or refreshing his Latin through the examination of classic texts. Like his peers, he drinks his share, but, unlike them, he does not revel in complex and carefully savored meals. He's not much for sports on television. His passions have always been other. Most nights he holds a glass in one hand and the remote in the other, flipping channels, never finding what he's after.

It is only when he has been in the company of the children that he feels fully engaged, fully awakened. He had become a priest with them in mind. He had wanted to engage with the children the way he had seen the priest of his youth, old Father Sullivan, do. The old man had something that few he ever saw in the old neighborhood had—unmitigated respect. Father Sullivan seemed, in John's mind, almost mythic. His gentle approbation was a gift that seemed to flow directly from God Himself. John knew, even early on, of his own baser impulses; it was a conceit of youth to think that they could be ignored, that wanting to be like someone else could actually make you *be* that someone.

But it was at the seminary where he saw that the path to holiness was indeed a difficult journey. His vow of celibacy came in some ways from both a pure fear of the sexual act as well as a sense of his own unattractiveness—that narrow face. At that age he could not imagine he was giving anything up at all. But in the dark, late at night in his narrow seminary bed, the impulses could not be denied. He was a very young man, for whom desire was already becoming a constant, coursing need. And he had pledged to God that he would touch no woman in that way, just as those around him had made the exact same pledge.

The quenching of those needs is something he remembers neither fondly nor sadly, but merely with the blank sense that this was, it turned out, how it was done. This was, in essence, an explanation. The furtive creepings in the dark; the first touch of flesh upon flesh, unspoken about in daylight. He was really still a child and, in his dark ruminations those nights, he felt it was an anointing that he had not anticipated but now accepted. His body in its youth could not have been expected to contain those very urges God had planted in him.

And as a young priest he found himself already yearning to be back at the seminary as he sat in his small room in that first rectory, trying to abide himself. He wanted to be Father Sullivan right away, but had already seen that it was a slow evolution, that mistakes would be made, and that no one had bothered to demarcate the boundaries. The first time he made an advance, he was nearly shaking with uncertainty, but it happened by him as it had happened to him, with slow and silent acceding. He had the sense for only a moment of God's eyes on him, but the sensation was followed by no sign or manifestation. His mind duly settled. Always without words, without acknowledgment, God's will.

It all made him feel closer to the children than their own parents were. He was the young priest at the parochial school, teaching religion to the delight of similarly young parents. Occasionally, there would be a young mother, divorced or in trouble with her husband, who would seem to come to him in an unexpected way, to make herself available. But he still had an oath to God, and he stood behind that in all possible ways.

Then, suddenly, began his personal migration. Abrupt and unexplained orders to pack and report to a new parish, this one out in a far, failing mill town; new connections and new duties and again connection with a favored child (he felt special provenance with those boys just coming out of their childhoods). Then, again, new dispatch to another bleak place. It occurred to him at that time that his commitment to the church and his superiors was making it too easy for them to exercise their whims and move him to yet another place, another small and even more remote parish, farm communities out west of the far suburbs, farther still from the corridors of power of the Archdiocese. There had been a period in the mid-Seventies when they tried him at an all-black parish down in Mattapan, but even there he had lasted less than two years before moving. He had been careful to take no stated position on the unrest in the city on the matter of race, an ideological absence that seemed to make his parishioners wary and silent. Through the Eighties and into the Nineties he was nomadic, a traveling show, never more than a few years anywhere, his friendships and connections made only to be quickly broken.

It seemed, in fact, that he could be no farther away from whence he'd come. But then the times were changing as well. As the old priests retired and died, there were few younger ones coming up to take their places. And after all those years of movement, it was an irony to him, but possibly not to Cardinal Law, when John received his new orders that fall of 1996: To return to the very parish in which he had begun, less than a mile from where he'd grown up. And to tend to the children of parents he had tended to as children.

Now, it is coming to a rapid end. There will clearly be no party. No acknowledgment, no thanks, no meaningful respect. Only a strange woman pounding on his door and her even stranger son watching him from a sidewalk bench as he drives by, a man of God on his way to attend to those who need him.

+ + + + + + + + + + + + + + + + + + + +

44

The phone message is a surprise. Jimmy lies in bed listening to his cell phone, as Shelagh tells his voicemail that, on the one hand, she thought they had fun that night, but on the other hand, maybe it wasn't as much for him, but on another hand, maybe it would be fun to connect again, but on another hand again, maybe it would be something that wouldn't be, but maybe friends, so who knows?

"But the real reason I called," she says, "is because I am just hoping you're doing all right with the drinking. You seemed to be doing so well."

It's just before three in the afternoon and he doesn't know when she called, because again he has awakened feeling nauseated and with no recall of anything past about eleven o'clock last night, when he knows he was working on Rafferty's notes at the office. Now he is here, feeling as bad as the worst hangovers of his life, and he has to know how it happened that he returned to drinking. He doesn't even know where it is he goes. He has come to realize that when he wakes up, most of the night before is erased, and he suspects that in all these years he'd simply not thought much about it. He thinks he was at the office, but further thought reveals that it isn't anything he's all that sure of, either.

He redials the number and Shelagh answers on the second ring.

"Jimmy."

"I got your message," he says. "Thanks."

"Just wanted to see how you're doing," she says.

"I don't know. Not good, I guess."

"What's going on?"

"I've had these incidents. I wake up in the morning and I'm not even sure where I've been."

"You've been drinking again . . ."

"Somewhere. Heavily. I wake up in the morning without a sense of where I've gone. I haven't been drinking here because I have nothing to drink here. But I've wandered off somewhere and then the whole night before is a blank. I'm not sure whether I've worked or not. It's like, when I don't drink for a week my body needs to balance by having enough for blackouts and memory loss. I feel like crap all the time."

Shelagh is silent on the other end.

"I have to ask this," Jimmy says. "Did I drink with you that night?"

"Jimmy, are you serious?"

"Meaning I didn't."

"You think I'd be taking you *drinking*?"

Jimmy says he doesn't remember and waits for her to answer, and after she is silent for a while he realizes it's not so much that she is silent as that she's not there at all, and when he looks at the screen of the phone there is no "signal lost" message, but rather the creeping possibility that she has actually and definitively hung up on him, as he most certainly must have deserved. He hits her number again but she does not answer and he does not leave a message.

He has nothing to do now until he goes to the office, after every-one else has left. He has not seen Rafferty in more than a month.

The security guard, whose name he has yet to learn, is his only connection to the building and to the sequestered room in which he types out Rafferty's rambling monologs. He is still on the first batch, still cleaning up the repetitions, the rare lapses in grammar, and the transparent modifiers. There are long gaps when Rafferty stops to think and the recording runs on, and at times Jimmy tries to interpret the breathy sounds that occasionally punctuate the silence. He is being paid well for this service, and really it seems too easy. He is, more than anything, a transcriptionist. But until then, he is getting in his own way. He knows he won't get back to sleep now.

He could walk, could try to maintain his resolve and move toward something roughly like health. He can feel, in his mostly sober state, the damage that has been irreparably done. He is still young, more or less, but his body has a kind of wheezing operational mode that doesn't seem at all right. The heart thumps heavily along with the occasional erratic beat; the breathing doesn't always come as easily as it probably should, and at times he can feel a floating of his mind that seems something like faintness. His florid ruddiness, the sweaty beefsteak red that his skin always seemed to glow with when he was drunk, has faded into a kind of yellowness that isn't a suntan but isn't exactly the whiteness he knew in his youth. His stomach aches, more than it should. He has no medical coverage and he has convinced himself that before he goes to a doctor he should give his sobriety a good six months. He's heard that there are many uncomfortable withdrawal pangs. He just wishes he felt the kind of non-awareness of his biology that he did when he was flat-out shitfaced at the end of one bar or another.

No, he decides, he will not walk; he will indulge himself in television and the puzzle of how this thing with Shelagh is going, which apparently went at least well enough for her to hang up on him for his lack of memory.

He flips through the channels. The *Oprah* show is indulging its viewers with a segment on easy Thanksgiving side dishes. He hasn't really registered that Thanksgiving is little more than a week away. It will be his first in years not standing outside Triple O's waiting for someone to finally wander over and open up. Thanksgivings spent drinking shots from plastic Dixie cups and watching the hot dogs dance on the rotary grill. But, on the other hand, it may force him to sit in his apartment all day trying not to think about how long it has been since that last Thanksgiving his father was still alive, when he got tanked on bourbon before the first course even came out. His sister had finally, in her own troubles, shouted at him to *just please leave*; his father had tried at first to get him to stay, but then finally saw that Jimmy could not possibly complete the afternoon with any kind of success. He finally called a cab to take Jimmy back to his apartment, for which the old man had lent him money and for which Jimmy had never repaid a cent. When the old man died, Jimmy drank on the couch all through the wake (his hip flask quaint and Irish to the old folks, his drunkenness abided) and then slept it off all through the funeral. When he awakened late that afternoon as the light died and his father was about to spend his first night of eternity under the fresh-turned dirt, he knew he would be hard-pressed to explain the absolute truth of it, which was that this was his legitimate and unique way of expressing his grief. The tears had been real, as had the pain; he did not call anyone and no one called him. That, in short, was the basic version of the estrangement from his family.

45

"I know now that I'm trapped," Colleen says, and Chuckie Connelly leans over his coffee to hear her more intently.

"After that policeman let me out of the back of the car, it was like I was just standing there paralyzed while my brain was trying to decide whether to have me cry or have me go back up and start screaming until someone really had to drag me away. But then I didn't do either. Good girl Colleen, never makes a peep. I didn't cry or scream in the end. I just went home. I got on the T and sat there without making a sound. Not a goddamned fucking sound. Didn't want to bother anybody. Didn't want to make a scene. Didn't want to be an *imposition*.

"What I'm doing as I sit there on the T is retreating, but what I think I'm doing, what I'm *telling myself* I'm doing is going home to make a plan. To figure out a way to get to him. The Cardinal. Bernard Fucking Law. To make him listen, so he knows. To find a way to him. So people like me can't be kept away."

Chuckie grunts assent.

"That fat fuck!" Colleen says. "That pig, that goddamned goddamned son of a bitch. And me putting my money in the church envelope every week so he can eat his lobster at Anthony's with all his lackeys. *I will*, I tell myself on the train home, *I will find a way*, and for that long at least I'm feeling almost good. I'm going to do something. I'm going to make noise.

"So I get home. I let myself in and go right to my son's door. It's locked. He's in there, I'm almost sure of it. I want to bang on that door and demand he come out and tell me what happened, even though I know enough now that I probably couldn't bear to hear it. But I'm not going to, I know it, because whatever is going on with that child is *my fault*; I've let this happen, and for the two of us to try to talk about it, to actually *discuss the facts of it*, is something neither of us would ever be able to do. It's something we will never be able to look each other in the eye about and get out in the open, where it can't ever be put back. My son will never allow me to have that kind of conversation.

"So instead I'm just plotting my revenge. I'm gonna make lots of trouble, see? I'll put up signs and picket the Cathedral for the Cardinal's Mass, right? I'll stand outside the chancery and force the police to put me on the ground and handcuff me, right? Well, then I'm thinking *Oh no, damn!* No, actually I won't do this because I'd be parading my son's shame out there, and that would end any hope between us. So here's reality: I'm not going to make a scene or call the newspapers or go to my fucking Congressman because it all goes to the same place, which is rolling it out, putting it in front of everybody, making everything worse than it already is. The bastards have me trapped, do you see how they do? All this has been done to my son and I have let it happen and now they have me trapped in it.

"You know what I remember most, and what I regret the most? It was telling him, when he was such a little boy, about his father. That his father was dead. It went badly, very, very, very badly. I screamed it at him. I had just dropped the phone and I screamed at my child, *Daddy's gone! Oh my god, Daddy's gone!* I just kept screaming it, sobbing, I was collapsing and I felt like I had a right to and I just did it. He was little, and that's when he just closed up, and I did too, and we've spent every day since in this kind of silence, in this routine, just going from one thing to the next. I'm bad at things, really fucking *bad*. I put him in that school and paid the money so someone could rescue him, so someone could help him be who he was headed toward being, before that day.

"I try to explain Barry to people and I can't even do him justice. I can't come close to it, and sometimes I think that it's the only way to save Barry, and I'm not good enough to do that either. I'm shit, at all of it. I had it there for a time that seems so short it just went right by, Barry and me and Christopher—all was as it was supposed to be. And you know what, Chuckie? It was that good. And this isn't idealization, or filtering the memories, or making the man into some kind of saint he really wasn't when he was alive. He was a good man! He was a simple, good man, something these bastards at the chancery could never understand from now to the Second Fucking Coming!

"And I can't do anything about this, can't scream or fight because it's their ballgame, they have all the power and they have all the secrets and I've finally come to the realization that there is no one out there who can help me with this.

"Where the fuck is *God*, Chuckie? Who the hell is God to let these people do this to my son? Is he even there? Do Bernard Law, or this priest whose name I cannot even let come off my tongue, or any of those others believe that God sees them? Is it all just shit?"

"I don't know," Chuckie says.

She shakes her head. "Is it even possible those people can believe in God *at all*?"

46

They find a parking lot off by the Port of Boston, late at night, after another basement photo session involving a man she has never seen before, whom Marty apparently found by placing a want ad on the Internet. Jeanmarie is tired, but she wants to do this, now, as she has been begging Marty for weeks. The parking lot at this hour is vast and empty, and Marty guides the Sedan de Ville to a spot as close to the middle of the lot as he can. He looks both ways.

"Okay," he says, "we're clear."

They each get out and circle the car, and each gets back in on the other side. Jeanmarie is sitting in the driver's seat of a car for the first time.

Marty, in the passenger seat of his own car for what is also likely the first time, is clearly nervous. "Just go easy at first," he says. "It's not that hard but don't think you know what you're doing, either. Put your foot on the brake before you put the car in gear."

Jeanmarie takes a deep breath and then begins. She puts the car into drive and, as she lets her foot off the brake, it begins to roll forward.

"Here we go," Marty says. "Now give us some gas."

The car is moving. Jeanmarie squeals with excitement. She's driving a car and there seems no end to the things in her life that are turning out well. Marty says he can get her a car for four hundred from a buddy of his, once she passes her driving test. Jean-marie, nervous as she is about tests of any kind, had at first balked at the idea that she even needed a license. But Marty seemed adamant about doing it right.

"Now you're going to turn," Marty says.

"Which way?"

"Either way you want," he says. "Just brake a little first."

Jeanmarie brings her toe to the brake and then turns left, feeling herself grinning as she does so. She is feeling absolutely flooded with joy for everything Marty has done for her. A few months after exiting her parents' awful house and her father's overbearing ways, she has her own apartment, new clothes, and is about to get her first car. And, beyond that, she is nearly a celebrity. She is Sandra Shields! When she thinks of her sour parents and their constant disapproval of everything she does, she wonders why they couldn't have lightened up and been more like Marty.

She understands what it is that is happening. Last week, finally, Marty showed her the website he has made with his pictures of her. He had brought her into his apartment for the first time (it was as dark and musty as she would have expected from a man like Marty), and to the big computer sitting on a table in the dining room, where he brought up the page and she nearly gasped with happiness. The main page of the site has photos Marty took of her clothed, if seductively so, with buttons directing paying customers within, and non-payers to some tempting samples. The pictures and the headlines and the colors make her look like someone else. When Marty clicked into the pictures of her in the act, it seemed at first that it wasn't even her; it was like looking at photos of other people in a magazine, but she kept on looking and finally told Marty she liked them. He had told her that he had only used photos in which she looked really beautiful. The men in these photos, crawling all over her in their feverish machinations, were sad really in their efforts, people she can hardly remember now. Like earlier tonight, as she repeated the now-familiar actions that men must never get tired of looking at, but which, for her, have become as mechanical as the things she would have to do on other jobs—making doughnuts, ringing up groceries, whatever. She takes birth-control pills that Marty got from somebody he knows, so none of that worries her now. That night, Marty had, after she sat silently looking at the photos, pointed at the hit counter at the bottom of the site's homepage. More than sixty thousand hits. "We have better than three thousand subscribers at $4.95 a pop," he said. "You're going to make some damned good money."

She is out there, in the world, and she is not stupid about it. She knows where it all is. This used to be something to be ashamed of, but not anymore. Half the senior girls at the high school seemed to have (or at least at the long lunch tables they bragged that they had) murky videotapes of themselves having sex with their boyfriends, turning the lenses on themselves with the videocams their parents had bought to tape Christmases and cookouts. The cameras somehow made them feel legitimized and real, or at least made their lovemaking with these acne-backed teenage boys seem somehow more meaningful, less like a love that they suspected was not completely mutual. Those girls, hard and nasty already and full of bravado, with their cell phones (I'm important!) and their cigarettes (I'm a grown-up!) seemed to know they had become more lofty because of it, more worldly than the tight confines of Southie would otherwise allow. They all knew more about sex than their parents, and waved that knowledge like a flag, with their tight clothes and high heels and makeup caked over their bad skin. But it is Marty who has taken Jeanmarie beyond that, who has bought her a whole life with it.

And so here she is, swerving through a parking lot in Marty's car at one-thirty in the morning. As she gets bolder she picks up speed, even as Marty grumbles at her to take it easy; turning one way and then the other with no particular direction in mind, she feels the thrill of acceleration.

47

The story of my burgeoning career is one that I hesitate to boast about, but the facts remain what they are: By my thirtieth birthday, I had become managing director of the firm, and I was preparing for my wedding to the woman who would become my first wife, the utterly repressible Mary Mead.

She was the daughter of Beacon Hill Republicans who had been made rich by the firm; in those environs, the one who makes you money is the one deserving of your love. I was, at this point in my life, undergoing something of a change that had started first with my ardor for the game of golf, at which I had become quite proficient, and through which I had developed a ruddy athleticism that I had not enjoyed in my days in the old neighborhood. I had also used a substantial amount of my own well-earned money to invest in the dental work that I hoped would rid me of the objectionable "rodent" moniker, which had lingered on even after Saltonstall's departure. Through my late twenties, I had secretly been receiving the services of an orthodontist on Park Place, who, through a combination of grinding and capping, and the fitting of a variety of night retainers, had brought a slow straightening to my teeth that no one around me had seemed to take as anything other than a young man's maturation into adulthood.

Not that this was a full solution, but it was part of a slow evolu-

tion that moved in the direction of this Beacon Hill girl and her parents. It was the kind of door-opening that usually came to people such as myself (Irish lads from the Lower End) in one of three ways: politics, joining the police department, or crime. And occasionally all three.

I honestly have never believed that Mary cared for me any more than I cared for her, although in those first months there was a kind of suppressed giddiness for both of us that may have mimicked actual affection. I know that for me she represented far more than simply a woman to be in love with. Even early on, I found her manner somewhat grating, and was really more smitten by the notion that I myself had gained some base level of attractiveness. I had never assumed that I could, by my own devices, attract a woman of real quality (and by that I mean the possessor of stunning looks that would show the world I was a chap of manly consequence). I honestly doubt most men do, in their hearts. Life is about what you can manage to obtain, and as I lay in bed in my now-somewhat-impressive apartment, I set out Mary's various qualities and faults as if filling a balance sheet. She was not truly stunning but had a kind of patrician attractiveness that would serve its purposes and probably last. She was easily frustrated and could be brought to a state of near-viciousness when her needs were not adequately served, but, even when nasty, she retained that well-bred dryness that could pass for drollery, unless what she had to say mattered to you. To me, it did not. I could float over it as my own well-placed nine-iron could vault a trap.

She had gone to Radcliffe and was very social, and with my rising eminence in my new country club—Brookline—I had gained a social entrée myself.

I spoke differently now, no longer the Southie way of expressing that was, to me, not so much American as a poorly transferred mother tongue, a kind of broken Irish, not quite here but not back there either, stuck like all of them with the narrow Channel to the west and the long ocean to the east.

Like my slowly straightening teeth, my accent had transformed almost imperceptibly from my Southie Cockney to a smoother and more Brahmin affectation. As had my vocabulary, which I had begun to stockpile in my days at Boston College but now burnished with readings of more British novelists. The stories were something I didn't much care for—I had to force myself and rarely finished a book—but within fifty pages I usually felt that a book's lesson had been absorbed.

At the same time, I slowly disavowed any link with my past. My childish domination of my peers at Southie High had led me to better places than the thugs and gangsters who could not seem to find their way across the Fort Point Channel and instead carried on their puerile wars with the other small-timers. Whitey and Stevie and the others were doomed to their own provincial attitudes about the world. The amounts of money they scrapped over were pitiable compared to what could be had legally in my line of work, and here I was courting the scioness of the Beacon Hill Meads. I had no reason to return to the old terrain. I doubted whether many of them would really understand what it was I had become.

And what did Mary Mead make of me? I had my guesses then, but my theory from this far vantage point of age is different. She saw me as someone who would take care of her, "taking care" of course being euphemistic in the way of monetary flow. Beacon Hill girls were not crass enough to openly chase money, but instead vocally pined for men who would "just take care" of them, as I indeed was showing that I could do. For Mary, the acquisition of clothing and accessories seemed her very raison d'être, and I did not see that being much different than most women I had encountered. I could not help but think of those pathetic poor women of the projects, women such as my mother, who had made their bets on dissolute men such as my father, men who carried on with their angry loftiness even as they sat in dark bars spending their trifling wages, men who had all the answers even as they could not seem to get out of their own sad way. Mary Mead had been born to expect certain things, and as our wedding day drew closer, I was already losing my giddiness and settling in for something flat and arid.

+ +

47

He pushes the doorbell and waits. When Jeanmarie comes up to the exterior door to see who it is, she is sleepy-looking and wrapped in a bathrobe, even now at four-thirty in the afternoon. She smiles and opens the door. Christopher has a backpack jammed tight with what he has brought.

"So here you are," she says. "Come on in, but I'm sleeping."

"Why?"

"I was driving all night," she says.

"Where?"

"Nowhere, just driving. Why do I have to be going somewhere?"

They go into her apartment, and Christopher is taken by surprise at how truly small it is. The bed nearly swallows up all the floor space and it's apparent he'll either have to sleep on the narrow space between the bed and the wall, or on the linoleum of the kitchenette.

"You just need to be quiet so I can sleep," Jeanmarie says, and when she takes off her bathrobe she is in her underpants and a tight belly shirt, and Christopher can feel himself blushing. She dives onto the mattress and pulls the blanket over herself. Christopher sits quietly, but then goes into the bathroom and shuts the door quietly behind him. He puts a towel on the toilet seat and sits on it, and finds it satisfactorily comfortable. He takes a library book from his backpack and begins to quietly examine the pictures of weaponry.

It's nearly dark when he hears her tap gently on the door. "Are you sick in there or something?"

"No," he says, opening the door a quarter of an inch. "Just reading."

"Well I gotta *go*."

He opens the door fully. Mercifully, she has her bathrobe on.

While she's in the bathroom, he sits on the bed and opens the backpack. He lays his folded clothing on the floor. Then takes out the gun and puts it on the middle of the bed. She comes out of the bathroom and when she sees it, she shouts, "What is *that*?"

"It's a gun."

"Jesus, where did you get it?"

"It was my father's. He was in the military."

"How did you get it?"

"My mother keeps it hidden. I doubt she's checked on it since he died. It was in the basement, packed up with a lot of his other stuff."

"What kind is it?"

"It's a .380. I never touched it before today but I knew it was there and I used to look at it."

Jeanmarie cannot hide her fascination, but neither can she seem to gather the courage to touch it.

"Is it loaded?"

"No. That's my small problem. My mother must have thrown away the clip. Or maybe there wasn't one in it. I need to figure out how to get one."

"Why did you bring it here?

Christopher looks at her, almost sadly. "It's to protect you," he says.

Jeanmarie laughs. "Well, you better get some bullets, honey."

The idea of an unloaded gun suddenly seems to hold much less interest for her. "Did you see my kitchen?" she says. "Isn't it cool?"

"I like it."

"It has better appliances than my parents have, the cheap shits," she says. "It's just that they're smaller."

"They look really good."

"I'm making dinner," she says. "You want dinner?"

"Sure. What are you making?"

"Grilled cheese sandwiches."

"I like those."

He sits on the bed while she makes the sandwiches. The electric burner is on too hot and smoke quickly begins to fog the room. When the smoke detector in the ceiling above the stove suddenly begins blaring, she shouts above the noise, "This is the way I like to make them." While Jeanmarie holds her hands over her ears, Christopher climbs up on the counter and pulls the detector off its mount, then removes the battery. Jeanmarie turns down the heat, then swings open the window above her bed to let the smoke out over the sidewalk. The place is hazed over and as the room gets colder, Jeanmarie pulls a coat on over her bathrobe and finishes up the sandwiches, which are a flat black on one side and soggy yellow on the other.

"I'm not used to the stove," she says. "It's electric. I'm used to a gas stove."

"It's okay," Christopher says. "I like them this way."

She puts the sandwiches on paper plates and carries them out of the kitchen. They sit at the foot of the bed and Jeanmarie turns on the tiny television. There is a show on about meerkats. As they eat, they laugh as the meerkats fight each other for control of their pathetic little burrows, which hardly seem worth the bloodshed.

"Can you do any better?" Jeanmarie suddenly says.

"Huh?"

"I mean can you cook anything."

"Well, yeah."

"You can?"

"Yeah. My mother works nights a lot, so she showed me how to do some things."

"Cooking? I'm not talking about milk over cereal."

"No, real stuff. I can make spaghetti and meatballs . . ."

"You're shitting me! You can do *that*?"

Christopher shrugs. "I mean, yeah . . . you roll the meat into balls and grill them, boil the spaghetti and then heat up the sauce."

"Exactly! That's what I mean . . ."

"Maybe I'll make some for you."

"Only if it doesn't make me fat. Marty says I can't be modeling if I'm fat."

Christopher nods but lets the conversation stop there. They watch cartoons on Nickelodeon for a while, but Jeanmarie quickly seems to get bored.

"So how do you get bullets for a gun?" she says.

"If you're old enough, I think you just buy them somewhere. If you're not, you figure something else out."

"Am I old enough?"

"I don't know. But you look old enough."

Jeanmarie smiles and flicks her hair back over her shoulder. "Why," she says, "how old do I look?"

"With all your makeup on and stuff? You look like you're eighteen, maybe even nineteen."

"Well," she says, straightening up from her less-dignified slump, "thank you *very* much."

+ +

49

Shelagh had finished telling Jimmy precisely what had happened, and he could only process the whole thing as being a bit far-fetched. Something like this had never really happened to him before, and now that it had, he couldn't remember any of it. Shelagh had told him that she'd met him outside the office at eleven, and they had gone to late dinner in the city, then walked through the Public Garden, kissed in the rain there, then walked back to her little apartment in the South End; they had, after sex, fallen asleep together until dawn, when Jimmy had quietly risen and dressed, kissed her goodbye, and let himself out. Sitting with him in a coffee shop for the first time since then, she just shook her head with that intrinsically sharp kind of female incredulity.

"Where does somebody find a drink at six in the morning? I mean, is there any such place?" she had said. "And why would somebody even need to?"

Jimmy could only shrug. He could have said that indeed he knew every place you could find a drink at six in the morning (as did the third-shift cops and firefighters and Boston Edison crews who were up all night on the interminable Big Dig), and that "need" was a particularly slippery word when one has been drinking inexhaustibly since his early teens. He is becoming more aware of his frequent memory lapses, like someone suddenly aware of a blind spot when his vision has almost gone. "Need," as it came off Shelagh's tongue, involved willful choice. *Need.* Why does a fourteen-year-old drink a six-pack a night, hiding them in the basement and swilling them warm, stealing change from his parents, sneaking into his friends' mothers' handbags, pulling loose pennies from the curb? Why does an eighteen-year-old drink himself into unconsciousness each night, sucking foam from the sputtering kegs at a college from which he will soon enough be expelled? Why does a twenty-three-year-old move on to bottomless scotch and sodas, begin to ignore food, sleep in three-day-old clothes, run up debt? And why does a thirty-year-old, now having scraped himself a place in the universe (based on two hours of decent work a day in an eight-hour-a-day job), graduate into straight vodka (and a thirty-two-year-old into Goldschlager and 151-proof rum)? What he knows as a fact about his apparent evening with Shelagh is that, nine hours after apparently exiting her warm bed, he had awakened in his own chilly apartment with a crushing headache, soiled pants and no memory of the previous three days. After hearing Shelagh's version of events, Jimmy has to acknowledge it seems as if nothing was fully behind him.

When he admitted to having no recall at all of the evening, she had taken on the wounded look of someone who might have thought well of the whole experience, who might have had reasonable expectations, and who might actually be skeptical that a man, even with heavy drinking in his recent past, could so easily forget such an encounter. He, by the same turn, could feel within himself the desire to believe that such an evening had happened, that Shelagh did not have some sort of bizarre agenda, that he really (upon close and more sober inspection) hardly knew her, and that he could not possibly ascribe all this to healthy and level-headed affection.

She also told him he needed to see a doctor.

So now he is being summoned from a gray-on-gray-on-gray doctor's waiting room to a leaning-toward-purple doctor's office, to talk. The room, as he enters, seems to have no personal affect at all, but is rather machine-like in its industrial neatness. The doctor, a young and slight man whose nearly unpronounceable Indonesian name is fading from Jimmy's head, and whose eyes through heavy-rimmed glasses do not move to meet his patient, motions Jimmy into the chair and continues looking over the lab results. It's all out of pocket, this stuff, but the Rafferty money will pay it.

"It doesn't look good," the doctor finally says.

"What doesn't?"

The doctor looks at him directly for the first time, as if it is something he has to remember to do at moments as this. "Your condition. You have a seriously advanced case of ALD."

"Should I know what ALD is?"

"Advanced liver disease."

"Oh. Yeah, ALD. I guess that makes sense."

The doctor moves forward, a man with many appointments, a man with patients waiting pensively in little rooms all the way up the gray hallway. "It's a funny illness," he says, "because you can exhibit very few of the symptoms but still have the disease continue to a very serious state. Looking at what I have here, I'm surprised your skin isn't completely yellow already."

"I didn't have any symptoms at all?"

"Oh no. You've listed them. A lot of them . . . blackouts, nausea, disorientation . . . bouts of psychosis that can leave someone delusional and incoherent. Memory loss."

"My logical assumption was that that was from the drinking."

"You've told me that you don't specifically remember the drinking."

"That's pretty much how it's worked, for years."

"What if I suggested you might not have been drinking at all?" The doctor seems intrigued by this, the shell game of symptoms and behaviors, the Friday-afternoon interesting case that helps shake off the drowsiness on a rainy day.

"But I had to have." There was, now that he thinks about it, no distinct evidence that he'd done any drinking at all. He has no real feel for what life is supposed to feel like not drunk. He can only, in his ruminations, go back to the familiar connections.

"You might not have. It may have been the disease."

"Wait a minute," Jimmy says. "Are you telling me I stopped drinking and then I got this disease?"

The doctor laughs. "Oh, no," he says. "You've stopped drinking much, much too late."

"But why did this happen after I stopped drinking?"

"I suspect it's gone on a while, but you were drinking too much to notice. Now you have some clarity."

Jimmy is still now, settling into this knowledge.

"You don't have medical insurance," the doctor says.

"No."

"That will be a hurdle."

"What will I need to do?"

"Other than a liver transplant, which without insurance may be very difficult? Not much."

"So how do I get a liver transplant without insurance?"

The doctor shakes his head. "I can't even go there. It's not my place. I'd refer you to a surgeon for this. I do know that people do things like fund-raisers, appeals for donations, sales of family assets. Money from parents, siblings, friends. But, really, I deal with patients with coverage. Uninsured patients have a different route to take in all this. So I can't help you with that."

"That's going to be really difficult," Jimmy says.

"Well, all I can say," the doctor says, putting the chart back into its folder and leaning toward him with a benign smile and an extended hand to be shaken, "is that you have to appeal to all those people out there who place great value on your life."

51

Sitting in Chuckie Connelly's car, she finds her breathing rising again and labors to suppress it. The car windows are beginning to fog; Colleen shifts nervously and wonders whether Chuckie has the right notion about what's about to happen. It's cold and there's an overcast as low as a ceiling, and it seems nearly ready to rain again. She shivers a bit, for more reasons than just the cold.

"Here he comes," Chuckie says, and she can see her son far down the street, enveloped in his hooded sweatshirt. He looks smaller, slighter, more delicate than in recent memory, even. She stifles the urge to sob. Christopher comes slowly up the low rise of road and arrives at his bench, where he sits, in what seems imprinted movement, like someone making the morning arrival in a long-familiar office. He sits without looking and, seemingly, without purpose.

"He comes here every day, always at this time," Chuckie says. "I don't know why." They have both taken their lunch hours late to be here, something that was easy for Colleen to arrange but apparently more difficult for Chuckie. As they sit, shielded by a parked car, Colleen can feel her heart thumping. She is slumped in her seat, sighting over the dashboard at her son.

"So shall we do this?" Chuckie says, and to Colleen he seems overeager for the confrontation, trying too hard to make something happen, perhaps for the wrong reasons: Bad motivation possibly leading to bad results.

"I'm not sure now," she says.

Chuckie lets out a theatrically long sigh. He is clearly itching for this, seeking completion. But now Colleen is deeply uncertain. This kind of action goes against everything she believes herself to be, but does not always like: A woman conditioned for passivity, fear, nonconfrontation.

Chuckie turns to her. "You promised me we would do what we said we would do."

"I'm still not sure."

"I had to call in some favors to leave work and be here right now," he says, the edge in his voice increasingly apparent. "Don't make it a waste of time for me."

"Why is it so important to you?" she says. "Why do you care?"

Chuckie sighs again, a man who needs to do this and get back to work.

"Truthfully? At first it was because I felt sorry for you," he says. "Here you were, a nice woman whose husband had died, trying to work and raise a kid, and feeling like it's getting away from her. So I decide to stick my neck out and help. Truthfully, and honestly, I felt like I could do more than what I do working at the airport, and I liked the idea of putting some of my skills to use. But then I start following the kid, and I see what a mess his life is. Truant, wandering the streets, hanging around with that prostitute, sleeping with his head on the table in the library. And he's thirteen years old . . ."

"Fourteen now," Colleen says in nearly a whisper. "He had a birthday."

"Fourteen," Chuckie says. "Still young. Still the exact same point. And the more I follow him, the more I get angry at you—just sitting back and letting this happen, afraid to make any trouble. Wrapped up in your own shit, which, while understandable, does not—*does not*—make this okay. So at a certain point I decide I will push you to do something. And take some personal risk in doing so. And all I get is this indecision, which I find very hard to take. If you just said, straight out, that you don't want to make the effort, then okay. Just don't go on with the 'I'm not sure, I'm not sure' thing, *please*."

The urge to cry has left her now. She feels harder and colder than only a moment before.

"Let's go ahead, then," she says.

"Now I've pushed you," he says. "Now you want to do it because I insulted you."

"No," she says. "We have to do this."

"Another day," he says. "We'll arrange to do this another day. You should go home and give thought to what you really want to do, not what I can guilt you into."

"You're messing with my head," Colleen says.

"Look," Chuckie says, "in the end, most of the risk is mine. We're going to essentially kidnap him off the street. But you're his mother and that makes it okay. But if you think the better of it later, if you decide you only went along with it because I pushed you, then I have to deal with the consequences."

"So now you're saying you're not going to help me."

"I am helping you," Chuckie says. "I'm trying to get you to think about what you're doing. I get the sense you've never done much thinking about what you want to do."

"Barry always made it easy for me," she says. "Since he died I've been completely lost." Now she bursts into tears. Chuckie sits, watching her cry.

"There are a lot of ways to try to deal with this situation," he says. "But you have to definitely pick one."

"I want to do this now," Colleen says. "Right now."

"No," Chuckie says. "Not now. Sit in this car and just look at your son."

So they do. They watch him sit on the bench, not seeming to be looking at anything, not seeming to be waiting for anyone, making nearly no motion at all in the cold late-autumn wind. A few cars roll by, but no humans approach. There are no children in the schoolyard across the street. He sits, staring straight ahead, and Chuckie checks his wristwatch and says, "Any minute now, he walks away." And, with that, without seeming to have any specific way of knowing the time, Christopher rises slowly from the bench, shoves his hands in his pockets, and walks across the street and away.

"Show's over," Chuckie says. "And I really have to get back to work."

52

All day she's had an unsettled sense of things. Out walking to get some groceries, Jeanmarie has had a buzzy sort of anxiousness she cannot fully shed. When she wanders along East Broadway she can see the men looking at her, on foot and in cars, and she knows that is her very power, her ability now to arrest and attract. She wears sunglasses, always, and from behind them she can look at the eyes of the men, searching them for that subtle sign of recognition that comes when one sees a celebrity in the flesh. Admittedly she is a minor celebrity right now, but she is on her way someplace, she is certain of that; and, on at least a few occasions, she believes she has seen that recognition in the eyes of these men, recognition of Sandra Shields. And that's only Southie. There are men all over the country—all over the *world*. It's all about sex, as it's always been; she is now one of those girls who doesn't play coy and act as if this isn't what it's all about. From every little slut running around at Southie High to the singers like Britney and Christina, it's all about sex and she is simply taking it to a more powerful and honest level. She imagines traveling to someplace far away—Tokyo or Paris—and having a man look at her with that glint of recognition, regarding her as someone he has been virtually intimate with. She wonders sometimes, walking past men, how many thousands have been nearly intimate with her, have imagined what she is like, how she smells, what her voice is like. She is that malleable vision, no one in particular but yet most definitely *someone*.

But no, today the vibes are more subdued. Maybe due to the weather, which has slid from the brilliance of the fall to a kind of pre-winter that makes her feel chilled and fluttery. Up her street and toward the front of the apartment building, she is thinking about getting inside and turning up the heat. She wants to be in her home. She wants the comfort she has finally earned, and which she had never been able to find with her constantly disapproving parents.

It has been months since she left and she still has no sense of whether they even tried to find her. She could almost imagine them relieved at coming home to find her gone. Her father seemed, all through her childhood, to be someone who needed to be out in the neighborhood, saying hello to this guy and good morning to that guy, How's your mother and What's new at work, almost busybodyish in his need to make those connections. Her father and his obsession with status, on these streets. Where is he now? She has hardly gone into seclusion, and while he may not recognize her now, she would certainly recognize him, but he hasn't appeared. Those first few weeks at Bobby's, she lived with that sense of expectation, of someone showing up for her, of a scene, of authorities and court orders, or of her father's guys. Somebody. But no one came at all, and she believed, completely, that her father knew enough people to find out exactly where she was, and with whom.

At the front of her building she takes out her keys and unlocks the entry door. She suddenly feels him come up behind her, grabbing her hair so that her head tilts back, moving his hand to hers and taking her keys.

"Get inside the fucking door," Bobby says.

"Let go of me," she says, and he shoves her in. He wrestles her down the hallway to her apartment door.

"How did you know this is mine?" she says as he finds the apartment key.

"I can see you right through your window," he says. "You should close your shades."

Inside, he lets her go, and folds his arms across his chest.

"Okay, so what do you want?" she says.

"I want to know what the hell your problem is," he says, breathing hard. "I want to know what the fuck has happened to you."

"You didn't want me around there," she says, calmly, understanding she is in control, knowing he needed her far more than she did him.

"That's bullshit," he says.

"Look, I didn't want to be with you anymore," she says.

"Look at what you are now," he says.

She laughs at him. "Yeah, I should thank you for getting me lined up with Marty. It got me a better place than you could come up with . . ."

He hits her so quickly that she falls without really having been hurt. He stands over her, seemingly unclear as to what to do next. She gets up, pushes by him and goes to the closet, and he just stands there, watching her rifle through her clothing. As soon as her hand finds the gun, she whirls around and jams the barrel in his face, so hard that she knows it hurts.

She thinks of every line from every movie, all the things she could say, all the clichés. *Make my day . . . Who's laughing now . . . Say hello to my little friend . . .* but then says nothing at all. She is staring into Bobby's eyes, not even angry, looking at his fear. She can hear dripping and when she steps back she sees the stain on his pants, the widening wet circle in the crotch of his jeans, the drips on his legs and sneakers.

"You're pissing on my rug," she says.

Bobby doesn't start crying, which seems at that moment a tremendous effort on his part.

"Drop my keys on the bed," she says, and he does.

"You need to leave and not come back," she says. "You need to stay away from me so I won't have to fucking kill you."

Bobby cannot find words. His lips are trembling. The front of his pants is now soaked. She wishes right then that she had a clip in the gun. She doesn't wish she could shoot him, there is no point in that, but she wishes she could feel in truth what she feels now in theory, which is the absoluteness of knowing there is a loaded gun in her hand, that she can make this happen, that she is in charge.

53

So I had indeed arrived. I was the protégé of and filial figure to Red Driscoll, I was a high operative of the firm, I was the husband of a Beacon Hill debutante (and the son-in-law of her powerful father), and I was an increasingly wealthy man. My earnings had so out-stripped my needs that I really had no wants at all in a material sense. My wife was not someone new to money, so even her needs, while prodigious, were consistent. I tried to find things to spend money on, but without even trying I made more money. After engaging an advisor I began investing in art, particularly by American artists. I owned Wyeths, Hoppers, Pollocks and O'Keeffes, all of which kept soaring in value. I assembled a collection as one might a mutual fund, investing both in sure-thing classics and then buying for a pittance works by new artists I was advised would bring big returns. I bought and sold Harings and Lichtensteins and Hock-neys, all of which made me money; I bought Dardens and Flacks and Rosenblooms that sat in my basement, realizing no apprecia-tion whatsoever. In fact, one of the works by this Rosenbloom (trust me, you never heard of him before) was actually one of my favorites, one of the few I bought because I actually liked it. It was a winter landscape that appalled my advisor to such a degree, I had to give her a rather stern warning about the consequences of repeating this judgment of my tastes to any of her art-dealer friends. I came to hate the art types even as they made me more millions.

I came to almost hate my wife, too, and her cheerless parents, which surprised me. The irony of working so hard to connect with a different kind of people is that, well, they're a different kind of people. Unlike my relationship with Red, who was aging rapidly thanks to his diet of bourbon and cigars, the Meads of Beacon Hill seemed, as I settled into the life I had so ardently pursued, to be dryly amused by me. As if I was a gifted mimic. As if I was adorable in the way I so convincingly acted as if I were actually one of them. I was a trick act, often introduced by my father-in-law as having come from Southie, to collective nods. The monkey in his bellhop outfit. It made me quietly furious. My wife, as we moved into the stasis of married life, seemed in some ways not to fully engage. She was steeped in her shopping and the Junior League and her charity work, all of which seemed to me to be as superfluous as she and her insufferable deb friends. There turned out to be many small ways in which I displayed my ignorance: I used a merlot glass to drink pinot noir; I sometimes tied my tie with a simple Windsor; I wore socks that were lighter than my suit. These were things that had never mattered to me because I did not even know such considerations existed, let alone that they were important. Now I was shown they were. I suppose I was only getting what I deserved.

So, after a round of golf one Saturday afternoon, I did not feel the desire to return directly to my home, a townhouse we had bought on The Hill, not far from the Meads' ancestral home to the northwest of the State House. Nor did I feel the urge to remain at the clubhouse bar with my golf partners, or to go out to the practice greens to work on my putting. I got in my car, a new white Cadillac that my Mercedes-obsessed wife had scoffed at, and found myself driving out along the edge of the city, looking at the shimmer of water out to the east, and the harbor islands on the horizon. I exited at Colum-

bia Road and continued up along Old Colony Avenue. I was very close to places I had not seen in years, and to which I'd had no intention of returning. But there I was, squeezing my car into a tight parking space along the seawall and getting out to smell air that had its own salt-and-smoke essence one did not breathe outside of this small enclave. I was in my early forties and feeling something that was not nostalgia as much as epiphany, that this place was as deeply wrought in me as a chromosome, a gene, my flesh itself. As much as I was loath to admit it, I was between two places with no other to which I could go. Standing as I was in my golf sweater and plaid pants with my Titleist cap on my head, I felt some sort of intuitive pull back. I walked down along neighborhood streets and then to a small drinking joint, Muldoon's, with its Kelly-green door and Guinness sign. At the bar I ordered a beer. This was the place, then. I was trying the feel of it back on, as if it were an old uniform taken out of a cedar trunk. For a summer Saturday afternoon the place was surprisingly crowded. Men in work clothes sat drinking and smoking cigarettes. There was not much in the way of conversation. The Red Sox were on the television and everyone more or less watched the game; the field over at Fenway was sun-scorched and yellowed at the edges, the light hard and glaring. But inside this windowless place it was as dark as at closing time, coolly air-conditioned and as otherwise unconcerned with time or season as a dungeon or a lair. I ordered another beer. The bartender eyed me a bit askance, but said nothing. I looked down the rail and not surprisingly saw a familiar face, although it was one that had aged more quickly than my own. I tried to place it; when I did, it was a surprise.

It was McX, my old nemesis. He had fattened considerably and his red hair was longer and slicked back over his head in a way *that seemed antiquated. He was dressed a bit better than the others, but chinos, an oxford shirt and a rough tweed sport coat—too tight across the shoulders—did not allow for easy interpretation. I doubted myself for a moment, thinking it could not be him, but then I came to the obvious conclusion that to find him sitting in a dark bar in Southie was hardly the same as seeing someone who looked like him in Bangkok or Sydney. Of course it was him.*

I sat and drank my beer and watched him watching nothing. It seemed as if he had not a friend on the planet, alone as he was. After a half-hour he got up, tossed a few more bills on the bar, and walked out.

I motioned to the bartender, who at first looked irritated to be beckoned by the likes of me, but finally ambled over.

"That man who just left," I said. "Who is he?"

"I don't know any man that just left," the bartender said.

"He was sitting right at the end there. Who is he?"

The bartender leaned into me and said, "Who the fuck are you, pal? You ask questions about my regulars, but who the fuck are you? You want to know who he is, ask him yourself, but ask at your own risk."

I smiled a little then, a smile that could not have meant anything to him, but which, in past days, would have portended grievously bad things. It's just that he didn't understand. I felt all the old imperatives asserting themselves again. I felt my blood coursing back through myself.

5 4

Christopher does not yet have a key, so when he wants to come back into the small apartment he must ring the doorbell and wait for Jeanmarie to come forth. It's after eleven and he hopes she isn't off on another "modeling" job for Marty, because that will leave him slumped in the cold on these front steps until two or three in the morning. Still, he has no grounds for complaint. He sleeps on the floor next to Jeanmarie's bed and, sometimes, when she is up and about, or out of the place to get food, he is allowed to crawl onto the bed itself and sleep more. It's just that outside it's getting cold now, this close to Thanksgiving, and he craves the warmth inside.

He presses the doorbell again and squints down the stairway to the narrow hallway, where Jeanmarie's bare feet approach. She comes up the steps, in sweatpants and a sweater, and she looks uncharacteristically angry.

"What is it?" he says as she opens the outer door.

"Get inside," she says.

He follows her. Inside, she shuts the door and locks it and says, "Sit."

He does. He can hear her breathing through her nose.

"Bobby came in here after me," she says. "He hit me in the face. Look."

Now that she points it out, Christopher can see a rising welt beside her left eye.

"Why did you let him in?" he says.

"I didn't fucking let him in," she says. "He got me coming into the building and forced me inside. And you know what I did? I pulled the gun on him. He thought it was loaded. He pissed his pants."

She grins and so does Christopher, but then she gets serious again.

"I thought the whole idea of you staying here was that I had a little protection," she says. "I thought you were going to help me if and when he came by. Then he did and where the hell were you?"

"I had someplace to be," Christopher says. "Then I came right back."

"Well, you fucked up!" she says. Her voice is rising into something more shrill than he's ever heard coming out of her mouth. "You're a disappointment to me most of the time."

Christopher hasn't cried since he was little. He didn't cry when his father died, and he didn't cry when his mother went into her sadness and he didn't cry when Father John started in with it all. He isn't going to cry now for this girl, as much as the situation might call for it. *Disappointing* is the word that hurts most, with its implicit suggestion that she's actually had expectations of him, that she had formed in her mind the theory that he was better than what he appears to be at this moment.

"I can leave," he says. "I can go away. I just need to say something first."

Jeanmarie throws her arms up theatrically. "Did I say to leave?

I thought I just said the opposite, which is that I need you to *be here* if Bobby comes back. He's fucking crazy, you know."

The moment to say what he was going to say, in all its bare feeling, has passed. "I know he is," Christopher says.

"Well, if you know, then don't leave me hanging out there. Now that this has happened, who knows what he'll pull next."

"I'll be here all the time you need me except for one thing I need to do every afternoon," he says.

"I put a roof over your head and this is what I get?" she says, and he doesn't know exactly if she's joking.

She doesn't either. She's heard that line before, so many times that it's like the long welt of a scar on otherwise smooth skin. So many times that having it leap from her own mouth is both awkward and painful, because this is the first time she has consciously realized she is channeling her father—his constant stream of disapproval, like an electrical hum or radio waves, something that simply hangs in the air even when he is not speaking. If he saw her now, and knew what she was doing to earn her living, he would be apoplectic in his gleeful disapproval. She always sensed he fed on that, the opportunity she gave him. Truth is, he would have been miserable with a good daughter. He would have had no purpose. But that would presume she should be ashamed now, as he would be ashamed of her. And she's not. Just in case no one noticed, everything now is about sex, and, in fact, if he could even possibly understand it, that every girl out there would be doing what she's doing if they were good-looking enough. She feels sorry for the girls she knew in high school, the ones giving blowjobs in cars and not having anything to show for them, the middle-school girls who are already dressing like strippers, and, worst of all, their fat forty-year-old mothers with their belly rings and cleavage and spiked heels, who would presume to look down their surgically altered noses at her. This town is full of them now, hypocrites, while she's simply doing something that allows her to live her own life. It's all headed that way, but her father, if he knew what she was doing now, would derive absolute glee from running her down for it. And now, here at this moment, she's spewing the same sort of junk at this kid in front of her. She draws a breath and then smiles, the punctuation to her change of direction.

"You know what we're doing tomorrow?" she says sweetly.

"What?"

"We're going to get some bullets for that gun. You know where to get them, right?"

"Kind of."

"Well, let's kind of go there tomorrow. It'll be an outing."

"I don't think we're old enough. Maybe Marty can get them for you."

"I'm not telling Marty I have a gun! He'll go apeshit."

Christopher sits on the end of the bed, thinking. Of course he wants to do anything she asks of him, but he also knows her well enough that she ought not to be messing with loaded guns.

"So you need to do this for me," she says softly.

"I will," Christopher says. "For sure."

+ +

5 5

He is not feeling well. John rises in the middle of the night in the cold rectory feeling squeamish and lightheaded, not right in himself. He presumes that the slow ravages of old age have been hastened by the knowledge of his retirement, by the disappointment of his lonely movement toward this transition, by the fact that he is almost imprisoned in this place, other than for his morning Mass (for which he has been told it is difficult to find anyone to sub for him) and his afternoon nursing-home visits. He's drinking more in the evenings, trying to settle himself. The nights now are punctuated by the awakening with burning stomach, the trips to the bathroom for milk of magnesia, the thirst he seems to have suddenly acquired, standing at the sink drinking glass after glass of water.

The weather is getting colder now, the chilled winds blowing from the ocean in these small hours of the morning, and it's a good time of the year to stay inside as the days go darker. He'll be gone by the New Year, the new millennium. His retirement party was a foolish thought, given the distractions of people in this day and age, the lack of appreciation for what he has done. It seems people are always quickest with their grievances, sadly.

She comes to the morning Masses now, the mother of the boy, glaring at him from the back of the church. He must, in such moments, work to maintain his serenity. He will not allow her a moment when he is not in the act of giving Mass, and she is not yet so foolish or so impious as to interrupt a Mass to get at him. Sitting on the toilet seat, drinking water from a glass, he sighs as he thinks about how awful people can become.

It had been for that very reason that he had always gravitated toward the children. Even in his own early adulthood he had come to mistrust the adults, had come to see in all of them—even his superiors—a certain crassness of living, filled as it was with pride and avarice. He had come from that world, here, of poor people doing everything they could to beat a nickel out of the next person, a world of scams and dirty deals, but it seemed to him not nearly as bad as what he slowly came to see in the hierarchy of the church, or at least in the Archdiocese of Boston that he came into as a young man, which, in its own way, was as dirty as the Boston police in those days. The archbishop was as rich as a king but called himself a shepherd and would do what it took to remain so; the priests who continued to try to live the simple life were the ones who never rose from the front lines of the poor parishes. It was the talented fund-raisers and the smooth talkers who were promoted out to Wellesley and Newton and Swampscott to bring more money in. He felt, himself, that pressure to produce, to meet unspoken quotas; the simple equations of love and forgiveness were largely meaningless in a business that claimed it was not one. The currency of that world was a job at the chancery or a teaching appointment at Boston College; humbler men were condemned to their foolish humility. He found himself wanting even more to be nearer the children. He found himself somehow connected to them, in particular the ones who were drifting and untethered, and he knew that they loved him in their own quiet way. He knew in his heart that he was their physical connection to God, and to Godliness, and it was with a sense of that underlying intimacy that he sought to move even closer to them. The boys, in particular, needed his guidance and his attentions, his touch. And when those connections began to seem more profound, it was always the parents, not the boys, who began to make trouble. What was it about them? Why could they not understand? What was it that instead made some of them turn on him in grim judgment and refuse to take Communion from his hand? In these small parishes of working people, it was too ingrained in them not to speak against the church, and they elected to keep quiet. They were afraid of the church's power. Fortunately. He always believed that, in his unconventional ways, he was simply being a better friend to these children than their own parents were. Over the years, though, most of the parents seemed not to be concerned at all— seemed excited, in fact, that a priest would show such attention to their child. The mothers without husbands especially. It would only follow, of course, that there was a certain physical contact, what he believed was his own expression to them of God's love of children. They never complained, those young boys. They were rewarded as well by their rising place in the hierarchy, with the most honored altar-serving assignments, with special duties in the schools, with gifts to help them on their way. He took them on camping trips and boat trips, to ball games.

It was only when they began to grow up that there was any trouble. He could only ascribe the change to some sort of teenage rebelliousness, the hubris of a certain age. Usually, a few well-placed dollars helped them on their way, so they would remember who

their friend was. He preferred that they keep their intimacies intimate; still, the fact remained, as always, that he had never once
been asked by any of his superiors to answer to the rantings of
some overreacting parent. Many of those young men went on to
become very fine people, in one way or another—men who kept
their mouths shut and their heads down, and who understood
what their lives were. He was proud of them for that. But walking
past them in their adult lives, he felt no connection at all, only the
wispy recollections of when they were more innocent. All things
must pass, and the adults could not be the same as they had been
as children, when he was first compelled to be their friend.

He is tired, and he wants his mind to settle into sleep. Not
much longer now anyway and he will have left this place. And with
that comes a new situation, one that is not better, but that will allow for the kind of retrospection he has never particularly gone in
for. He wonders what the future holds for these late years of a life
he has always tried to make holy.

56

Shelagh has begun to cry, a raspy and heartfelt kind of gasping, which seems strange to Jimmy, given how little they know each other. He knows that, in effect, she is crying for whatever aspirations she might have held about them. Her grief is theory-based. To judge by the volume of tears, which stream into her Kleenex even as she quiets into shoulder-wrenching silence, he suspects that she must have thought there was a fair bit of "whatever" there. The only other explanation is that she hates to hear that *anybody* is this ill.

They are sitting in the same coffee shop on Tremont, and people are looking over as he tries to quietly console her. He suspects that the other customers infer that he has just dumped her, rather than told her of his impending demise. She seems so surprised. *But you stopped drinking!* He cannot say he is at all surprised. His sobriety, he suspects, was somehow less about resoluteness than about his liver being in the process of shutting down, his body somehow freeing itself of its own need for the poison, although, of course, he has no medical facts to back this up. The notion that he had simply willed himself off twenty years of constant drinking seems laughable now. Butchie Morrissey's accident, he now concludes, was a crutch that made him ignore his own symptoms.

Shelagh's eyes are fluttering as she dabs her paper napkin to them, and she says, in a wavering voice, "What are the treatments?"

"Well, pretty much a liver transplant," Jimmy says.

"So you have to get on a list and wait, then."

"That's how it would be done."

"Until then, what?"

"There would be short-term treatments, but without a transplant, I just sort of, you know, *die*."

The word "die" sets Shelagh off on another jag of tears. He gets another paper napkin from the dispenser and hands it to her. Finally, after a series of protracted breaths, she looks at him through now-rheumy eyes and says, "When do you start?"

"I don't know," he says. "We'll see."

"Do you have insurance?"

"No."

"You should call your mother. She'll help. She has to."

"I'm not calling my mother," he says. "It isn't the thing to do, to put that on her. I'm on my own on this."

"I'll help you," she says, and he smiles.

"I'm on my own on what happens now," he says, "although it's nice to know you care. I'm going to take care of it."

"So what do you need to do to get treatment?"

"Well, I'm looking into it."

She slowly absorbs this and then says, in almost a silent mouthing of the words, "You are getting treatment, right?"

Jimmy hands Shelagh another napkin.

"I don't think so," he says.

She doesn't cry now, but rather sits blinking, apparently too taken aback even for sobbing.

He appreciates the generosity of her grief over this, even as he wonders where it comes from. He regrets as well that he has not been able to recall their night together, even as he wonders why his mind, albeit affected by his illness, has apparently chosen to purge it. That would be a little too random.

"Look," he says, "I know I should, and I guess it's more than the fact that I have no insurance coverage, or that I could get myself waiting on a liver and die before it ever comes, or that I worry that if I get a new liver I'll just ruin it with the drinking. It's more than that."

"Then what is it?"

Jimmy sits back and gives her a weak smile.

"It's probably not something I can fully explain," he says. "But I'm a man in his thirties who has been defined by one thing, which is the drinking. It's funny, I remember when I was a kid, it was almost a matter of pride that I started drinking before anybody else my age, or that by the age of fifteen I could drink anybody under the table, or that in college, when the name of the game was getting as drunk as possible as often as possible, I always won that game. It was who I *was*. It was what I did, more than a job or a sport or a hobby. I was pretty much proud of it. I could live in it. Every stupid thing I said or did was okay, because, after all, I was drunk. I didn't have to have a conscience, or any ambition, or any direction.

"The drinking was something that solved the problem I had, the problem of those expectations. I was *smart*. I had *talent*. I was supposed to *accomplish things*. It was all I ever heard when I was younger. I had tested well. I seemed to exhibit some kind of aptitude that had to be acted upon. I was supposed to amount to something more than anyone else. No one really said it; it was just there. My parents seemed preemptively proud of what I would eventually become. Something even better than what my father was, presumably. That was the shadow I stood in.

"But my father was somebody I already knew I could never be. I don't mean success, either. I mean who he was. I couldn't live up to it. Some stuff happened. Stuff I don't even want to talk about. I already knew that wasn't in me. Then I had my first drink. It solved everything. This was what I could be, to avoid having to be what I couldn't be."

Shelagh sits looking at him, not blinking at all now.

"So now they told me this, that it's time. I know I shouldn't, I know it's awful to think this, but since the doctor told me, I can only think of all this is as being . . ."

"Being what?"

Jimmy straightens up and looks in her eyes.

"Being a relief," he says.

57

She sits in the pew of an unfamiliar church, waiting. In the confessional toward the back, an old woman whispers on and on, reciting what could only be a laundry list of those venial sins realistically still within the grasp of someone so elderly. The priest behind the red velvet curtain, whom Colleen does not know and whose age and appearance she has no sense of, grunts on in his boredom.

The church is in East Boston. She has walked up here from the airport at the end of her shift, seeking someplace different, hoping. It's a rainy Saturday afternoon. She can hear the drops ticking against the stained glass windows. Colleen is the only one of a dozen repentants who is under the age of sixty-five. Apparently no one younger feels the need to explain themselves; apparently no one younger feels guilt for the acts they have committed. Who feels guilty about anything anymore, except for the odd ones who cling to the old notions of right and wrong? Or the old, who do it out of habit more than as a result of committing actual sins.

She hears the slide of the confessional's little portal closing, and the creak of the priest's bench as he shifts on it in his blessed darkness. She waits, quietly. When the old lady finally emerges, laboring to the altar rail for her penance, another old woman rises and shuffles into the booth. The others, two men and a woman, whisper companionably about the weather, apparently a regular klatch here at the Saturday confessional. They seem alarmed that she is here at all. Apparently this is a real sinner in their midst. She wants to be the last one. She has all night if need be.

While she waits she contemplates the building, which is small and neat but festooned with holy trappings, with hand-carved piety. Saints, major and minor. Angels and cherubs. She wants to believe in it all, as she did when she was a child and it seemed like a dour carnival, all colors and smoke and chants and bowing of heads. She wants to believe that there really is some order to this, some sense of a system of belief and action, some clear dictates. She wants to believe that someone is listening. But right now she sits in a cold place trying not to overhear the poor soul nattering on behind the curtain, something about throwing out her daughter's horrid sweater and then claiming she had no idea what had become of it.

Colleen stands and walks toward the baptismal font. The water looks as if it hasn't been changed in weeks, dust seeming to skin its surface and lending a dullness to it. Putting an infant into this, she thinks. Touching them with filth. She goes back down to the far pews, still aware of the old people watching her, and sits, quietly, feeling no urge to pray. One of the old men, going on about the rain, stops in mid-sentence when he sees it is his turn. On his cane, he nearly drags himself to confess. What sins could he possibly hold within him? The one old lady who's left looks over to Colleen, probably accustomed to being last in line. Colleen stands and backs off again, waiting.

The old man coughs and grumbles inside the box. The word "gambling" comes through audibly. Colleen wonders if, at a certain age, certain sins become much less so. But she knows nothing of this man or his life; maybe damage is still being done. The statute of limitation on sins, she thinks, must be measured by the amount of pain still suffered.

Finally he emerges and the old lady, after trying to wait Colleen out, shrugs and makes her way to the confessional. Birdlike, nervous, she catalogs her sins in whistly sotto voce as the priest stays with her, uh-huh, uh-huh, probably at this moment in his Saturday routine beginning to think of other things, of dinner in the rectory, of simply standing and stretching. When the old lady emerges, Colleen is quick to enter, before he can assume that all is done. The space is warm and stale, the air all used up by the people before her. There seems a hesitance on the other side of the portal, another creature of habit thrown by her arrival, possibly bringing dismaying news of real sins. The little door slides back and through the screen she sees the priest, white-haired and small for the deepness of the voice she had heard from beyond the curtain.

"Go ahead," he says.

"Bless me, Father," she says, and stops.

They wait, now. In her silence he prompts her line: "*For I have sinned.*"

"Bless me Father, but I'm here to talk about the sins of others, the sins that are going on in the church."

He sits upright, and, though the church is empty, whispers fiercely, "*That's not what we're here to do.*"

"I've spent a long time trying to get anyone to acknowledge what's going on," she says. "I'm from South Boston, from Most Holy Trinity. Do you know the priest there? Father John?"

Silence.

"Do you know what he does? *Do you know what he has done to my son?*"

"Now wait a minute," the old priest whispers. "I don't really know him, I know *of* him."

"Well, I've come here to tell you what he's done to my son, so that you can know that and carry it. I am here to put the burden on you so that you will carry this forward."

"I'm not the man's superior. You need to contact his superiors."

"You don't think I've tried? I can't get near them. They won't even hear me out. This is the only place anyone will hear me. I need for someone to carry this."

"Look here, there's nothing I can do about that."

"Then I'll go to another church," she says. "I've been to four already. None of you want to hear. I'll keep going until someone is willing to hear about real sins and do something about it. I can't say it out loud because it will ruin my son, but I'll say it here, in the dark, to put it on you . . ."

The priest is silent, trapped and thinking.

"Now listen," he says. "Do you have any of your own sins to tell me about?"

58

The gun shop is down on Columbus Avenue, down toward the black part of town, which makes Christopher nervous. Almost any part of town that isn't Southie makes him nervous. Jeanmarie seems not to be worried at all, and so he follows her down the street as she clacks along on heels that seem yet higher than the ones he's seen before. She isn't close to seventeen yet, but seems nonetheless to be in possession of something far beyond his reach.

The shop, like many down here by Mass Ave, has rusty bars covering the windows, and in the display he sees an assortment of weapons laid out on a green felt blanket, something that might be wrapped at the base of a Christmas tree. He can name every one of the guns, and can also name the ammunition each would take. He has gone over it with Jeanmarie on the subway ride over, the name of this, his father's gun, and the clip it requires.

"Do you want me to wait out here?" he says.

"I don't know," she says. "I mean, yeah, I guess."

She enters and Christopher hears the buzzer go off. She slams the door shut behind her and he is alone on the sidewalk. He moves away from the front window and watches the traffic on the avenue. It feels so strange to be outside the tight confines of the neighborhood. But he appreciates the true anonymity of other places, the kind that is real, not like in Southie. He cannot, even in his abandonment of school and home, even sleeping on that narrow patch of floor next to Jeanmarie's bed, shake the sense of what everyone knows, or knows of. He cannot say with any certainty what it is that people know, how they know it, or whom they tell, but the sense that it is there hangs over him in Southie, in a way that it wouldn't in a place like this, only a few miles away. There is liberation in that thought, here.

He waits until it feels as if Jeanmarie should be coming back out, but she does not appear. He sits on the topmost of a set of granite steps going down to a basement door, and waits. He pulls the hood of his sweatshirt up, warding off the chill of the breeze gusting from the avenue, and hunches in on himself.

He has constricted his life to a tight pod, cocooned in the little cylinder of space he takes up in the world. But the next question becomes how to move back outward, and when. He actually misses parts of school, the reading and learning part, the pictures in the books and the maps on the walls of the shifting borders, countries given colors as if the demarcations were really so profound. He liked that, the part that was apart from the people he had to be around. But he's out now. He knows he's going to have to find some kind of job. He sometimes imagines finding something at which he can work hard and where it won't matter that he's fourteen, and that he and Jeanmarie will find themselves a bigger place.

She still has not come out of the shop. He stands and goes to the window and looks through. The rifles are locked in their racks, but he sees no one. He goes to the front door and opens it. The buzzer goes on and then off when he closes the door. He is alone in the store. He walks to the counter and sees no one.

"Jeanmarie?" he calls. No one answers.

He stands waiting, but as the minutes go by and no one appears, he feels himself getting either frightened or angry, he's not quite sure.

"Hello?" No one.

He now goes behind the counter and finds the stacks of ammo. He looks around again, but the place is just as empty. He stuffs four boxes into the pocket of his sweatshirt, then goes to the guns displayed in the front window. He takes the .380, the .38 and 9 millimeter, tucking each one into the waistband of his jeans and then pulling his sweatshirt back down over them. They're deeply cold, even through his underwear. There's a little gun, too, rubber-handled, a .22 Derringer he thinks; for good measure he stuffs that one into his pants pocket. The buzzer goes off again as he leaves, summoning no one, and he walks down to the corner and leans on a newspaper box. Thanksgiving is this week, the next occasion for potential trouble with his mother. The metal of the guns warms slowly in his clothing, and he wonders what it would be like to shoot one, for real. Maybe he could go down to the woods off the Expressway and try firing into the dead trees.

"Hey . . ." Jeanmarie is standing next to him, smiling. "You ready?"

"Yup." He wants to demand to know where she was, wants to know what she was doing, but he also knows he cannot ask, that his place in her apartment—and, by extension, her life—is still tenuous. He is still proving himself, and he knows she will not answer to him.

"You got the clip?" he says.

"Of course I got the clip," she says. "Ready to go home?"

They walk down to Huntington Avenue to wait for the T, and he says nothing.

"You want to hold the bullets?" she says.

"You go ahead," he says. "I'll put them in the gun when we get home."

"What's the matter with you?"

"What do you mean, what's the matter with me?"

"You seem, like, angry. Sorry you had to wait so long, but that's the way it goes, you know?"

"Yeah, I know."

"So quit acting angry," she says.

"I'm not angry."

"You're not lying either, right?"

Christopher knows to say nothing. She has that leverage. He has no other place to go.

"Can we just forget it?" he says. "I'm not angry, and I'm not lying."

"But now you're angry," she says.

"Can we stop now?" he says. "Please?"

+ + + + + + + + + + + + + + + + + + + +

5 9

I had never given much thought or credence to the notion of being a family man, and I suppose it showed. I quickly got bored with it. I had a wife with whom I could not have a conversation and two daughters who seemed only to stare at me from their silence. What kind of understanding did I have of parenting, growing up at Old Colony with a father down at the corner bar and a mother sitting out on the steps smoking with the other women while their children ran wild? But of course that's very much an excuse. Had I wanted to be better, I could have been better. I just really couldn't get myself in a family mood. They were trappings, more than anything. I had an insatiable desire to keep moving forward, and in my thirties I was understanding that success somehow had a hollowness unless it had to do with all the old grudges and scores of the neighborhood. Don't get me wrong, I didn't want to be around any of them, but I needed for this knowledge to somehow flow back to them. This was not an easy realization. I was almost distraught when this understanding finally crossed a threshold into my consciousness. I had spent so long trying to get away from them.

That day in the bar I had finished my drink, left a decent tip, gotten in my car and driven back to my Beacon Hill home. I ate dinner with my family, letting them natter on about their day of shopping while I rolled with only one thought, which was McX. There was a *tremendous sense of victory for me, seeing him silently downing his beer in that place, his failures in life rather apparent to the neutral observer. But the trick was this: I had to let it be known to him that I had risen to a station in life that he could only envy. And I had, in the distance I had come, lost all way of getting back there.*

The nature of the Beacon Hill Meads was such that any show of wealth at all was regarded as vulgar. My in-laws lived behind a high wall in their stupendous affluence, making a point of being sure that no one had ever heard of them. They made anonymous charitable donations, engineered the social order of The Hill from the confines of their parlor, and paid people to keep them out of the newspapers. My own wife, despite her liberal spending, dressed in a way that was like a secret code—just clothes to the rest of us, but something the other young wives of Beacon Hill could read like a hieroglyph, as a measure of sophistication and wealth. It was also clear that any desire of mine to obtain perfectly normal professional recognition had, for them, an air of nouveau riche, an air of, well, Irishness, to it. By that book, the fact that I had even known who Red Driscoll was at the moment I met him showed a vanity on the old man's part that would have been unforgivable in these horn-rimmed circles.

I went to bed that night and arose the next morning still contemplating McX, roosted at the end of that bar. I had nursed my resentment for years, and given the fact that our clash had the feel of a draw, I could not imagine it did not cross his mind from time to time. Him, in a layabout bar, was all I needed to know where he stood. But I was still curious. I felt the need for specifics.

Of course, I had so long ago turned my back on the place, the job of getting information was not an easy one. I did it simply, by hir-

ing an expensive private investigator whose contacts were legion and whose fee was commensurate. He was an ex-Boston cop named Lydell Barrett. I made the call myself, leaving my secretary out of the loop, and arranged to meet him at a restaurant in the North End where I would not see any of my usual associates. He came to my table clearly thinking this was another cuckolded husband needing someone to tail his wife. When I began to tell him I was simply trying to find out what had become of an old high school classmate, he looked even more indifferent.

"Why don't you just call your high school and see if they have an alumni directory?" Barrett said. "I'm not a social director, you know."

Lydell Barrett didn't know who I was, but I hadn't expected him to. What he saw was a soft-looking Beacon Hill guy who had some reason to find some other soft-looking Beacon Hill guy, some old buddy from Choate. I would forgive him that, for the moment.

"If I pay you what you charge to investigate, you call yourself anything you want," I said. "But I'm paying you what you charge because, first, you keep your mouth shut, and second, you just find out what I need."

Barrett sat back. "Okay, what high school did you go to?"

"Southie High."

"You're from Southie?"

"Old Colony Housing Project."

Barrett grunted, apparently impressed now. "And who do you want to find?"

When I told him McX's full name, he smiled broadly.

"You want me to tail James McX, is that right? You know this guy?"

"Jimbo McX, yes," I said. "But how do you?"

Barrett leaned in and smiled again. "You could read the newspapers and not come across his name but I'm surprised you being from Southie don't know this," he said. "McX is one of the most powerful guys in the city. We're talking about James Joyce McX, right?"

"Jimbo McX," I said. "Played football at Southie High. A big dumb shit. We must be talking about a different guy. This guy I spotted drinking a beer by himself at some dive called Muldoon's."

"I can hardly believe it," Barrett said. "We are talking about the same guy."

$+ +$

60

He waits outside the house until he sees his mother leave. She pulls the door closed and keys both deadbolts, making that habitual glance around, something she seems to do now without actually looking. Christopher observes her with a dispassion that seems harsh to him at times, but also somehow warranted. He has not so much persecuted his mother as simply become too uncomfortable around her, the way she picks around the edges of things without stepping forward or backing off, the way she inflicts her silent anxieties on him, the way she refuses to see where she fits into it all. He watches her now, craning around as if she hopes to avoid life entirely, in whatever form it may come at her.

He feels his anger creeping up on him again. He feels angry all the time and doesn't really want to. But in its own subtle way it has always been there, at least since his father died, and it has never really abated. And mostly it has been directed at her, something he is not sure is quite fair but is definitely a feeling he cannot dispel. She, the helpless; she, the nervous; she, the passive. Coming back to this place now gets him tight and furious, and as she comes to the sidewalk and begins her walk to the bus stop, he wills her to simply go away.

He waits until she is clearly out of range, then waits a bit longer for good measure. He goes around to the back, where he can go up the fire escape and then through his own bedroom window. He has his key with him but chooses not to use it, as if it would leave evidence. Inside, he unlocks his bedroom door then stands in the silence of the apartment, which has become, by slow degrees, a place completely foreign to him. There is food but he will not eat. He removes the boxes of baseball cards from his closet and opens them, throwing the stacks of cards in a pillowcase he has taken from the linen closet. He puts the filled pillowcase on the upper shelf of the closet, behind the sweaters he has outgrown, then takes the guns from his waistband and puts them in one of the boxes where the cards had been. The money is still there at the bottom and he will not touch it. He puts the guns in on top, closes the box and puts it back in the recesses of the closet. He has a system now, so that he can come into and leave his room leaving no evidence of its having happened.

He crawls back out the window and slides the window and then the screen down, leaving just enough finger space for reentry, something his mother will never notice. It is a little after nine in the morning and he has no idea where to go next. He doesn't want to get in the habit of going to the library in the mornings because people will notice he isn't in school; he has some money in his pocket and he could go ride the subway. He has taken to that, paying his eighty-five cents and then riding the Red Line up and down the line as it crashes through the dark, killing the hours by watching people crowd off and on, getting out only to wait on the platform and reboard another train, and continue his destinationless journey through each day.

By afternoon he will end up at the library. He will pull out his favorite books and some new ones, and use the computer to do his research. He is working on a secret project. He hasn't even told Jeanmarie, nor will he. This is not about that, not about making some announcement to the world. Rather, it is about simply making certain things right. With his money he will gather his supplies and wait until the time is right.

He doesn't feel anything like a child anymore. That is done with, and he has no desire to go back. It was in his childhood that he was still waiting for someone to make things right for him. He doesn't fondly recall the helplessness of it. He hates the responsibility he had after his father's death, to somehow be something for his mother, to somehow cheer her out of her funk, to be more than he otherwise would have had to be.

When he sits on the bench at his appointed time each afternoon, he can sometimes see the kids down in the schoolyard, playing. Kickball, tag, free the box, whatever. They are still children, and maybe it fits them better. He tries not to imagine how their lives have been different. Down at the Most Holy Trinity schoolyard, maybe they are not that much different.

But for now, he has a day to kill. He has begun to think it is time to try to find a way to work. He can lie about his age but he'll need to find someone who will let him tell that lie. The Liquor Mart is no good because Bobby works there, and Jeanmarie, for all her confidence in her own savvy, doesn't really have any connections. He'll have to find a way around that, because he definitely does not look older than he is.

He walks up toward Broadway, gripped again by the odd feeling that someone is still watching him.

+ +

6 1

Jimmy hasn't been returning Shelagh's calls. She's become much too optimistic in all the wrong ways. She believes in an answer, in a cure, in a miracle. She has become evangelical about holistic solutions, about mango juice, about the amazing nature of surgery these days and the fact that he is among the youngest of liver-transplant patients and is therefore more deserving. He would argue that this makes him less deserving, to have burned off a major organ at such a young age, and then to presume to ask for a new one. She keeps mentioning Rafferty. "The man is worth at least a hundred million," she said during their last phone call, which she probably didn't know was their last. It's all become too intrusive, despite her apparent good intentions. It's just that every time she petitions for him to live, he can't settle into the dying.

"You don't think he'd consider a charitable donation? We can start a charity in your name and he can deduct it from his taxes," she says. "I mean, if you report directly to the guy then he must have some respect for you . . ."

Of course, having been transcribing Rafferty's recollections and organizing them into a manageable narrative, Jimmy knows not to be so foolish. If Shelagh knew more, she'd probably be advocating blackmail, whereas he is just doing a job and trying not to give it much thought. So he does not answer or return her calls.

He is serious about wanting to just do this alone. She is someone he hardly knows, and he has come to see that this essential alone-ness he has occupied from such a young age is something you don't free yourself from so easily; with so little time with which to do anything with the results. It's over, more or less; he just needs for her to figure that out. He doesn't want to die waiting for a liver to come to him, or thinking about how he would pay all the bills after, or who really would be there to help him. He doesn't want to die with some sort of pathetic hope still flaring inside him.

Oddly or not, he feels no desire to drink. The doctor has told him that he is now experiencing edema, the buildup of fluid in his body that his liver isn't processing, and he goes through the day feeling bloated and without needing to drink anything. He has be-gun to earmark some of his earnings from the Rafferty job for the heavy painkillers he will certainly need, and for the nurse he may need to hire. He thinks of how he may simply, when the time comes, dump himself on the emergency room of Boston City Hospital and let them ferry him to the other side, where the bill collectors apparently do not venture. He'd be a cheap date: Lay him in a bed, pump him with morphine and let him slip away. He craves, already, the release.

The phone rings again. The only person who would be calling him would be Shelagh. He lets it ring eight, ten, twenty times, and when it does not stop ringing he pulls the cord from the wall and sits in the silence, working himself back to calmness. It would seem odd for him to be bothered by his own disappearance from the world. There has never before been a question of mattering, to anyone. He lost that when his father passed, when he lost the old man's benevolent worry, the quiet observation that seemed to be gathering itself for some advice never delivered. That was when it was becoming apparent that Jimmy, a man in his twenties, wasn't at all outgrowing the drinking. Those were the days when the other reasons for the alcohol—the buddies, the girls, the music, the noise that would keep someone from confronting their worries—simply gave way to the constant silent feed of the substance. Sometimes, stumbling home from one bar or another, he could understand the unencumbered serenity of the man sleeping in a cardboard box wrapped in a dingy blanket, not worrying about being bothered because nothing more could be taken from him. It was at that point in his life when the drinking could not be fully hidden, but was something oozing from the small crevices of a young man with a decent entry-level job, living in his first apartment. He had, in many ways, anticipated his father's first halting approach to the situation. Then the man was gone, and, with him, whatever words that might have made a difference.

He needs to go to his father's grave. Some one of these days. He probably needs to send word of his own imminent demise to his mother, and his sister. It is a time for the settling of things. It occurs to him that the holidays are not far off, and then the new year, a new millennium, and then whatever comes after, whatever finality. There are matters to be attended to, soon, and one of the first is to return to Triple O's and give Tommy Morton his three-twenty back.

+ + + + + + + + + + + + + + + + + + + +

62

She goes to confession, constantly, some Saturdays three times a day, three different churches, and she is sorry for nothing. She seethes through gossamer screens at the dimly lighted and nodding heads of priests, watching for their reactions, hoping that even one will act. She wants her voice to go right through them, wants her raspy whispers to be the ghost that haunts them. The days fade early now and lend themselves to the sense she has of herself as a specter, keening from dark places, some sort of conscience in a void where there would otherwise be none. She is their personal banshee, a voice scything through the dark.

Tell someone, she says, *tell them what's happening. I've done this at other churches, to other priests. Tell those people who would do something about it.*

"I can't," one of them finally hisses back. The others, invariably, have said nothing at all, have slid back their little doors and shut her back into her own chamber, until the push of others awaiting absolution flushes her out—or, if she is the last of the repentant, as she tries to be, she hears their own flight, their hasty footfalls and the echoed shutting of heavy doors.

"What?"

"I said I can't. I *cannot* repeat what is said in confession," he says in his throaty confessor's brogue. "What is said in the confessional can never be repeated. None of the others can repeat it, either."

"This is the only way I can do this," she says, faltering. "I want you to tell them."

"I won't," he says. "Neither will the others. This is confession."

"But I'm not confessing," she says, letting her voice crack into what feels like shouting. "I'm here to tell you."

"Then you're abusing the sacrament," the old man barks, his face a death mask in the blue light. "Get out of this confessional. Get out of this church."

"You should be ashamed," she says.

"Of what?" he says. "Of what? Some voice I don't know giving me vague accusations about someone I don't know? I know none of the facts but I'm going to be the prosecutor? And how do you think that makes my position any better? If you want to say something, say it out loud."

"But I can't," she says. "I can't do that to my son."

"Your choice. Yours and your son's. And let me ask you one thing."

"What?"

"How do you know this man has not asked for God's forgiveness, and received his absolution? How do you know he has not found his way to a better place?"

"It's not enough," she says. "He's still out there."

"It's enough in this church," he says. "Anything other than that, you need to go to the police, or the district attorney. In this church, absolution is enough."

"How do you live with yourselves?" she says.

"You need to leave now," the old man says.

So again she finds herself, in the dawn hour, entering Most Holy Trinity Church, a place she enters now with the bile rising in her, no holiness left in this place. She moves to the front-left pew, her now-usual place, and around her are the same people in the same spots for their morning Mass. She is by far the youngest one here, and they seem not to like her. They sense the edges. They have watched, on those mornings when a young substitute priest emerges from the sacristy, as she gets up and walks out.

She waits now in her pew, drowsy as the sudden rustle around her signals the beginning. She stands with the rest and this morning it is indeed him, Father John, shuffling out to the altar and mumbling his invocations. It is all rote to these people, their daily petition. She had believed so much. She can still recall, as a girl, going to her First Friday Masses, being told she would go to Heaven because she had strung nine of them together like beads on a rosary. She was ten, and for years after that she had gone forward with this knowledge, that she had her reservation made, that she was untouchable. This was her article of faith, and it stayed with her until her teenage years, when she began to realize that it was her mother who had told her all this. Colleen can recall resorting to a furious leafing through the Gospels, trying to find any reference, any intimation that this was at all true. Of course there was none at all. She confronted her mother in the kitchen.

"It's not true?" her mother said, as if she had just been kicked. Colleen, suddenly unshielded, her halo ripped from her head at fifteen, actually cried about this.

Will she go to Heaven now? She sits in the front pew, trying to will this man to have the guts to actually look up, to meet her burning eyes, which he does not and will never do. Is he untouchable?

Is he absolved? Will he go to Heaven? She wants that acknowledgment, wants to stand and give testimony, scream and condemn. She wants to harm this man, in every way possible. She wants to derail his path to a presumed hereafter, the way a hunter might pot a rising bird and watch it spiral into the muck. At every turn of this unendurable Mass she wants to explode into something.

But, in silence, she watches once again. He shuffles through the Mass as if drugged, as if having drunk before leaving the rectory. The hands shake, palsied; the head nods; the balance at times seems to waver. It is as if the very lightest push would send him tumbling apart, but yet with the gleaming crucifix hanging over him and the elderly mouthing their millennial incantations, she is only more aware of her own dire incapacities.

6 3

The line at the Registry of Motor Vehicles is out the door and down this dingy Quincy street, and Marty leaves her standing there, saying he'll be drinking coffee at the café down the block, and that her plan to be here so early as to avoid the crowds is obviously flawed. A black woman in front of Jeanmarie, folding back another page of her magazine, chuckles at the notion that crowds can ever be beaten at this place.

"What are you here for, dear?" the woman says.

"I'm taking my driving test," Jeanmarie says.

"In those shoes?"

Jeanmarie, tottering on her high wooden mules, says, "Oh, it's no problem. I've been practicing."

The woman smiles wanly and goes back to her magazine, and Jeanmarie is alone, with no one to talk to and nothing to read. Marty wants this done with, wants to get home and sleep, because they have a late-night gig tonight that isn't at his house. He's promised her that if she passes the test, she can drive the Caddy down to Dedham, where the Holiday Inn is just off the highway ramp.

She's tired. More of the photo shoots are now in places in and around the city, and Marty works only with a camera and flash, and none of the lightstands or umbrellas he uses at his own little studio. She is not an expert on photography but she wonders how the pictures are turning out. She also wonders why he can't hire some better-looking guys to do it with her. Not that it matters much to her, she hardly pays attention, but from time to time she suggests that a better-looking couple would be more appealing to those who purchase their work.

"Oh, not at all," Marty had said. "It works better when the guy is average-looking, or older. It's the whole, you know, *milieu* you're trying to create. Your appeal to your *fans*, Sandra Shields' *fans*, is that you have this attainable quality."

She finds herself grinning when she thinks of her *fans*. She's begun to understand that there are real stars in this business. She hears the top performers earn hundreds of thousands of dollars. Marty says that in another couple of years, when she's eighteen, he'll take her to California, to The Valley, and get her connected with the right people in the film industry. Places like Encino and Van Nuys. It seems an interminable wait, but, for now, the work pays. Beyond covering her expenses, Marty feeds her lots of cash. She puts most of it away so she can get her own car, soon. A convertible.

The line moves a bit and she begins to feel nervous. She is already realizing that in the scripted reality Marty creates for her, she can feel as if she has all the power, but in lines such as this it fades quickly. She is an actress playing a role. It has come to feel as if the photo sessions, with their theatrical lights and the urgency of the popping flash, are like a service in which she is the deity, as the famous are deities. She imagines at this moment that she would be recognized, standing in a line, that she would create a murmur, that she would be the subject of a sighting. But of course if she were that famous she would never be standing in this wretched Registry of Motor Vehicles line.

"Jeanmarie?" a Registry officer calls, looking into the line for the face connected to the name. He is a sour, late-middle-aged man with grayish skin.

"That's me," Jeanmarie says.

"Driving test, right?"

"Yeah."

"Okay, where's your car?"

She is shaking as they find their way to the Caddy. The Registry man looks at her, and then at the car, and snorts. Jeanmarie will be a story over dinner tonight, a break in the tedium of endless days.

Jeanmarie gets behind the steering wheel and the Registry man slides into the passenger side. "Okay, up to the corner," he says. Jeanmarie starts the car, puts it in gear, and lets her foot off the brake. The car floats out into the driving lane, just as she's practiced. Marty has told her that the test is a breeze, as evidenced by the number of total idiots on the road possessing Massachusetts driver's licenses.

At the stop sign, she comes to a complete halt, and then waits. He's filling out the paperwork already.

"Left turn," he says.

She makes the turn and goes down the narrower street; at the end of it, he says "Left again" and then they are on a somewhat more comfortably wide and quiet street that backs onto a school and is lined on either side with parked cars.

"Three-point turn," he says.

She lets out a breath. This is the hard part, but Marty has shown her how to do it. She noses the car sideways, puts it in reverse—her foot shaking on the brake—then creeps backwards until she is up to the bumper of one of the parked cars.

"What was that?" the Registry man says.

"What?"

"You hit that car."

"I *touched* that car," she says. "That's the way you do it."

"Put the car in 'park,'" he says, his tone one of disgust.

They get out of the car and examine the bumper of the parked car.

"There's not a mark," Jeanmarie says. "I touched it. I *kissed* that car. Which is how you have to make a three-point turn."

"Not here you don't," the Registry man says.

"Well, you sure as hell do in Southie," she says.

"Look," he says tiredly, his humorous after-dinner story beginning to evaporate. "You fail the test. Just come back and try it again."

"I *touched* the fucking car," she says. "I did not fail this test."

"I believe you did," he says.

"What is this shit?" she says.

"Watch the attitude, honey."

"Oh, yeah, *honey*? There's something more you want from me, isn't there? Is that what you want from me? A little something to help change your mind?"

He looks her up and down, in her heels and tiny skirt and fake-fur jacket and makeup, and says, "The test is now over. I am walking back to the Registry. If you drive that car from here, you will be doing so illegally."

"Yeah, fuck you," she says.

Outside the car, he shrugs and turns, and after he rounds the corner she gets in the car, seething. She puts it in gear, but this time she's confused and furious and she puts it in reverse, and hears the true crumple of something behind her. No matter. She roars up the street, swings around the corner past the walking Registry man, and slams to a halt in front of the café. She honks the horn loudly until Marty comes out.

"The hell is the matter with you?" he says. "What did you do to my Caddy?"

"Just get in the goddamned car!" she screams at him.

+ +

6 4

What I found out from Lydell Barrett was that McX had made his bones the old-fashioned Southie way, dipping down below the somewhat abstract line of what one might reasonably define as law-abiding behavior. To wit, he was a Teamster captain. And he was not unlike many of his fellows in one sort of criminal behavior or another, in that his earnings could not be properly paraded, something that always amused me—they could rob people blind but still had to live their outwardly shabby lives, apparently for appearances' sake. The money was hidden somewhere, almost another abstract concept: Other than a few cheap women on the side and the occasional all-inclusive vacation cruise, one had little opportunity to enjoy one's acquired wealth. I suspected, too, that there was a lack of imagination present, that inability to see beyond life as lived in The Neighborhood. McX had always been plagued by that absence of inspired thinking, and had found his successes, always, in more physical displays. He was big and strong and, while he'd gone to fat, I had seen, observing him on that barstool at Muldoon's, that he had kept a suggestion of brawn intact, a lumbering and witless product of his origins. Ergo, McX lived in the small house in which he had grown up, supporting his elderly parents, his wife and daughter; he drove a black Lincoln he'd bought used and wore clothes that were appropriate to the working man he purported to be. I told the pri-

vate investigator to give me everything he could find on McX, some-thing that seemed to make Barrett regard me as someone ventur-ing into things that were best left alone. Maybe he was right that I should leave those sleeping dogs, but I was feeling the pump of get-ting back into a game that had satisfied me more than anything I had been doing in my life over on the Beacon Hill side.

Not unexpectedly, what Barrett told me was this: Under the aus-pices of McX and his crew, there was an unfortunate amount of "leakage" from trucks and warehouses at which these Teamsters worked. And, it seemed, no one whose inventory was evaporating seemed able to raise much of a complaint. The Boston police would conduct tepid investigations that came to nothing. There was one particular trucking company, King of the Road Moving, that seemed akin to the magician's box in which all manner of items could be made to simply vanish.

Of course this had to do with me in only the most tangential of ways. I found myself sitting on the end of my bed with a glass of scotch in my hand, wondering why I had such an itch to reengage. My upper-crust life was unfulfilling, and I contemplated ways to re-lieve the torpor. I was in my middle forties and there must have been some requisite taking of stock. Red Driscoll was nearing retirement, and I was making so much money that I was "redistributing" in real estate, art and wine. I had several girlfriends, all in their twen-ties and fully satisfied by an arrangement that put them in Marl-borough Street apartments and left their weekends free. They all worked in public relations and marketing, that last bastion for the attractive-but-dim modern woman. I'd met them as they handed out press packets at corporate events, or manned the booths at in-dustry functions. I made it clear to each that I was a Catholic and *my faith forbade me to divorce; they seemed easily accepting of that. I was a way station to someplace else, real or imagined: I covered bills they otherwise could not. The sex was after work, usually, before I showered in their bathrooms and walked home in the dusk to my townhouse on The Hill. It was all right, and most certainly my due at that point. My wife now occupied her own bedroom, as was the apparent tradition of the gentility, unlike my own experience, listening through thin walls to my parents rolling grumbling and rancorous into their old featherbed at the end of each bone-weary day.*

But the women were not enough. Nor was the house or the artwork or the closet of suits or even the golf. Everything lacked the kind of engagement I had once known, the secretive and eventful kind. I was preparing to pick at all the old scabs, despite myself.

Lydell Barrett took on a more subdued affect each time I asked him to dredge up further information on McX, but he also couldn't walk away from this, given the money I was paying him. He expressed, more than once, a certain nervousness about even being noted as someone gathering intelligence on this particular man, a fellow who had many subsidized "friends" within the Boston police. Someone was going to ask sooner or later, Barrett said. But I liked it, as I thought about it. I was about to move my first pawn.

"Barrett, if someone were to ask you, what would you say?"

"I would say I don't reveal who my client is," Barrett said.

"In this case, you certainly may," I said. "If anyone asks, you can tell them that Terrence Rafferty wants to know."

Barrett, florid in his cheap suit and sink-washed rayon shirt, looked like a man hoping no one would ask. Ever.

+ +

65

Christopher has had jobs, but they're the kind always doled out to boys his age: shoveling snow from walks, raking leaves, carrying boxes. The kind where someone slips you a ten for three hours of work and thinks you should be happy. The kind where afterwards you get a piece of pie in somebody's kitchen, a tousle of the hair. But now he needs a real job, and he is too young to do so legally. He can only think of a few places where he might have a chance. The Liquor Mart, except for Bobby. The supermarket, if they will allow him to lie about his age to bag groceries. Except that his mother shops there. King of the Road Moving, where he has heard they hire extras for busy days and don't ask much about who you are.

He sits in the back reaches of the library; the book in front of him is open to the page on medieval ramparts, but he cannot concentrate on it. Jeanmarie went off with Marty in the late afternoon, leaving Christopher free to wander from the confines of the apartment. But here in the library, the pleasure of his studies is fading as he worries about more important things.

He needs to bring in money, especially now that Jeanmarie has gone into her extended pout. She seems irritated by him, and the fact that she hasn't gotten her license, and that without her license, Marty won't get her the car. It has made the small apartment seem utterly claustrophobic. As he occupies his small patch of space on the floor, he senses her eyes on him, her unrelenting irritation. He needs to purchase his own worth here. It has occurred to him more than once that he basically needs Bobby to show up and make trouble. But Bobby has been frustratingly absent. Christopher sometimes walks by the old apartment, and from the outside, looking up from the sidewalk, he can only discern the blue cast of the television's tube lighting the room. He sees no girl in any window, and hopes Bobby still has it in him to come forward. The gun, loaded, is in the night table next to Jeanmarie's bed, but she is clearly afraid to touch it now.

He needs money, even as the thousand dollars sits in a box with baseball cards at the bottom of his closet. He will not touch that, will not sanctify it by putting it into circulation. From the moment he first opened that envelope, it has paralyzed him. It makes him wonder who he is and what exactly he has done, and whether he can possibly not be complicit, by virtue of its delivery. Is he, though, through his silence and inaction? Christopher had thought it was over, when he finally could not bear any more and had demanded to be released from that school and its silent indictments. He thought he had indeed been set free from the wary attentions of the nuns, and of his classmates. He had wanted to be washed clean of the worry of how much they knew, and what it was, exactly, that they knew. The arrival of that money, cloaked in the language of gifting and with its last line's intimation of bribery, was a stark reminder of the ongoingness of it all, of the way that secrets do not fully die but, rather, remain embedded more deeply than one can fully comprehend. The inextinguishable flame of memory. He sits in the library with a book open before him and tries to steer out of the thought, back to something more practical.

Without a job, and without the opportunity to repel Bobby in some heroic manner, there is the material fact of the saleable commodity that is his stash of stolen guns. He has no idea what he could sell them for, or to whom. But it seems that it should be possible, and that enough money could be made to stave off the ejection he fears will come at virtually any moment. He has almost forgotten why he feels as he does for Jeanmarie, but it has become his primary article of faith. All actions are now permissible by fact of his devotion to her. It's been a long time since she's been nice to him, a long time since she's been nice at all, yet, still, all the choices he makes center on his need to be with her, even this way. His worry that she'll get back with Bobby is only surpassed by his fear that she will find a new boyfriend, one who will not warm to the idea of a fourteen-year-old boy sleeping on the rug next to the bed. When he is in the shower masturbating to the thought of her, he yearns as well for his body to fill out to match the strength of his desire for her. In all the pictures of his father from his high school days, Barry Cooney is tall and muscular. Christopher is terrified by the notion that he will never grow to occupy his father's dimensions.

So there are the guns. He had never had any intention to steal, but now he has. It was easy, not just from the logistical end of it, but morally as well. He has come to see that balance more easily now, more complex than the simplistic lessons administered at Most Holy Trinity. Christopher has lived in Southie long enough to see that right and wrong are relative positions on a sliding scale. The trick is in proper calibration. Stealing is wrong, clearly, but not so much when you're stealing from a man gone off to the back room with the girl you want to be with. Doing bad things to bad people carries, instead, the happy sense of extemporaneous justice. One can spare oneself the guilt of nearly any indiscretion on the simply conceived basis of a greater good. One, in fact, can make oneself feel completely better.

The trick, then, is in determining who is worthy of what would otherwise be criminal attentions. He can start with Bobby, but the problem is that he has no sense of what Bobby has that he can take. He can try the rectory, if he can find a way in. He knows exactly the hours when it lies empty, and presumes many expensive items to be there for the taking. He can also try Marty, who, from what Jeanmarie has told him, has a lot of expensive photographic equipment down there in his basement. Christopher might, in the act of theft, put an abrupt end to Jeanmarie's modeling. It is both a problem and a motivation.

He lays the book down on the library table. There is something he must finally do. Over near the reference desk are the computers, almost always occupied through the day by the aged and the homeless. But today, mid-afternoon having gotten unseasonably warm, there is a computer terminal sitting free. He slides into the chair and clicks in. The man next to him is dressed in layers of wool and emits an odor that might otherwise drive Christopher away. Except that he finally needs to know. He types a name into the search field. *Sandra Shields*. Scrolling through the results, he passes those that are clearly irrelevant, Sandra Shields the Ph.D. student in Oklahoma, Sandra Shields the store manager in Alpharetta, Georgia. Way down low, he sees the heading *sandra-shieldsxxx.com*. He clicks the mouse. *You must be over 18 to enter.*

He clicks. And there she is, nearly unrecognizable in her makeup, so heavily applied. *See my free pictures.* And he clicks. And there she is, smiling at the camera even as these things are done to her by these men. There she is, unabashed. There she is, thumb-nailed, offering herself to everyone but Christopher himself. He feels as if he is going to scream, looking. But he can't not look. Then the hand is on his arm, and he realizes how long he has been sitting there, staring.

"*What are you doing?*" she says in a fierce whisper that is heard by everyone. The librarian, the one who has seen him so many times when he should have been in school, and has never made trouble.

"I wasn't doing anything," he says.

She reaches over and clicks off the website. *Disgusting*, she says. *Inappropriate*, she says. *You can't come in here anymore*, she says. *Banned*, she says, as she pushes him out onto the street.

+ +

66

The door of Triple O's holds no sway for Jimmy today as he
stands before it, no effect one way or the other. It summons neither the palliative bodily hum he once knew when pulling open
that door, nor the disquiet he thought he might feel in doing so
now. It hasn't been that long, but the place seems, from the other
side of all this, to be nearly an antiquity. It is decorated for Christmas already, though the effect is one of uninspired convention,
with a chewed-up length of plastic garland nailed around the
weathered doorframe. It seems only acknowledgment, not at all
celebration. The work of men who will soon enough be home,
and cursing, as they try to untangle Christmas tree lights from a
mildewed box.

He has again awakened sick this morning, the past two days
again expunged, all gone but for the notes he now takes in case
something important has happened. According to the words of
his own cramped hand, nothing at all has happened. Days are
evaporating, and he is torn as to whether he should be eager for
them to pass or trying to do something better with them. He has
been prescribed an assortment of medications that don't help; he
feels no real pain other than the vaguely hangoverish pall that is
not nearly the pain he will need to manage later, but for which
there will be much morphine. He isn't afraid of all that, although

he isn't sure why. Shelagh tries to call but he resolutely ignores her; she will only remind him of what lies ahead, as she attempts to persuade him to avert it.

He still dutifully goes up to the offices of Driscoll, Irving, Rafferty. He transcribes and organizes, cleans up the small burrs of language that Rafferty occasionally stumbles into in his long recorded ramblings. The man seems to have fallen, in his disclosures, from the high tetchy tone of Beacon Hill back to a Lower End bark. Jimmy has not seen Rafferty in many weeks now, just keeps on with the work. The checks come in regular disbursements and Jimmy has few places to spend them.

Today the detour to work is at this door, through which his former life seemed to thread itself as through the eye of a particular needle. He has in his pocket an envelope containing three hundred and twenty dollars in cash. After the momentary hesitancy he had expected walking down, he pushes through and into the bar, to no response. In this place where he had sat for years shoulder to shoulder with these men, drinking, no one even registers his return. He cannot even claim a shunning, which would have had some bite to it. What he sees is simply himself, the tilting of heads over glasses, the talismanic touch of a sweating beer bottle. The devotional act, heads bowing up and down the line. The blare of television over the silence of daytime drinkers. The numbing of all beyond it.

Jimmy sees Tommy Morton down at the far end of the bar, already glassy and remote of spirit, as if his body had been left behind. Jimmy comes up almost to him before he turns. Looking at the man while sober, he can see how gone Tommy really is, so early.

"What are you here for?" Tommy says. "Gonna knock me down again?"

"No," Jimmy says softly. "I just came to give you your money back."

"Oh. Okay."

Jimmy takes the folded bills from his pocket and puts the money into Tommy's hand. Tommy does not count it and does not look at Jimmy.

"I have to ask you something," Jimmy says. "Did I say what the money was for?"

"You said you needed to get rid of somebody. Or something like that."

Jimmy thinks about this for a bit. "Did I say who?"

"No."

"Do you know what I meant by 'get rid of'?"

"I took it to mean in the not-so-good kind of way."

"Wow," Jimmy says. "And you gave me the money to do it?"

"Hey," Tommy says, "I was clearly shitfaced."

"And was I?"

"Hell, yeah. We were drinking together. You were working me for my money the whole time. I was so tanked I actually listened. I shed a tear for your problems."

"I don't remember anything. When was this?"

"Long time. Long time without my money back. I had to borrow from my brother-in-law, who is never going to let me off the hook on this one."

"When was this, Tommy?"

"Back in the summer. Labor Day weekend. I had just come from Mass and you were on me. You took my money and flaked on me. You took my money and all of a sudden never set foot in this place from then on."

"I actually decided to give up drinking," Jimmy says.

"More bullshit from this guy," Tommy Morton says in general proclamation.

"Did I say why three-twenty?"

Tommy shrugs. "It's just what I had. You said you needed more than that. You were tanked, going around here, telling everybody you needed money. Everybody else was sober enough to tell you to feck off. Me, stupid. I'd just cashed my check. You said you'd be back the next day."

"I'm sorry, Tommy. Thanks for lending me the money. So I said I had to get rid of somebody."

"Yeah, I was a drunk giving his money to a drunk," he says. "You didn't use the exact words 'get rid of,' you were telling me you had to make peace. 'I have to make peace,' you kept on, almost crying about it. It sounded like it was something you were about to do, right then, that minute."

"Look," Jimmy says, going into his wallet and extracting more bills. "Here's another sixty for the trouble."

When he leaves the place, Jimmy feels some relief that it had happened before he stopped drinking, and that he had apparently not acted on whatever he had drunkenly conceived. It wasn't like he hadn't done things like that in his drunkenness. *No harm done*, seems the resolution. Money borrowed and repaid, with interest. But as he walks, a dry and dying man easing into the peace of clear endings, he now puts it together: where it was he'd been driving toward, drunk out of his senses, the day Butchie Morrissey fell from the back of that car.

+ +

67

At home, Colleen finds herself restless, constantly up and moving even though there is little to occupy herself. She comes home from work, makes herself a simple dinner, and then, most nights, sits flipping cyclically through the channels on the television. Each day seems to organize itself around her efforts to be heard. She has gone through the phone book making lists of every church in Boston, then each one in the suburbs, then at the outer reaches of the Archdiocese. She believes the moment must come when someone will listen, and act. These are priests after all, not criminals. They are men who cannot plead neutrality to matters of sin and conscience. They are men who have been blessed and consecrated; men who, by virtue of their black clothes and their collars, seem different than they would otherwise be—sad, overweight, dank-smelling older men who, without the script, might actually find troubles in the daily human discourse. But they are more than this by virtue of their circumstances, of their benediction. They would not have a rational way of acting as if this did not matter to them. And it has always seemed to her that, if they know that this has happened to even one boy, they will rise against it, as they (always) say the Gospel says, as she had heard in every dusty, light-rimed Sunday morning homily of her childhood.

Most of them believe she's a nut, or badly want to. Chuckie has clearly come to some negative judgment of her as well. This man, whom she had thought all along was trying to ingratiate himself with her, now steers past, politely but clearly, for the most part done with it all. He seems in fact to be disgusted by her. At the airport he makes his due rounds, but where he once found a way to wander by, to strike up a chat, to have a concern, he now takes the opposite tack, pushing on with an opprobrium she never saw in him before. And there is no doubt that she feels stung by it, the scorn of this man who for so long she had felt the need to put off and be careful with. It makes her appreciate his character, if not his proposed methods. She knows what he wanted to do, and she couldn't do it. She knows that he wanted to pull her son off the street and somehow wrestle him back into his bedroom, as if by doing that everything could go back to being as it was. As if going back to that was the answer. She cannot do that; she now holds out in the vague hope that someone will simply come along and help. But that was also what she was thinking when this kindly older priest presented himself, offering to spend "one-on-one time" guiding her eleven-year-old son. Now she has the wistful notion that it might be different, that there are still good people out there, that things can turn.

Christopher's bedroom door is locked and there is food missing from the fridge and cupboard, giving her the hope that contact might still be made. Despite what Chuckie has told her, she believes her son still lives here, that he indeed comes and goes in spectral silence. Her faith in that is brought to bear by the nearly unnoticeable absence of items: a missing cookie, the disappearance of a can of spaghetti, a half-inch less milk in the bottle when she lifts it from the refrigerator. The bedroom door now remains locked, a message she isn't quite sure how to interpret.

What he has apparently never realized is that there is a key for that door, old and tarnished, that has always sat in the messy drawer in the kitchen. She never knew it actually worked. The first time she tried it, there was no give; but in her need to be in that room she had sprayed WD-40 into the lock again and again until one day it mercifully gave. She negotiates the room as if at an archeological site, trying to disturb nothing, taking in the stale odor as if in a freshly cracked sarcophagus. She is now, as always, led to the closet, for that revisiting, for that touching, to check, to puzzle.

She slowly opens the closet door. She kneels in front of it. She has a system for this now, a way of moving and stacking, so that, when she is done, each item is back in its place, leaving no evidence of her incursion. The opening of one box and then the next, the careful stacking of the old baseball cards, and then to the final box, the one with the money. But when she opens that last lid and sees the guns, she nearly slumps back onto her haunches, struggling to breathe. She cannot bring herself to touch them. Shaking, she restacks the boxes quickly, trying not to think at all until she can leave the room and lock it and retreat to her own bed. Turning the lock back into place, she feels almost as if she will involuntarily urinate, but she works to control herself and makes sure to replace the key in its properly concealed spot. In her bedroom, she shuts the door and sits on the end of the bed, shaking nearly in convulsions. The guns lie in there, only a wall away, predators in wait. It feels as if everything around her is about to somehow and instantly explode.

68

The motel is even worse than the others, a dingy place up on the ridge in Walpole, the City View, apparently so-called because the buildings of downtown Boston lie clustered and barely visible on the far north horizon, with expanses of storage warehouses and auto-parts stores in between. It's a cold late afternoon, end of November and the days short; when Jeanmarie gets out of Marty's car, she can feel the bite of the wind.

"It's Room 38," Marty says, pointing along the drive-up accommodations. "Down at the end."

"Why are we doing this here?" Jeanmarie says. "Why aren't we just doing this in your studio?"

"Can't have the same background every time," Marty says. "We're 'on location.' Don't you know what that means?"

"I guess. But I'm freezing."

"We'll be inside in a minute, so lighten up," Marty says as he gets his camera bag out of the trunk.

She can sense, almost always now, the bite of Marty's tone, and indeed hers to Marty has the same edge of irritation and condescension. He's never tried to make a move on her, but there is now the lingering sense of them as bickering couple, as ball and chain. She finds him virtually insufferable at times; but then again, Marty was always a loser. She can feel duly disturbed then that he has become her benefactor. She thinks at times about breaking away from him, but lacks the contacts to do so. She could go to a modeling agency or maybe to a real photographic studio, but she really has no sense of how to even start that process. She could head out to California, on her saved money, but she needs a contact there and Marty isn't ready to give her one.

Marty has gotten the room key already, and she shivers as he opens up. The room is as cold and bleak as it is outside. The tamped-down carpet seems completely beaten of its color, the beds concave beneath threadbare covers. Marty turns the heater under window to High and then finds the remote and pops on the television. A game show is on. Jeanmarie sits on the bed with her coat on and questions her motivation.

"This place totally sucks," she says. "Why are we here?"

Marty lets out a long breath, as if he finds her impossibly dull and is tired of having to explain. "Like I said, this is a *location*. It's that it sucks is why we're here. Don't probe into the dark fantasies of men."

She answers him only by turning the channel to "Montel." Jeanmarie has become something of a talk show addict, sitting on her bed learning the currency of empowerment and sex-positive lifestyle and having the courage to dream. If she told Marty about those dreams right now, he'd probably laugh at her. A couple of months ago, he would have told her he'd get her there. Montel is revealing to a young husband and wife that they are actually, and unbeknownst to themselves, half-brother and half-sister. The audience shrieks.

Marty opens his camera bag and begins getting his equipment ready. He pops the flash a few times and screws the camera body onto a tripod. Then he turns to look at her, in her furry coat and gray sweats and heavy boots.

"Why don't you go in the bathroom and get yourself ready?" he says. "The guy will be here anytime."

She takes her coat off and throws it on the bed, then kicks her boots onto the rug and goes into the bathroom. The tiles on the floor are like ice. She has in her bag the requisite costuming—the stockings and bustier and panties—and the gun, loaded, which she has become less afraid of and carries just in case.

She decides not to put on her costume until the place gets a whole lot warmer. She starts with her makeup, laying it on thick and heavy. She loves the transmutation she sees in the mirror at moments like this. Her habit is to do her right eye completely, then her left. People from her past life would probably never even recognize her in one of these photos—part geisha and part burlesque, the adaptation into a more amplified version of her own essential self.

She has one eye done when she hears a knock, and Marty's muffled greeting, then the slam of the door. Then silence. The heat is not kicking in and she doesn't want to undress until it does. She comes out of the bathroom, halfway into character, the half-face of Sandra atop the sweats-clad body of Jeanmarie, but the room is empty. At the window, she looks out to the parking lot and sees Marty in discussion with her apparent co-star, a skinny, middle-aged man who is vaguely unappealing. The man looks overly nervous. Marty holds out his hands, as if calming him, and then, by the way their heads bow in toward each other, it seems their voices must have dropped. The man looks around, then takes a clump of cash from his pocket and hands it to Marty.

When the two of them come into the room, she's sitting on the bed, one eye made up and the other not, still in her sweats.

"Why aren't you ready?" Marty says.

"Why is he giving *you* money?" she says back.

The man looks instantly alarmed. "Hey, what is this?" he says to Marty.

"Why is he paying you if you're selling these pictures on the Internet?" she says.

The man says, "You're selling these pictures on the Internet? You said only I would get them."

"Fuckin' A," Marty says, groaning out a breath.

"Who the hell are you?" Jeanmarie says to the man.

"Me? I'm leaving, that's who I am," he says.

"Hang on, let me explain," Marty says to him.

"No need," the man says. "Can I please have my money back?"

"Look, it's fine," Marty says. "Just wait."

"Can I just have my money back?" the man says.

"Give him his fucking money back," Jeanmarie says.

"I can't give it back to you," Marty says. "I already paid for the room."

The man knows he has choices, but none of them seem as appealing as just walking. His face is flushed in fury and frustration, and, as he opens the door, he says to Marty, "This isn't over."

The man closes the door behind him and Marty watches him walk to his car. Marty turns and says to Jeanmarie, "Why don't you wipe that fucking look off your face?"

"Why is he paying you?"

293

"Look," Marty says, waving her off dismissively, "you just don't understand revenue streams."

"You said this was a modeling gig. That's what you told me."

Marty just laughs. "What the hell is the difference? You're getting paid to have sex. How could it possibly matter what you call it?"

"I want you to take me home," she says. "I'm not working with you again."

"Then I'm not going to be paying for that apartment."

"You're a liar. You said you'd get me lined up in LA."

"You're still underage," Marty says.

"Yeah," she says. "I'm fucking *underage*. I should call the cops and tell them what you've been doing to me."

Marty straightens then. "You'd do that to me, after all I've done for you?"

"What have you done for me?" she says.

"You're making a mistake, saying that," Marty says. "You don't want that kind of trouble."

"You'd be the one in trouble," she says. "It wasn't the deal, what you're doing. How many of these guys have been paying you?"

"A lot," Marty says. "You think I'm making this money on the Internet? There are a million girls out there. Half the girls from your fucking high school class are showing their tits on the Internet these days. For free!" Marty snorts. "That's a good joke, what you just said. I did what I had to do to help you not be living on the damned streets."

"Take me home right now," Jeanmarie says. She is in the bathroom, packing her bag.

"I'll take you home when you stop mouthing off at me."

"I'll mouth off all I want," she says. "Maybe I'll tell the cops, and then I'll go to California on my own. Maybe I'll tell my *father*."

"I'm telling you only one more time that you're making a huge mistake with this," Marty says. "So just get in the fucking car."

+ + + + + + + + + + + + + + + + + + +

69

The building of one's reputation is a curious thing. At Red Dris-coll's funeral, a succession of speakers had come forward to eulogize a grand and wise old man. I sat silently contemplating that he'd been a man who had probably never stopped thinking of himself as a city kid who had to do what he had to do, who got by on scrappiness and the willingness to fight dirtier than everybody else. Leaving that church for the ride to the cemetery, I was only beginning to fully grasp that I had become a man with a certain reputation, thanks largely to my art collecting and my careful charitable donations, which were meant to create the image of a publicity-shy do-gooder—exactly the image to generate even more press and accolades. Like Red, however, I sometimes fell back on the probably truthful notion that I was still, at my core, just a Southie dirtbag playing out the same old grudges.

There was something sporting about the way I had reengaged with the infamous McX, who had built his little empire on the more usual muscle and fear, with no flair or elegance whatsoever. McX, I learned, was bent on unapologetically shaking down anybody with money, and tended to pinpoint the especially fulsome wellsprings of money. When a Hollywood film was shot in Boston, McX and his gang virtually took it over, sabotaging equipment and vehicles until the stunned Hollywood types, used to far more mannerly vicious-

ness, put McX and his crew in obscenely high-paying no-show jobs. When cargo ships came into the docks, the pirates were the ones sitting in trucks at the water's edge. And from what I could gather, the only people who engaged King of the Road Moving were insurance fraud types who knew that the Boston police were either too frightened or too well compensated to pursue such matters.

And it was this intriguing business concern that I slowly circled in on, planning my next move in this long-dormant match. Lydell Barrett was my nervous agent, someone I knew I could trust because of his being fully implicated, which was exactly why I retained him.

By then I had purchased a home in Vermont, to suit the interests of my skiing children and their non-skiing mother, for whom this had become a fashionable necessity. And it occurred to me that a transfer of expensive art from my Beacon Hill home to my Vermont chalet was just the job for the men at King of the Road. It was my wish that Mr. Barrett, armed with a list of my holdings and their insurance value, should arrange for said transportation within a week. It was to be mentioned that I was the owner, but with no mention that I understood this to be McX's company.

When Barrett returned, ashen, to say that the move had been scheduled, he asked me why.

"You know what this is about and who this man is," Barrett said. "So why would you do it?"

"To get my paintings up to Vermont, of course," I said.

I brought in packers to lay the works into carefully sealed crates that, once closed, could not be opened without leaving some telltale sign: signatures across seals, airtight vinyl sheathing, brass screws. I was not going to allow the works to be quickly eyeballed. There was going to be a challenge to this. The insurance people had come and photographed each work, at my behest; my art advisor came and fretfully watched the removal of each work from my wall. When they left that evening, eight separate crates stood leaning against the wall of my foyer, my de Koonings and O'Keeffes and Pollocks, my Picasso drawings and my Eakins. Each was marked with a number that corresponded to a description on the list I had made "for my own reference purposes." At the same time, I was having a new alarm system installed in the Vermont place. My wife had argued against moving the paintings, concerned that I would adorn the walls with the horrid works I kept in the back of the basement, but I had assuaged her by promising that our walls would soon be filled with new and greater works, something she sounded deeply suspicious about, making me feel again the taint I could never fully exorcise, that of the incorrigibly uncultured. All was in place, and I awaited my opponent's response to my gambit.

The movers came in early the next morning, paying what seemed to be undue attention to my home, a place of a type into which they had most likely not ever tread. And who could blame them, coming from the shag-rug-and-plaid-couch world they lived in on those narrow Southie streets? They were young men in some godforsaken apprenticeship with McX, regrettably their apparent best bet.

One of them, in an attempt to strike up conversation, said, "Is this all the artwork you own?"

"All the valuable artwork, at least. I have more in the basement that aren't so expensive, but truthfully they're far more to my liking. One in particular is probably almost worthless, but still I like it more than all the others. That's why it stays here."

"These, however," I said, patting the top of the crate of O'Keeffes, "are worth a king's ransom, so I beg you to be gentle."

"That's why we're here, sir," he said, and when I realized he was fishing for a tip, I duly rewarded him with a twenty.

The moving of the crates to the King of the Road truck idling outside was quick and silent, and soon enough the truck was rolling down onto Charles Street and on toward the Expressway. I wondered what it might have been like if I were really seeing my prized art for the last time, and if I were such a person as to love the art for itself. Unfortunately or otherwise, I did not; it was simply another trapping, fully insured. We, Mary and the girls and I, were being driven, then, in a limo, a ride that promised the usual bickering and boredom. But my heart felt merry, for the anticipation is often as succulent as the resolution. I had put many chips on the table this time, and had in my mind constructed a perfect game.

I watched my wife and daughters chattering on as we rode. I was aware, as they were not, that it would be a weekend of disruption, one that would, more than likely, bring in police, insurance investigators and probably reporters. For what McX (I was betting) did not understand was that the theft of great art is more a public violation than a private one, and that men such as myself are never truly thought to own the works as much as provide stewardship for them. I also knew that I could resolve the matter quickly and with a flourish, for this would indeed be my last flawless move.

We arrived in Stowe, in the driveway of the chalet, to find my art advisor and Lydell Barrett, looking at me without apparent affect, with the faces of people about to break very bad news. I emerged from the car with my own face of chipper resoluteness.

"Everything all right?" I said, as my art advisor cleared her throat.

"The crates arrived on time, with no problem," she said.

I looked at Barrett, who gave me a nearly imperceptible shrug. "Lovely, then."

"But they were the wrong crates," she said. "It's all the worthless art they brought up."

I looked at Barrett as the blood drained from my face, for it had been he and I who had switched the crates late the night before, moving the good art back to the safety of the basement and the bad art to the place by the front door. It had never been my plan to allow my great art to be stolen, but rather to imagine McX's face as the true junk was revealed. But they had not touched it.

"And there's something else," Barrett said. "Your house was broken into, probably not long after you left to come here. Your neighbor noticed the front door had been open for hours. The police are there now. Your house has been ransacked."

70

He sits clenched at the end of his bed, his jacket on as if he is about to suddenly go somewhere, although he is not close to making a move. Christopher has sat in this apartment with his jacket on for three days, has not eaten and has barely slept; still she has not appeared. Her clothes are gone, nothing left in the small closet but the jangle of wire clothes hangers. He has desperately searched the apartment for his father's gun as well, and it is not here. He is becoming infused with a grieving anger, a place to which he has been many times before and through which he had come to this apartment, with her, trying to escape. And the only place he can imagine her being now is back with Bobby, up in that apartment without having left any word as to what's going on, as to *why*.

The first of these three nights he has slept in his usual spot on the floor, but never fully descending into sleep, one part of his mind vigilant for the sound of the key in the door. It was only when he had swung open her closet door to find her things gone, that, with nearly weeping desperation, he'd begun to hunt for his father's .380, running his hands along the carpet under the bed, and then between the mattresses, and then beginning the crashing hunt through cabinets and drawers and under the sink, and then, gasping for breath, his brain screaming at itself to *think*, where would someone hide a gun, where would someone like Jeanmarie decide to hide a gun, because she would not, ever, under any circumstances, leave *him* and take *it*. Did she not understand that this was *his father's gun*. He had removed it from its place and brought it to her, to protect her. There could be no betrayal to him more profound than this. He tries to push the thought from his mind on the grounds that this is probably all perfectly explainable and that, if he lets thoughts of such betrayal take hold in his mind, it might actually harm their friendship, which, at this moment, could perfectly well be just fine, just as much as it could be devastatingly over.

So he waits. He does not recall sleeping at all last night, although he might have. He had moved to the bed, but slept on top of the covers. The hours had come to seem interminable, the uncountable glances, despite himself, at the red LED glow of the alarm clock; he had spent it mostly fighting the specter of what came next, where he would go, and how he would survive. He had exited life with his mother at least in part because of the promise of this one, and now she seems gone.

Out the high window to street level, Marty's car has rolled by several times, slowly, and Christopher has waited for what he thought would be the inevitable slam of the car door, the next slam of the outside door, and the keying in the lock that has never come. Marty has always been a puzzle to him, all this about modeling and shoots and gigs. He doesn't want to think of her giving it away to the entire world, opening herself to that loser Bobby, maybe even to Marty, giving it to anybody who asks or has a dollar, except him: shutting herself to him, the only one of all of them filled with something that might approach real love for her. He doesn't want to imagine himself once again pushed out of the kind of world that comes so easily to those who deserve none of it.

He wants to be sitting here waiting and simultaneously out hunting for her. His immediate desire is to go back to his old bedroom, get the stolen guns, and lay siege to Bobby's. Let them try to shoot him with his father's gun, it wouldn't matter. He would wipe them all out. He would cut them up and end their miserable lives, which would deny them of nothing and deny no one of them. He can sometimes imagine a moment like that as a release of every sin that has ever lived in him, a sudden decompression on the other side of which is peace, simplicity, a brain without the same coursing thoughts he has tried to run from. He has never actually shot a gun but he has read everything there is about how to do it. It would be easy. He would wear gloves to avoid leaving prints and fling the guns, afterwards, into the landfill. He would find a way out of the city, without money, and he would disappear. There is no way he would be found. He doesn't even have identification. And if he is found, the worst he would ever pull would be Juvy Hall. Unlike the world of his knights—his noble warriors fighting under God's eyes for those things that were meaningful—pretty much everybody gets away with everything these days, and nobody at all is paying attention.

71

He enters the place the same way as before, not exactly a sneaky ingress, but fully mindful of being noticed. Up the back stairwell, Jimmy is not even sure that Butchie Morrissey is still here, or even among the living. But at the door he sees Butchie in exactly the same position as he had been weeks ago, on that first visit. The television is on, tuned to some nattering daytime fare, but Butchie only stares blankly off toward nothing. There seems none of the thinker at all in Butchie, no intellect to be used and cultivated. Just a dumb fuck from Southie whose stupidity—that little brain that allowed him to roll off the back of a car and snap his neck—is in its own hell now, lack of movement without the compensation of meaningful thought. He lies there in his bed wishing someone would enter this room and kill him. That's his best plan, even after months of around-the-clock thinking. *Kill me. My mind has nothing to offer. I should not exist.*

Jimmy has no idea whether Butchie is a religious man, and he doesn't know whether, in his desire to die, Butchie simply seeks blankness, the ceasing of all consciousness, or an alternate unclenching, the sense that there is an afterlife to which he will be delivered. But given Butchie's track record, he seems screwed either way: Petty thief, apparent rapist, who knows what else. What would he be delivered to, unless he thinks his paralysis is indeed his penance?

Jimmy has no idea, but knows he has done his best not to think too hard about what comes after. Jimmy nearly resents Butchie for his accident, which brought him to this, a sober clarity about how sick he is and where it all goes. He wonders whether he'd have been happier staying in his drunken oblivion, then simply stopping like an unwound watch, one last tick and then silence. It is, after all, the reason he began the drink—not to think, to escape contemplation. He was young but he had a right.

He enters the room, and Butchie does not look. Jimmy presumes it could not possibly matter to him. But Jimmy stands at the foot of the bed and Butchie's eyes finally shift to him.

"What do you want?"

"I'm here to see if you still want me to kill you."

"Now?"

"No. Not now. Later, maybe."

"You're just here to talk about killing me."

"Yes."

"This isn't like the rest, trying to get me to want to live. Playing head games."

"No."

"What's your name?"

"I'd rather not say."

"So you won't get caught."

"That probably doesn't matter. I just would rather not say. It makes it too personal."

Butchie considers this. "So what made you change your mind?"

"I'm going to die. Soon."

"Of what?"

"Alcoholism. Liver disease. Advanced."

"No options?"

"I chose not to take them."

"Why is that?"

"I'd just rather get it over with. That's my choice. I have no medical coverage anyway. I don't want to fight for the right to live and die anyway."

Butchie contemplates this. "Then if you kill me," he says, "you better not get caught."

"Why?"

"Because if they put you in jail for killing me, you'll get all the medical attention you need. They're obligated."

Jimmy nods. "I guess I never thought of that."

"They'll give you the best medicine, maybe save you, and put you in prison for most of the rest of your life."

"If I get caught."

"Yeah, if you get caught."

"I never thought of *that*," Jimmy says.

"So you kill me and get your life saved, maybe."

"And go to prison? Forget it."

"So that makes two of us," Butchie says. "Two who want to die. So what is your problem you don't even want to try?"

"I'm just tired," Jimmy says.

"Oh." Butchie Morrissey seems to be getting angry that Jimmy won't even try. "Tired of what?" he says.

"I've been a drinker pretty much all my life. It wears you down. I don't really even know how to live sober."

"Yeah, well, I'm tired, too," Butchie says, as the respirator hisses on.

"When I was driving behind you and your friends, I was completely shitfaced," Jimmy says. "You were in my way. I had to go somewhere. I only remembered a couple of days ago where I was even going."

"Oh yeah? Where?"

"To return some money. Some money I had taken from someone years ago. I felt guilty about it ever since. It happened when I was a kid. Just before I started drinking. I used up the money thinking I'd feel better, but I didn't. It had always been on my mind. That day I was trying to take another shot at squaring it. But of course I was completely drunk. If I told you what my actual plan was, you'd tell me it makes no sense. But it made sense to me that day, that drunk."

"Yeah, I was really drunk, too," Butchie says, and looks off toward the light of the window. Looking at him, Jimmy finds it hard to think of him as a kid; he has aged considerably in only a few months. His neck has the distended bloat that makes his chin sink turtlish into the soft flesh; the arms seem not the same ones he recalls from that day, no more tan or muscle but the purplish crosshatching of blood vessels.

Jimmy waits a while but nothing is said. He turns and moves quietly toward the door.

"Hey," Butchie says.

"Yeah?"

"You'll come back, right?"

7 2

When Chuckie sees her approaching on the concourse, he tries to evade, turning in a manner meant to be casual, as if he simply hasn't seen her. He heads down the way, nodding at travelers, his security-guard shuffle just a touch too quick, and he seems to be making a point not to glance back. She has to call his name twice until he finally looks at her.

"I'm sorry to bother you," Colleen says. "I know you don't want to be bothered."

"You know I already tried to help you," Chuckie says. "I really did but I can't keep doing this."

"Just this once," she says. "I need you to look at something. Out in the parking garage."

"I'm working here," he says.

"Just this once," she says.

"Just this once," he says.

She goes back to the ticket desk and takes a small gym bag from a cabinet, pulling it over her shoulder. She tells the other girl at the desk she's taking a ten-minute break; Chuckie can't help but see the roll of the eyes from the other girl, and from the long queue of passengers with their bags.

Up the escalator and through the two sets of sliding doors, across the sky bridge to Central Parking, they walk in silence. He follows her up the concrete stairwell to Level 4, and then out past the parked cars to where there are a few rows of empty spaces. When they come to what seems a dead end out by the far wall, he says, "So where's your car?"

"I don't have the car. I just didn't want to do this inside. You know, the security cameras and everything."

"That doesn't sound good," he says. "I'm asking myself what I'm even doing out here right now, when you tell me something like that."

"I just need you to look at something," she says. She puts the bag on the concrete and unzips it. She opens the mouth of the bag as widely as she can and looks up at him.

"Holy shit," he says. "Are you crazy, bringing these into the *airport?*"

"I was hoping maybe they aren't real. Are they real?"

"Of course they're real," Chuckie says. "Are they loaded?"

"I have no idea. All the way out on the bus, I was terrified they'd go off."

Chuckie reaches in and takes out the topmost gun.

"This is a Tec-9," he says. "It's not loaded." He looks at the others. "None of these are loaded. That's a Galena and that's a Smith & Wesson. Where did you get these?"

"They were in Christopher's closet. With the money."

"Then you need to call the police. The kid is too young to be stashing guns. Obviously, something really bad is going to happen."

"I can't call the police. The police won't help. It will only make things worse."

"Then I can't help you. I won't. Look at us out here, with *guns.* Do you have any idea how much shit this could get us both into?"

For the first time, he sees her begin to really cry. He can't help but think about all her rebuffs, back when he was simply trying to be friendly. Now she looks at him in imploring desperation. "What do I do now, Chuck? Just tell me what to do now . . ."

"My opinion? Throw the damn guns into the harbor right now. Or go to the police and drop them off in a bag. Just don't put them back where they were."

"But then he'll know that I know. I don't know what he'll do when he knows that I know. The only reason I touched them was so you could look at them."

"Look, those are real guns," Chuckie says. "Really dangerous guns. You need to do something with them."

"I'm not sure," she says.

Chuckie shakes his head ruefully. "You can't come to me anymore. I can't help you. I ought to take them from you right now and get rid of them, but with my luck someone'll find them on me. I don't need that kind of problem."

Colleen is still crying. She pulls the zipper shut and nods, blinking back her tears.

"You need to not come near me anymore," Chuckie says. "If you can't do what needs to be done, no one can help you, and no one can help your son."

"I know," she whispers.

"Look at him, for Christ's sake. Hanging around with some skeevy prostitute, staying out of school, hiding guns that came from who knows where."

"I know."

"I understand what you think happened to him," Chuckie says. "I'm not sure that's still an excuse."

She lunges at him, slapping and screaming, and, with his arms up to fend her off, he feels one of her fingernails break skin, drawing blood. She is pounding at him with ineffective fists, shrieking. He backs up and pushes her away and brings his hand to his cheek where he can feel the drip of blood.

"What the fuck?" he says. "I can't go back to work like this . . ." He looks at his fingers, red with blood, and says, "Give me a Kleenex or something."

She goes through her bag and finds a paper napkin crumpled at the bottom. He takes it and presses it to his eye. "Now please go away," he says. "I'm begging you to. Go do something to the people who really ought to be getting their eyes gouged. I'm just too easy a target, aren't I?"

"Yes," she says, almost inaudibly.

He takes the napkin away and sees how much blood it has already soaked up. "Goddamn it. Now I'm going to have to take the rest of the shift off, and you know what? My boss will be pissed, on account of all the other shifts I took off. So just go away, and leave me alone. I like my job, and don't want to have to find another job because of you."

"I understand," Colleen says.

"And get those damned guns out of this airport before there's real trouble."

"I will."

"Then that's it, for you and me," Chuckie says. "I'm just not listening anymore."

+ +

73

The irony, in the end, was that McX had outmaneuvered himself. He had seen my ploy for what it was, and had at least grown up enough that he didn't go for it. Instead, it seems clear, he had someone break into the house nearly the moment we left—if they weren't already inside, having possibly slipped in as they packed the truck. They'd cut the electricity to disable the alarm system (which, I had to later admit, was not as up-to-date as it might have been—having come with the house's hefty price, I had assumed better of it). But what they did then was unanticipated. They had exacted visible damage with limited effect, overturning furniture without breaking it, cracking windows that could be easily replaced, and pulling things out of drawers to create a look of chaos and harm. It was a psychological invasion, in essence. But, ignorants that they were, they had found their way to the basement, to my supposedly cherished but worthless works of art, to make a point. By slashing them into ribbons. And of course what they had done was vandalize millions of dollars' worth of art, because they were too uneducated to understand what they were even looking at as they put their box cutters to it. When we went to the basement, my art advisor burst into wailing tears, although my assumption was that it was loss of commissions she grieved. Her love of art was really no greater than mine.

I had suddenly been made into a very public and sympathetic victim. It wasn't just the cost to me—I would have been a fool not to have had all of it heavily insured—but that I was seen, as many art collectors are, as being merely a custodian of something that really belonged to the ages, this great art, now lost to future generations. The Globe's headline read, "Art destroyed in home of Beacon Hill philanthropist," and described how I had intended to ship the works to Vermont before a last-minute change of heart, a "premonition."

The event was not something that would be taken lightly. The public outrage was more than I would have expected. Art, destroyed! The mayor, clearly having heard from spooked Beacon Hill residents (without whose generous donations, both legal and otherwise, he could not flourish), made it a sudden priority for the Boston police, who requested assistance from the State police and the FBI Crime Lab. The heat was on, and when I told the detective the name of the moving company that had been in just that morning, he hyperventilated a bit, thinking about it.

And again on a Saturday not long after that, I made my way from a late-autumn round of golf back down into the old neighborhood, back to Muldoon's, to the seat at the end of the bar where McX was, apparently as usual, camped on his stool. I said nothing, and he did not so much as glance over, although in that quiet establishment you could hear the nearly pneumatic issue from his nostrils. I ordered a beer and slowly drew the foam off the top. If you'd been standing there at the bar you would never have known that anything had transpired between us. But it had. Very much so.

I knew McX would never be brought to justice, but I also knew that he suddenly found himself on a short leash with the people he once had in his pocket. My insurance company, after repeatedly prodding the police to make an arrest, finally threw their hands up after being made aware of who the prime suspect was, and how his arrest could only make things more difficult for everyone. It was a subtle turning, and meanwhile it happened that my paintings had been appraised as being even more valuable than I'd thought. The two million or so I netted on the settlement became a donation to the Museum of Fine Arts, for which I was celebrated in a Globe editorial and given a delightful cocktail party by the trustees of the museum. My wife could not contain her delight at this arrival, and I hinted that more donations could be in the offing. A short time later, I was invited to join that august board myself, which I happily did.

I also knew that the game was clearly back on. I once again felt purpose and passion in life. It was clearly time for my move if the game was to continue, despite the fact that his countermove had been disastrous. My wife and daughters had been living in terror since the break-in, but I couldn't help being curt with them, telling them, in essence, to suck it up. A new alarm system had been installed, which appeased them a bit, but their whining was of little concern to me now. I was learning that the gap between them and me could never be bridged.

The time came, some months later. The Museum was to lend several Vermeers and Breughels to the gallery at Columbia University in New York. These were the kinds of paintings to which the word "priceless" is often ascribed. I was at my first board meeting, and as the discussion went on, it was my suggestion that there was no better firm to transport the goods than King of the Road Moving. "They moved art to Vermont for me and it went off without a wrinkle," I said. "I only wish, on that day, I'd put my better works in their care. In fact, I'm so confident in them I'd be happy to pay for this move."

Odd request though it was, I was the newest donor with less of an entrée but far more money than nearly anyone else at the table. It was put to the vote. Agreed. I called Barrett the next day and asked him to make the necessary arrangements. He shook his head, ruefully; I knew he would have been inclined to resign right then and there if he could have made even a fraction of the money I paid him somewhere else.

A few days later, I had Barrett describe to me the expressions on the faces of the front men at King of the Road as he explained the contents of what was to be shipped, the value of the works, and the seriousness of the task with which they were being entrusted. It was, he had told them, an extremely important task, which, if it were to go wrong, would be a huge and possibly devastating embarrassment to the Museum's newest board member, one Terrence Rafferty . . .

74

When, on the fifth day, he hears the key in the apartment door, it is almost startling, like a bomb going off. The lock hasp turns, and then the knob. Christopher sits up to receive the entrant.

From the dark hallway comes a squat, white-haired man, moving with some effort and trundling a plastic bucket stacked with cleaning agents and rags. He is inside before he realizes Christopher is there, and, when he sees him, he does not react visibly. He only says, "Who are you?"

"I live here," Christopher says.

"No, that's not right. Nobody lives here."

"I've been living here with Jeanmarie."

"Who?"

"The girl who lives here."

"I don't know about any Jeanmarie. Like I said, nobody lives here. But someone's moving in tonight. And I don't think it's you."

"No, I'm serious, Jeanmarie has been living here for almost two months," Christopher says more firmly. "Who are you?"

The man puts the bucket down, with the affect of someone who has just spotted trouble. It is something he seems not particularly worried about. He plants his feet a little more widely, the practiced movement of someone who has had to deal with certain situations and irritations.

"I work for the owner," he says. "And what he told me is that this place has been vacant for months. And now someone has rented it." He looks around, and then says, "It doesn't look like anyone lives here. Except you. So how did you get in here?"

Christopher holds up his key.

"Go figure," the old man says. "I probably don't want to know anything about why you have a key to this apartment, because it's only going to get the both of us in hot water. But you have to leave anyway."

"Does the owner know Marty?"

"Marty who? How should I know who the owner knows? He owns a lot of units and I get hired to do cleanup. That's what I know. How old are you, anyway?"

"Fourteen."

"Well, you better run home now," he says. "Or I'll have to call somebody to come get you."

Christopher nods and gets his things together, of which there are few. The old man watches him and then holds his hand out for the key, which Christopher duly surrenders.

"Maybe I misunderstood," the old man says. "Maybe you were living here, got the key, whatever. But I know for a fact that a new tenant is coming in tonight. You wouldn't have wanted to get in trouble."

"Do you need any help?" Christopher says.

"What's that?"

"I'm looking for a job. I wondered if you needed any help."

The old man shakes his head. "I'm barely hanging on to this job," he says. "Sorry."

When Christopher comes out onto the street, it feels somehow different after five days inside. It is late afternoon and already dropping into darkness. The weather has turned cold; it seems as if there has been some definitive shift, winter now, Christmas season, something he has not ever had to contend with in this way. He has slept very little and the tiredness brings him more easily to shivers. He ate the last of the food two days ago, spooning margarine into his mouth and washing it down by holding his mouth against the faucet.

He needs to get the guns. He needs to figure out where he can sell them. With the right connections, the hundreds of dollars he can get will at least bridge the weeks until Christmas. He needs a place to stay, to hide, someplace where no one will think to look for him, if anyone is indeed looking. He has finally shaken off the odd feeling that someone is following him, which, in some ways, saddens him. But he has to assume he will be sought—if not by his mother, then at least by somebody from the school, where he has not shown up in two months. He needs to assume that someone is looking for him, that there is somebody for whom his absence from the world would be meaningful. And then he must hide from that person. He needs to find cover. He has no idea where that would be.

But first he wants his father's gun back. He cinches the hood of his sweatshirt tightly and begins to walk toward Bobby's. He is formulating a plan as he goes, and what he realizes is that it will take a gun to get one. He veers now toward the house, walking and thinking. If she is indeed at Bobby's and he shows up with a gun, he is likely to find a loaded gun pointed right back at him. He veers back in the direction of Bobby's, thinking now about first simply asking. But that thought has begun to infuriate him. Jeanmarie, after all this, with that gun, up there with the guy she supposedly needed the gun to protect herself from. He veers again, his direction now clear. His mother is at work and this is the time to go there.

He has full-body shivers now. He can feel how thin he has become, the looseness of his clothing, the slack in his belt. He knows there is food in the house, and he will take from it in a way that won't be noticed, small draws off many tops. He doesn't want to feel that anything is owed, but he also needs to eat, badly.

The walk has warmed him by the time he gets to the house. Outside, he circles several times, looking through the windows for movement. When he is satisfied that the place is empty, he goes around back and slides through his bedroom window. On his hands and knees, he moves to the closet and roots down through to his box. When he opens it and looks inside, he feels a tingle coming up the back of his neck. The guns are gone. He feels along the back of the closet, sliding his hands under the piles of clothes, trying to convince himself that he must not have put them in the box. But he did. And they are gone. And next to the space where the guns had been sits the money, and the note. Now seen by someone other than him. There is the same numb remove he always feels at such moments of violation; the slow rise of the curtain, the widening of distances. He closes the box, puts it back in the closet, and goes out the window.

+ +

75

And so Jimmy begins the route again, this time not from a bar but from his apartment, this time in the winter chill and not the heat of summer, this time not drunk but sober, this time not fighting himself but calm, the future foretold and the details to be attended to. He merges onto Day Boulevard, the feeble waves of the harbor running gray and icy up the flat sand. He approaches L Street, the Bath House on the right, the light. He has traveled this road thousands of times but, since the day of Butchie's accident, driving through this intersection has felt like punching through a membrane, like breaking through water to air. It is today that the journey will reach its completion.

He has the money in his pocket. Not *the* money, spent so quickly so many years ago and then such a source of torture, but *the* amount: Six hundred. How many times in his cups had he sought relief from that ache, and begun such actions? Uncountable. Drunk away. Forgotten by morning. It is the broken resolution, endlessly repeated. But now to be dispatched.

He drives past five more streets and takes a left. The destination of his many attempts was never the same geographically, and always the same philosophically. But today it is indeed the same plan, geography and philosophy, as that Sunday before Labor Day, the mirroring of the mission. All those scattered attempts go back to the source, like a river.

He is thirteen when he steals the six hundred dollars from his father's dresser drawer. He comes across it while looking for cigarettes, and, after holding the cash in his hand and feeling its weight and substance, he cannot put it back. He stands for long minutes at the open drawer in the empty house (where his mother was that day is lost to memory), and his mind runs through its gymnastic, Olympian rationalizing. He has no idea what kind of money his father actually earns, but he tells himself that this amount must be nothing, that it's little more than loose change, rolled up in a rubber band with the socks.

He pockets the cash. He does not close the drawer, leaves it open a hand's width. What he does do is open other drawers, pull out clothing, throw some on the floor. His mother's jewelry is locked in the cabinet in the wall, but the effect he is creating is one of attempt. He is improvising now, staging a burglary. These were the days when people didn't lock their back doors, when such an intrusion was as easy as it was unthinkable. He goes down to the dining room now. The good silver is in a locked cabinet, a place of substance. He finds a hammer in the basement and, holding it with the cuff of his sweater pulled over his hand, gives the cabinet a few well-placed blows. He drops the hammer nearby, as evidence of thwarted effort.

He hides the money, then exits the house through the back way, leaving the door ajar, a finishing touch that will be the first troubling sign. He is on the street and not wanting to be seen; he goes around to the back of the houses and pushes through the hedges, working his way out under the cover of shrubbery, until he's down by a brook and crashing through the water, away.

He comes home to find his mother overwhelmed and crying,

although nothing of hers is missing. It is the intrusion that has made her hysterical, a man in this house when she might have been home alone. She is going on about calling the police, but his father says No, nothing was taken. He sees Jimmy looking at him, then Jimmy looks away, feeling his face flushing, warm into burning. It occurs to Jimmy then that his father can't have looked in the open drawer, as illogical as that would seem. He spends the evening waiting for the discovery, for his father's reaction. At that moment, the money is in a paper bag in the back of the basement. The money has not left the house. Jimmy can still go to it and find a way of bringing it back, and somehow undo this. But he knows its reappearance in the sock drawer is his own indictment. Or maybe his urge to have the money is the simplest fact.

His father says nothing, and never says anything. It is as if the money has never existed. It is in the basement, like a spark that can spread into bad fire. It cannot remain. So Jimmy goes to work spending the money. On nothing. On subway rides into the city where he eats, goes to movies, takes cab rides. In the neighborhood, where he buys new friends by lending them money they will never pay back. It is hard to spend six hundred dollars on nothing, but over time he chips away at it, and one day he reaches into his pocket and there is nothing at the bottom of it. But he has freed himself of nothing, either.

His father seems to soften in those days as his mother hardens. He can feel her seething disapproval but she seems unable to simply say something out loud. She does not allow disrespect to her husband, and her barely contained rage seems all the greater for not being on her own behalf. His father, always kindly, becomes yet more solicitous, more available than he has been before that, with his work and his clients. He asks after Jimmy more often, takes a stronger interest, seems to demand less than what would seem fair—Jimmy's grades are decent but could be better, he offers little to his parents in the way of help or consideration, but avoids outward rudeness. He realizes one day that his mother no longer speaks to him directly, and only then in the presence of his father, as if it is now an obligation. It feels unbearable, on both accounts.

Not long after, he is invited to join three older boys in the woods, boys to whom he has lent money. They have apple wine and they offer it, the apparent squaring of obligations. It seems in their circuitous conversation that they are looking for money, but when it becomes clear he has no more, they still offer. Perhaps against future accruals. Jimmy drinks, and it is in a matter of short moments that all is lifted. It is the thing that frees him of his own sins. It is his own armor.

And now, driving, he pulls up to the front of the Most Holy Trinity Church rectory. He goes to the front door but does not ring the doorbell. He takes from his pocket the envelope on which he has written, *To help those less fortunate.* He pushes it through the slot and hears it hit the floor with a weighty slap. Despite all those times when he has imagined what this moment would feel like, it feels like nothing.

76

She has tried, truly. She has stood at midnight at the rail of the Charlestown Bridge, staring down into the waters with her bag over her shoulder, filled with guns. She has wanted to simply end their presence, to damn them to dark waters. She has wanted to scour them from her son's life. But she cannot. What hangs over all of it is what they both know, but are not supposed to: She, that he has had this happen; he, that she knows. This is the thing that prevents all else. It forbids her from real action, or from peace. It hovers, like a spirit, everywhere and all at once. It pushes out God and fills the space, silent.

She has stood on the bridge in the cold for better than an hour, trying. Between the late-night cars and the occasional pedestrian or a weaving couple straggling back from downtown, she has slipped her hand into the bag and let it slide around the metal, the surprising heaviness. She has told herself that, if she can send one down into the black water, then the others will be easy; she has told herself to do it until another car or another late-night walker comes upon her and she loosens her grip and holds her breath. She has imagined correctly that she could get in trouble with these weapons in her bag, unregistered and from who knows where. She has shuddered at the thought of knowledge so awful it will compel her to make these guns available again to her fourteen-year-old son, instead of puncturing that thin film of separation, to let him know that she knows.

She cannot find a taxi. She walks down off the bridge and onto Atlantic Avenue, and then to Summer Street, then across the channel back into Southie. It's after one now and the bars have closed and the traffic has picked up again, but she keeps her head down and trudges on. The police are a real worry now; she also cannot help thinking that it would serve her right, that she would benefit from the perception that there are consequences, that there are balances. But no one bothers her. No taxis come. The blisters come up on her heels and over the small toes. She arrives at her dark home past two in the morning, exhausted, her shoulder throbbing from the weight of the bag. Just inside the door she drops the bag and the guns inside make a solid knock on the hardwood floor that startles and frightens her. The guns have not gone off. She has to believe Chuckie is right, that they aren't loaded. But she knows nothing about guns. For all she knows, he is wrong. Her legs are shaky from the walking, but she is not ready to sleep. She sits on the couch looking at the bag for a while, as if it might go somewhere if she isn't paying attention. But it sits right there and after a long time she takes it into his room and puts the guns back in the box.

She misses her husband all the time, unceasingly, but right now it is as palpable as she has ever known. You have those people who are your guides through life, and she has lost hers, never to be replaced. And without him she can't be who she was, she can only be this, which is not good enough, not even close. She had thought at first, after his death, that it would be all right, that he had brought her along enough that she could carry on from there.

That would have been tribute to him. It wasn't as if he had come from the best of circumstances, but he had somehow developed a sense of things, a quiet certainty about the decisions he was making. It was more than sensible. Each step he took seemed another on the same straight line; since he died, she has felt trapped in a geometrically growing decision tree that has taken her far out to the edges. With every seemingly common-sense choice she has made, she has brought herself further ruin.

It is three in the morning and, outside, the first early snow has begun. Where is he? Where is her son? She imagines he might come back when the weather gets cold; maybe they can try to build something better. She opens the drawer next to the sink and takes out the straight razor she keeps there for cutting tags out of clothes and for peeling off labels. It was Barry's; he'd had a brief period in which he had tried shaving with this old tool, a long blade that folded into its own ebony handle. He'd gone back to a double-blade after a few too many nicks and tissue-stanched slices; but she'd liked it, that brief time in which he had seemed older and they seemed more real as a couple, because he stood in the bathroom and shaved like that.

She runs the bath. The water steams as it rises, and she takes her clothes off and puts them in the hamper, then sits on the toilet seat waiting for the tub to fill. When it is done, she turns the old ivory handles shut and gets in. She eases into the water, which is so hot it reddens her skin almost immediately, bringing a rising flush to her face. She sinks in to her neck and, when the water stops sloshing, the house is silent save for the drip from the faucet and the intermittent clank of the radiator. Outside, the snow falls lightly and will not stick, too early in the winter yet; she hopes

Christopher is somewhere where he can feel some happiness he does not have here.

She takes the razor from the sink top and opens it. She feels useless in a way that she can hardly bear. She has lately thought more about this, of how to put it all to its conclusion. She wonders whether it will be good for her son, whether it will afford him some kind of lifting she cannot fully grasp. She waits for the wisdom to enter, the kind Barry had that would make the choice seem obvious. But he is gone. She begins to cry, as she allows herself to in water, when she knows she won't be heard. She takes the blade and lays it across her wrist where the veins seem most vulnerable. How will it be? She is right there, right at that moment.

She moves the blade and the sting overwhelms her. It's only a small cut, away from the veins, and it lays there white and exposed. Clean-made edges. A non-reaction. Then, as suddenly, the blood begins to fill the gap and spill out and the pain makes the tears begin to sear her eyes. It hurts too much, yet it is almost nothing. She gets out of the tub with the blood filling her cupped palm and stands naked and shivering at the medicine cabinet, trying to find the bandages.

+ +

77

He's been drinking too much. John has never minded a drink or two in the evening, but his tolerance must be lower now, what with the stress of recent weeks and months. Events have unfolded in ways that have made him feel almost bitter, something he does not want for himself. To have expressed love to the ability one can is to carry no remorse; he spends his evenings in quiet contemplation, trying not to succumb to those who have hatred in their hearts.

He gets drunk now more easily, and doesn't quite know why. Maybe he isn't eating enough; maybe the strain of recent developments has begun to wear him down. Lately, upon finishing a drink that would have had little effect on him a few years back, he finds himself nearly staggering to bed at night, only to awaken feeling wretched and dry in the middle of the night. He remembers the time a few years ago when the housekeeper at that time, an elderly lady named Mrs. Mulvaney, had found rats in the basement (or at least she had imagined them there). The exterminator had come to lay poison in the crevices and crannies, and had explained how the poison, when ingested, would give the rats a powerful and insatiable thirst that would compel them to flee outside in search of water, where they would die. As he is older, and as he drinks, he awakens often in the night with the inexplicable combination of a papery mouth and painfully full bladder. He finds himself almost never sleeping through the night. He finds himself instead in the white glare of the bathroom, alone in this dark rectory, peeing and then standing at the sink, drinking glass after glass of water. It is then, and only then, attending to his ruined body, that regret may begin to announce itself. There, in the night's silence, without distraction or defense. But regret at such a late hour cannot be allowed to stand; he will, in these instances, go to his room and turn on the lights, brightly, then open a book or turn on the small portable television that sits on his nightstand. There's usually something to distract him, some old movie or sports highlights or even just those endless infomercials, with miracle cleansers that can lift almost any nasty stain.

His retirement looms and he has begun to accept it. He has made the first jaunts to the suburbs to buy civilian clothing, which, unlike some of his brethren, he has really never bothered with all these years. He was always proud to wear the priestly black. But now he is collecting a new wardrobe. Khaki trousers and button-down shirts and cardigan sweaters, regulation old-man issue. That is the change he faces, and when he lies in his bed late at night with his mouth dry and his stomach rumbling, he tries not to let himself wonder what comes after. He fights the urge to wonder what it was he was supposed to have heard, what inside game he was supposed to have been part of. John has never heard anything but his own urges and his instincts. Maybe it is in that way that He communicates with His earthly charges. After all, He has endowed each of His children with certain minds and marrow. He would not be so cruel as to endow on someone a way of living that cannot be tolerated but also cannot be overcome. For that is a damnation that contradicts all that has been taught. At the funerals he presides over, John murmurs the usual recitations, the comforts and summaries, wondering if any of it amounts to anything.

John is woozy and disoriented; he shuts his eyes these strange nights and tries to recede into something blank and undemanding. Whatever thoughts may seep into him in the small hours, it's too late anyway. He has confessed what he can. He has, in past years, been asked to kneel in the presence of the archbishop and confess things in which he felt he had committed no sin at all. To wash away events, to make clean a new assignment. He has bowed and received absolution from the hand of His Holiness, his superior, who has in each instance spoken no further words before leaving the room to his minions, those who unfolded each successively more remote assignment. How strange it had been that last time, three years ago, to be called inward again, closer to the center. Back home. He'd been told that there were not enough priests anymore, that everyone was stretched thin, that he would now be alone in a rectory in Southie that had once housed four priests, of whom he had once been the most junior. Now, alone in the night, he feels the presence of something like ghosts, if memories can be ghosts. He felt them, indeed, when he had found the envelope stuffed with cash lying on the floor beneath the mail slot. *To help those less fortunate,* whomever they may be and however one might define them. He only truly senses the ghosts when he'd rather not believe in them, when he slips the envelope into the inside pocket of his coat, its destination to be determined at a later date. This has been the way it's worked for as long as he has known, and by virtually all the people he has known. The righteous skimming. The auxiliary account. The necessary contingency fund. When he sits at his bedroom desk counting out the bills, he is as haunted as he will ever be, to the point that he sometimes even hears footsteps, the movement through rooms of people who only live on in his memory, so loud as to be nearly real.

+ +

78

The truck departed the Museum of Fine Arts, carrying the paint-ings bound for New York, with an escort of two State police cars that had been arranged by another board member who apparently had just not liked the feel of what was going on. I was home that day, set-tling into my study to spend the day monitoring both the stock mar-ket on my computer and the progress of the paintings by phone from Lydell Barrett, who was following the convoy in his own vehicle at a safe distance back. If something was going to happen, it was go-ing to be ugly; I must admit that, sitting in my lair in the back of the house, I was nervous with the certainty that something would in-deed happen.

But as the day wore on and I received no reports from Barrett, I became first giddy with the idea that McX had finally been had, then anxious with the thought that the game was finally over. I had not fully absorbed the notion of how badly I needed my enemies and foils, who afforded me my opportunities for rage and resentment, without which I felt sadly hollow. Serenity only suited me as affect, as part of my cleverness. The day ended with a call from Barrett, quietly confirming that all had indeed gone without incident.

I was in my manse with a new alarm system surrounding me like the wireframe rendering of my own risible paranoia. I'd done this to myself! I slept fitfully that night, and awakened with the small notion that there was to be some yet-unexecuted coup de grace, an unexpected finale. But I went to bed that night having seen none. I held some small hope for a couple of weeks, but even I had to admit that any action now would be surprising. I felt the decompression of a man without a place for his passion. At my firm, I had so thoroughly put distance between myself and anyone else that I would have been merely toying with people; across the city even my ostensible peers wanted nothing to do with me. I spiraled into a depression that caught me by surprise and seemed to give my wife momentary pause, as if she might for a moment stumble into some tender regard. Based only on that I pulled myself up enough to at least feign my usual flintiness. Girlfriends failed to raise my mood, or even my usually dependable protuberance.

I waited. It was indeed the nature of the struggle to attack that which is most vulnerable. It is the weakest spot that is best hit, the one that to others might seem insignificant but to its victim is most searing. A television set. A varsity jacket. It occurred to me in the middle of one night, koan-like, that it was in taking no action that McX had pierced that softest of flesh. I was allowed no comeback. As there are rules to all sport, I was proscribed from further action, which would have then become childish harassment. The ball was taken from my hands. I checked with Barrett for updates, but he had none. It seemed his well-paid gig was becoming an irrelevancy.

It suddenly occurred to me that I was in the prelude to my old age. I was into my fifties now and at a loose end. I had long since gone bald and my mouth had become creased into an even more rodent-like countenance, which I had never truly registered. Now, age was not so much visual as corporeal. My body had begun to express its turn toward home in a panoply of small aches and pains, in bed and on the golf course (where, even there, seeking some suppuration of my despair, I found none) and in my office chair when I did not move or stand enough.

It was a few months later that Barrett called, his voice grave with portent, asking to come to my office and share some news. I spent the next hour in restive silence. When Barrett arrived he was brought into my office, where he cleared his throat in what sounded like pre-apology.

"I'm not completely sure if this is anything you want to know, or care about," he said. "I just thought I'd mention it."

I nodded, waiting.

"There's been a change up at Most Holy Trinity Church," he said. "They've brought in a priest who I think you know."

"Is that a fact?"

"They had that Mexican priest in there temporarily, but he's been moved up to Cambridge. They've brought in an older priest who's been away a long time. Father John Rafferty?"

I said nothing.

"Your brother, right?"

It took me a while but I finally nodded. "Yes, my older brother," I said. "I haven't spoken to him since we were kids. He left home and that was it. He's a lot older than me."

"He brings a certain history back with him," Barrett said. "Some people still remember him."

"What the hell does that have to do with me?" I said.

Barrett shrugged. "You're a well-known man now. You have a reputation. This could lend a taint to it that you wouldn't want."

I stood and went to the telescope at my window. I didn't need to actually look through it. The landscape had not changed in a long *time. Through the glass I would still be able to see those old projects, as glyphed and scored with shared history as a Great Pyramid.*

"Is McX behind this?" I said, almost hopefully.

Barrett remained uncomfortably silent.

"Is this part of it?"

"I don't know about that," Barrett said in a measured tone. "I mean, it's the Catholic Church."

"As if they're a match for the Teamsters," I said.

Barrett held up his hands, as if in surrender. "I don't know anything about McX," he said. "I just heard this and thought you'd want to know about it."

"I do want to know, so there can be an appropriate response," I said. "Thank you."

I had not, I realized over the next few days, done as much as I could have for the Church. And so, like a straggling penitent, I arranged some calls that would make good my standing, and perhaps even entitle me to some amount of consideration and accommodation. Indeed, while my endowment was sought and encouraged, my petitions went unanswered. I held my checks in lieu of movement. It was absurd that they didn't even want to hear me out. The fact that, as the months went by, my money remained firmly in my own possession, made me understand both my dilemma and my enemy.

+ + + + + + + + + + + + + + + + + + + +

79

The old furnace runs on oil and is, behind its greatcoat of as-
bestos, a wonder of valves and tubes and pipes that often absorbs
Christopher as he lies behind it, bedded into a pile of musty blankets that seem long-abandoned from whatever use they formerly
had—maybe from as far back as when other people lived up above
in those many rectory rooms. Down in the dark he sits with its
flames. When the furnace kicks up and he can hear the water trick-
ling through its belly and then bubbling up the pipes, he feels his
own rising temperature, enough warmth to finally unnumb his
fingers and joints, which had seemed nearly to petrify after he'd
survived nights outdoors in the gathering winter, had seemed to
be in permanent freeze until he finally cracked a window down behind the shrubs and entered the basement of this place. He has
stacked some boxes beneath that window and wedged some cardboard along its frame so that he can come and go without leaving
much of a trace. He is a nighttime creature now, sleeping with the
lightness not of the predator but of the quarry, despite all else. He
burrows into his warren, and watches the water level in the glass
tube rise and fall as the boiler empties and refills itself. The first
biting cold of the winter has arrived, and, with it, a speckling of
snow; the long haul of what will happen is something he cannot
allow himself to think about yet. When he's done with what he

needs to do, a quick exit will be his only choice; he is young but he thinks of Florida, where he could sleep on the beaches and eat oranges from the trees. He is half-starved and the thought of food is a constant undertone, although he has somehow managed to get by: slipping fruit into his pocket at the supermarket and eating it in the back aisles before he leaves; swiping half-eaten pastries from the counter at the coffee shop when he goes to look for Jeanmarie. Sometimes, even, allowing himself food from the rectory pantry.

If he's ever found down here, he will need to fight his way out of it, but there is a reason why he is here and he will see it through, too. But he doubts he will be found. There's nothing but junk and discarded supplies, blankets and drip-covered paint cans and some car supplies—fluids and solutions and treatments. Early in the morning, he hears the first clacks of the housekeeper's feet on the back steps, and then the rattling of keys in the double-locked door; it is then that he steps up onto the boxes and bellies out onto the cedar chips that hem the hedges. His habit is to crouch low until he is certain the street is free of traffic or pedestrians, and then to simply walk back out into the world, with the hood of his sweatshirt cowled up around his head. He washes himself in the men's room of the supermarket and changes down behind the long King of the Road warehouse, where he has stuffed clothes into a waterproof pack that he then slides down between the cinder-block wall and a rusted-out dumpster. All his clothes are filthy now, but somehow there is in his daily shivering, as he changes out in the junk and weeds, a sense of some kind of self-sufficiency.

He will not go back to his mother's again. He wonders what she has done with the guns she has taken from him, whether she has told anyone, whether the police have been called. But he walks the streets anyway, searching. It's been eight nights since he left Jeanmarie's apartment, and he doesn't know how much longer this will all go on. He is still waiting for Jeanmarie to turn up, and has taken to brazenly walking all over Southie, even during school hours, in the hope she will materialize. He has stood for many hours across the street from Bobby's, hidden in a deep-set doorway, looking up at the windows and watching. Bobby apparently has another girl now, and he arrives home each night with almost mechanical punctuality, his pilfered liquor under his arm. Christopher has also frequently wandered in the vicinity of Marty's house, and has seen something more of what it is that Marty does. The girls who come and go from his basement look drugged out and vacant, the men furtive. In the basement windows, which have been blocked with cardboard, the sputtering flash of strobes etches and re-etches the thin spaces at the edge of the windows, like a summer lightning storm flaring from behind its veil of rain-fat clouds.

He wants his father's gun. Once, when Marty had driven off in his de Ville, Christopher tried to work the edges of the windows and doors, but with no luck. Marty has lots of cameras, and has secured his place accordingly. Christopher has also snuck up into Bobby's dismal apartment after making sure that everyone has gone, and has searched through everything with no luck. He walks the neighborhoods with more rage, more despondency, and more of a sense that there is nowhere to go from here.

So he finds his way back into the basement of the rectory late at night, and in the darkest parts of night he crawls up the back stairs and into the kitchen and slowly slides open cupboards and drawers; he walks sock-footed and with such care and slowness that he barely elicits a creak from the old, warped floorboards. He walks in darkness, his hands spread to lightly guide himself, his ears pricked for the slightest of noises. At the liquor bottles on the silver tray on the buffet table, he slowly removes the crystal stoppers to empty, each night, an unnoticeable amount, just a slow swallow he fights down with little pleasure.

He feels a power in what he is doing, a power that none of the Bible stories and sermons and prayers—none of those endless invocations—has really ever vanquished. The dark knight, in the dark night, clad in his knowledge that he hides just down below, unbeknownst.

+ +

80

"I'm surprised you're back," Butchie Morrissey wheezes when he becomes aware of Jimmy, in the doorway of his room, watching him. "One by one, pretty much everybody stopped coming."

"That's too bad," Jimmy says. "I don't even know why I did come."

"Did you decide you want to live?"

"Nah. I'm good."

"You here to do me the favor I asked?"

"I don't know. I'm not sure you really want that."

Butchie lets off an airy laugh, a laugh that is leaden with his frustration.

"Can you just do it? What do you have to lose?"

"What if they catch me and I get sentenced to live?"

"Who's going to know? Who's going to care? You know, I deserve to die."

"Oh, yeah."

"Do you know that I was up for trial when this happened? That I was out on bail?"

"I think I heard something about that," Jimmy says.

"Do you know what for?"

"More or less."

"I was up for rape. I raped a girl."

"I guess she must be happy this happened, then."

"She and her family would be happier if I were dead."

"I wouldn't know," Jimmy says. He's come thinking about granting Butchie his wish. He has come with a vial of the pain-killers from his own doctor, has come ready to feed them to Butchie one after another, to wash them down with water, to gather the blankets around him and help him be comfortable as his breathing slowly abates, to be in the car and going home by the time Butchie's heart stops, confident that he has done the right thing, feeling perhaps as well that he has closed a circle that had begun with each of them changing. But he also doesn't want to be caught, to be examined and medicated, treated and saved. The Christmas decorations have already gone up here in the linoleumed and fluorescent hallways, and he has stood in the doorway looking for security cameras. He sees none but the sense of himself being watched is palpable, even as the nurses far down the hall natter to each other, oblivious to his presence. The sense that there are eyes on him as he goes through these finals days is unshakable—maybe part of the illness, tricks played by his own plagued mind. He drifts back to the fact that Butchie Morrissey is talking.

"I pulled her arm so hard that I separated her shoulder," he says. "I had her down on the pavement behind the school. She'd been walking through and I was back there, strung out, even though that's no excuse. I slammed her down hard and she was bleeding. It was hot out that night, July. She cried."

"Why are you telling me this?"

"You need to feel all right about putting me out, don't you?" Butchie says. "You need to know that it's worth ending it for me."

"You're confusing me."

"No, no. That's what I was. I was never ashamed. The girl went forward and I was so trashed I wasn't careful enough. Not just drinking, all kinds of shit. Have you ever had meth?"

"No."

"It really fucks you up."

"So you didn't feel responsible."

"No, no. I was. Because of the meth, I got caught. I'll tell you something else."

"Yeah."

"That girl wasn't the first. It was the first time I got caught. The other times, I did it right."

Jimmy is staring at Butchie, both hands in his coat pockets, his right hand on the bottle of pills. He doesn't want this, to be forced to pass judgment, to be pushed into acting out of spite. He had come up the back stairwell with a certain amount of peace in his heart, but now things are getting complicated. He has never been one for vindictiveness.

"The other girls, they didn't really even know who it was," Butchie says. "I'd see them, afterwards, around the neighborhood. I could see what it did to them, how they had changed. I didn't care. I felt like I had some power. That was the only power I had, and it made me feel strong. To hurt people, to terrify people."

"That day, when you were riding on your buddy's car, you didn't look too worried."

Butchie grunts. "That's how it looked, didn't it? I wanted everybody to know I couldn't be touched. Of course I was denying everything, saying the cops were just looking for an easy bust.

I was telling everybody that the cops said they needed to just make an arrest, and after things cooled down the charges would be dropped. They didn't say that, but we're talking about the Boston police here and a lot of people bought it. Are you listening to me?"

Jimmy has drifted into a consideration of his own sins. Back into his lies and his hubris, from so long ago. What would he have done to himself, for crimes so brutal? He wonders now whether he has, for all these years, been asking for the same thing Butchie is asking for now. He wonders, too, with a bottle of these pills in his pocket and very little to attend to any more, why he doesn't just do it himself: quick, fogged, black—the sleep he craves.

"You listen to me," Butchie Morrissey says, his voice cracking in impotent fury. "At least give me that much."

Jimmy straightens. "I can't do it now," he says. "You should have just kept your mouth shut, and you'd already be gone. But now you have to go and make it some kind of moral judgment. I don't want to do that anymore. And I'm afraid that if I really think about all this, and really want to do the right thing, I'll just leave and let you get what you deserve, because what you deserve is to just live in your own thoughts."

"Kill, me, motherfucker," Butchie says. "Fucking *do it*. Put a pillow to my face and just let me fucking *go* . . ."

"No," Jimmy says. He takes his hand out of his pocket and shakes the bottle of pills, its rattle like a life knell for this man who wants the silence of death. "And that's the sad part. Doing nothing at all is probably the most awful thing I've done with my life."

343

8 1

She had gotten into bed with the bandage wrapped tight and three ibuprofens. Still there was the insistent pulsing sting of the cut. It was no longer than an inch and not all that deep, but had cost her sleep nonetheless and made things difficult at work the next day. Chuckie seemed to notice at a distance that something was wrong, but made no effort to move forward, to investigate. Whatever illusions she had about some sort of painless exit from the ache of life, the ache from that small slicing of the skin has chased her back from something she had probably never really intended. And it was the chilling afterthought of how long she would have lain there in the cold blood-and-water soup of her suicide before anyone found her, something that should not have logically mattered, but most definitely did. She had been naked; in bed awake at five that morning, bandaged and in the warmth of a flannel nightgown and clean sheets, she shuddered at the immodesty of it. She thought about how horrifying it would have been for Christopher to find her, bled out to bone white, shriveled and naked. Who knew with what expression on her face, what death mask she would have effected. By five-thirty she had come to the most disturbing realization: that she might secretly have hoped that Christopher would indeed find her, that he would see the pain she had suffered, and that a bond would thereby be renewed between them in a way it could not be in life. At six, as the sky lightened and the first glint of sun touched her curtains, she realized she was now in her bonus life, and something had to be done with it, with absolutely nothing to lose. If harm was to come to her, it would have to be someone else's encumbrance. Her heart has become full of hate, and no one seems to have paid any mind to it. The coldness of life is something that stuns her, as if everyone else knew but her.

She has one of the guns, the medium-sized one, in her bag as she drives. It would seem that her mission is indeed medium-sized, when compared to what's on the news every night. She has begun this journey with no clue as to how one buys the bullets, or puts them in, or how one properly fires. She will go to the public library and look up the last of these, but in the phone book she has found a place where one buys such things. She still doesn't know if she's serious about what she wants to do, any more than she knew as she drew razor against flesh, but she feels there will be clarity when these devices are actually loaded, when they assume their natural state, when things are suggested and acted upon by the very virtue of their presence. She drives north on the Expressway, her wheezing old trap of a car unused to the speed; in Lowell she finds her way off the highway, reading from the directions she had written down as the man went through them over the phone. Down along the expanses of warehouses and body shops, she sees the place, pulls along the sidewalk, then parks down the street as if anyone cares. She is, in her rehearsed banter, simply a woman who lives alone who feels better having a gun in the drawer, ready. She has gone through this all the way up the highway and it still sounds false. She just wants the bullets, chambered, to see what happens next.

The shop seems all that she expected, dour and sepulchral, hemmed by bars and roll-up doors, as square and solid as an ingot. She pushes the door open and a big Doberman trots up to investigate her.

"Lefty, get back," the voice behind the counter says, a very heavy man with an unshorn beard and the affect of purveyed violence, ecclesiastic behind his glass cases and padlocked racks. Lefty whimpers and returns to his bed in the far corner. The man is looking at her, askance, making her feel both self-conscious and of the mind that this truly is a place a woman like herself never goes.

"Can I help you?" he says, a different voice than the one on the phone earlier, the tone seeming to indicate that he is trying to figure out what she's really here for: looking for some other place, most likely . . .

"I need bullets for my gun," she says.

"Oh, you do," he says, not without a hint of amusement.

"Yes," she says.

"Bullets . . . loose? Do you mean a clip? Or shells . . ."

"I don't know. I have the gun with me, though."

"It's *your* gun?"

"Of course it's my gun," she says. "Actually it was my husband's, but he died, and I don't feel safe."

"Do you have a permit?"

"Yes. But not with me. It's somewhere at home."

"You're supposed to keep it with you when you're carrying."

"I know that," she says. "I just didn't want to lose it."

"Is your gun loaded now?"

"I don't think so," she says.

The man takes a step to his right. "Okay, why don't you take the gun out, pointing it away from me—and away from Lefty—and put it *slowly* on the counter."

She nods and, with a trembling hand, reaches into her bag. The weight of the gun surprises her every time. When she puts it on the top of the display case, even gently, it makes a resounding crack that, for a moment, makes her think it broke the glass.

The man picks it up and opens the chamber. "You know how to use this, right?"

"Yes."

"And you're not just bringing this in for someone else?"

"I don't know why you'd say that," Colleen says.

"I have to go in the back," he says. "Just wait here and we'll get you set up."

He goes through a door behind the counter that seems to lead to a storeroom, and Colleen stands still, shaking a little, as Lefty raises his head and seems to take a greater interest in her. She looks into the case at all the weapons. The accumulated promise of bad things, a litter of them. Caged animals, each of its own mind. Not dedicated to the abstract propositions of self-protection and security, but each, dark and oiled and sharp-toothed, meant for specific acts: A score to be settled. A robbery somehow rationalized by need and circumstance. The simple desire to inflict and observe pain. The need to fire a bullet into someone or something to assert one's existence on a cold planet.

Lefty, who Colleen is beginning to understand is an old dog, lifts himself arthritically from the pillow and ambles toward her. She tries to even out her breathing, to dampen her show of fear. But Lefty simply nudges her hand with his snout, looking for nothing more than a good scratch. She sinks her fingers into the looser skin of his neck, getting her fingernails in there so his head lolls, thoroughly pleasured.

The man is taking a long time back there, and she wonders if the bullets she needs are hard to find. She looks at her watch, thinking now about getting to work on time. The bells on the entrance door jingle, and she sees a Lowell police officer, a fat and fiftyish man, entering. "Hey, Lefty," he says with enthusiasm, and the dog releases from her grip to sniff around this new arrival. The officer, patting Lefty along the back, looks at Colleen without saying a word, and then yells, "Richie?"

From the back comes the man carrying her gun. He hands it to the policeman, who says to Colleen, "Whose is this?"

"Mine," she says.

"You sure about this? Because it comes up stolen from a gun shop in Boston, which is where you're from, and that's pretty serious stuff."

"It's not really mine," she says.

"Then whose is it?" he says, still scratching Lefty's back.

"I can't say," she says, somehow holding out in her mind that this statement will solve all this. "Actually, it *is* mine."

"Well, that's different, then," the policeman says, releasing the dog and straightening. "Because then I have to arrest you."

+ +

82

The nights grow longer, darkening like a candle slowly burning to its root; the prelude to Christmas, which, for him, carries no pleasure. Thanksgiving was spent alone in the rectory, eating a dinner left the night before by the housekeeper, shrouded in foil, with a note regarding temperature and time. Thanksgiving has always been so, in its secular glory, the Thanking of God without the true inclusion of God, save for a hurried Grace said by a child or a tepidly executed toast to no real effect. For him, annually, just silence. No calls, no visits; it seems even quieter than usual this year, even as Christmas approaches. Three years now since his return from the far territories, that surprising turn of events that was followed by little. It never really seemed to take. Even the old people at the nursing home, most of whom have no one else, sense his impending departure and distance themselves with polite nods and briefer conversations, maybe out of some sense of self-preservation. They are too pious to say so, now as ever putting their bets on something over on the other side. But they have heard that the new priest will be arriving in the New Year, and they behave accordingly.

His calls to Bernard go unanswered, even by the minions. The chancery is all but closed to him now, the Cardinal withdrawn behind his gilded curtain and his lobster dinners. The detailed arrangements for John's relocation to the desert arrived in the mail, the same day as that envelope full of cash came through the slot. He will have to use that cash, where it is patently necessary. It seems to him, as with other cash he has had to use similarly, that it doesn't go a very long way as compared to a lifetime of service and obedience.

Things are quiet now. The woman has suddenly stopped appearing at his morning Masses. The boy is gone from his bench by the school. Whatever ritual was being enacted, it is over now. Solved, or so it would seem; he really doesn't know. And he considers why he was part of it. Why, when he could have turned a corner and driven a different route to the nursing home, he chose the same unwavering path and that wordless, gestureless daily exchange. He is still the boy he was, after all; in some ways, John has not yet shed himself fully of the old wants. Even now as his physical capabilities decline, he cannot cast off the core of it, the base urges. He feels the disapproval in Bernard's silence; if he were an angry man, he would feel the betrayal of someone for whom the equation had changed. No one ever seemed to have minded before.

He drinks more now. There had been brief times in his life when he had kept to the point of near abstinence, but it seems to him that late life must now be enjoyed and in his isolation it is a welcome comfort. He mixes his nightly concoction at the tray atop the buffet, where his housekeeper keeps all his green cut-glass decanters well filled, his liquor chest stocked and organized. It is mostly bourbon now, usually with Coke, an old vice now revisited, an old pleasure resurrected. He is not without some pangs and discomforts, a bit of upset in the stomach or a pounding in the head. But then the alcohol's fog rolls in. He has been resolute through the years about avoiding doctors; somehow to stand naked before them represented a shift in some essential power he did not warm to. He has taken his chances, health-wise; he has left such matters in God's own hands, as it were. Now, the boiling in his stomach is tamped with antacid and diversion: television, mostly, the cacophony of nonsense that somehow pulls him away from his own thoughts.

He has, in more abstemious incarnations, allowed himself to ponder the paths he might otherwise have taken. Had he fled that sad home as a young man to simply ease the oppressiveness he felt in his heart, or was it the need to be afforded that third-party sanctity he could not otherwise find? He had hated Da's honed disapproval; the man never laid a hand on him but yet the disgust seemed like a stinging blow. Even at his ordination, Da sat in his stiff gray suit, shaking his head dolefully. Ma was no help, and young Terry, his brother, was simply a child to whom little mind was paid. Perhaps in his wealth he enjoys a peace that John now knows he himself has not found.

In bed, late at night, he falls asleep with the television blaring, and wakes in the smaller hours, three and four and five, to shift and groan and move his hands across the other side of the bed, seeking the remote, to put an end to the din. The sounds he hears— the shifting of the old place, the urgent clanks of the hissing old radiators, the creaking floors bearing the weight of countless ghosts—do not frighten him. In a few weeks' time, he'll find himself in some noiseless cinder-block retirement tower, acclimating to its utter silence, the whoosh of the ductwork, the hush of carpeted floors.

He rolls over in bed, the burning in his stomach competing with the pleasant hum of his drunkenness—the necessary penance for a necessary pleasure. Sleep will come soon, then another day to pass. On the television, some pointless show with pointless romance already bores him. His celibacy has entitled him to certain attitudes. His life of simplicity has reaped certain privileges. He can congratulate himself, in that, on the simple rewards of the life simply passed.

+ +

8 3

I had contacts all over the city, but the least of them were in the Archdiocese, which I had avoided rather scrupulously for obvious reasons. I didn't want any part of something that would have a part of him. From an early age my brother's ordination had seemed an object lesson in what that church filled itself with; I had endured in my brief catechism days the glancing blows of one old priest or another, deserved or not. When my older brother drifted from our stifling house to that seminary, it had been, to me, nothing less than a punch line to a joke we all knew.

My trusted man Barrett had no particular entrée into that world, either. And it seemed to me I required a liaison who wouldn't need to know all that much. So I called from my middle-management ranks a young fellow named Malloy, who, while not someone I fully trusted, seemed to have a bit of The Anger. He had actually migrated up from a boyhood in Garden City, Long Island, which I suspected may not have been much different than my own. Malloy entered my office with wary silence. I asked him if he was a religious man and he said Yes in the way you have to say Yes, which I liked. I shared very little, simply telling him that I was considering a rather large donation to the Catholic Charities Appeal, but that the message was to be delivered in a somewhat abstruse manner. And, also, that there was one condition: The removal from duty of one particular priest, whose last name, coincidentally, was the same as my own. I gave Malloy no other information, and instructed him that the donation would come from him, using money I would put into his accounts. I explained to Malloy that he would benefit from being listed as a major donor in the Appeal's list—not a bad thing—and that they would need no explanation as to the reasons for the bequest. Malloy nodded, seeming to understand.

This was not a game. I was not countering McX as much as asserting my will in a matter I had thought resolved many years before, when I had made certain similar arrangements to make sure he would not remain in Southie and be a taint on the reputation I myself intended to build. Money had been exchanged, and petitions had been answered. I had a canceled check, but what did that mean? And in those days, influence could be bought relatively cheaply. I sweetened the pot considerably this time round, sending forward a sum that exceeded the entirety of what my income had been back in those nascent days. Back then, I had laid out the facts of the case; with the money involved now and my brother's curious movement from place to place, no explanation seemed necessary.

Of course, I fully intended to answer McX, as soon as I could determine whether he was actually behind this, or whether there had been, up at the chancery, some kind of inexcusable clerical error in which they had effected this transfer without checking the dossier (and had also completely forgotten the point of my earlier contribution). But then again, organizations like that don't shake out more money by continuing to celebrate the money already tendered. That doesn't work well in any business.

Malloy was someone about whom I had not given extensive thought, but I was beginning to realize that I was at the age that Red

Driscoll had been when he began to bring me under his auspices. I had no sons, and my daughters had demonstrated no interest or aptitude in the making of money, although they were quite talented spenders. I admit I had not had much to do with them; this Malloy, although well into his thirties, was someone who had an indefinable edge to himself. I imagined that his upbringing in Garden City must have had in it a workingman father and a healthy infusion of alcohol; as I had a father but needed Red, I wondered too if this young man, in his quickening climb, would benefit from my mentoring. As I explained the task, I sensed that he understood that, while this was far from being company business, it was exactly this sort of thing that created loyalties that could benefit him for a long time to come. He clearly had that hardness, but it was finesse that I also wanted to find in him.

A few weeks later, he came to my office, and asked if he could shut the door behind him. I said yes; he did so and sat in the big chair across from my desk.

"They took the money," he said, "and assured me that they wanted to make me, as a donor, happy."

"Did they ask you why you wanted this done?"

Malloy shrugged. "They seemed to already know," he said. "They said that after an appropriate amount of time, arrangements would be made."

I sat straight up on that one. "Tell me, Malloy, what you defined, in your conversation with them, as 'an appropriate amount of time'."

"There wasn't exact language," he said.

I smiled. "Well, I'm sure that they understand, right?"

Malloy nodded. "I thought so," he said.

I sent him on his way, already certain he'd been jobbed. There was no point in yelling or screaming; it had never been my style. In an appropriate amount of time, he'd be "promoted" into something he'd eventually understand to be a dead end, and he would leave. No pain, no mess. Just the eventual understanding of missed opportunities. Barrett monitored the situation, using his contacts to make sure Malloy had indeed given the money, which he had—the check had been cashed the next day. But after eleven months, there had been no movement. Sitting in my office late on a Tuesday night, scotch-rocks in hand, he told me that very little seemed to have changed.

"Do they know who they're screwing with?" I said, really just thinking out loud.

"I think they answer to a higher power," Barrett said. "The International Brotherhood of Teamsters."

84

There were rules about these sorts of things back in the day, back in the era dealt with in his favored books. Challenges made and met. Paces counted off and then distance closed. But at this point, sick of it all, Christopher just goes ahead and hits Bobby with the board as he comes out of the doorway onto the street, catching him in the least effective place: The two-by-four he'd selected from behind King of the Road movers had seemed weighty and dangerous when he hefted it, but it smacks sideways against Bobby's upper arm, which is well padded by his down-filled jacket, only startling him and apparently doing no harm.

"What the hell?" Bobby shouts at him, eyes wide. Now Christopher isn't sure what his intention was in the first place. But as Bobby advances, he realizes it's a moot point, for sure. Bobby isn't much better at fighting than Christopher is, but he swings anyway and makes connection, overextending, his forearm landing up along Christopher's jawline. Christopher loses his footing and grabs a handful of Bobby's jacket, and Bobby, nearly instinctively, keeps him from falling; Christopher accepts the help and gets his feet back under him. The fight abruptly halts, in the confusion.

"And why are we doing this again?" Bobby says, checking the fabric of his jacket for damage.

"I want to know where she is," Christopher says. "I want to know where my gun is."

"You call your gun 'she'?"

"Jeanmarie, idiot. *And* my gun. I brought it to her, the gun that used to be my father's. And now she's gone, and so is the gun."

"Thanks for giving her a gun to stick in my face. Really, that's awesome. Well, she's not here. I got a new girlfriend. She's way better than Jeanmarie ever was. And she has a car."

"A month ago she was asking me to protect her from you."

"A month ago I wasn't as smart as I am now," Bobby says.

"So where is she, then?"

Bobby shrugs. "I have no idea. Why would I have any idea, after the way she treated me?"

"You haven't seen her, walking around the neighborhood?"

"I don't walk around the neighborhood. Like I say, I have a girlfriend with a car. And a job."

Christopher is at an absolute loss. He stands dumbly as Bobby picks up the board and tosses it against the building.

"Where are you living now?" Bobby says.

"Nowhere."

"'Nowhere' as in you're living with your mother, or some other kind of nowhere?"

"Some other kind," he says quietly.

"What was really all that wrong with living with your mother, anyway?"

"I just don't want to be there."

"You want to be with Jeanmarie, right? Except you don't even know where she is. Think she's avoiding you?"

"Right now, I just need to get that gun back. If it's not you she's with, it must be Marty. Him I'll hit with more than a board."

"Whoa, whoa," Bobby says. "I'd be really careful about messing with him."

"But he's such a loser," Christopher says.

Bobby is getting cold, even with his jacket on, and he motions for Christopher to come up to the apartment. The place is empty, and warm.

"Where are the guys?" Christopher says.

"Moved out," Bobby says. "My girlfriend makes decent money and I got some new things going for myself."

"Like what?"

"Like just moving a little weed around. Nothing serious."

"Do you need help?"

"Maybe. But here's the problem. I work for people who are tight with Marty. And Marty may be a fat loser, but he is someone you definitely don't want to play games with. Beyond the fact that he carries a few pieces himself, he's connected. He's so connected, you wouldn't even understand the connections."

"I want to know where she is."

"She doesn't want you to know though, does she? Think about it. Look how she just disappeared on me. Haven't you figured out you have to look out for yourself?"

"I guess."

"You know, maybe you should work with me. You haven't even gone to high school yet. I could use you in there, and I bet I could pay you enough that you could afford to get your own place with some buddies."

"I don't have any buddies."

"That's a problem. But maybe you can solve it. Then we can try to work something out."

"How much do you sell?"

"Enough to live here with the heat on and without two guys in my living room. But more importantly, I'm in the system now."

"But aren't those the guys who killed your father?"

"Hey, I didn't even know my father," Bobby says.

+ + + + + + + + + + + + + + + + + + + +

8 5

It's something he notices slowly, standing in the bathroom in the half-light of fading afternoon, just out of bed. It's like a bloom, clouding outward in a delicate pinkness, tendrils reaching out toward the edges of the toilet bowl, then fading into themselves. The doctor had said the blood would come, and now it has. He had waited for it as one awaits some intonation; the color does not hold but rather fades into the rest. He observes the yellowing of his skin, and the tiredness, and the disorientation. He has taken to writing it all down, as if these scrawled notes have any applicable use.

There are moments of passage in this journey. In his bathroom at dawn, sober yet with throbbing head and aching stomach (muted as much as it can be by the medications), he considers this to be another. Irrefutable evidence of the roiling inside, of the continuing failure. The body's progress in dissolving itself, amazing if one can keep objective distance. Jimmy stands looking down at the mix of blood and water and urine, and in doing so feels abruptly overcome by a deep sadness, something akin to nostalgia for a time in which the body had seemed to withstand any onslaught and somehow soldier on. There was something almost charming about that, something amusing. It is the sadness of thinking about something that once was but can no longer ever be. That odd simplicity, gone.

He turns on the shower. He will wash and dress and then he will kill off a better part of the evening doing mostly nothing as he waits to take a cab to Rafferty's office. He will come home afterwards and sleep and probably not remember much of what happened today. He finds, oddly, that he thinks very little of the illness, which is now gathered like a storm at the edge of a sea, blowing. He watches television mostly, numbed to the problems of the people both fictional and real, screaming away at one another on the progression of shows that blare across the channels and fill the early gathering darkness. It doesn't stay in his head now anyway. His brain is a like a leaky basket. Christmas is not far away, but it holds little import to him. He feels drained and delivered, by the simplicity of stuffing an envelope of cash through a mail slot. As if it were a divesting of his own packaged sins. He recalls the church, at least the one of his childhood, in which all intentions could be subsumed into the concrete, the rituals, the touch of water, the smell of smoke, the taste of wine. The jangle of the chalice and the rustle of the heavy robes, the gilded finery.

There is almost no point in struggling downtown to finish this thing with Rafferty, but there is a ritual feel to it that he must answer. He has, in some ways, done very little, other than type, smooth and edit, excising the ramblings of the spoken word, the echoes of recollection. He has to go to the doctor anyway, in the morning, after work. They are treating him, to the degree it is treatment, on the pay Jimmy has accumulated over these months; the only point of order is to effect comfort. The muting of pain, the abridging of symptoms as far as is possible, and the useful explanation. To know what will come. The doctor has once or twice inquired as to any change of heart, vis-à-vis the transplant list, but seems relieved when Jimmy shrugs it off. When he leaves the doctor's office, Jimmy has that rising sense of true aloneness that he must work to shake off, which he does by reminding himself that whatever connection he seeks cannot be symmetrical. The other, whomever it might have been, would have to go on, alone. He expects to be in his grave by the first warming days of spring. In a few weeks it will be a new millennium, and besides some of the Y2K panic he reads about in the paper, he sees what seems to him an unwarranted excitement. The passage of time, he thinks, if measured usefully only in oneself, in the slow seeping of one's allotted days.

86

It was seeming to me that sixteen months was absolutely sufficient to be considered, by anyone's measure, an "appropriate amount of time." It was certainly enough time for me to have worked into a rather substantial boil. I did not like having my wishes ignored, from the Pope on down. I was giving them money to do something that was, all money aside, the moral thing to do. And still they were not budging. The only possible benefit of this was that I had been given sufficient time to consider my response to McX, which would be discrete from this action. I realized that there would have to be some truly emphatic conclusion to all this, for if he had engineered this thing as some sort of joke, it was no longer a joke. There was such deep wrongness to it. McX and I were both getting older; as much as you think you can step back and look at such things as being childish, they are the very fuel that can keep one getting out of bed in the mornings. And this thing he'd done as an answer to me was simply unconscionable on so many levels. Simply put, it just wasn't the least bit funny anymore.

I was beginning to see, as well, that my life, so diligently con-structed, had borne no absolute benefits. I saw this clearly now, as if it were a vision. I might as well have never left the neighborhood: It was those old spites and slights, those old vulnerabilities, which continued to matter. And as I sat shuttered in my office, with the old terrain stretched out far below my telescope, I began to wonder whether I had simply been focusing on the wrong enemies. Who was McX, after all? Some two-bit Teamster hack, sitting on a barstool at Muldoon's, his squirreled-away wealth something that could not be displayed but had to merely be implied. Really he was not much different than myself, in that the wealth hardly mattered at all. I had already come to understand from Barrett, thanks to his investigations, that much of McX's money seemed devoted to an escape plan: The moment when he would, as I had long ago, leave this place and arrive at some presumed reward, most likely for him a retirement in a gated community in South Florida with a condo on a golf course: I doubted the extent of the man's imagination. I could have gone to Muldoon's and sat on the stool next to him and told him a secret, which was that it wouldn't be enough.

And what came over me was a sense of assessment I had never before allowed myself. I found myself trying to dig back to the roots, to unearth what it was that had made me the man I had become. It was simple in some ways: Unlike Beacon Hill, I had come to see early on that the way out of Old Colony never came from simple belief and effort. We all had to find our way or be damned to living with our principles; some of the most noble people I had ever known lived on as poor and beaten down as they had started out. And where were they getting such ideas? The Church, which they believed in absolutely, which they believed was inextricable from He whom they worshipped, inextricable from the teachings we had all been awash with in our simpler youth. These people at the chancery had used exactly that; my own brother had used exactly that. It was a great ballgame they had going—nearly perfect, in fact.

I called Malloy back up from his cubicle on the lower floors. He

365

had after all this time not gone away, which showed my poor judgment. But I told him he had one more visit to pay, one in which several discussion points would be covered in full. Firstly, where did the money go? Secondly, why had that move not been made? And thirdly, did they truly understand who they were fucking with? Names could be named, I said. Malloy nodded grimly and said nothing. "You need to understand," I said, "that what we're trying to do is actually the right thing." And I was surprising myself, understanding that this was true. A week and a half later, with no word back, I called down to Malloy, but his line transferred to the receptionist, who told me he had abruptly resigned the previous Friday.

I called Barrett and had him meet me in a tourist bar down by Fanieul Hall. He had been a stealthy figure in my life, and indeed I admit now that his name is not actually Lydell Barrett. Such things are best kept quiet in the wake of certain acknowledgments. And indeed this might well be one.

In the late summer of this year, through the usual indirect means, I put together a package for Barrett that I knew he could not possibly refuse. It involved a fund that would allow him, much to his surprise, the same earthly reward of more highly placed men, namely that condo on the golf course in Florida. It was a pittance to me but to him it was everything. With his police pension and the pay he had already accumulated from me, he would no longer need to do anyone's bidding. Sitting with him and explaining all this, he seemed clear on the fact that what I was having him do was not insubstantial. He knew exactly what I meant; we never actually said it aloud. He seemed not to mind at all.

He moved to Florida only a few weeks later, and I have not heard from him since, as we agreed. The transfer of assets took place qui-

etly, off the books, and with the kind of neatness I had always appreciated in financial matters. And the clock had begun to tick. Barrett would simply see to certain matters, if necessary. No names were mentioned but the message was delivered nonetheless. He would arrange for the deployment of certain paid subcontractors, the kind who, for significant but untraceable amounts of money, can put certain problems quietly to rest.

The millennium draws near, and it seems as good a final deadline as any (and if the people at the chancery do what is necessary —and already paid for—before the strike of that momentous midnight, no harm will be done and Barrett will have the further pleasure of a retirement without ever having to fear the dreaded tap on the shoulder). It seems that it is, in the end, an inspired deed. And it seems, additionally, to be something that would likely hardly be investigated. It would simply be too ugly. The list of suspects, we knew, would be long, and far-flung, both strange and very familiar.

And so, having made these arrangements for an outcome that does not even have to be named, and having come to the conclusion that, if I keep my mouth shut, it will all simply fade away, I feel instead the desire for disclosure. I undertook these recollections honestly; as I finish now in these days before Christmas, I feel no guilt and have come to understand as well the uplifting nature of confession, even into this microphone, which I hold right now and am finally ready to put down, for good, and even for a man with such tepid Belief as mine. These nocturnal ramblings wait to be transcribed by a young man at the other end of life, a young man who can do with them what he wishes. I say to you now, that I didn't start out thinking I'd tell so much of my story. That I'd tell all of it. I ask you to forgive me this indulgence.

But it has come to seem that saying it out loud, to an audience of one, has helped me unburden myself more than I could have ever anticipated. I don't know where it will go, or whether my audience will feel, given his own shortened prospects, his own need to disclose, or perhaps to edit, or even to delete completely. But I do know this: That for which I am most indictable might turn out to be my first Holy act.

87

The assistant says Rafferty will see him now, and Jimmy pulls himself to his feet and follows her in. The old man is sitting in his big chair, with that searching grin of his.

"You don't look good," Rafferty says. "Are you drinking again?"

"No."

"Are you lying to me?"

"No."

"Your skin looks strange."

"What can I say?"

Jimmy sits in the usual chair, Rafferty in his. The old man looks in expansive mood.

"Are you sure you're all right?"

"I'll be fine," Jimmy says. That's not a lie, exactly; his illness seems to move cyclically, a wavering descent, and this is definitely a down week. He expects he'll come out of it a bit, and for now continue. He needs to. He intends to put aside as much money as he can, because once he becomes really ill, he may need it.

Rafferty shrugs, and says, "Are you to the end of it all?"

"Pretty much," Jimmy says.

"When can you get it wrapped up?"

"A couple of weeks?"

"Okay, as long as it's before the New Year," Rafferty says, but there is a rustling uneasiness to him, something in his shifting that is unusual. Jimmy sits in the silence Rafferty has left for him.

"Is there anything else?"

"Not yet," Rafferty says. "Why don't you go home and get some sleep?"

"Okay," Jimmy says, getting to his feet.

On the train back over, Jimmy feels the lolling unsteadiness he must have had as a drunk, but was probably never conscious of. He is aware of people looking at him. When he gets out at Broadway and begins the walk home, he feels there is nothing left in him. There will be a day where he simply can't make this walk, a day when he can't rise from his bed. The money he has set aside will cover some time at a hospice; as long as he dies on schedule he won't be getting himself into debt.

He has no will, and nearly no assets. His estate will be easily disposed of, and as long as things don't drag out there may be enough left over for a burial. He tries not to think too hard about that. He wants to keep trying to work, for the money and because he wants to see it through for Rafferty. But as he struggles up West Broadway like the derelict he is, dry now but still what he is, he now knows he won't be able to finish the job. He has barely made his way through the first six or seven recordings, and there are more than twenty left. He doubts he'll ever get to the end of the story. The man has turned out to be far more effusive than Jimmy had expected. He has tried, as the job has required, to be more than a transcriptionist, has tried to save old Rafferty from himself. The art of clever euphemism is a tiring one, but he believes Rafferty will be pleased with the way he has muted things.

So be it. He feels he can barely make it up his street. And when he takes his keys from his pocket and looks up, there she is, Shelagh, sitting on his stoop.

"I came to see how you're doing," she says.

"Getting along."

"You look like it," she says. "Can I come up?"

"The place is a mess," Jimmy says.

"I won't try to talk you out of anything," she says. "I just can't bear the thought of you, like this, by yourself."

Jimmy stands, nodding. "It's really a mess up there."

"Is that a no?"

"It's saying to prepare yourself," he says.

When he opens the door to his place, she comes in and says, "It's not that bad."

"It's awful."

"I grew up with brothers," she says. "This is nothing."

She is watching him, and he is nearly staggering. He finds his way to the couch and eases down onto it. "Why are you here?" he says. "I hardly know you. I don't mean that in an insulting way, but this whole thing has been . . . a surprise."

"I'm just concerned about you."

"In a somewhat abstracted way, it seems. Not your friend who's dying, but a *person* who's dying, and you have that kind of compassion."

"I know you. Or at least I knew you."

"You knew me back then? For that one semester I was in college?"

"Yes. Is that so odd?"

Jimmy laughs out loud. "I don't even remember it. It's all totally blotted out."

371

Shelagh shrugs. "Just because you don't remember it doesn't mean it didn't happen. You were completely drunk all the time, but there was a kindness in there."

"There was . . ."

"One night I had a big fight with Jack," she says. "Because Jack could be a real asshole. What were we, eighteen? It felt like the end of the world. I burst into tears and went out the door of the dorm, running down toward Beacon Street, knowing that the reason I was doing it was that I wanted Jack to chase after me and ask me if I was all right. And I heard the footsteps behind me, the breathing. It was you. You looked absolutely stricken. And you were in that kind of constant drunkenness you were in—I'd guess that for you it was cruising altitude—but you kept asking me if I was okay. You asked me about a thousand times. *Are you okay? Are you okay? Are you okay?*' And you brought me back."

"To the party?"

"No, you brought me back from an awful place, which was that utter loneliness. Hey, I was a freshman in college. It felt like the absolute end of the world."

"And . . . ?"

"And that's it. You were really drunk, *really*. And then I heard you flunked out."

"I don't think I ever even showed up for half my classes, and I know for a fact I never showed up for a test."

"And there was something I used to wonder about."

"What was that?"

"I used to think a lot about what you'd be like if you were sober. And then one day, years later, I look up, and there you are, standing there."

"So what am I like sober?"

"Other than being a bit elusive, you're what I thought you'd be like sober. I like that. Are you sure you don't want to keep on with it?"

"I think the only real reason I can stay sober is that my liver is shutting down," Jimmy says. "I'd hate to waste one that somebody else could really use. I don't really have much faith about being much better."

"Will you think about it? Will you consider trying to get better?"

"Well, dying is a lot more uncomfortable than I thought, physically."

"So you'll think about it?"

Jimmy shrugs, which is the best he can muster right now.

"Maybe," he says. "Definitely maybe."

88

They've brought in construction lights, running on gas generators, to allow the work, down in the shadows beneath the Expressway where it hurdles past the gas tanks. The noise of the equipment gives his own workings a machinelike drone, as if the throbbing of valves and gears is inside the casing of his skull. The yellow police tape has been run out along the road, strung from phone pole to phone pole, and then to a coterie of police cruisers beyond that. But he has been allowed down, because it's possible he is family. The captain from the Boston police who is charge of the job keeps saying not to think anything yet, that they're not even sure what they have here other than that it's human remains. But his tone seems unconvincing.

James Joyce McX stands with his hands in the pockets of his lumberjack coat; no gloves, no hat. He has his cell phone in his pocket but he will not call his wife until he knows exactly what it is that's going on here. He won't make her suffer the slow unfolding. He doesn't bother anyone and has brought none of his guys with him. He stands alone. The fact that he's been allowed down here is not just because of who he is, but because of who it may be in the poorly covered grave that was sniffed out by a dog on its late-afternoon walk. Someone had come to get him, more than two months after he finally put the word out through the cops that he wanted his daughter located.

It is in these moments, in which the past might be irretrievable, that we most want to retrieve the past. This is what he is thinking. He had let her go from that house because, with her, went the chaos; after her departure there was peace, and it was easy to accept. He knew she was probably down there on West Broadway with her two-bit boyfriend, and while he might have gone and dragged her back, it seemed best to simply let it play out. He wanted her to come back and beg to be forgiven, so he could be both magnanimous and the one to make the rules. One of the reasons why he had found himself nearly hating her, his only child, was his absolute inability to control her. He had spent the better part of his life learning how to clamp down on men; he had learned to take control and then he did it. But this child would not be brought into line by all the threats, retribution or withdrawals he could bring against her.

He was playing the hard guy, as always. After a month, his wife had finally sat him down and demanded to know where she was; he had sent one of his guys looking, and it turned out she was not living with the boyfriend as they had assumed—as, after all, McX's unwillingness to accept this boy had been the purported reason for her departure. His wife laid into him on that one and still he was still the hard guy. But beginning to worry a little as well. He would make some looping drives through the neighborhood, checking with his men down at the docks and then crossing side streets, meandering, keeping an eye out. But there was no sign of her, this furious girl in her sweatshirt and sneakers and matted hair. He'd stop down at the Liquor Mart and see the boyfriend coming in and out of the walk-in, but whatever impulses he had to throttle the kid and demand to know things were suppressed both by the fact that the Liquor Mart was territory in which even he needed to tread lightly, as well as the fact that for him to show such desperation was to lose the most intangible and valuable thing he had—namely, the perception by all below him that there was not a hint of desperation in him. Without that, he could not be.

The weather has gotten deeply cold but the ground beneath has yet to freeze, and the earth turns easily under the trowels they have now begun to use. The body comes out of the hole wrapped in heavy-gauge plastic contractor bags, one bag over the head and another over the feet, taped at the waist with duct tape. The detectives have told him that the coroner has used a scalpel to make a small slice along the bag to ascertain that it is indeed a body, one of recent vintage, and more likely than not a woman. McX came as soon as he heard, and, although he never filed an official report, the police have let him stand and wait. But the captain has also told him that there are a lot of lost people, both listed and not, both local and not. It could be anybody in that bag, the captain has said in his underlining inflection.

So he stands, alone. Thinking of how he might have done so much differently, and did not. Thinking of what has happened to his daughter. And thinking of who would have done such a thing, and why, and what he will do to make things even again.

89

He hears the footsteps on the floorboards above, compression and release, the squeaking trail. Christopher waits, burrowed in his place in the basement, thinking of the past. It is the day before Christmas Eve and he thinks of his father, as he always does at Christmas, although the memories are vague and he knows he is reconstructing much of them, the way a fossil is fleshed out into something that might have been, based primarily on an impression. Taking equal parts of his own recollections, his mother's stories, the old family photos and a large chunk of his desire for what might have been, he creates a father who is the person who would find a way to keep him from doing what he has done.

Christopher has come through the window and found his way to his blankets and to his waiting. The waiting is all that's left now. There is a calmness to it that comes with resolve. Above, the footfalls are unsteady, without an established meter. They form brief patterns that as quickly dissipate. The man is alone up there, coming to the end of things. Christopher knows, following the echoes above his head, that the old man is coming back now to repour from his crystal decanter. Again. Christopher listens to him up there alone in the old house and begins to see the veil being pulled back: That this man is nobody special. That his mortality is at hand. That this man, in his robes and his trappings, has no greater claim to God than Christopher himself.

It has been a long experiment. Christopher has tinkered with the mix, made mental notes, studied the ebb and flow of the liquors in those containers. He has mixed to taste, spitting and rinsing out in the basement sink, trying to find the effective dose. And he believes this is the night. He hears the labored steps above him, beyond drunk, into something new. The rusted antifreeze can on the basement shelf (Red Indian brand, decades old, clear and still pungent) is nearly empty now. But this, Christopher is certain, will be it. He has researched it thoroughly on the computer at the library, the new library he walks to over in Dorchester. The dosages he has found have been mainly intended for lesser targets, such as annoying dogs and small, invasive pests. There is a sweetness to the fluid, syrupy and clear, that is almost like a temptation to all manner of animals.

He thinks again of his father. He thinks of the man apart from the home videos or the wedding pictures or the photo album, the man apart from his mother's fabulistic stories that stopped being told before he wanted them to stop. He thinks of this man made of pieces, the shards that can be realigned into something close to what might have really been. He had started forgetting, but now he remembers again. The ghost was fading but now reforms itself. It is what Christopher has. All he knows of the future is as far as tonight. There is no plan, no expectation. His father's eyes are on him again, on what he has now done.

Above him, the steps slow almost to nothing. The creaking of the floor implies some effort to steady, some seeking of balance, some urge to *get hold of oneself*. Then the silence. The vatic silence; the final accounting of all that came before this.

Then the slam of heavy body to floor that startles him even as he has been waiting for it. Then a new silence. So quiet it seems as if it is colored a depthless black. A silence of release, of appraisal, perhaps even judgment. Christopher waits, for some final struggle, but there is none.

His father is truly close at hand now, across some nearly bridgeable threshold, the way ghosts only haunt us in our dark hours, when both sins and holy acts bring their eyes upon us. Christopher could speak out, could utter something aloud that petitions the spirit world, that presumes such a connection. He does not.

He could go up to inspect, to see the man laid out and done with. But he will not.

He should leave now and begin to erase every connection to this, to begin to feel the slow shedding he must believe will come. But he lingers, the flames in the cellar furnace shedding light and warming his face. He feels it all, not as he had thought it would be but how it really is, right now, one instant in his life that is already passing to the next. He is afloat in the moment, the moment after which all other moments can start, finally.

He is in his new life, on the other side of God.